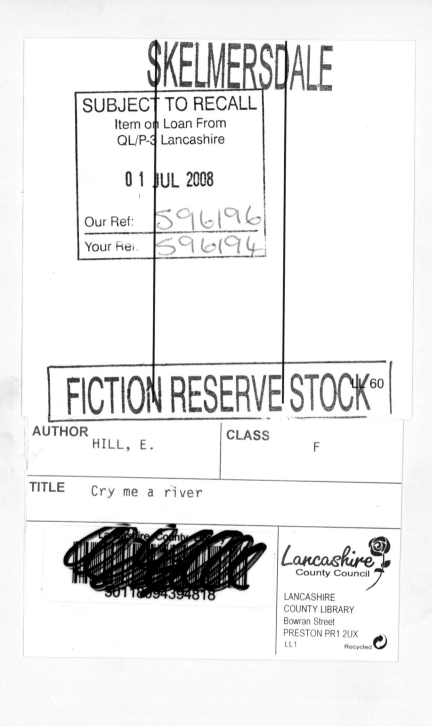

Cry Me
a
River

Cry Me
a
River

ERNEST HILL

Dafina
BOOKS

KENSINGTON PUBLISHING CORP.
http://www.kensingtonbooks.com

This book is a work of fiction. Names, characters, places, and incidents either are products of the author's imagination or are used fictitiously. Any resemblance to actual events or locales or persons, living or dead, is entirely coincidental.

DAFINA BOOKS are published by

Kensington Publishing Corp.
850 Third Avenue
New York, NY 10022

All Kensington titles, imprints and distributed lines are available at special quantity discounts for bulk purchases for sales promotions, premiums, fund-raising, educational or institutional use.

Special book excerpts or customized printings can also be created to fit specific needs. For details, write or phone the office of the Kensington Special Sales Manager: Kensington Publishing Corp., 850 Third Avenue, New York, NY 10022, Attn Special Sales Department. Phone: 1-800-221-2647.

Dafina Books and the Dafina logo Reg. U.S. Pat. & TM Off.

ISBN 0-7582-0277-6

First Hardcover Printing: April 2003
First Trade Paperback Printing: May 2004
10 9 8 7 6 5 4 3 2 1

Printed in the United States of America

For my father, Charley Hill Jr.
The ultimate dad

Acknowledgment

Thanks to my agent, Frank Weimann; my editor, Karen Thomas; my family and friends; and all of the dedicated souls who make up the Kensington family.

Chapter 1

Dazed and confused, Tyrone backed the truck out of the yard, pulled the lever into drive, depressed the accelerator, and sped toward the main highway. As the truck raced past the lake, he gripped the steering wheel with both hands and stared into the twilight. Though his eyes were clear and his vision was unobstructed, he saw nothing. Not the beautiful, orange July sun that had risen just above the east bank. Not the flock of wild birds dancing in the treetops. Not the stand of fresh honeysuckle that ran parallel to the still blue water and decorated the roadside well past the point at which he turned onto the highway leading into Brownsville.

No, he did not see because he could not see. And he could not see because he was remembering the sound of the soft leather soles of his sister's slippers sliding across the surface of his mother's old wooden porch. He was hearing again the soft, steady tapping of her bare knuckles against his closed bedroom door. He was seeing the pain in her wide, bloodshot eyes just before she asked the question: "You heard about your son?"

He had suspected that something was wrong even before she told him. He did not know why. Maybe it was the way she had averted her eyes before she spoke. Or the way she wrung her fingers in her hand. Or the way she shifted her weight from one foot to the other. Or maybe it was because in forty years of living he had learned that good news never came this early in the morning.

"No," he said, alarmed but trying not to think the worst. "What about him?"

"He killed a white gal," she said, immediately dropping her gaze again before adding, "So the law say."

The meaning behind her words was clear. The impact instantaneous. He felt his knees buckle. His head became light. He opened his mouth to speak, but shock rendered him silent.

A space of time passed in which he tried to listen to her, but his mind could not focus. Too many thoughts came too quickly. She said a lot of things, but all he could remember was . . . "He killed her . . . He raped her . . . And they done set the date. . . . He gone die in eight days."

A thousand times he had driven this route. Ten miles through the swamp . . . a left at the traffic light . . . right onto Hospital Road . . . a double curve . . . a stop sign . . . a sharp right turn . . . a half mile north on Highway 17 . . . left across the tracks . . . a short drive through the projects . . . Chatman Avenue . . . Death Row . . . home.

His old house came into view, and instantly the last ten years of his life dissipated. Suddenly, he was hearing again the fading sound of his wife's shoes striking the bare concrete floor outside his tiny cell. He was remembering the sight of her tear-stained eyes, seeing her frail, trembling hands clutching the cold steel bars, hearing the tone of her unsteady voice as she mumbled, "I can't do this no mo'."

He parked his truck on the shoulder of the street, ambled out, and bound toward the house. No sooner had he crossed the yard and climbed the steps onto the porch than he heard someone call to him from the adjacent house.

"Who you looking fo'?"

Instinctively, he turned and looked in the direction of the voice. The woman was sitting on a screen-enclosed porch. The mesh wire from the screen obstructed his vision, and he could not identify her.

"Mrs. Stokes," he said, instantly wondering why he had said Mrs. Stokes and not my wife.

"Pauline?" the woman questioned him.

"Yes, ma'am," he said.

Now he recognized her voice. It was Miss Leona.

"She ain't there," Miss Leona said. Her voice was friendly, but Tyrone was sure that she still did not recognize him. But how could she? Ten years had passed since he had been sent to prison. He had been a youngster then. Now he was a man.

"You know where she at?" he asked.

"What you want with her?" she wanted to know.

"I come for her," he told her.

There was an awkward silence, and Tyrone was sure that now she was remembering him. *You the one they used to call Deuce . . . You the one killed that man over yonder in Cedar Lake.* Suddenly, Tyrone heard the latch on her screen door snap shut.

"What your name?" she asked.

"Tyrone," he told her, ever aware that she had asked simply to confirm what she suspected.

"You Pauline's husband, ain't you?"

"Yes, ma'am."

"She up to her mama's."

"Thank you," Tyrone said. He turned to leave, but the sound of her voice stopped him.

"You ain't moving back here, is you?"

"No, ma'am," he said. "I ain't."

"Good," she said. Then, quickly added, "I mean . . . 'cause ain't nothing 'round here for you to do 'cept get in trouble. And ain't no sense in looking for trouble if it ain't looking for you."

"Yes, ma'am," he said, descending the steps and making his way to his truck. As he walked, he understood. He and his family were pariahs. They were trash to be collected and discarded. He started the truck and headed into the country, vowing that his son would be executed over his dead body.

Chapter
2

It was seven A.M. when he stopped at the gate leading onto his in-laws' property. It wasn't much of a gate (a few pieces of scrap lumber held together mostly by wire) but it was enough to keep the chickens and cows and horses and hogs from straying.

He got out and opened the gate, then got back in, drove the truck through, and got out again. Though it was summer, it had been an unusually hot, dry month, and the long, winding road was covered with fine, loose dust. It was the kind of dust that aggravated the grown-ups. Especially if the wind was blowing, or if they had laundry hanging on the line, or if they wanted to sit out on the porch and eat a sandwich or nap during the hot part of the day.

But for the kids, these were ideal conditions for rolling tires, or riding bikes, or playing war, or engaging in any type of activity that would cause the dust to rise in their wake, adding tangible evidence of the trail of smoke conjured in their overactive minds. How many times, on days like this, had he watched as his son raced barefooted down the old dirt road, climbed the gate, retrieved the mail from the box on the opposite side of the street, and raced back to the house?

He shut the gate, climbed back behind the wheel, and hastily guided the truck through the shallow, dry ruts toward the small wood-frame house. Directly through the gate, on the right side of the road, was his brother-in-law Levi Jackson's house. (Levi and his family had lived there together before his wife took the kids and moved to St. Louis.) Behind Levi's house was a cow pasture. On the opposite side of the road, just beyond the long, straight rows of cotton, the roof of Joe Jackson's small two-bedroom trailer was barely visible. Either Levi or Joe had been plowing the field when the news came this morning. He could tell by the way the old John Deere tractor sat halfway down the center of a row with the blades of the plow still deeply embedded in the partially tilled soil.

Flanked by a thick cloud of dust, he stopped just east of the front porch and parked underneath the large tree where the chickens roosted. He killed the engine, pushed the door open, and slid to the ground. He paused for a moment, staring at the simple gray house with the tin roof and the small open porch that was supported by four wood studs. More than ten years had passed since he had seen either his son or his wife, but in a way that he could not explain, it seemed like only yesterday that he had stood across the street from his house, watching the police watching for him, all the time longing for one last glimpse of the woman to whom he had pledged his life and one last word with the son who, because of what he had done, would have to come of age fatherless in the cruel, unforgiving world they called home.

Plagued by a sense of uneasiness, he walked toward the house, ever aware of the tightness in his arms and legs. He, unlike the prodigal son, was returning to a world that had once rebuked him and that perhaps still did not welcome his presence. With each step forward, he fought against the mounting desire to turn back, and he clung to the faint voice calling from a remote part of his brain, counseling him to continue, persuading him to push on.

As he approached the steps, a strange noise caused him to halt. Startled and wide-eyed, he watched a large black dog with eyes ablaze and teeth exposed burst from underneath the house and race toward him. Instinct told him to run, but experience hastened a slow retreat. With his eyes glued to the advancing animal, he slowly eased backward until his back was pressed firmly against the bed of his truck.

Tense and motionless, he eyed the large animal whose lean, terse body was now positioned only inches from his legs and whose loud, rapid barking had given way to a low, threatening growl. As the animal crouched down, indicating his intent to attack, Tyrone leaped onto the rear bumper and stepped over the tailgate into the back of the truck. Instantly, the dog advanced, barking wildly and holding him at bay. As he watched the animal prancing back and forth, angered by his presence, he realized that he was now a stranger trespassing on territory that the animal had been trained to protect.

From the safety of the truck, Tyrone heard the sound of the screen door opening, and he saw his father-in-law emerge from the tiny house, wearing a pair of overalls and leaning on a walking stick.

"Git on back here!" he heard his father-in-law yell forcefully. "Git on back here, Blue."

The sound of the old man's voice calmed the animal. His eyes softened, his ears fell forward, and his tail began to wag. In the twinkling of an eye, the large, powerful animal was transformed from a fierce predator circling his cornered prey, threatening attack, to a docile house pet obediently responding to his master's every command. Relieved, Tyrone watched the dog whirl and run toward the sound of his master's voice with his tail held high above his back, exposing the large, taut muscles in his round, powerful haunches.

"Good boy," he heard the old man say as the dog leaped onto the porch. "Good boy, Blue," he said a second time, cheerfully rewarding the dog's obedience by patting the animal's head and rubbing him about the neck.

Assured the animal was under control, Tyrone stepped from the truck and eased forward, feeling his father-in-law's eyes upon him. His father-in-law's stare made him uncomfortable, and he felt awkward and stiff as he mounted the steps and paused before the old man. He could tell by the confused look in his father-in-law's eyes that time had rendered him unrecognizable. Yes, his was, indeed, the face of a stranger.

"You looking for somebody?" his father-in-law asked.

"Miss Leona say Pauline up here."

The old man looked at him, bewildered, but did not speak.

"Papa Titus, it's me. Tyrone."

There was an awkward silence. The old man narrowed his eyes and studied Tyrone's face, looking for signs of the young man who once wore that name.

"Is she in there?" Tyrone asked, looking beyond the old man. The window curtains were drawn, but through the partially opened door, he detected a faint light glowing in the tiny living room, and he was aware of the sound of muffled voices emanating from deep inside the belly of the house.

"Git back in your truck," his father-in-law said. "You ain't welcome here."

"Papa Titus, I just want to talk to Pauline."

"She don't want to talk to you."

"I need to see her," Tyrone said, moving toward the door.

"Don't make me turn this dog loose," his father-in-law said, lifting the dog by the collar and pulling him forward, threatening release.

Tyrone halted, staring at the large dog with wide, fearful eyes.

"What you got against me, Papa Titus? I ain't never done nothing to you."

"You got bad blood in you," the old man said, staring at Tyrone with cold, piercing eyes. "And you rotten to the bone."

"I ain't never done nothing to you, Papa Titus," Tyrone said again.

"Why you come back here?" the old man asked.

"I need to talk to Pauline," Tyrone answered.

"She don't want to talk to you." He dismissed Tyrone's statement.

"I heard what happened," Tyrone felt compelled to tell him.

"That ain't none of your concern," his father-in-law said coldly.

"He my son, Papa Titus," Tyrone said, attempting to appeal to his father-in-law's conscience.

"That ain't his fault," the old man responded.

"Papa Titus, you don't understand—"

"No," his father-in-law interrupted. "You don't understand," he said sternly. "That's my child in there, and she done cried enough."

"But, Papa Titus," Tyrone tried to speak, but now his father-in-law was not interested in listening. He had heard all that he would hear.

"You shouldn't have come here," the old man said. "She got enough to deal with without having to deal with you."

Suddenly, Tyrone was besieged by a feeling of reality. His father-in-law was right. Things were as they had always been. Ten years ago, she had buried him in that part of her consciousness that denied his existence. His death, however symbolic, provided her a type of peace that their life together never had.

"She with family now," he heard the old man say. "We'll get her through this. You just need to go on back where you come from."

Wordlessly, Tyrone descended the steps and retreated across the grassless yard on wobbly, unstable legs. As he neared his truck, he heard his mother-in-law call from inside the house.

"Titus, who that out there?"

"Nobody," his father-in-law replied.

Tense and anxious, Tyrone pulled the door open, slid behind the wheel, and stared straight ahead as his large brown eyes fought back pending tears.

Chapter
3

Somewhere between exiting the gate leaving his in-law's property and entering the city limits of Brownsville, Tyrone decided to find Beggar Man and see what he knew about Marcus's situation. There was in him no anger toward his father-in-law or animosity toward his wife, for he knew that neither anger nor hatred would change the state of things between them. In him was simply a resolve to find the truth about his son with the hope, however small, that what he had heard had not been true, and what he feared would happen would not be done.

When he turned off the main highway and crossed the tracks, he found himself driving directly into the bright yellow sun that had risen just above the thick woods a few hundred yards east of the projects. Through squinted eyes, he gazed at the world that he had once called home. Some things about the neighborhood had changed while others had not. People still parked their vehicles on the street, and women still hung their clothes on the line. But now there were fences around more yards and bars over more windows. Trees that were saplings had matured, and now their large branches extended far beyond their trunks, shading the cluttered yards and the run-down shacks that lined both sides of the long, narrow street.

At the far end of the street, he pulled to the shoulder and rolled to a stop in front of Beggar Man's tiny wood-frame house. He killed the motor and looked around. A strange sensation enveloped him. He was home, traversing streets that for the past ten years he had only been able to see in his dreams. A thousand times, he had tried to imagine this moment—the joy, the exhilaration, the excitement. But never, in his wildest dreams, had he anticipated a return not only void of joy, but filled with such pain, such fear, such dread, such sorrow.

Outside the truck, he leaped the small drainage ditch that separated the narrow street from the tiny yard, then mounted the steps to the porch and knocked. The force of his hand caused the rickety screen door to vibrate on its loose, rusty hinges. He paused, then raised his hand to knock again, but before he could, he heard Beggar Man's loud voice boom from inside.

"Who is it?" He seemed annoyed that he had been bothered so early in the morning.

"It's me," he said. "Tyrone."

Instantly, he heard the sound of feet moving. The chain rattled. The knob turned. The door flew open.

"Well, look what the cat done drug in," Beggar Man said, a wide smile etched across his face. "If it ain't my old buddy Tyrone." He threw his arms about Tyrone's shoulders, and the two men embraced, then released each other.

"Man, how long you been home?"

"Not long," Tyrone said.

Beggar Man looked at Tyrone as if he were about to say something else, but then realized that Tyrone was still standing on the stoop.

"Man, come on in and sat down," he said.

Tyrone followed him into the house, then paused as Beggar Man stopped to straighten the old bedspread that had been draped over the worn living room sofa. When he moved aside, Tyrone plopped down. A loose spring prodded him through the cushion, and he discreetly shifted his weight, ever aware of the foul odor rising from the badly soiled sofa.

From his seat, he watched Beggar Man cross to a plain wooden chair that he had positioned directly in front of the television and re-move a plate of food that he had placed on the seat. His movements disturbed a fly that had been lingering nearby. Tyrone watched the large black and green insect rise into the air and land next to the light bulb that hung from the ceiling.

Unconcerned, Beggar Man sat on the chair and rested his plate on his lap, then bellowed, "Want some breakfast?"

Tyrone looked at him, then at the plate. "What you eating?"

Beggar Man lowered the plate so that Tyrone could see. "Beer and eggs," he said.

Tyrone squinted. "For breakfast?"

"Sho' you right." Beggar Man smirked, then lifted the can of beer to his lips, took two gulps, and let out a loud, pretentious belch.

"Nigger, you ain't changed a bit."

"Changed," Beggar Man chided. "Why mess with perfection?"

Both men chuckled; then there was silence.

"Well, do you or don't you?"

"Do I or don't I what?" Tyrone asked, puzzled.

"Want some of this?"

Tyrone looked at the plate again, then shook his head. "I'll pass," he said.

"You sho'?" Beggar Man said. "Got plenty."

"I'm sho'," Tyrone said. "I ain't hungry."

"All right," Beggar Man said, then scooped a large forkful of eggs from his plate and stuffed them in his mouth. As he ate, Tyrone stud-ied him. He was a big man, well over six feet tall, and nearly three hundred pounds. His head was bald, and his clean-shaven face bore the marks of a man who still lived life hard. There was a scar on his left cheek, and another on his neck, just below his Adam's apple. But other than a chipped front tooth and a few extra pounds, he looked the same. He drank from the can again, then looked at Tyrone.

"Me and the fellows was just talking about you," he said, lowering the can and wiping the corner of his mouth with the hem of his shirt.

"How is everybody?" Tyrone asked, more out of politeness than concern. He was anxious to talk about his son, but he could tell that Beggar Man wanted to visit.

"Man, Byrd in the army."

"What!" Tyrone said, a little louder than he had intended.

"Nigger a sergeant somewhere over there in Europe."

"Is that right?"

"As God is my witness," Beggar Man swore.

"What about Pepper?" Tyrone asked, his curiosity piqued. "What he doing now?"

"Driving tractors for Mr. John."

"Pepper!" Tyrone said, his tone indicating disbelief.

"Nigger married and got six children."

"Six!" Tyrone exclaimed. "My Lord."

"Ain't but two of 'em his," Beggar Man said, laughing. "Married one of them ready-made families."

"Who he marry?"

"Nigger, you'll never guess in a million years."

"Who?" Tyrone asked again, not bothering to guess.

"You remember Pumpsi Greene?"

"Who?" Tyrone did not recognize the name.

"Old tack-head from up the Quarters," Beggar Man said.

Tyrone frowned.

"You know her," Beggar Man said. "Joe L.'s oldest girl."

Tyrone paused, concentrating. Suddenly, he remembered her.

"What!" he said, shocked.

"Nigger say he was drunk when they married, but I don't know. He sho' act like he love that old ugly girl. Been with her going on five years now."

"Five years?" Tyrone said with a faraway look in his eyes. For a few seconds he was transported to a time when he and the fellows were running wild through a world that they did not respect and that did not respect them. "Married," he mumbled softly. "Pepper married."

"Yep," Beggar Man said, then reached down and lifted the can of beer from the floor next to his chair. "Nigger done tied a knot with his tongue he can't tear loose with his teeth."

Tyrone chuckled but did not speak.

Beggar Man tilted his head back and took another long swallow. He lowered the can, and the two men's eyes met.

"Well, what about you, Beggar Man?"

"What about me?" he asked.

"Yeah," Tyrone said. "What you doing for yourself?"

"Just running the club."

"What club?" Tyrone asked.

"Luther's place," Beggar Man said. "Working security right now. Just a little something to pay the bills. Plan on opening my own club one of these days." He paused. "Soon as I git my money right."

"Your money still funny, hunh?" Tyrone joked.

"Don't you hear it laughing?" Beggar Man teased.

Tyrone chuckled; then Beggar Man looked at him and smiled.

"Nigger, it's sho' good to see you," he said. "We figured you was dead or something, seeing how ain't nobody heard from you since God knows when."

"Naw, man, I'm still alive and kicking."

"When you get out?"

"Yesterday, but didn't make it home 'til last night."

"You seen Pauline?"

Tyrone shook his head. "Spent the night at Mama's."

"Well, I know she was glad to see you."

"She was. But to be honest with you, we ain't had much time to visit yet. I didn't get there 'til little after ten last night. My bus was late."

"You took the bus all the way from Texas?"

"That's right."

There was silence.

"Well, don't look like prison life done hurt you none," Beggar Man said, smiling. "'Cause, nigger, you sho' look good."

"Well, I was feeling pretty good 'til this morning."

"What happened this morning?" Beggar Man asked.

"Marcus," Tyrone said. "Just found out a little while ago."

Beggar Man lowered his eyes and began fumbling with his food.

"Came by to see what you know about it," Tyrone said.

"Just what I heard," Beggar Man said, averting his eyes.

"What's that?"

"Word on the street he did it."

A lump of terror rose from the pit of Tyrone's stomach and lodged in his throat. He looked at Beggar Man, and Beggar Man lowered his eyes.

"That's hard to believe," he said.

"That's the word," Beggar Man assured him.

"What happened?" Tyrone asked.

Beggar Man sighed and leaned back in his chair.

"It happened five years ago. White girl come up missing," he said, with a look in his eyes that a person had when he was remembering something that he had long since tried to forget. "Looked for her for three or four days straight. Finally found her in a ditch beside one of ole man Peterson's tater fields . . . butt naked."

He paused and looked at Tyrone, but Tyrone did not respond. Beggar Man lifted the can to his mouth and took another swallow.

"They say Marcus grabbed her from that grocery store just west of town. They say he took her down one of them back streets. They say he raped her and killed her and dumped her body out there in Peterson's field. Ole man Willis found her Wednesday evening. Police picked Marcus up that Friday night. They say he the one. They say ain't no doubt about it; he the one."

"Who is they?" Tyrone asked.

"The law," Beggar Man told him.

"What make 'em think it was Marcus?"

"Say somebody seen him."

"Who?"

"Two white girls."

"Must've seen somebody else," Tyrone insisted. "Wasn't Marcus. Couldn't've been. No way. Just couldn't've been."

"Man, he was on the tape."

Tyrone looked but did not speak.

"Had a camera in the store," Beggar Man explained. "Your boy and the girl was on the tape. She left; then he left right behind her. They say he didn't even buy nothing . . . just followed her out the store. She walked a piece-a-ways 'round the corner, and that's when them two girls say they saw him grab her and throw her in his truck and drive off."

"Naw." Tyrone shook his head. "They lying."

He rose from his chair and walked to the window and looked out. An old lady, with a huge straw hat atop her head, was walking down the street, leading a small child by the hand.

"Can't see it," he said, refusing to believe what he had been told.

"Can't see Marcus killing nobody. Not the Marcus I know. I just can't see it."

"He changed, Ty," Beggar Man said. "When you got locked up, look like he got depressed or something. He took to keeping to hisself. He went to acting real strange like he didn't care 'bout nothin' no mo'. We figured he would've been all right if he could've seen you. But Miss Pauline wouldn't allow it. Ty, maybe he killed that girl so he could be with you. Maybe he didn't figure on them giving him death like they did. Maybe he thought he'd just go to the pen . . . seeing how he was only seventeen."

"I don't know, Beggar Man. I—"

"Ty, there's something else you ought to know," Beggar Man said. "They found a pair of drawers behind the seat of his truck. They say they belong to that dead girl." He paused, then added, "And they say he failed a lie detector test."

Tyrone looked but did not speak.

"It looks bad, Ty. I hate to say it, but look like they got him dead to right. Look like his time short. Look like it's real short."

"Where they got 'im?"

"Over in Shreveport."

"They allowing visitors?"

"Couldn't tell you," Beggar Man said. "But I know who can."

"Who?"

"Captain Jack."

"Who?" Tyrone asked.

"His attorney," Beggar Man said.

Chapter
4

Captain Jack's office was located on Elm Street in a converted building just north of the post office and just west of the courthouse. Like most streets in Brownsville, Elm was not marked with a street sign, and like most streets, it was not difficult to find. Not only did Elm cross Main Street, but it was also one of the streets forming the popular configuration the locals called the Courthouse Square.

When Tyrone turned off Main Street onto Elm, he did not park at Captain Jack's office. Instead, he drove to the end of the street, turned left onto Bowman Avenue and pulled into the large parking lot surrounding the courthouse. In his mind, things were moving too fast. It was as if he could hear the ticking of an internal clock, and he could see the sun literally rising higher into the sky. Death was on her way. She had selected her prey. The day had been chosen. The hour had been set.

What did one do when his fate had been sealed? What did he do when there was no place to run? What did he do when there was no place to hide? What did he do when there was nothing to do?

Feeling powerless, Tyrone pushed the door open and stepped to the ground. The bright yellow sun had disappeared behind a huge white cloud, and the warm morning air had given way to a cool summer breeze. Nervous and anxious, he hurried to the street, checked for cars, then dashed to the other side. He looked at the building into which he would enter. It was old and poorly kept. There was a small metal placard on the solid wood door bearing the name Jack Elroy Johnson, Attorney-At-Law. Tyrone flinched; the door opened, and a young white woman came out followed by a middle-aged white man. Tyrone nodded and spoke, then stepped aside. They cleared the doorway, and a second white man appeared. He looked at Tyrone, and Tyrone waited for him to speak.

"What can I do for you?" he asked. His voice was strong and professional, and his tone was pleasant but authoritative.

"I'm looking for Captain Jack," Tyrone said, then quickly added, "I mean, Mr. Jack . . . I mean, Mr. Johnson."

"I'm Johnson," the man said. "How can I help you?"

"I heard you my son's lawyer."

Captain Jack furrowed his brow and tilted his head, but did not speak, and Tyrone realized that he was waiting for him to say more.

"Marcus Stokes," Tyrone said, then paused.

"Ah, yes," Captain Jack said. "Come on in."

Tyrone edged through the door, observing Captain Jack as he entered. He was an older man in his late sixties or early seventies. He wasn't fat, but he was slightly overweight. His silver hair was combed to the back and neatly cropped just above his ears. His clothes were neat, but they did not appear to be expensive. He wore a plain white shirt, with a bow tie, and a pair of dark-colored slacks that were secured with a pair of bright red suspenders.

"Come this way," he instructed.

Tyrone followed him through the small room into an even smaller room.

"Take a seat," he said. "I'll be with you in a moment."

Tyrone took a seat in a plain wooden chair that had been positioned before an old oak desk that seemed too large for the quaint, little, windowless room. Captain Jack excused himself, and Tyrone looked over his surroundings. Besides the chair that he sat in, and the file cabinet behind the desk, the only other furniture was a bookshelf that someone had set in the far right corner. The papered walls were bare save for a clock that hung on one wall and an arrangement of frames containing Captain Jack's diplomas that hung on the other.

Tyrone heard a toilet flush followed by the sound of water running. Then he saw the door open, and he watched Captain Jack enter the room and take a seat behind the desk. The lawyer closed a folder that was sitting before him, pulled open a drawer, and slid it inside.

"So, you would be Tyrone Stokes, correct?" he said, after he had closed the desk drawer and leaned back in his chair.

"Yes, sir," Tyrone said. "That's me."

"Well, what can I do for you?" he asked, then waited.

"I want to know where things stand with my son," Tyrone said.

"Not good," Captain Jack told him. "The court handed down its ruling late yesterday evening. Our appeal was denied. The verdict stands."

"Now what?" Tyrone asked, then slid to the edge of his chair and stared deep into Captain Jack's eyes, anxiously waiting to hear some clever legal trick that would save his son's life.

"We will petition the governor for a stay of execution."

"And then what?"

"That's all we have left."

"Will it work?"

Captain Jack did not answer immediately. He cupped his hands behind his head and stared at the ceiling.

"He is not showing any remorse," he said, after a brief silence.

"Because he didn't do it." Tyrone was adamant.

"There will be no stay without contrition."

"So he'll have to lie to live?"

There was silence.

"Mr. Stokes, even then, he would most certainly die."

"Do you believe he's innocent?" Tyrone asked.

"I believe I did all I could to defend him," he said. "There was just too much to overcome. The evidence . . . his life . . . you."

Tyrone opened his mouth to speak, but he was interrupted by the sound of the door opening behind him. He turned and watched a young black lady poke her head through.

"Oh, I'm sorry," she said. "I didn't know you were with a client."

"That's okay," Captain Jack said. "Come in."

Tyrone followed the woman with his eyes as she entered the room and paused before Captain Jack's desk.

"Janell, this is Tyrone Stokes," he said. "Mr. Stokes, this is Janell Rainer. She is my part-time paralegal."

"Hi," Janell said, extending her hand.

"Hi," Tyrone said, rising and taking her hand in his own. "Pleased to meet you, Miss Rainer." He released her hand, then sat back down.

"Janell, Mr. Stokes is Marcus's father. We were just discussing the status of his case."

"I didn't mean to interrupt," she said apologetically.

"That's okay," Captain Jack said. "Did you need something?"

"No, sir," she said politely. "Just letting you know that I am here." She turned and left the room, and Captain Jack resumed.

"Mr. Stokes, the courts are not perfect. Neither are the people who sit on juries. They're just ordinary folk subject to the same biases that affect us all."

He paused, let out a deep sigh, then resumed again.

"You have a pretty sordid history. And because of that, it didn't take much for the prosecutor to convince the jurors that Marcus was just another pea in a pod. His father was a ruffian, and so was he. The acorn didn't fall far from the tree."

Tyrone looked at him but did not speak.

"Mr. Stokes, I hurt for you, and I hurt for your family. God knows I do. But I can't say any more to you right now than I was able to say to your wife. A jury has said that Marcus brutally raped and murdered an innocent young girl. And for that, a court of law has ruled that he must pay with his life. And so he will, if the governor says the same."

"There has to be something."

"If so, I don't know what," he said. "I have done all that I know to do. I filed an appeal based on the fact that we were denied a change of venue. I filed a separate appeal based on the fact that our petition to have the jury sequestered was denied. I even challenged the composition of the jury. Mr. Stokes, as far as the appellate courts are concerned, your son had a fair trial, and the verdict will stand."

"What about a DNA test?" Tyrone asked.

"There is nothing to test."

"Didn't they say he raped her?"

"No semen," Captain Jack said.

"How could that be?"

"Prosecutor's explanation . . . He could have worn a condom."

"What about—"

"Mr. Stokes, I will petition the governor. That's all I can do."

There was a long, awkward silence.

"I want to see him."

"I can arrange that," he said. "The warden is an old friend of mine." He paused. "But I can't do anything before tomorrow."

Tyrone rose to leave, then stopped.

"How is he?"

"Scared," Captain Jack said. "Real scared."

Tyrone looked at Captain Jack, but Captain Jack was no longer looking at him. Instead, he had begun fiddling with some of the papers scattered over his desk. For him, the conversation was over. He was thinking of something else now—his next meeting, his next client, his next case.

"How will I know?" Tyrone asked.

"Know what?" Captain Jack responded, looking up briefly.

"When I can see him."

"Leave your number with Miss Rainer," Captain Jack told him. "I'll call you as soon as I know something."

Chapter
5

When he left Captain Jack's office, he did not go straight home. Instead, he drove to the small church just west of town. He did not attempt to enter the church, but rather walked around back, crossed the small, wooden footbridge, and passed through the short stand of trees that led into the tiny cemetery. Toward the middle of the cemetery, a fresh grave had been opened, and the loose, dry, excavated earth had been heaped to one side of the grave and covered with a sheet of thick white plastic. The sight of the open tomb made him uneasy, and he pressed on, navigating his way between one headstone after another until he finally stood before a well-manicured grave.

"Hi, Papa," he said, then lowered himself to the ground, pulled his feet underneath him, and looked away. From where he sat, he could see a small herd of cows grazing in the lush green pasture just east of the graveyard, and beyond the pasture, he could hear the low, dull roar of a tractor plowing in one of the adjacent fields. On the far end, he could see the old man everyone called Dirty Red. He had been mowing the cemetery; but it was breaktime now, and he had parked the bush hog underneath a tree and was sitting on the ground resting.

Just beyond the headstone marking his father's grave, he saw a tiny rabbit emerge from the sparse woods, pause, rise to its hind legs, and begin nibbling on the leaves of one of the low-hanging branches. The sight of the small furry animal caused him to smile. It was ironic, but the cemetery, this most dreaded place of death, calmed him. It was so quiet, so peaceful, so tranquil.

"You got a nice spot here, Papa," he said, glancing at the headstone, then looking away. Two black men had entered the cemetery and were inspecting the grave that had been opened. One of them wore a pair of black slacks and a short-sleeve shirt, and the other wore a dark blue jumpsuit.

"I'm sorry I wasn't at your funeral . . . I wanted to pay my respects. But . . . I—"

Tyrone's voice became heavy. His eyes became full. A tear fell from one eye, then the other. He picked up a small stone from the graveside and threw it into the woods. The sound of the stone tearing through the trees startled the rabbit. It fell to its feet, scampered a few paces to the right, paused, then disappeared into the darkness of the woods. Tyrone reached up and wiped his moist nose with the back of his hand. He filled his lungs with air and let out a deep sigh.

"I didn't want to disgrace the family no more than I already had by showing up at your funeral in handcuffs and chains."

Again, his misty eyes filled, and a long stream of tears fell from the corners of his eyes. He paused a second time, took a deep breath, then compressed his lips and struggled to maintain control of his voice.

"Mama, Sarah Ann, and René all doing fine. Mama and Sarah Ann act like they happy to see me, but René act like she don't know if she ought to be happy I'm out or scared I'm gone do something else to hurt the family."

Tyrone was interrupted by the roar of an engine. Breaktime was over, and Dirty Red had climbed atop the little red tractor and resumed his work. It was hot, and though he had not removed his shirt, he had unbuttoned it down the front and pulled it out of his pants. He did not have on work gloves, but he was wearing a straw hat on his head and a pair of dark shades over his eyes. A slight breeze was blowing, and Tyrone could smell the sweet fragrance of the freshly cut grass riding the wind, scenting the air. Involuntarily, his gaze fell on the tombstone, and inside his head, he heard himself reading: *Albert Stokes. October 22, 1923–May 16, 1997.*

Suddenly, his hands began to shake; his lips began to quiver. He opened his mouth to speak, but no words came. He let out a deep sigh, then paused, trying to compose himself. He stared in the direction of the woods, but he was not seeing them. He was imagining his dead father, dressed in his favorite suit, lying in a coffin, his eyes closed, his arms at his sides.

"Aw, Papa," he said. "I need you so much . . . Why did you have to die?" The anger came from a place deep inside of him. A place that he no longer recognized. "Why did you leave me?" A floodgate had been opened; now he sobbed heavily.

His mind began to whirl; his head began to ache. He snapped to his feet and turned away from the grave. Was this the fate that awaited his son? Would his body soon be laid to rest in a place like this, before people like him, who were powerless to stop the powers that be from doing the unthinkable? On that day, would he gather at his son's grave, seeking solace in a soul-wrenching spiritual, or a God-inspired word, or a gentle touch from a friend or relative? Would he be there when they rolled him into a room, strapped him to a table, and injected him with the serum that would eliminate him forever? Suddenly, he couldn't breathe. His chest felt tight. He took a deep breath, paused, then walked away.

When he again became aware of himself, he was walking up the front gallery of his mother's house. Both his oldest sister, Sarah Ann, and his mother were on the porch. Sarah Ann was sitting on the swing piecing a quilt, and his mother was sitting in a rocker drinking a cup of coffee.

When he pulled the screen door open and stepped onto the porch, neither one of them said so, but he knew that they were waiting for him.

"How you feeling, Mama?" he asked.

"Oh, I'm doing fairly," she said, then paused. He leaned forward, and she kissed him on the forehead.

"How you, sis?" he asked.

"Making out," she said.

"You ate?" his mother asked.

"No, ma'am," he said. "I ain't hungry."

"You ate since last night?" she asked.

"No, ma'am," he said.

"Well, you need to eat," she insisted.

"Mama, I ain't got no appetite right now."

"It's some grits and eggs and bacon and sausage in there."

"I ain't hungry."

"You find out anything?" Sarah Ann asked.

"Some," he said. "Not much."

She was quiet, and he knew she was waiting for him to tell her more.

"His lawyer gone try to git 'em to let me see 'im tomorrow," he said.

"You need to put something in your stomach," his mother said. "You want Sarah Ann to fix you some toast?"

"I can't eat right now, Mama," he said. "I just can't."

"You need to force yourself," she said. "You ain't gone do nothing but make yourself sick."

"Mama, he gone eat directly," Sarah Ann said. "Ain't no sense in you carrying on so. He gone eat."

"He gone git sick if he don't," she said. "Don't make no sense sitting 'round worrying on a empty stomach."

There was silence.

"Maybe I should've made Pauline bring him to see me," Tyrone said.

"You did what you thought best," Sarah Ann said.

"But what if—"

"What if, nothing," Sarah Ann said. "You ain't the blame for this. If he did what they say he did, you ain't the blame. He is."

"Sarah Ann, why don't you fix your brother a plate," his mother pleaded. "I sho' would feel better if he ate something."

"I ain't hungry, Mama," Tyrone said a third time.

"Mama, I told you. He gone eat when he ready."

"He didn't really know me," Tyrone said, speaking to no one in particular. "He should have known his daddy."

"Did he know right from wrong?" Sarah Ann asked.

"I'm sure he did," Tyrone said. "I'm sure Pauline saw to that."

"Then, he knew all he needed to know."

"Want some coffee?" his mother asked. "Ought to be some in there. Pot still on the stove. You welcome to it now."

"Naw, Mama," Tyrone said. "I don't want nothing."

"People sho' can git theyself tangled up in some mess," Sarah Ann said.

"I got to know," Tyrone blurted.

"Know what?" Sarah Ann asked.

"Whether he did it or not," Tyrone told her.

"How you gone know that?"

"I'm gone ask 'im."

"What make you thank he gone tell you?"

"I just know he will."

"How you know he gone tell you the truth?"

" 'Cause he don't lie."

There was silence. He raised his eyes and looked at Sarah Ann.

"You think he did it?" he asked.

"I don't know what to think," she said.

"Baby, why don't you go lie down cross the bed," his mother said. "Try to rest your nerves."

"Yes, ma'am," he said. "I believe I'll do that." He rose to leave, then stopped. "Lawyer say he'll most certainly die."

"Don't make no difference what that lawyer say," his mother told him. "Only matter what God say."

Chapter
6

He lay down in the bedroom just beyond the living room. This had been his room when he was a child, but now, it was a spare room, open to anyone who needed a roof over their head or a momentary place to rest their weary bones. Inside the tiny room, there was a bed, a night stand, a space heater, a chair, and a small dresser. The floor, like those throughout the house, was covered with a cheap, light-colored linoleum. The paneled walls were bare save for a large picture of the *Last Supper* that hung on one wall and an outdated calendar from the local feed and seed store that hung on the other. The only window was the tiny opening cut in the top half of the rear door, and the only other source of light was the single bulb that hung from the center of the ceiling.

Besides the entrance off the main hall, there were two other ways to enter or exit the room. There was a side entrance that led into the adjacent bedroom. That room had been shared by Sarah Ann and René when they were children, but now, the twin beds had been removed and replaced with the queen-size bed that René shared with her husband, Jimmy. There was also a rear exit that led out onto a small side porch. Someone had left the side door open, and from where he lay, he could see outside. There was a large pecan tree just north of the porch and a fig tree just south of the porch. Beyond both trees was a fence, inside of which was a garden, and outside the garden was a road. Directly across the road, he could hear a group of neighborhood boys playing softball in a vacant lot. He started to go out onto the porch and watch, but reconsidered. Mentally, he was drained. He needed rest. He had just closed his eyes when he heard the loud, cracking sound of the bat making contact with the ball. Someone had just gotten a hit, and he could hear the others yelling frantically, encouraging him to run, willing him to score. In his mind, he could see the boy crossing first base, passing second, rounding third, heading home.

Tyrone was listening to the cheering of the excited children when he heard the sound of feet on the front steps followed by the sound of the screen door opening and closing.

"Morning, Miss Hannah," he heard someone say.

"Morning, Brother Clayton," his mother responded.

"You looking mighty fine this morning, Miss Sarah," Mr. Clayton said in a tone that indicated more than a greeting; he was flirting.

"Clayton, I ain't studin' you," Sarah Ann said sternly.

Sarah Ann had just turned fifty, and her mother was in her early seventies. The two women favored each other, only Sarah Ann was short and heavy-set, whereas her mother was tall and thin. Neither of them was dressed fancy. Sarah Ann wore a plain, bland duster that hung just below her knees, and her mother wore a multicolored shift, the length of which must not have been satisfactory, for she had draped an old towel across her lap to cover that which her dress did not. Neither of them was wearing shoes. Sarah Ann did have on a pair of house slippers, but her mother's feet were bare.

"Pull up a chair, Brother Clayton, and sat down," Tyrone heard his mother say after a brief silence. "Take a load off your feet."

"Aw, I ain't gone stay long," Mr. Clayton said. "I'm just checking on y'all."

"We making out all right," Miss Hannah said.

"Well, thank God for that," he responded.

Tyrone heard a deep sigh, and he could tell by the series of creaks that Mr. Clayton had sat in the flimsy wooden chair that sat between Sarah and his mother.

"Clayton, what you got in that bucket?" Miss Hannah asked.

"Brought y'all a mess of fish," he said.

"You fished today?"

"Yes, ma'am. Fished Gasoway this morning."

"They biting good?"

"Pretty good," he said. "Caught some real nice perch."

Tyrone heard the sound of a chair scraping the floor.

"Yeah, Clayton," he heard his mother say after a brief silence. "They is nice. Real nice. I'm gone get René to fry 'em soon as she come home from work."

"Want me to clean 'em for you?" Clayton asked.

"Naw," she said. "I'll get Tyrone to clean 'em when he git up."

"He here?" Clayton asked.

"Yeah, he made it in last night," she said. "He in there lying down."

"How he look?"

"Done aged some and done put on a little weight," Miss Hannah said. "Other than that, he look 'bout the same."

"He know 'bout his boy?"

"Told 'im this morning."

There was silence, and Tyrone knew Mr. Clayton was turning things over in his mind.

"He take it awright?" he asked.

"Well as can be expected," Miss Hannah said. "He went to see the lawyer this morning, but I don't thank he got no satisfaction. Way that old lawyer talk, ain't too much nobody can do. He say, mo' than likely, they gone kill that child."

"Well, Miss Hannah, I suspect he right."

"What make you say that, Brother Clayton?"

"You know Mike Buehler, don't you?"

"He the one that own that little catfish house over in Brownsville?"

"Naw, now that's his brother Dale. Mike the one that own all them grocery stores. He live in Brownsville, but he got stores in Wilmington and Pinesboro, too."

"Mama, you know 'im," Sarah Ann said. "He married Mr. John's oldest daughter. Miss Annie Lou."

"He a kind of heavy-set fellow?"

"That's him," Mr. Clayton said.

"What he got to do with this?" Miss Hannah asked.

"Old boy that work at the lumber shed told me that gal is kin to 'im."

"Sho' nuff?"

"That's what he say."

"Close kin?"

"I don't thank she supposed to be close kin, but she kin. Now, he told me that Mike Buehler done talked to the mayor, and the mayor done talked to the governor, and the governor done fixed it so that it ain't no way in this world that Marcus gone git out of this thang alive."

"I sho' hate to hear that."

"Well, I hate to say it," Clayton said, "but that's the way it's being told."

He said that, and then it was quiet. Tyrone had been lying on his back, but now he rolled onto his side and propped his hand underneath his chin, listening.

"Well, I tell you what I hate," Sarah Ann said. "I hate to see Tyrone have to go through something like this so soon after getting out the pen. I'm scared it's gone send him right back to dranking and smoking that old dope."

"He just gone have to stay on his knees," Miss Hannah said. "Lawd ain't gone give 'im more than he can stand."

"I know that's right," Mr. Clayton said.

"It might be right, but I still hate to see it," Sarah Ann said emphatically. "It already look like he done just about worried hisself to death."

"That's why I made 'im go lie down," Miss Hannah said. "I'm gone make 'im eat, too, soon as he wake up."

"Well, all y'all can do is look after 'im."

"We gone do that."

"If there is anything I can do, let me know."

"We'll do that, Brother Clayton. We sho' will."

"Well, I better be gitting on."

"Ain't no sense in hurrying."

"I promised Phoebe I'd clean that fence row for her today."

"Now, don't you git out there and git too hot."

"I won't."

"Tell Phoebe I asked about her."

"I'll do that."

"And you tell her, when she see Fred, be sho' to tell him that that oldest boy of his passed here the other day and ain't bit mo' opened his mouth to speak than that tree over yonder."

"I know he didn't," Clayton said, his tone indicating shock.

"Baby was sitting right here when he passed," Miss Hannah said, then added, "These children today, I just don't know. Look like they ain't got no respect for the old folks. None at all."

"Well, I'm sho' gone tell her," Clayton said.

"Good," Miss Hannah said. " 'Cause I know Fred raised him better than that."

"He gone git on 'im," Clayton assured her. "Soon as he find out, he gone git on 'im. You can count on that."

"He need to."

"Well, I'm gone run."

"You gone take supper with us this evening, ain't you?"

"Thank you, but I'm gone have to pass."

"You know you mo' than welcome."

"Some other time."

"I'm gone hold you to that."

"Yes, ma'am, I know you will."

Tyrone heard the screen door open and close.

"Brother Clayton."

"Yes, ma'am."

"Thank you, hear."

"Aw, you welcome."

Chapter
7

Not long after Mr. Clayton left, Tyrone heard Sarah Ann in the kitchen preparing lunch. He did not hear her pass in the hall, so either he had dozed off or she had walked around the house and entered through the back door. Though he did not see her pass, he knew it was her. For that was the routine. Not only did she prepare their mother's lunch, but she also ran her errands and helped with her laundry. René, on the other hand, cooked breakfast before she went to work (she kept house for one of the local white merchants) and she cooked dinner when she returned. Their father had taken care of the yard, but since he passed, Jimmy had taken over those responsibilities. He washed dishes at the hospital during the week and tended the yard during the weekend.

Tyrone heard a noise, and he went to the door and saw his mother easing down the dim hallway, leaning against the wall for support.

"Did I wake you up, honey?" she asked as soon as she saw him.

"No, ma'am," he told her. "I wasn't asleep."

She eased closer, and Tyrone stepped into the hallway.

"You need some help, Mama?" he asked, extending his hand in her direction.

"Naw, baby," she said softly. "I'm just going to the restroom. I can make it."

She pulled up even with him, and Tyrone stepped aside to allow her to pass.

"You gone try to eat something now, ain't you?" she asked.

"Yes, ma'am," he said. "I'll try."

The kitchen was toward the back of the house. There was only one room farther back, and that was René's room. Past her room was the door leading into the backyard. The outer door was open, and Tyrone could feel a cool breeze circulating through the screen door, cooling the hall. He turned into the kitchen and saw Sarah Ann standing in front of the stove. Her back was to him, but he could see that she was frying potatoes in a cast-iron skillet. Like most of the house, the kitchen was simply constructed and sparsely furnished. It was a rather large, rectangular room. There was a table and four chairs in the corner next to the rear window. The make of the table was not readily discernible, for it was covered with a simple white tablecloth that hung nearly to the floor. Besides the stove, the only other appliance was the white, single-door refrigerator positioned in the corner just off the entrance. There were two sets of homemade cabinets. One was located below the sink, and the other was on the wall just left of the sink. There were four windows. Two on the back wall, one on the side wall, and one directly above the sink. Though each window was open, the outside breeze was no match for the heat emanating from the stove. The kitchen was a virtual furnace.

"Lunch ready?" he chided.

Sarah Ann turned to face him, and he could see the tiny beads of sweat running down both sides of her face.

"Almost," she said. "I fixed some bologna sandwiches and fried a few potatoes. You must finally be hungry."

"Not really," he said. "Mama sent me in here."

"She still on you 'bout eating, hunh?"

"Yeah."

"Well, you might as well eat, 'cause you know she gone keep on 'til you do. Want me to fix you a plate?"

"Naw," he said. "I can do it."

Tyrone moved to the double sink next to the stove, removed the bar of soap from behind the faucet, and washed his hands. He dried them on the rag that Sarah Ann had draped over her shoulder; then he took a plate from the cupboard next to the sink and a fork from one of the drawers. Sarah Ann had put the fried potatoes in an aluminum mixing bowl and placed them on the stove. Tyrone put a few on his plate and took a sandwich off the dish before taking a seat at the table.

"It's some Kool-Aid in the box," Sarah Ann said. "If you want some."

He went to the cupboard, removed a glass, filled it with Kool-Aid, and then returned to his seat at the far end of the table. While he was up, Sarah Ann had placed a box of salt and a bottle of ketchup next to his plate. He sprinkled some salt over his potatoes, then doused them with ketchup. From where he sat, he could see into the backyard. A clothesline had been strung from the far corner of the house to a pole that had been posted about fifteen feet out. Just beyond the pole there was a small building. It had been a woodhouse before the main house was converted to gas. Now, instead of being filled with cords of wood, it was filled with old furniture and other large keepsakes that required storage. To the left of the wood house was a second fig tree; it was twice the size of the tree on the west side of the house. To the right of the wood house, and a few yards up, there was a little toolshed, and just beyond the toolshed, there was a pear tree loaded with pears ready to be picked, ready to be canned.

"You know Mama don't mean no harm, don't you?"

"I know she don't."

"She just call herself looking out for you."

"I know."

"You know when she make her mind up you can't tell her nothing." Sarah Ann said that, then started to laugh. "Guess what me and René used to call her behind her back when we was chil'en."

"What?" Tyrone asked.

"Miss I Know," she said, then howled with laughter. "I mean, she thought she knew everything. Couldn't tell her nothing. Still can't."

Tyrone laughed, but he did not say anything.

"We didn't sass her or nothing. You know for yourself we was all raised better than that. But we sho' did call her Miss I Know. And it fit her to a T."

Tyrone heard someone stirring about in the hall behind him. He turned in his chair and saw that his mother had made her way to the kitchen and was standing in the doorway, looking toward the stove.

"I know that little something to eat ought to be done by now," she said. Hers had been more statement of fact than a question.

"Yes, ma'am," Sarah Ann said. Then both she and Tyrone howled with laughter.

"What's so funny?" their mother wanted to know.

"Nothing, Mama," Sarah Ann said.

"I know y'all laughing at something," she blurted.

"Naw, Mama, we ain't laughing at nothing."

Confused, their mother began examining her clothes. "Y'all act like I done peed on myself or something."

She said that; then they all laughed.

"Mama, I told you it ain't nothing."

Their mother turned her attention to Tyrone. "Child, why you eating in this hot kitchen?"

"It's all right, Mama," he said. "It ain't that bad over here by the window."

"Well, it's too hot in here for me," she said.

"Go 'n back on the porch, Mama," Sarah Ann said. "I'm gone bring yo' food to you."

"Don't fix much," she said. "I ain't that hungry. I just want a little taste."

"Yes, ma'am," Sarah Ann said. "I know."

Their mother left, and they both laughed again.

"Ought to be a little piece of sweet bread over there if you want it," Sarah Ann said after she had stopped laughing.

"I don't want none," he replied.

"I baked a pie at the house," she said. "I intended to bring it, but I went off and left it."

"What kind?"

"Sweet potato."

"I wish you had."

"I'll bring it when I come tomorrow."

He smiled but did not speak.

"Mr. Clayton brought Mama some fish this morning," she said. "You feel like cleaning 'em?"

"Yeah." He nodded. "I'll clean 'em."

"When you git through, I'm gone season 'em so René won't have so much to do when she come in."

"I'm sho' she'll appreciate that."

"Reckon y'all gone want potato salad with that fish?"

"I don't," he said. "But they might."

"Well then, I might as well peel a few mo' potatoes while I'm at it."

She removed a few potatoes from the bottom cabinet and placed them in the sink. Then she turned on the faucet and began to wash them.

"Can I ask you something, sis?"

"Yeah, what?"

"I heard Mr. Clayton talking a little while ago."

"Un hunh."

"Reckon it's possible?"

"Is what possible?"

"That they've already decided about Marcus."

"I don't put nothing past them people."

"Guess that's why Captain Jack didn't say much. Maybe he already know."

"Could be."

Suddenly, his doubts rose. His concerns grew. He wondered about Captain Jack. Who was he? Was he competent? Had he been hired or had he been appointed? How vigorously had the attorney fought for his son's life? Had he really fought at all?

"I was thinking about going back over there," he said. "What you think?"

"For what?" she wanted to know.

"To see that lawyer again."

"Well, I don't 'spect you gone be able to rest if you don't."

Chapter
8

He received the phone call from Captain Jack's office by eight o'clock the following morning. He wasn't asleep when the call came. He had gone to bed and had tried to sleep, but when sleep would not come, he passed the night lying on his back, listening to the soothing sound of crickets chirping outside his bedroom window and the loud, monotonous ticking of the small wind-up clock sitting atop the television in the adjacent room. When twilight dawned, he was still lying in bed fully conscious of the sounds of a well-rested world rising to face another day.

At five he heard Mrs. Alberta's rooster crow. At five-fifteen, Mr. Lonzo's old Ford truck rumbled past. He was on his way to work; he had to be at the plant by six. By five-thirty, the trash collectors arrived. He heard the garbage truck when it pulled off the road in front of his house and he heard the men talking amongst themselves as they worked.

"What time is it?" Tyrone heard one of them ask the other.

"Too early to start watching the clock," he heard the other respond.

"Look like it's gone be a hot one," came an unrelated observation.

"Weather man say it suppose to rain," the other retorted.

"Well, he didn't tell the good Lawd, 'cause it ain't a cloud in the sky."

Suddenly, the men were quiet. Then Tyrone heard a loud grunt followed by the sound of trash hitting the bottom of the truck. A few seconds passed before the empty barrel hit the ground. The engine roared, and the truck rolled on.

At six-thirty, he took a shower. By seven, he had dressed and eaten a simple breakfast—two slices of bacon, one slice of toast, and three scrambled eggs. He had spoken to Janell by eight, and he was on the road by nine.

As he drove, his mind was preoccupied, and his actions were mechanical. He passed through towns without seeing them. He stopped at signal lights without thought. Instinctively, he drove over hills and through curves, automatically adjusting his speed to negotiate turns or to execute lane changes. With dulled senses and a muted mind, he pressed onward until some abnormality forced in him a temporary state of awareness. Just outside the small village of Epps, it was a slow-moving pick-up truck driven by a middle-aged white man with curly black hair. There were three black boys riding in the back. One stood against the cab, and the other two sat on the railing. They were farmhands. He could tell by their dirty bodies and their tattered clothes. Maybe they drove tractors, or hauled hay, or tended livestock. But more than likely, they worked in a potato field; after all, this was potato season, and by their appearance, they had already spent the early part of the morning riding a potato setter.

In Wilmington, it was a freight train, the Southern Pacific, going who knew where, carrying who knew what. He sat at the crossing for what seemed an eternity, clutching the wheel, counting passing cars . . . two engines, fourteen flat cars, forty-two boxcars, and finally the caboose.

The train passed, and he guided his truck across the tracks and through the center of town. There were a few people milling about Main Street, but not many. It was Tuesday. Most of the adults were at work, and most of the children were in school. He drove another two or three miles before turning off the highway and onto the ramp which led onto the interstate. Again, his tense body relaxed. He loosened his grip and leaned back against the seat, his mind lulled by the hypnotic motion of four rubber tires gliding over the smooth concrete highway. Physically, his tired body yearned for rest, but his hyperactive mind, fixated on the plight of his son, yearned for answers to questions, the implications of which meant the difference between living and dying. The sound of a siren made him check the mirror. Flashing lights caused him to change lanes. He slowed and pulled to the right. An ambulance raced past, and he watched it disappear into the horizon. In a brief moment of awareness, he recognized that it was a beautiful day. The medians were green; the air was fresh; the sky was blue.

He arrived in Shreveport at eleven-fifteen, and from high atop the interstate he could see the skyline of the city with its tall, majestic buildings glistening under the hot summer sun. Two miles outside the city limits, he exited the interstate and drove down a long stretch of country road. The prison was twenty miles hence in what for most people probably seemed the middle of nowhere, but for inmates like his son, it had become the center of everything.

When he arrived at the penitentiary, he parked his truck in the large lot just outside the gates and climbed out onto the pavement. To his left and through a haze of heat loomed a series of drab, gray buildings neatly situated behind a tall chain-linked fence. From where he stood, he could see the sharp, menacing razor wire spiraling ominously across the top of the imposing fence that circled the compound and fortified the prison. There were two guard towers rising high above it all, manned by men who watched all who came and who no doubt gave final approval to all who would depart. As Tyrone walked toward the entrance, he inclined his head and looked toward the tower. There were two men on each tower, one armed with binoculars, the other with a high-powered rifle. All of them wore uniforms. Navy blue pants, baby blue, short-sleeved shirts, and shiny gold badges. Three wore hats; one did not.

He felt their eyes on him. His tepid skin flushed hot as searing blood surged through his pulsating veins and spiraled to his light, giddy head. He approached the gate cautiously, ever aware of the small surveillance camera mounted just above the entrance. The gate swung open, and he followed the sidewalk to a huge metal door. His

stark eyes fell on the bold black letters posted on the wall: No weapons. No drugs. No alcohol. All visitors will be searched. All violators
will be prosecuted.

He pulled the door open and stepped inside. Directly ahead of him
was a second door. To his left a uniformed man sat in a small office
behind a large Plexiglas window. He was a portly man, in his mid-to-
late fifties. The hair on his balding head was black save for the tiny
patches of gray about his temples. His pale white skin had begun to
wrinkle, and the whites of his sky blue eyes held a jaundiced tint.

"Can I help you?" the man asked. His tone was gruff; his stare, cold.

"I'm here to visit a inmate," Tyrone said.

"Ain't no visitation today!" the man said in a thick southern drawl.

"They told me I could see him."

The old man stared at him for a moment. Then he narrowed his
eyes and furrowed his brow, confused.

"They who?" he asked.

"His attorney," Tyrone said. "Mr. Johnson."

The man sighed, leaned back in his chair, and rubbed his short,
grubby fingers over his bald head.

"Who you trying to see?"

"My son," Tyrone told him. "Marcus Stokes."

He watched the old man push a coffee cup aside, then touch his
thumb to the tip of his tongue and begin looking through a stack of
papers, agitated.

"You Tyrone Stokes?"

"Yes, sir."

The old man eyed Tyrone coldly, then slid a piece of paper
through a slot underneath the Plexiglas.

"Sign in," he said.

Tyrone signed his name, then looked at the clock hanging on the
wall behind the man. It was ten minutes until one. He noted the time
and slid the paper back through the slot. He heard a buzz, then a
click. The large metal door opened. He walked through, and the door
clanged shut. Waiting in the corridor, behind the door, was a second
officer. He was a young man, tall and athletic with grayish eyes, short,
dark brown hair, and thick, bushy eyebrows. He had a pistol strapped
to his waist, a metal detector dangling from one hand, and a tiny

bucket in the other. Their eyes met, and the officer extended the small bucket toward Tyrone.

"Empty your pockets."

He seemed serious, but not gruff. Stern, but not mean. Tyrone removed his keys and his loose change and dropped everything into the bucket.

"Is that it?"

"Yes, sir," Tyrone said. "That's it."

"Raise your arms above your head."

Tyrone lifted his arms high above his head, and the officer ran the scanner underneath his left arm, down the outside of his left leg, and then up the inside before switching to the other side and repeating the same.

"Turn around and face the wall."

Tyrone turned and stared at the wall. It was a plain cement wall that was bare save for the round mirror in the corner just below the ceiling. Through the reflection in the mirror, he watched the officer slowly drag the scanner down his back, over his butt, and about his ankles. Satisfied that all was safe, the officer returned his things, then uttered, "Follow me."

Tyrone followed him, fully expecting to be led deep into the bowels of the prison, traversing a maze of slamming doors while walking past hordes of half-dressed, tattoo-covered men peering at him from behind steel bars. Instead, he was led down a long hallway, through two sets of solid steel doors, and into a moderate-size room. Inside the room, there was a long row of chairs, each in its own tiny cubicle, and each neatly aligned behind a thick glass partition that spanned the full length of the wall. He took a seat before the glass and stared wide-eyed at the empty chair on the other side. The door opened and two officers escorted Marcus inside. "My God," Tyrone mumbled as his gaze fell on the frail shell of his son hobbling toward the empty chair, swinging the chains girting his hands, and dragging the shackles binding his feet.

One of the guards loosened his hands, and, as if in a daze, Marcus eased into the chair, then lifted the phone from the hook and placed it to his ear. He looked at Tyrone, and his large, empty eyes revealed the hopeless soul of a broken man. His hair was long and unkempt.

His face unshaven. His teeth dingy. His body bent. He was living, but he was no longer alive.

"How you doing, son?" Tyrone asked. He did not look directly at Marcus, but at the two officers who had led him into the room. Neither left. Both stood back against the wall watching Marcus, guarding the door.

"Awright," Marcus mumbled. His voice was unemotional, lifeless.

Tyrone parted his lips to speak, then paused. Lingering just beneath the surface of his iron constitution, his frayed emotions threatened to erupt and release an avalanche of raw, naked emotions. His mind counseled him to be calm. Inside his head, he heard himself trying desperately to still his pounding heart and relax his wretched nerves. He swallowed, feeling a glob of saliva slide off the back of his stiff, thick tongue and down the hollow of his parched, throbbing throat. He concentrated on trying to steady his trembling hands and calm his shaky voice.

"They treating you awright, son?" he asked.

Marcus nodded, but did not speak. Again, Tyrone looked at the guards; only this time, they were looking at him. Though he knew they could not hear what he was saying, he sensed that they were aware that he was talking about them.

"You need anything?" Tyrone asked.

"No, sir," Marcus said, then averted his eyes.

There was an awkward silence. Tyrone shifted his eyes to Marcus. Marcus looked at him briefly, then looked away.

"You seen Mama?" Marcus asked. His head was bowed, and one of his hands clasped the phone while the other lay across his lap.

"Not yet," Tyrone said uneasily.

"This been hard on her," Marcus confided, his voice tinged with regret.

"I can imagine," Tyrone said in an understanding tone.

There was a pause. Marcus raised his head for the second time. The whites of his puffy eyes were red, and the skin of his chestnut-colored forehead was marked with several thin, dark lines. He seemed tired; he looked old.

"You back home?" he asked softly, timidly.

Tyrone shook his head, then paused. He saw Marcus furrow his brow, and he knew that the boy was confused. He had not understood. He wanted an explanation. "Cedar Creek," Tyrone told him. "Least for the time being."

"Grandma Hannah's."

"Yeah," he said. "Got out a few day ago. Been there every night since."

Marcus looked at him; then his sullen eyes dropped submissively.

"Glad you got out," he said. His voice was dry and mechanical. "Don't reckon I ever will. Least not alive."

"Don't say that, son," Tyrone said. "Don't ever say that."

Marcus raised his head, and there was a faraway look in his gloomy eyes.

"I had a dream the other night." He spoke in a frightened whisper. Tyrone looked at him but did not speak.

"It happened." He paused, and his eyes widened. He was reliving the dream. He was seeing the whole thing. "They strapped me down. . . ." His heaving chest began rising and falling. "And they did it . . ." His hands began to shake. The chain began to rattle. "They killed me."

"Naw, son," Tyrone said, shaking his head slowly. "That ain't gone happen."

Marcus's quivering mouth hung open. His head was perfectly still. His unfocused eyes were staring straight ahead, looking at nothing, seeing nothing.

"I went to this place . . ." He said that, and his voice trailed off. "It was dark . . . so dark."

"Son, you just scared," Tyrone said. "That's all. You just a little scared. It's gone be all right. I promise you that."

"People were crying," Marcus continued as though in a trance. "I heard moaning." His twitching eyes narrowed, and he slowly looked about. "Daddy," he whispered in a voice laced with terror, "I was so scared."

"It was just a dream."

"I don't want to die."

"You ain't gone die."

"I keep asking God why this happening to me. But he don't tell me nothing."

"Marcus!"

"I just want it to be over."

"Marcus!"

"I just want to go home."

"Marcus!" Tyrone shouted into the phone. He leaned forward, his tensed face against the thick glass separating them. "I want to help you, son," he said. His voice was stern; his teeth, clenched. "But you got to pull yourself together."

Marcus stared blankly at his father; then his moist eyes dropped, and he slumped in his chair, quiet. Tyrone looked at the guards. There was a smirk on what had been stoic faces. This was what they wanted. Now that the day had been chosen and the time had been set, they wanted to see him squirm. They wanted to see him cry; they wanted to see him suffer. They wanted him to beg like that little girl had begged. He had shown her no mercy, and now the state would show him none.

"Tell me what happened, son."

"I don't know what happened," Marcus declared fervently. His eyes searched his father's face, pleading for understanding. "I swear to God I don't."

"Why were you in that store?"

"Mama sent me," he said. "She was cooking." His voice had become soft, childlike. "She needed some onions and pepper and a can of milk."

"But you didn't buy anything."

He had heard that line of reasoning before, and hearing it again caused his tired, dreary eyes to well. It had been his downfall. Proof offered by the state that his had been a devious plan, hatched in a sick mind, executed by a cold-blooded killer. The store was a ruse. He was a stalker. She had been his prey.

"I was checking prices like I always do," he explained. His voice was deflated, and the tears from his eyes rolled down his face and connected underneath his chin. "That's all," he said. "Just checking prices."

"So when you left, you went to another store."

"Yes, sir," he mumbled.

"Did anybody see you?"

"I don't know."

"Think, son. Think!"

Marcus's wet eyes were blank. Several times he opened his mouth as though he was going to speak, but no words came.

"Did you buy anything?"

He nodded.

"What?" Tyrone wanted to know.

"Onions, pepper, milk." He was talking, but he was no longer there. The words were coming from a place deep inside of him. A place that was dark, lonely, painful.

"Can you prove you were there?"

He dropped his eyes and shook his head. He frowned. His mind flashed back, and again, he was rambling. "He tried to get me to make a deal." He raised his head and stared straight ahead. "He wanted me to plead guilty." Marcus paused, thinking. "I didn't know what to do. He kept saying if I didn't confess, I was gone die, but I couldn't. I didn't do what they say I did." His voice faded, and he became introspective. "Maybe I was wrong. Maybe I ain't gone get another chance. Maybe I'm gone die. But I just couldn't say I did something I knew I didn't do . . . I just couldn't."

"Who told you to confess?"

"Captain Jack."

Stunned, Tyrone opened his mouth to speak, but out of the corner of his eye, he saw the guards moving toward his son. He saw one whisper something to the other, then yell, "Time!"

Marcus rose clumsily to his feet, and they grabbed him by both arms. He turned and looked back at his father with sad, pleading eyes.

"I'll be back, son," Tyrone mouthed. "I'll be back."

Marcus nodded, and Tyrone watched him hobble away.

Chapter
9

After leaving the prison, Tyrone drove back to Brownsville with a staunch determination to know the man whose charge it had been to save his son's life and to rid himself of the nagging questions gnawing deep within his troubled soul. There was in him the feeling that the contest for his son's life had not been a battle in which Captain Jack had fought to win, but a game in which Captain Jack had played not to lose. There had been no knights, or pawns, or kings or queens, but there had been talk of deals, struck between friends, in quaint little rooms, over cordial glasses of brandy or stiff shots of gin.

When he pushed through the door of Captain Jack's office, Janell was sitting behind the desk up front, with her head bowed and her arms folded before her. There was a cup of coffee on one corner of her desk, several large books on the other, and an open file lying before her. Their eyes met. She smiled at him, and he approached the desk, ever aware of the lingering scent of her perfume in the cool, dry air.

"Can I see Mr. Johnson again?" he asked.

"I'm sorry, he's out of the office until tomorrow," she said. "Can I help you with something?"

Tyrone hesitated before answering. He had looked at her earlier, but he had not seen her. She was tall, five-seven or five-eight. That, he had noticed before. But he had not noticed her straight white teeth, or her big, beautiful brown eyes, or her long black hair that was pulled back and clamped behind her head, exposing her high cheekbones and her smooth brown skin. He had noticed her professional demeanor, but not the exquisite manner in which she dressed. She wore a navy blue skirt, a matching jacket, and a white shell. Her nails were sculptured and finished in a French manicure. She did not slouch, but sat tall with her back straight and her shoulders erect. She had a thin herringbone chain about her neck and two tiny gold studs in her ears. Her fingers were bare save for the single pearl that she wore on the ring finger of her right hand.

"I was here earlier," he said. "I'm—"

"Marcus's father," she interrupted. "I remember."

Tyrone nodded but did not speak.

"What can I do for you?" she asked.

Her question caught him off guard. He had not anticipated Captain Jack being away from the office; therefore, he had not anticipated a conversation with her. There was a window to his right. Through the window loomed a gas station. A pig farmer had pulled a truck and a trailer filled with hogs next to one of the pumps and was filling his truck with gas. Tyrone was looking at the oversized man, who was adorned in overalls and wearing a big cowboy hat, when the man set the nozzle back in place and screwed the cap back on the gas tank, but he was not seeing him. He was collecting his thoughts; he was formulating his next question.

"Did you work on my son's case?" he asked after a brief silence.

"Well, yes and no," she said. "I was not working here when his case was tried, but I did work on his appeal."

"Then, you're familiar with the case?"

"Very," she said. "Why do you ask?"

Tyrone glanced at her, then looked away. Her desk was in the corner on the left side of the room. It was too large for the space and had been turned catercorner with one end extending to the far wall and the other to the door leading into Captain Jack's office. There was a couch and a few chairs on the right side of the room, next to the window. A plain, wooden coffee table that had been covered with several rows of neatly arranged magazines sat in front of the couch. There was no television, but there was a small radio atop her desk. It was on low, so low, in fact, that it was barely audible.

"Who hired Mr. Johnson?" he asked bluntly.

"Marcus's grandfather," she said, seemingly confused by the question. "Why?"

Tyrone paused again and measured his words. He didn't want to say the wrong thing. He didn't want to offend her.

"I heard the governor has given his assurance that my son will die."

"Given assurance to whom?" she asked, her tone indicating shock.

"The victim's relatives."

"I don't believe that."

"That's what I heard," Tyrone said, looking deep into her eyes.

"That's unlikely."

"But is it possible?"

"Yes," she said. "It's possible."

"Is it legal?"

"It's legal."

"I don't understand."

"Sir, both sides have a right to argue their case before the governor," she explained. "He can listen, if he chooses, but he is not obligated. Ultimately, it's his decision."

"How well do you know these people?"

"What people?" she asked.

"The governor . . . Mike Buehler . . . the girl?"

"Not well," she said. "I'm not from around here."

"Where you from?"

"Monroe," she said.

"That's a long ways from Brownsville," he said. "How in the world did you find a job way over here?"

"There was a job bulletin posted at the law school for a part-time paralegal. It seemed interesting, and since I've always wanted to practice law in a small town, I decided to give it a try. I called Mr. Johnson, he hired me, and I've been here ever since."

"You a student!"

"Yes, sir."

"You ain't a real lawyer?"

"No, sir, not yet. I'm a third-year law student."

There was silence.

"How well do you know Mr. Johnson?"

"Excuse me!" she said, probably louder than she had intended. Tyrone hesitated. She was black like him, but how honest was she? Could he speak to her freely? Would she be forthright?

"Why did he ask my son to cop a plea?"

"Have you ever tried a capital case?" Hers was a rhetorical question that required no answer. "Do you know what it's like to have somebody's life in your hands? Yes, he advised Marcus to plea. But his motives were not sinister, as you seem to be implying; he was simply trying to save your son's life."

"But he didn't try to get him off, did he?"

"The town was in an uproar."

"So, he sold him out?"

"He fought for your son's life," she said. "I've watched him sleep in this office for days at a time, looking for an angle, or a mistake, or anything to save Marcus. And he's still looking."

"Looks to me like he's done gave up."

"He's doing everything he can."

"Do you really believe that?"

"Yes, sir, I do."

"Would you feel the same way if Marcus was your son?"

"Yes, I would," she said, looking at him with stern eyes. "Let me tell you something about the man whose character you are questioning."

"No," Tyrone interrupted her. "Let me tell you something about the person they trying to kill. I was hard, but not my son. I stayed in trouble, but not him. He was always a good kid. A do-gooder. A mama's boy . . . Yesterday, a friend of mine tried to convince me that he has changed, but I know better." He paused. "Does he have a record?" he asked, then quickly added, "I mean, before all this happened?"

"No, sir," she said. "But you know the prosecution's response to that, don't you?"

"No," Tyrone said. "What?"

"They contend that his clean record does not mean that he has not done anything; it simply means that he had not been caught."

"He ain't done nothing," Tyrone said emphatically. "Not Marcus. No way."

"How can you be so sure?" she asked.

"Because I know him," Tyrone told her. "When he was a little boy, I tried to change him . . . I tried to make him tough . . . I tried to make him mean. But no matter how hard I tried and no matter what I did, I couldn't. He just stayed the same . . . wouldn't hurt a fly."

"Why did you want to change him?"

"Where exactly in Monroe do you live?"

"Castle Rock," she said.

"What kind of place is that?"

"A quiet place. Peaceful."

"Suburbs?" he asked.

"That's right," she said.

"Crime?"

"Not much."

"Ever seen a rat?"

"Sir, what does that have to do with anything?"

"Everything!"

"Mr. Stokes, this is not about me."

"You're right," he said. "It's about my son, and me, and where we're from."

"I don't understand."

"Where we live, you have to be tough to survive. Get them before they get you. That's what I tried to teach my boy. But he couldn't learn it. It just wasn't in him. That's why I know he didn't kill nobody. It ain't in him. He couldn't hurt a fly. It just ain't in him."

She looked at him but did not speak.

"Ma'am," he said. "The state got my boy, and he running out of time. I just need somebody to tell me what to do."

"He's exhausted his appeals," she explained.

"I understand that," Tyrone said.

"We've petitioned the governor."

"There has to be something else."

"There is," she said.

"What?" he asked.

"Prove he didn't do it."

"I want his file."

"Yes, sir," she said. "Come back in an hour."

Chapter 10

O utside the tiny office, traffic was beginning to build. It was three-thirty; the Glove Factory had just let out, and a long stream of workers were slowly making their way through town. Some of them stopped to do a little shopping, but most continued on, eventually connecting with one of the various highways leading them away from town and carrying them home.

He hadn't eaten since morning, and since he had close to an hour to burn, Tyrone decided to pass the time at the little deli just east of town. As he sat in traffic, inching along, he noticed a black lady sitting in the gazebo on the courthouse lawn, just beyond one of the many large oak trees that populated the property. She appeared to be fifty-four or fifty-five years old. She wore the clothes of a domestic—a white dress, brownish-colored stockings, white flat-soled shoes—and she had a rather large purse sitting on the bench next to her. Perhaps she worked in one of the large homes nearby, and now that her long, arduous day was over, she was waiting on her ride, in the cool, peaceful solitude of the courthouse square.

Some school children were huddled in front of the tiny ice cream stand just east of the courthouse. Like the old lady, the difficult part of their day was over, and now it was time for a chocolate malt, a vanilla shake, or a strawberry cone, or a bag of chips, an ice cold soda, or any small treat to celebrate another day endured.

Drained by the events of the day, he methodically navigated his truck through one signal light after the other, slowly creeping past the old abandoned theater and the hardware store, before finally turning off Main Street into the large parking lot surrounding the deli. The deli was not only a deli; it was also a gas station, a grocery store, and a drop-off and pick-up point for passengers traveling on the local Trailways bus line. Like many of the commercial establishments around town, the deli was not fancy, but it was clean, inexpensive, well stocked, and located in a perfect spot for stranded travelers looking to pass a little time. There was a Wal-Mart department store next door, and beyond Wal-Mart, there was a supermarket, beyond which sat an old train depot that had recently been converted into a pizzeria. Across the street, there was a large Methodist church where the white folks worshiped. Next to the church, there was a bank and a car lot, across from which was a dollar store. When he was a kid, the dollar store had always been a favorite hangout of his. Only then it had been called the Five and Dime. And though he had rarely patronized the store in the truest sense of the word—hard, cold cash for merchandise—it had been the primary establishment that he and his contemporaries frequented to kill a little time or to replenish their dwindling stock with a comb, a brush, some penny candy, a comic book, or anything that they could snatch from the shelves and stuff underneath their shirts without being detected by the watchful eye of the attending cashier.

As soon as he pulled into the lot, he could tell that for them, today was a busy day. There were cars at both of the gas pumps out front, and there were cars waiting behind each of the cars being serviced. There were two elderly men sitting on a bench that had been positioned in front of the building, against the wall, underneath the large bay window. The few front parking spaces were filled, and he had to circle the small building twice before finding a spot close to the rear in one of the side lots.

When he entered the building, he realized that not much about the deli had changed since he left. On the right side of the room were the same shelves of food and assorted merchandise. On the left side were the same tables and chairs, and up front was the same service counter and deli. There were between ten and twelve people inside the deli. Some were milling about the shelves of food, but most of them were sitting at the tables, eating.

Two white women stood behind the counter. Both were middle-aged, and both wore full-body aprons. One was working the cash register while the other filled orders. Through an open door at the rear of the deli, he could see three other people. One, a short, robust black man, appeared to be tending the fryer, and the other, a young white fellow with long, stringy blond hair, was making sandwiches. The third man seemed to be in charge. Perhaps he was the supervisor, or maybe he was the manager. Like the others, he also wore a full-length apron, but unlike them, his appearance was more formal. Underneath his apron, he wore a white dress shirt, a tie, and dark-colored slacks. There was a pen in the front pocket of his apron, and he was holding a clipboard in his left hand.

As Tyrone approached the counter, he nodded at the woman behind the register, then focused his eyes on the huge menu board hanging on the back wall.

"May I help you?" she asked.

"Three-piece chicken dinner," he said, then added, "All dark."

"Anything to drink with that?" she asked.

"Coke," he said.

"Here or to go?" she asked.

"Here," he said.

She ran her hands across the keys of the cash register, then paused and looked up at him.

"Anything else?"

"No," he said. "That'll do it."

She rang up his bill, and while Tyrone was paying her, the blond lady dished up the food and placed it on a serving tray—two thighs, a leg, one ear of corn, and a small container of mashed potatoes and gravy. After he finished paying, she placed the tray on the counter and gently slid it to him.

"Enjoy your meal," she said. Her voice was soft. Her tone, friendly.

"Yes, ma'am, I will," he said. "Thank you."

He moved to an empty table next to the window. Not the large bay window at the rear of the store, but the small window on the east side of the building. From where he sat, he could see into the large Wal-Mart parking lot. A stock boy had collected a long string of stray shopping carts and was pushing them from the far end of the lot back to the store. Tyrone watched him for a minute, then lifted a piece of chicken from his plate.

He had just sunk his teeth into the warm, tender meat when he heard someone say, "You Tyrone Stokes?"

Startled, he looked around. Standing in the aisle behind him was a white woman. She was of average height, five-foot-four or five-foot-five. She was slender and appeared to be in her early forties, but she could have been older. Her hair was dark, slightly curly, and hung well below her shoulders. She wore plain clothes. A white blouse and a simple, multicolored skirt that fell about her ankles. She had on some make-up, but not much. He did not know how she knew him, but he did know that he did not know her.

"Yes, ma'am," he said. "I am."

"You got some nerve coming around here." She did not avert her face, but looked directly at him. She had pretty brown eyes, but now they were hard, cold.

"Ma'am, I'm just trying to eat a piece of chicken."

"Eat it somewhere else!" she demanded.

"I bought it here, and I'm gone eat it here."

The man with the clipboard must have heard him, because as soon as Tyrone said that, he hurried from behind the counter and rushed to the table.

"What's the problem, Maude?" he questioned.

"Jake, you ought to be more particular 'bout who you let in here," she said.

An eerie silence fell over the room, and though Tyrone did not turn and look, he could feel the eyes of everyone on him.

"Mister," he said calmly, "I don't want no trouble."

"You are trouble," the woman said.

"Maude!" the man said in a stern, terse voice. Tyrone could tell by his tone and by the confused look on his face that though he did not fully understand the nature of her problem, nevertheless, he wanted her to keep her voice down.

"Jake, this here's Tyrone Stokes," she explained.

The man studied Tyrone but did not speak.

"He the one that stole Danny's truck a few years back. His boy killed Buddy's daughter."

She stopped talking, and Tyrone could feel the tension mounting. Suddenly, there was in him a keen awareness of the force of his pounding heart and the tingling of the skin on his nape.

"Mister," he said. "I'm just trying to eat my dinner." Again, the pitch of his voice was low; the tone, calm.

"Not here you ain't," the man told him.

"Excuse me?" Tyrone said.

"I'm gone have to ask you to leave."

"Soon as I finish eating," Tyrone said. His defiance angered the man, and he saw the man's smooth tanned skin flush a dull shade of red.

"Don't make me lay hands on you, boy."

"Mister, I wouldn't advise that," Tyrone said, his tone serious.

"You threatening me?"

"No, sir," Tyrone said. "Just telling you. That's all."

A moment passed and Tyrone knew the man was pondering his next move. He had inched closer to the table and now was staring directly into Tyrone's eyes.

"You best watch yourself," the man issued a warning. The tone of his voice was low, threatening.

"Yes, sir," Tyrone said. "And you best do the same."

"Jake, you gone let him talk to you like that?" the woman asked.

"Maude, why don't you go on back over yonder and sat down," the man said. He raised his voice for the first time, and Tyrone could tell that the situation was beginning to get next to him.

"Not long as he in here, I won't," she said angrily.

"He got a right to be here," the man told her.

"What you defending him for?" she wanted to know.

"I ain't defending nobody," Jake snapped. "I'm just stating the fact. This is a public place, and long as he ain't breaking no law, or causing no trouble, he got as much right to be here as you or anybody else."

"You act like you scared of him."

"I ain't scared of nobody."

"Jake—"

"Maude, please!"

She looked at Jake, then at Tyrone. But before either of them uttered another word, a second man approached the table.

"Need a hand, Jake?" he asked. He was a big, burly fellow, well over six feet. He wore a large cowboy hat, a pair of faded blue jeans, a work shirt, and a pair of worn cowboy boots.

"What I need," Jake said, "is for y'all to sat down and relax."

"Not long as he in here," Maude said for the second time.

"Well, Maude," Jake said, his voice filled with impatience, "suit yourself."

"I'm disappointed in you, Jake," she said. "Real disappointed."

"Sorry you feel that way," Jake said. "But you still gone need to sat down."

"Jake, I won't be sitting in here, today or any other day," she said. "From now on, me and my family will do our business elsewhere."

She walked out, and Jake turned to the man.

"Sat down, Bobby Joe," he said. "Please. This ain't helping nothing."

Bobby Joe looked at Jake, then at Tyrone, and like Maude, walked from the deli. Jake sighed, then slowly turned to Tyrone.

"I'd thank you not to come in here no more."

Tyrone looked at him but did not speak. He slowly lifted a piece of chicken from his plate, took a bite, then looked out the window. Outside, a few dark gray clouds were moving in from the east. It looked like rain.

Chapter
11

Janell was with a client when Tyrone made it back to the office. She was not up front, as before, but was holding conference in Captain Jack's office. The door was ajar, and Tyrone could see that Janell was sitting behind Captain Jack's desk, and the white man was sitting in the same chair that Tyrone had occupied the day before. Janell and the man talked for a while; then the man left, and Janell entered the room, carrying a small cardboard box.

"Sorry to keep you waiting," she said politely, then set the box on her desk.

"That's all right," Tyrone said, rising from the couch. "I know you busy."

"Try swamped." She smiled.

Tyrone returned her smile. He watched her move behind the desk and open the lid of the box.

"This is everything we have on your son's case," she said. "The D.A. keeps the real evidence. All we have are odds and ends."

She reached into the box and removed a thick document, and Tyrone moved closer to the desk.

"These are the trial transcripts." She held the documents up, and when she was satisfied that Tyrone had seen them, she put them back into the box and removed a second item.

"These are sworn depositions."

Tyrone nodded, and she put them back, then lowered her head and continued thumbing through the box; only now she did not remove anything, but simply verbalized what she saw.

"We also have witness lists, interviews, photographs, etcetera."

"Seems like a lot to me," Tyrone said.

"Not really," she said. "Besides, most of it is pretty incriminating. We just couldn't find, or offer, much in the form of exculpatory evidence."

"You think he's guilty, don't you?"

"I didn't say that," she said quickly. But he could tell that his question had made her uncomfortable.

"Well, what are you saying?"

She sat down and folded her arms on the desk before her.

"The prosecution put on a very strong case. They didn't make any mistakes. And we weren't able to find any cracks. It's as simple as that."

"Did you look?" Tyrone asked.

"Of course," she said, insulted.

"Where?" he wanted to know.

"Everywhere," she said adamantly.

"Like," he pressed.

"Mr. Stokes, why are you attacking me?"

"Why are you trying to make me believe that this is hopeless?"

"I'm not," she said. "I welcome your help. I really do. I just want you to understand what you are up against."

"I know what I'm up against," he snapped. "I'm not stupid."

"Sir, I didn't say that you were."

He gaped at her with a long, angry stare.

"Listen," she said. "There are a lot of documents here. But most of them are worthless. The most damaging piece of evidence against your son was the testimony of the two eye witnesses. They both swore that they saw the victim get into your son's truck."

"They lied," Tyrone said.

"Maybe," she replied. "But they were extremely credible."

"So, you believe them?"

"Sir, what I believe doesn't matter," she said. "The jury believed them, and there is nothing in that box, or anywhere else that we've searched, that can challenge their testimony."

"They still live here?"

"Yes, sir, but they won't talk to you," she said. "We've tried on any number of occasions. They're very hostile."

"I'll get them to talk." Tyrone was emphatic. "You can bet on that."

"Mr. Stokes, even if you did, it probably wouldn't matter."

"Why not?"

"They testified under oath."

"What difference does that make?"

"All the difference in the world."

"I don't understand," he said.

"The courts take testimony given under oath very seriously," she explained. "So, unless we could offer proof that the witnesses lied or proof that they were coerced into making a false statement, their recantation would most likely be rejected. The prosecution would simply argue that they were having difficulty coping with the reality that their testimony had resulted in a person being sentenced to die. Their saying that they lied simply would not be enough."

"Their word can kill him," Tyrone said. "But it can't save him."

"Exactly," she said. "The verdict has been upheld under appeal. So unless the governor intervenes, or unless we find conclusive evidence of your son's innocence, he will be executed."

There was silence.

"And I'm pretty sure that the evidence we need is not in that box," she added.

"No reasonable doubt here," Tyrone said, dejected.

"Mr. Stokes, we've moved beyond the need for reasonable doubt," she said. "Now we need unequivocal certainty."

"And you don't think it's here."

"If it is," she said, "I haven't seen it. And between Mr. Johnson and me, we've looked through the information in that box a thousand times."

"Well," he said, "I'm still going to look for myself."

"As you should," she said.

Tyrone lifted the box and turned to leave, then stopped. In his mind loomed a memory of the deli: he was seeing the woman again; he was hearing her words, feeling her anger, remembering the tension that had hung in the room like a thick cloud of dark, billowing smoke lingering over a hot, blazing fire. He set the box back on the desk and turned and faced Janell.

"Can I ask you a question?"

"Yes, sir," she said.

"You said things got bad around here, right?"

"Right," she said.

"How bad did they get?"

She hesitated before answering, and he sensed that his question had spurred in her images or memories that she had long since suppressed. Her beautiful brown eyes glossed with a moist, vacant tint, and he was sure that she was remembering.

"I can tell you only what I've heard," she said, still not looking at him. "Like I said before, Mr. Stokes, I wasn't working here when the case was tried."

"I understand," Tyrone told her. "Just tell me what you heard."

"There was no violence, or bomb threats, or anything like that." Her words were slow, precise, methodical. "But there was a lot of anger, most of it directed toward your son; but some of it was also directed toward your wife, and Mr. Johnson, and anyone else who associated with the Stokes family."

"What kind of anger?" Tyrone asked.

"Verbal taunts, mostly," she said. "The way I understand it, people started riding past your wife's house at all hours of the night, swearing and cursing, and keeping up all kinds of racket."

"Did anybody touch my wife?"

"No, sir," she said. "At least not that I know of. But it still got to be too much for her to deal with. So she moved—"

"Up to her parents' house," Tyrone said. A light went on, and now he understood. She had not willingly moved to her parents' house; she had been forced out of her own home.

"Yes, sir," Janell said. "At least off and on. She stays at her house sometimes. And she came by the office every now and then. But, by and large, she rarely leaves her parents' house. If we need her, we go to her; she does not come to us. She said that she just can't take the ugly stares and the whispering anymore. So, we try to accommodate her as best we can."

"So the town turned on her before he had even been tried."

"Yes, sir," she said. "From my understanding, it was before the trial." Then she paused, thinking. "Yeah, it was before," she said with assurance, then began again. "Because once the trial started, things escalated."

"Escalated how?" Tyrone asked.

"Well, according to Mr. Johnson, two days before the trial, large groups of people began holding all-night vigils outside the courthouse."

"White people?" Tyrone asked.

"Probably," she said.

"A mob?"

"More like demonstrators, or protestors," she said. "Not a mob. From my understanding of things, they were peaceful. They burned candles and sang, prayed and chanted, and displayed crime scene pictures of the victim. There was a lot of anger," she said. "But there was no violence."

"Just good old-fashioned jury intimidation, right?" Tyrone said.

"That's what we argued on appeal," she told him.

"And," Tyrone said.

"We lost," she said.

"Were the jurors sequestered?"

"No," she said, slowly shaking her head. "Mr. Johnson petitioned the court, but that petition was denied as well."

Tyrone grew tense, and he felt his slumping spirits sink as the reality of his son's twisted ordeal registered in his weary mind and fueled the anger in his raging heart. In his mind, the picture was clear. His son had not been tried, but persecuted by a court eager to right a wrong and calm a town by slaying the deviant that lived among them.

"He was railroaded," Tyrone said. "Pure and simple."

"Possibly," she said. "But from what I've seen, Mr. Johnson did the best he could with what he had."

Tyrone looked at her but did not speak.

"He defended your son like he was defending his own."

"Hunh," Tyrone grunted. "I don't think so." His voice was low, cynical.

"He really did," she said. Her eyes were narrow; her expression, serious.

"Would he have asked his own to cop a plea?" Tyrone asked. His question caught her off guard.

She hesitated a moment then quickly said, "Probably."

"Yeah, right," Tyrone mumbled.

"He had no choice," she said, looking at him with wide, pleading eyes.

"Why?" Tyrone asked. "Because he thought my son did it?"

"No," she said. "Because he knew that he could not prove that your son didn't. It was that simple."

"What ever happened to innocent until proven guilty?" Tyrone mumbled, more to himself than to her.

"That's theory," she said. "This is reality."

Tyrone started to respond, then stopped. He lifted the box from the desk and cradled it in his arms.

"I'll look through this tonight and bring it back tomorrow."

"Keep them long as you like," she said. "We have copies."

Chapter
12

It was five-thirty when he arrived home. His mother was no longer in her bedroom but had moved across the hall into the tiny living room and was sitting in the recliner with her feet propped up. Her eyes were closed, and a damp cloth was draped across her forehead. She was resting, but he could tell by the slow, steady rocking of her left foot and the occasional twitching of her closed left eye that she was not asleep.

"How you feeling this evening, Mama?" he called to her softly, as he slowly approached her chair, his eyes fixated on the callused soles of her bare feet, and his ears keenly tuned to the pained sound of her heavy, labored breathing. The sound of his voice aroused her, and she opened her eyes and slowly turned her head toward him. Their eyes met, and she smiled, then grimaced, before her lips parted and she answered his question.

"Head worrying me some," she said. "Other than that, I do all right."

He moved closer to the chair on which she sat and took her hand into his. Instantly, he felt the grip of her warm, moist hand tighten, followed by the soothing sensation of the tip of her tiny thumb gently caressing the back of his large, hairy hand. The skin covering her old, wrinkled hands was no longer soft. Years of cleaning white folks' houses had made her skin hard, tough, leathery.

"Mama, why don't you go lay down?" he said, looking deep into her tired, blood-shot eyes. "Least 'til your head quit hurting."

"I will directly," she said, and he felt the tension in his arm as she pulled herself upright. "Been in the bed better part of the day. Just felt like sitting up awhile."

"Need me to get you anything?" he asked, then waited. All was silent save for the sound of her struggling to catch her breath. Pulling herself upright had winded her.

"Just sat with me," she said. "Keep me company."

He released her hand and sat on the sofa next to her. Beside the large sofa on which he sat, there was a much smaller one pressed against the short wall on the opposite side of the door. A few feet in front of him was a plain wooden chair, the back of which stood against the window that overlooked the front yard. To the right of the chair, crammed in one corner, was a television. To the left of the chair, crammed in the opposite corner, was a space heater. The curtains on the window behind his mother's recliner were open, and from where he sat, he could see out into the garden. As he stared through the window, absentmindedly eyeing the short rows of tomatoes, the tall stalks of corn, and the full, round heads of plush green cabbage, he could feel her eyes on him, examining the back of his neck, studying the side of his face, becoming reacquainted with the lone lost son that she had prayed for, and worried about, every day for the last ten years.

"René home yet?" he asked.

"She in the kitchen, cooking," his mother replied. "You need her?"

"No, ma'am," he said. "Just didn't see Jimmy's truck out there."

"Went to town," she said. "Ought to be back directly."

Tyrone nodded. His mother was quiet, but on her face was the look of someone who had a lot to say and didn't know where to begin.

"It's so good to have you home, son," he heard her say in a low, quiet voice. He knew she was happy; but somehow, her soft, sweet voice seemed weary, and he immediately felt guilty for all he had put her through.

"It's good to be home, Mama," he said.

She reached toward him, and he instantly felt her hand lying prone on the back of his own.

"Son, we missed you so much," she said.

"I missed y'all, too," he said. "More than you'll ever know."

Again, he felt her hand gently caressing the back of his own.

"Just hate you had to come back to so much trouble," he heard her say. "Just wish things could've been better. Never thought it would come to this."

"Somebody should've told me," he said. "Maybe I could've done something."

"Wasn't nothing you could do."

"I had a right to know."

"We just didn't want to worry you."

"I'm his father."

"You were in the pen," she said. "What could you do?"

"He needed me."

"You needed to deal with your own problems."

"Mama, he is my problem."

She looked at him but did not speak.

"Somebody should've told me," he said again.

"They wanted to," she said. "Sarah Ann and René. But I wouldn't let 'em. You my child, and I wouldn't let 'em."

"I had a right to know."

"And I had a right to protect you," she said. "You had done more than half yo' sentence, and I wasn't gone let nobody give you a reason to do something crazy and run up your time. Kept thinking that child might get off. Kept thinking he'd get a new trial. Kept hoping it'd work itself out. But it didn't."

"I had a right to know."

"I did what I thought best."

"Somebody should've told me."

She turned her head and looked away. She started to say something, but at the last minute, seemed to change her mind.

"Visit went all right?" she asked after a brief silence. But he could tell that that wasn't what she had been about to say.

"Yes, ma'am," he said. "It went all right."

There was silence.

"Didn't have no trouble?"

"No, ma'am. They let me right in."

"Guess he was glad to see you."

Tyrone paused and took a deep breath. "Yes, ma'am," he said. His voice began to trail off. "He was."

There was silence.

"He making out all right?" she asked.

Tyrone hesitated. His bottom lip began to quiver.

"No, ma'am," he said. "He ain't doing good. Ain't doing good at all." Tyrone brought his hands to his face and began to sob. He took a deep breath, trying to collect himself. He felt his mother's hand gently massaging his trembling knee.

"It's gone be all right, son," she said with the conviction of someone who knew. The words came from deep inside of her, and he knew that for her, they were not idle words spoken with the slightest bit of doubt. No, hers was not a guess, but a belief rooted in a long tradition of trust that was based on a faith that had been tried and tested. Yes, for her, everything would be all right if the Lord said the same.

"Don't know what God got in mind," he heard her say. "But I do know he got a reason for everything he do."

"What reason he got for killing an innocent child?" Tyrone asked, lowering his hands, looking her directly in the eye.

"Son, I don't question his wisdom," she said. Her weak voice had become strong, steady. "Neither should you."

"Well, what should I do, Mama?" Tyrone asked, his intense eyes studying her face, pleading for an answer. "What should I do?" he whispered again.

He continued to stare at her, but now his troubled mind was no longer there; it was on the box that he had left sitting in the hall next to his bedroom door. He heard her say something, but what, he did not know. Though he heard her voice, he wasn't listening to her. He was pondering, thinking, planning. Suddenly, he heard the quiet, tense whisper of Janell's discouraging words echoing through the quiet recesses of his overactive mind: I'm pretty sure the evidence we need is not in that box.

What if there wasn't a way to get his son off? The thought was strong, the impact immediate. His tepid skin flushed warm; his frightened body shivered. What would he do? What could he do?

"I should've been here for him," he said, his eyes in a daze.

"You ain't the blame for this." His mother's response was quick, forceful. "You hear me? You ain't the blame." She had turned in her chair, and now she was facing him. Both of her hands were clutching the soft, plush arm of the chair on which she sat. Her eyes were narrowed; her brow, furrowed; her lips, pursed.

"I should've set a better example," he said. His eyes were distant, vacant.

"Ain't no cause in carrying on like this," she said. "You made a mistake, and now you done made amends for it. That's all there is to it."

"That ain't all, Mama," he said; then his voice quieted. "Now my son paying for it." He looked at her with still moist eyes. "How am I supposed to live with that, Mama? How?"

"Yo' trouble ain't his troubles."

"People say he got convicted because of me."

"You can't pay people no mind," she said. "You ain't the cause of this."

"If Pauline would've just let him come see me. Maybe—"

"Maybe nothing," his mother interrupted. "Pauline was hurt, and she was scared. And she did what she thought was best for that child. She ain't the first woman made up her mind not to ever let her child walk through the doors of the penitentiary." His mother paused, and Tyrone knew she was remembering her own pain—pain that he had caused. "It's hard to see yo' love ones caged like some kind of wild animal," she began again. "You free, but you suffer just as hard as they do." She paused a second time and looked Tyrone in the eye. "You can't fault Pauline for trying to spare her child. Nobody can."

"I let him down, Mama."

"You let yo'self down," she said. "Now you got to pick yo'self up and go on."

"How," he said. "How can I go on without my son?"

"Same way I had to go on without you," she said, in a tone marked by a wisdom that came only from experience. "When they put you in that jail, look like my whole world stopped. People tried to comfort me. Some of 'em told me they knew what I was going through. But I knew they didn't. They meant good. But I knew they didn't."

"What did you do, Mama?" Tyrone asked more for himself than for her. Her suffering was over; his was just beginning. "What did you do?"

"Talked to God," she said. "And he told me that I had to keep on living. And that's what I did. And that's what you got to do."

Tyrone looked at her but did not speak.

"Don't you thank I blamed myself just like you doing?" she began again. Her eyes were distant; her voice was low, soft, calm. "Told myself I should've got between you and them old drugs anyway I could've. Told myself if I would've, then you wouldn't've tried to rob that store. And if you wouldn't've tried to rob that store, you wouldn't ever shot that man. I know you wouldn't've 'cause you ain't no bad child. You was just under the spell of something evil. And I should've got between you and it before it got hold of you."

She paused, and Tyrone could see that her eyes had begun to water.

"It's gone be awright, son," she said again. "God gone make a way somehow. I know he is."

Tyrone opened his mouth to say something, but through the open door, he heard footsteps in the hall. He turned his head and looked. René appeared in the doorway. She still wore the same white, loose-fitting dress and low-cut, flat-soled shoes that she had worn to work that morning. Balanced on her left hand was a plate of food, and in her right hand was a glass of something. It appeared to be like tea.

"Ready to eat, Mama?" she asked.

Tyrone saw his mother nod, and he watched René slowly enter the room, holding her tall, lean body rigid and walking stiff legged, taking care not to drop the plate or spill the tea. He looked at the plate. There was one pork chop, a small portion of black-eyed peas, a square of corn bread, a few mustard greens, and a tiny slice of sweet potato pie. As René placed the plate of food on their mother's lap and the glass of tea on top of the space heater in the corner next to their mother's chair, he quietly rose to his feet and moved next to the door.

As soon as she began to eat, he would excuse himself and retrieve the box from the hallway, then go to his room and review the papers.

"René, fix your brother a plate," he heard his mother say.

René frowned. She had not wanted him here, at least not until he had proven he had changed, and she certainly did not want to serve him. No, she did not hate him or wish him ill will. But their mother wasn't well. Her heart was bad, her pressure was high, and any more trouble would kill her for sure. No, she had not wanted him to come, and she did not want him to stay.

"I ain't hungry," Tyrone said in a low, meek tone. "I ate at the diner."

René looked at him out of the corner of her eye to let him know that she had not planned on serving him anyway.

"Ain't no sense in wasting good money on something to eat and we got plenty food in this house," his mother said. "Son, you at home." She emphasized *home*, then looked at him and then at René to make sure that they both understood. "You want something in this house, you welcome to it, hear?"

He nodded and glanced at René, then looked away.

"Mama, you need anything else before I go?" René asked.

"Naw, baby, this fine."

"Then, I'm gone go on in the back and rest," she said. "It's been a long, hard day, and I'm good and tired."

"Okay, baby," Tyrone heard his mother say. "See you in the morning."

René approached the door, and Tyrone moved aside. When she passed, she rolled her eyes at him but did not speak.

"Son, you better come on and have some," Tyrone heard his mother say. He looked in her direction. She had broken off a small piece of corn bread and had begun eating the bread and the greens with her fingers.

"No, thank you, Mama," he said. "I got some reading to do."

Chapter
13

Hurt and dejected, Tyrone excused himself and hurried to his room, carrying the box of documents he had brought from Captain Jack's office. Since there was no desk or table in his bedroom, he sat atop the bed with his tired, anxious body slouched lazily against the solid oak headboard and his weary, tear-stained eyes focused on the stack of papers resting against the back of his uplifted knees. As he sat sifting through the hoards of documents, trying to reconstruct the case against his son, he could hear the sound of René's slippers sliding across the floor in her bedroom next door. Though he could not see her, he was sure that she was pacing. In his mind, he could picture her slowly sauntering back and forth, her arms folded across her chest, and her agitated eyes cast downward in a concentrated gaze. And though she had not told him, he was certain that the source of her anxiety was an acute annoyance with his presence, rather than concern for the chaos created by his son's situation.

Slightly distracted by the sound of her monotonous pacing, but determined to plow through the box before morning, Tyrone shut the noise out of his mind and concentrated, pausing only to ponder the details of something he had just read, or to note a fact, or date, or time sequence that needed further investigation. He had just paused to jot something in the corner of one of the documents when the door connecting their rooms flung open and René emerged. Startled, his bent body flinched. Instinct told him to look, but he did not, choosing instead to keep his eyes focused on the paper in front of him.

"How long you planning on staying here?" she demanded.

Her voice was low. Her tone confrontational. And though he did not move, he could feel her angry eyes on him, daring—no, beseeching—him to look. He had no plans to oblige her. But in spite of his resolve, he unwittingly felt himself submitting to her will, and, as if hypnotized, his sheepish eyes slowly strayed from the paper and looked up. René, now garbed in a long pink and white housecoat, and wearing a pair of fuzzy pink slippers, stood staring at him.

"I don't know," he said, then lowered his eyes and gazed at the paper on which he had been writing.

"What you mean, you don't know?" she asked.

"Just what I said," he retorted.

"Well, that ain't good enough," she said. "I need a answer."

"Can't tell you no more than that," he said.

"Then, let me tell you something, mister," she said. "You can stay here a little while, but you can't live here."

He looked up a second time, and she was still staring at him. Only now her large brown eyes were narrowed, her brow was furrowed, and her teeth were clenched. Perturbed, he started to respond, but reconsidered, opting instead to bow his head and avert his eyes.

"You hear me?" she asked.

"I hear you," he said.

There was silence.

"You seen Pauline?" she asked.

He raised his head and looked directly into her eyes. "Why?" he asked.

There was quiet again, and he watched her watching him. She stared for what seemed an eternity before she spoke again.

"You still doing drugs?" she asked, ignoring his question and countering with her own. He chuckled softly, then slowly shook his head in disgust.

"Been clean going on ten years."

"I don't believe that," she said.

"Believe what you want to," he said. "That's your business."

"You quit?"

"That's right."

"Well, now, let me see," she said, bringing her hand underneath her chin. "How many times does this make? There was the time Papa had you locked up. Then there was the time Pauline left you. Then there was the time Mama dragged you out that crackhouse. Then there was the time—"

"René, I don't have time for this," he interrupted her.

"You better make time," she said.

He looked at her, then looked away.

"That was then," he said. "This is now."

"Oh, this time is different?"

"That's right," he said.

She looked at him with hard, cold eyes, and he knew at that moment the depth of the contempt she felt for him. He opened his mouth to say something else, then thought better of it.

"How'd you get clean?" she asked, but he could tell by her tone that she was not asking out of genuine interest. She was asking to prove a point.

"Dried out in prison," he told her.

"Didn't know they had a drug treatment facility in the penitentiary," she said.

"No facility," he said. "Just methadone."

She looked at him again with mocking eyes. Her tongue was still, and her lips were silent, while her eyes screamed liar.

"You had counseling?" she asked.

He shook his head, then looked away.

"You ain't had no counseling, but you cured."

He continued to look away. She had made up her mind, and there was no need to say more. She did not believe him, and she would not believe him, no matter what he said. No matter what he did.

"How can that be?" She continued to push.

"People change, René."

"I'm not talking 'bout people," she said. "I'm talking 'bout you."

"Why you so interested in me all of a sudden?" he asked, reluctantly loosening the reins on his emotions and giving in to the rage he felt festering deep inside of himself. "When I was down, did you ever do anything for me?"

He paused, and his fiery eyes challenged her, while his naked, unbridled emotions triggered something in the remote part of his brain. He resumed; only now, as he spoke, he was not hearing himself. Instead, he was remembering his incarceration. He was reliving the loneliness, the dread, the fear, the horror.

"Did you ever come see me? Did you ever write? Did you ever send me anything? Did you?"

He paused, and she stared at him with large, combative eyes.

"You got some nerve!" she said. "Asking me something stupid like that. Did I make you break the law?"

He looked at her but did not respond.

"Did I cause you to get locked up?"

She paused again, and again, he did not respond.

"No, I didn't," she answered for him. "You did that all by yourself. Now, if you were any kind of man, you would've took responsibility for your actions and did your time all by yourself, instead of making Mama, and Papa, and everybody else suffer for something you did. Naw, I didn't come, and I didn't write, 'cause I didn't feel sorry for you then, and I don't feel sorry for you now. I pity you."

"I don't want your pity," he said. "I just want you to leave me alone."

"And I just want you to get out," she said.

"This ain't your house," he said forcefully. "I got just as much right to be here as you do."

Suddenly, they heard the sound of their mother's concerned voice floating from beyond the thin living room wall.

"Everything all right in there?"

The sound of her voice forced a temporary halt, and in unison both of them sang out in perfect harmony.

"Yes, ma'am."

They paused and awaited her response, but when none came, they resumed their conversation, only now careful to keep their voices low.

"You ain't gone lay up here and kill Mama like you killed Daddy," René said, low, but forcefully.

"What!" Tyrone whispered, shocked by her words, stunned by their implication and hoping against hope that what she said wasn't true.

"You heard me," she said.

"I wasn't even here when Papa died," Tyrone defended himself.

"No, but you killed him just the same."

"Girl, you crazy."

"Crazy nothing," she said. "You worried that man to death."

"You don't believe that."

"No, I don't believe it," she said. "I know it."

"You don't know nothing."

"I know it, and you know it, too," she said. "You killed him with your trifling ways, and if we don't get you out of here, before too long, you gone do the same thing to Mama."

"I love Mama."

"Please."

"I do."

"You don't love Mama or nobody else," René said. "That boy of yours in the fix he in right now because you don't never think about nobody but yourself."

"I love my son," he said. His voice began to shake. His eyes began to water.

"That's why you left him and Pauline here to fend for theyself."

"That wasn't my choice."

"Whose choice was it?" she asked.

He didn't answer.

"Yeah," she said, her voice filled with sarcasm. "You've change all right."

"I made a mistake, René. That's all."

"No," she said. "You made a choice. And Pauline and that boy paying for it."

"I love my family," he said again.

"What kind of example you set for that child?"

He did not answer.

"What kind of reputation you left him?"

He dropped his head, and large, wet tears barreled down his face.

"A boy need his daddy," she said. "A boy need his daddy to teach him how to be a man." She looked at him with mean, contemptuous eyes. "Where were you when he needed you? Where?"

He opened his mouth to speak, but no words came. A large, hot mass churned in the pit of his stomach. He folded his arms tight across his midsection and slowly rocked back and forth, riveted by the pain, convicted by her words. Again, he tried to speak. His lips began to quiver, his hands began to shake, but still, no words came. He raised his head, and she looked at him with disgust.

"You pathetic," she said.

He felt the sting of her words, and rising, hot emotions caused him to leap from the bed. Guilt and anger made him unstable. His legs wobbled, and warm, salty tears poured from his eyes and passed over his still quivering lips. He took two steps, then leaned against the foot of the bed for support. He looked at René with red, swollen eyes. Then he raised his arm and pointed an incensed, unsteady finger.

"Don't you dare talk to me like that," he said. Anger made his voice crack, and he closed his mouth and swallowed. He could feel his heart pounding, his chest heaving, his frail nerves raging.

"Am I supposed to be scared now?" she asked defiantly. "Touch me and see if I don't send you straight back to the penitentiary."

Shame replaced anger, and he lowered his hand, then dropped his gaze and tried to relax his stiff, taut body. What was wrong with him? He was on probation. He had to do better than this. He had to control his emotions, not let his emotions control him. He looked at her with repentant eyes. His lips parted.

"I'm sorry," he said.

"You can say that again," she mumbled.

"I don't want to fight you, René," he said. "I just want to help my son."

"It's too late for that now," she said. "When you could've done something for him, you didn't. Now it's too late."

"No," he said.

"What can you do?" she asked.

"I don't know," he said. "But this thing won't happen. I won't let it."

"It's gone happen," she said. "And you gone have to live with it."

"You act like you want him to die."

"I'm just telling you how it is."

"You think he guilty?"

"Who knows?" she said.

"I didn't ask you what you know," he said. "I asked you what you think."

"I think he's your child," she said.

"What's that suppose to mean?" he asked.

"Like father, like son," she told him.

He heard a noise behind him. He whirled, and straightened. Jimmy was standing in the hallway next to his bedroom door, a bag of groceries in one hand, and his hat in the other. He looked at Tyrone, then at René.

"What's going on in here?" he asked. "I could hear y'all clear down the hall."

"Nothing," René said.

Jimmy looked at her for a few seconds before he spoke again.

"You sure?" he asked.

"I'm sure," René said, then turned and disappeared into her room.

Jimmy looked at Tyrone as if he was about to say something, but before he could, Tyrone turned toward the bed and began collecting the papers he had been reading. He didn't want to talk anymore. He had too much to do and too little time to do it. He could feel Jimmy's eyes on the back of his neck. He heard the bags ruffle, then the sound of Jimmy's heavy footsteps die away on the hall and disappear into the kitchen.

Next door, he heard René's bedroom door open and close, and he knew that she had gone to put the groceries away and to give Jimmy his supper. Tyrone decided to shut his door to blot out the noise, but no sooner had he reached the doorway, than his mother emerged from the living room, carrying her empty plate in one hand and the empty glass in the other.

"Mama, I'll take that for you," he offered.

"That's all right, baby," she said. "I know you got things to do."

He stood in the doorway and watched her wobble down the hall on weak, unsteady legs. He felt his heart sink. Yes, she had aged while he was away, and he could not help but wonder how much time he and his troubles had stolen from her.

When she turned into the kitchen, he went back into his bedroom and sat on the bed, but he did not close the door. Instead, he waited until he again heard her shuffled footsteps in the hall. When she was close, he returned to the door and bid her good night, then watched her cross the hall and disappear inside her bedroom. When she was completely out of his sight, he eased the door shut, gathered the paper that he had been reading, and resumed his work.

A space of time passed in which he toiled in silence; then a strange noise made him stop and listen. Next door, Jimmy and René had returned from their sojourn to the kitchen, and he could hear the muddled sound of their voices through the paper-thin walls. They talked awhile; then their soft murmuring gave way to silence, and their silence gave way to the faint, rhythmic sound of creaking bedsprings. Embarrassed, he rose to leave; but the bed on which he sat creaked, and he reconsidered, fearing that the sound of his moving about would betray him, causing undue embarrassment to them, and further embarrassment to himself.

He heard his sister begin to pant; then she began to moan, and at that moment he longed to be anyplace other than the place in which he was. He looked down at the papers and tried to ignore what he was hearing, all the time struggling to stave off the unwanted images fighting to creep into his consciousness. He opened his mouth and began to read softly to himself. He heard himself calling words, but what they were meant to convey escaped him.

Through the walls, the sound of the creaking bed became louder; René's breathing, more rapid. He thought of Pauline. His body flushed warm. The hair on the back of his neck began to tingle. How long had it been since he held her, caressed her, loved her? A dark cloud of silence engulfed him, and he pictured himself lying with her in love, their hot, naked bodies wet with sweat, their fiery loins pulsating with passion.

The thought excited him; then in an instant, a huge wave of hot shame brought him back to reality. In his mind loomed a brooding image of Marcus lying in his cell, longing for a sleep that would not come and listening to the all too familiar sounds of dangling keys and clanging doors, while dreading the impending sound of the prison whistle blowing morning into existence and telling him that he was one day closer to his imminent death. Tyrone focused his eyes again and began to read, while next door, the passionate moans gave way to silence, which soon gave way to the sound of two people sleeping.

"The answer is here somewhere," he mumbled softly to himself.

Hours passed; then somewhere around two A.M., it began to rain. All around him was quiet save for the soothing sound of the tiny drops of water pelting the roof of his mother's house and the soft whisper of the wind rustling the leaves of the large pecan tree just outside his window. It was extremely late. Though he had long since been tired, the anxiety he felt, and his keen awareness of the obvious time constraints, had inoculated him, enabling him to press forward. Now, in the early hours of the morning, his mind rebelled, and his tired, depraved body finally surrendered to sleep.

Chapter
14

He awoke to the smell of frying bacon and to the muttered sound of people talking in the rear of the small house. He looked at his watch; it was five until nine. He had overslept. He snapped upright and stared about. Scattered around him, on top of the unslept-in bed, were the papers he had been reading the night before. In his sleep, he had unknowingly pushed the box flush against the far wall and had somehow kicked his shoes off his feet. One lay on the floor at the foot of the bed, while the other lay against the base of the dresser in the rear of the room.

Tired and drowsy, he picked up a document and stared at it absently, then put it in the empty box. By now, he had not only read through the case files, and trial transcripts, but he had also constructed a simple time line chronicling his son's activities from the time he left home, en route to the store, until his arrest two days later. The deeper he had delved into the box, the more concerned he had become. His son had had time, and he had had opportunity, and there was nothing in the testimony of the two eye witnesses that one could deem inconsistent or render not credible.

Yes, his guilt seemed certain, and there was no rational reason to think otherwise; yet there was in Tyrone a belief—no, a feeling—that this thing could not be so. The exculpatory evidence needed to illuminate this crime and make sense of the senseless had to be camouflaged, chameleonlike, somewhere amidst the pieces of "irrefutable" evidence pointing to his son's guilt.

As his spiraling emotions continued to sink, there was in him a mounting desire to talk to the witnesses. He knew their names, but what he did not know was where they lived or how to contact them. Janell knew. She would tell him. She had already said that she would.

A plan of action made him rise to his feet. His awakening body made him yawn and stretch his arms above his heavy head. The muscles in his arms were taut; the back of his neck was stiff. He opened the rear door of his bedroom but did not go out onto the porch. Outside, the rain had ceased, and there was a fresh, sweet scent in the cool morning air. The feel of the gentle breeze on his face made him yawn a second time. Yes, he was still tired, and his weary body still craved sleep; but now there was no time.

There was no closet in his room, or in any of the rooms for that matter. A broom handle, which served as a makeshift garment rod, had been affixed, catercorner, between the walls in the far corner of the room and was filled with a long line of clothes dangling from a series of wire hangers. He removed a pair of slacks, then turned to the small dresser and removed a clean shirt, some fresh underwear, and a pair of socks. Compared to most convicts, he was lucky. His family (mostly his mother and father, and Sarah Ann) had provided for him while he was incarcerated, and they continued providing for him now. He was broke and without means, yet he still had food to eat, a place to stay, and clothes to wear. When all of this was over, he would make things right. He would give back that which had been given to him. He would be the son his mother desired; he would be the brother his sisters deserved; he would be the father his child never had.

In the hallway, the lingering scent of food and the strong aroma of freshly brewed coffee hung heavy in the air, but instead of following the urges of his rumbling stomach, he stayed his course and angled toward the bathroom. Halfway between his room and the bathroom, he stepped on a weak spot in the floor, and the floor creaked. Down the hall, the low sound of murmured voices ceased, and he heard his mother's lone voice rise above the silence.

"That you, Tyrone?"

The sound of her voice caused him to stop. He opened his mouth to respond, but before he could, he heard his mother's voice again.

"We in the kitchen."

With clothes in hand, he walked to the end of the hall and turned toward the kitchen door. What he saw made him stop abruptly. Sarah Ann and his mother were sitting at the table, but they were not alone. His maternal aunt, the one they all called Babee, was sitting with her back to him, drinking a cup of coffee. When he saw her, he immediately turned to leave, but before he could, Sarah Ann spoke and foiled his plan.

"Well, look who done rose from the dead."

Startled, he moved to the side of the door and peeped around the corner. Both his mother and his aunt had turned in their seats and were looking at him. He felt awkward. His hair had not been combed, his teeth had not been brushed, and he still wore the clothes he had worn the day before.

"Excuse me," he said sheepishly. "Didn't know we had company."

"Company!" his aunt said.

Tyrone glanced at her, then lowered his eyes. She was a big woman, close to two hundred pounds. She wore a dark-colored dress, brown stockings, and a pair of black orthopedic shoes. Her walking cane hung on the back of her chair, and there was a single strand of shiny, reddish brown copper wire twisted about her wrist. She swore it drew out the rheumatism.

"Child, when I started being company?"

Tyrone looked at her and forced a faint smile.

"Well, come on in," his aunt said.

He stepped through the door, then stopped.

"Come on," she said. "I ain't gone bite you."

He walked closer to her chair.

"Ain't you gone hug yo' auntie's neck?"

"After I freshen up some."

"Freshen up!" she said. "Boy, if you don't hug my neck, you better."

He bent low, and she wrapped her large arms around him and

pulled him close, patting him on the back the way a person did when they hadn't seen you for an extended period of time. He pulled away, then dropped his gaze.

"Turn around," she said. "Let me look at you."

He turned in a circle and stopped. He could feel her eyes on him, studying him closely, looking for a hint of the young man she had known ten years ago.

"Done fill out some, ain't you?"

"Yes, ma'am," he said. "Little bit."

"Don't see how," his mother said. "Won't half eat."

He smiled again.

"Well," his aunt began, but before she could finish, her sister interrupted her.

"Babee, let the boy sit down and eat his breakfast 'fo it git cold."

"That's all right, Mama," he said. "I'm running late."

She looked at him strangely, and he knew she wanted an explanation.

"Got business in town," he said. "Need to catch Captain Jack before he leave."

"You gone put something in your stomach 'fo you leave here, ain't you?"

"If I have time," he said.

"You need to make time," she said. "You can't do nothing on no empty stomach." She looked at her sister. It wasn't a long look, just a glance. A glance that said, See what I told you.

Tyrone sighed softly.

"René fixed bacon and eggs 'fo she left this morning. Some sausage out there in the freezer if you rather have that. Sarah Ann can fix it for you."

"Bacon fine," he said.

"Don't call yo'self on no diet, do you?" his aunt asked.

"No, ma'am," he said. "I eat."

"Like a bird," his mother added.

"Don't know where he got that from," his aunt said. "You know good as me, all us Thompsons big eaters."

"Got it from his daddy," his mother added.

"Albert?" his aunt asked.

"Child, partner drank a little coffee and munched on a few soda crackers. But he wouldn't eat worth nothin'."

"Is that right?" his aunt asked.

"None of them Stokes boys eat worth talkin' 'bout."

"Well, I like me a man with a appetite," his aunt said. "Look like it do me good to see a man what can eat." She paused briefly and smiled the way a person smiled when they were remembering something nice. "That's what I like 'bout my late husband, David," she continued. "Girl, when he was living, he'd walk a mile, barefoot, on a blacktop road, in the heat part of the day, to get hold one of my hot, homemade butter biscuits. That man natural love him some biscuits."

"Ain't never been much on making biscuits," his mother said. "But I was the devil on some corn bread."

"Girl, hush yo' mouth."

"And fried okra."

"Hush now."

"Babee, 'member how Mama used to fry it?"

"Do I?" his aunt said. "Girl, that was some good eating."

They paused, remembering.

"Folks these days don't 'preciate a good home-cooked meal like we did when we was coming up," his mother said.

"Raised on that old junk food," his aunt said.

"Ain't raised at all," his mother said. "That's the problem."

"Don't know when I is done had me some okra," his aunt said. She was no longer listening. Her mind was wandering, contemplating.

"They don't respect nothing and nobody," his mother said.

"I sho' nuff got a taste for some," his aunt said.

"Look like they mad at the world," his mother continued.

"Wonder where us can get some?" his aunt wanted to know.

"Ripping and running and causing nothing but trouble."

"I'm talking 'bout fresh okra," his aunt said. "Right out the field."

Sarah Ann, who had said very little, politely cleared her throat, and their mother looked up.

"Son, sat down and eat yo' breakfast."

There was an empty chair at the head of the table. On the table before the chair was a plate that someone had filled with food and covered with an aluminum pan. Tyrone looked at the plate, then at his mother.

"Yes, ma'am," he said. "Want to wash up first."

As he turned to leave, he heard his aunt say, "Yeah, he done filled out nice."

He made his way to the bathroom and pulled the door open. Inside, he laid his things on the sink and removed the tiny stopper from the edge of the tub and inserted it into the drain. He did not have much time and would have preferred to take a shower; but the house was old, and the tiny bathroom contained no shower, only a tub, a sink, and a toilet.

He turned on the faucet. The pipes rattled, and a long, steady stream of crystal clear water gushed from the nozzle and fell with a heavy thud against the bottom of the tub. He tested the water with his hand, and as the tub began to fill, he turned toward the mirror and stared at the reflection staring back at him. Yes, he was tired. His eyes were red, the lids puffy. With trembling hands, he began to slowly undress. Why had his aunt stopped by today of all days? She was nice enough. And she had always been good to him. But she was a talker, and right now he just did not have the time. She would want to visit, and pray, and tell him the importance of doing the right thing, now that he had a second chance at life. She meant well. And any other time he would not have minded. But right now, he had to find those witnesses, and he had to find them fast.

He got into the tub, and his naked body sank underneath the warm, soapy water. He stretched himself lengthwise and laid his head against the back of the tub. The invigorating water felt good, and the muscles in his taut, stiff body began to relax. He closed his eyes and tried to formulate a plan. How would he convince them to see him? How would he get them to talk? Not only was he black and they white, but for them to learn his name would immediately cast him not as a friend, but as a foe. Not as one with whom they should cooperate, but as one they should hate.

In the hallway, he heard the sound of shuffled feet and the tap of his aunt's walking cane gently striking the floor. They had finished eating, and he was sure that they were going out onto the front porch to sit in the air and talk. He washed and rinsed his body, then toweled off, got dressed, and returned to the kitchen.

To his surprise, Sarah Ann had not left with the others, but had remained in the kitchen and was at the sink washing dishes.

"They on the porch?" he asked.

"Believe so," she said without looking around.

The plate was as it had been before he left, sitting idly on the small table underneath the aluminum pan. He took a seat and removed the lid. On the plate were several slices of bacon, two fried eggs, a biscuit, and some grits. He lifted his fork and began to eat.

"Git you some coffee?"

He looked up. Sarah Ann had turned from the sink and was facing him.

"If it ain't too much trouble."

"Ain't no trouble," she said. "Pot sitting right here."

She wiped her hands on her apron, then removed a cup from the cupboard.

"Still take it black?"

He nodded, and she filled the cup with coffee, then handed it to him. The cup was hotter than he expected. He took a sip, then quickly set the cup on the table next to his plate.

"So, you going back to Brownsville, hunh?"

"Soon as I get through eating," he said.

"You gone talk to Pauline?"

"Naw," he said. "Gone talk to them witnesses. Gone try to find out what they saw. Gone try to find out why they said what they said."

"Be careful," she said. "Ain't gone do nobody no good for you to go get yourself back in trouble."

"I'll be careful," he said, detecting concern in her voice. "Just want to ask them a few questions. That's all."

From the porch, he heard his aunt laughing.

"They waiting on me?" he asked.

"Thank so," his sister said. "Aunt Babee want to talk to you."

" 'Bout what?" he wanted to know.

"Didn't say. Probably just want to visit."

"She know 'bout Marcus?"

"Everybody know."

"They don't act like it," he said.

"They just happy to see you," she said. "Been waiting a long time. Just happy you out. That's all."

"Ain't sad for him?"

"Sad for you," she said.

"But not for him?"

"Don't know him," she said. "Least not like they know you."

"He family," he said. "Just like me."

"Still don't know him," she said. "Done made up they mind it's gone happen. They wish it wasn't. And they hurting for you. But they still don't know him."

"Didn't Pauline bring him to see Mama?" he asked.

"Not after—" She paused.

"After I went to the pen," he completed her statement.

She nodded. Then there was a long, awkward silence.

"We ain't seen 'im but once or twice since you got locked up," she said. "Don't remember exactly how old he was then."

"Six," Tyrone said. "Almost seven."

"We went to the trial, and we visited him once or twice when they had him in jail. But we was strangers. He didn't know us. And we didn't know him. Hurt Mama that it was so. But Pauline his mama. And she raised him as she saw fit. Wasn't nothing we could do 'bout that."

She paused and waited for him to say something, but he did not.

"We don't mean no harm," she said. "Just don't know 'im."

He looked at her, and his eyes began to water.

"Neither do I," he said. "He's my son. And neither do I."

Chapter
15

The two of them were still sitting on the porch when he made it out there. His mother was in her favorite rocker which sat just east of the door, and his aunt was sitting on the opposite side of her, near the far end of the porch. They had been talking, but as soon as they saw him, they stopped abruptly, as though they may have been talking about him or about something they didn't want him to hear.

There was a third chair positioned against the back wall, but he didn't sit in it. Instead, he walked next to the screen door and leaned against one of the wooden studs that supported the roof and let the box he was carrying rest on the center of his thigh. He was in a hurry and wanted them to know that he wouldn't be staying long, not even long enough to sit.

"Get plenty to eat?" his mother asked.

"Yes, ma'am," he said, then looked away.

The clear blue sky was still cloudless, and though the wind had settled some, the air was still cool, fresh, clean. It was early, and the Quarters were still quiet. Out near the streets, a tiny brown sparrow had come down from its perch high atop the large pecan tree and was bathing in a small puddle of water that had collected just off the porch. Tyrone was watching the tiny animal when his aunt spoke and broke the silence.

"Look like the good Lawd done seen fit to bless us with another beautiful day," she said.

"Any day above ground is beautiful," his mother retorted.

"Amen." His aunt nodded her agreement.

"Even if it ain't your best day," his mother continued, "don't make no difference."

"Don't make a bit of difference," his aunt agreed.

"You know why?" his mother asked. She was no longer looking at her sister; she was looking at Tyrone.

He returned her gaze, but did not speak.

"He don't know," he heard his aunt say. "You gone have to tell 'im."

"'Cause he gone send you another one in the morning," she said.

"It's already on the way," his aunt mumbled her agreement. "Be here first thing in the morning."

"Bright and early," his mother said. "He done fixed it that way."

"Well, it'll be here then," his aunt said with assurance. " 'Cause when he fix something, it's fixed."

She said that; then it was quiet. Tyrone studied both women. His mother was looking out across the street, and his aunt was looking down the Quarters.

"Aunt Babee, you wanted to talk to me?"

He had addressed his aunt, but before she could answer, his mother spoke.

"Called that man yet?"

Her question confused him. He looked at her, then narrowed his eyes and furrowed his brow.

"What man, Mama?"

"Man from the parole office."

This was his fourth day out. He should have called. He was supposed to have called. But he had not.

"Not yet," he said, then averted his eyes.

"Need to call that man, 'fo he call you."

"Yes, ma'am," he said. "I know."

He paused, then opened his mouth to say something else, but his aunt spoke first.

"Was you at the deli mart yestiddy?" she asked.

He thought the question strange. He looked at her with curious eyes.

"Yes, ma'am," he said. "Why?"

"Folks at the beauty shop say you was popping off to some white folks."

"What folks, Aunt Babee?"

"Just some folks I know."

She paused, but he didn't respond.

"They say them white folks say they gone teach you a lesson. Say they ain't gone rest 'til you back where you belong."

Now he understood. His aunt had stopped by to issue him a warning.

"White folks don't scare me," he said. His voice was low, his tone calm, his words matter-of-fact.

"She ain't telling you to scare you," his mother said. "She telling you so you know to be particular. Honey, them folks watching you."

"And I'm watching them," he said defiantly.

There was silence. He looked at his mother, and she averted her eyes. He could tell that she wanted to say more. But she was being careful. Both she and his aunt were being careful.

"Was a big fellow there?" his aunt asked. "Big, stout white fellow?"

He paused before answering. He knew that she knew. And he knew that hers was not a question posed to gather information, but one intended to give it.

"Yes, ma'am," he said. "Believe his name was Jake. He did most of the talking."

"Not him," his aunt said. "He the manager. Was anybody else there?"

Tyrone did not answer right away. He knew that she knew.

"Some guy they called Bobby Joe," he said.

"That's him," she said. "That's the one I'm talking 'bout."

"Who?" his mother asked.

"Benny Goodlow's boy."

"You and him had words?" his mother asked.

Tyrone shook his head. "No, ma'am," he said.

"But you had words with somebody."

Tyrone nodded.

"Who?" his mother asked.

"Some white lady."

"What white lady?" she asked.

"I don't know," he said, trying to avoid a lengthy conversation. "Some white lady I ain't never seen before."

"She be Miss Irene's gal," his aunt said.

"Irene Goodlow!"

"Irene Goodlow," his aunt said. "She be her oldest gal."

"Good Gawd Almighty," his mother said. "Them Goodlows is trouble in the worst way."

"Way I hear it, they ain't satisfied with the way this thing been handled," his aunt said. "They say it been dragged out too long. Now that it's close, they say they don't want to see nothing else get in the way." She paused and looked at him. "Or nobody else."

His mother looked at him with wide, fearful eyes. "You seen that man 'bout your driver's license yet?"

"Not yet."

"Don't need to be on that road 'thout no license."

"I'm gone git 'em," he said. "Just trying to help my son first."

"Can't help nobody if you locked up."

"I just need to see Captain Jack 'fo he go."

"You need to dot yo' i's and cross yo' t's," she said. "Them people ain't playing with you."

He opened his mouth to speak, but reconsidered. He paused, then sighed.

"Mama, I got to go."

He turned to leave, but the sound of his mother's voice stopped him.

"You gone out of town?" she asked.

He turned back in her direction.

"Yes, ma'am," he said. "Need to catch Captain Jack 'fo he go."

"Wish you'd go 'n and get them license while you there."

"Right after I see Captain Jack," he said.

He tucked the box underneath his arm and pushed through the screen door. The door slammed shut. He descended the large concrete stairs and took two steps toward the truck. Something urged him to glance at his watch. He lifted his wrist and lowered his eyes. It was almost ten. Terror gripped him. There was in him an unsettling feeling that time was moving too fast. His reeling senses cautioned him to run. He quickened his pace and lengthened his stride. Behind him, he could feel their eyes on him, beseeching him to slow down, begging him to be careful.

Near the makeshift shed under which the truck had been parked, he fumbled in his pockets for his keys. Once he had located them, he retrieved them, then pulled the door open and slid under the wheel. He started the engine, then in one hurried motion pulled the truck into gear. He depressed the accelerator. The tires screeched, and the truck lurched forward. In his haste, he had pulled away too fast. He quickly depressed the brake and turned his head to look toward the porch. His mother was leaning forward. Her brow was furrowed, and he saw her wide, piercing eyes watching him closely. Yes, she was worried, and his reckless behavior was doing little to allay her fears. He lowered his head and pretended to search for something, then slowly raised his head. Their eyes met, and he forced a faint smile. Her face relaxed. She leaned back in her chair, and he eased off.

At the curb, just east of her house, he glanced in her direction again. Though he could not see her face, he could see that she had turned in her chair and was still watching him. He crept along until he was well past her view. Once he was convinced that she could no longer see him or hear the sound of the truck's engine, he depressed the accelerator and sped toward Brownsville.

He had expected the files to reveal answers, but when they had not, he had found himself overcome with fear and haunted by a growing sense of hopelessness. And though the prospects of talking to the witnesses kept alive in him a waning hope and helped stave off a total sense of desperation, he was aware that festering just beneath the surface of his overactive mind was an overbearing feeling of panic fueled by the prospect that like the box, an interaction with them would prove futile.

At the office, he pushed through the door. Janell was there, and he could tell that she had not been there long. Her large purse still sat atop her desk, and she had not yet taken her seat or clicked on her computer. He moved to her desk, lugging the box and inhaling the lingering scent of her perfume. He stopped short, and she looked up.

"Good morning, Mr. Stokes," she said. Her lips parted, and she flashed a warm, but professional smile.

"Good morning," he said, placing the box on the corner of her desk. "Can I see Mr. Johnson please?"

"I'm sorry," she said. "He's out for the day."

"Is he ever here?" Tyrone asked. The frustration in his voice hung heavy, suspended somewhere between indignation and full-blown anger.

"He's just swamped right now," she offered as an explanation. "That's all."

Her words registered, and he could feel the rage rising inside of him.

"What case he got more urgent than my son's?"

"We're doing all we can do," she said.

He looked at her strangely, and she felt the need to say more.

"It's in the governor's hands now."

"I made it through the box, and I want to talk to him."

"Won't be back until tomorrow."

"Tomorrow too late."

"Can I help you with something?"

"I want to talk to the witnesses."

"Excuse me!"

"I need their addresses."

"They won't talk to you."

"Like to try anyway."

"They won't talk, I'm telling you."

"I'll get 'em to talk."

"How?"

"I'll figure out something."

There was silence. She studied him a long time before she spoke again.

"Handle this wrong and you'll do more harm than good," she said.

"Don't see how that's possible," he grunted. "They can't kill 'im but once."

Guilt would not let her speak. She looked away briefly, then turned back.

"Information you want is in the files," she said in a low, sad voice. "Have a seat and I'll get it for you."

He sat anxiously on the edge of the sofa next to the window and watched as she disappeared inside Captain Jack's office. He heard her heels cross the room. He heard the drawer of the file cabinet screech open. Then there was a long period of awkward silence in which he could not help but wonder what was taking her so long. In his zealous mind loomed an image of her standing before the open drawer, thumbing through the files, looking but not finding that for which she was searching. He glanced at his watch. It was twenty-five minutes after ten. He leaned back into the softness of the sofa and let out a deep sigh. He closed his eyes and had just begun gently massaging his temple when the sound of her voice aroused him.

"Theresa Weatherspoon lives just east of town in a blue and white trailer."

Startled, he opened his eyes and snapped upright. She was standing before him holding an open folder. Their eyes met, and she handed him a piece of paper, then allowed him a moment to examine it. It was directions to Theresa's house.

"What about the other one?" he said, rising to his feet.

"Don't know where she lives," she said. "We don't have her address on file. But she works at the bank. She's a teller."

"Which bank?"

Janell glanced at the file to refresh her memory.

"First National."

He looked at her, then squinted.

"It's on Main Street," she said. "Just east of town."

He turned to leave, then stopped. "You got a pen and pad I can use?"

She heard his question, then paused, thinking.

"Let's see," she said, turning from him as she spoke. "Should be one on my desk."

He lingered by the door and followed her with his eyes as she hurried to the desk and retrieved first a pen, then a legal-sized yellow pad. She hustled back and presented them to him.

"Will this do?" she asked.

He took them and nodded. He turned to leave, but the sound of her voice stopped him.

"Be careful." She issued a warm warning.

He turned and glanced at her, then lowered his eyes. "I will," he said sheepishly. "I will." He turned toward the door, then stopped. "Thanks," he mumbled.

"You're welcome."

He entered the streets and stood on the sidewalk reading the information she had given him by the glare of the blazing sun and mentally mapping the quickest route to his destination by rote. Though his impetuous nature impelled him onward, all the wisdom he knew counseled caution, warning that any success, minuscule or grand, hinged on his ability to do that which the others had not been able to do—get her to talk.

Several miles outside the city limits, he drew near her house, traversing streets that skirted the outer edges of town, bypassing acre upon acre of sprawling farmland, and twisting and turning through miles of desolate habitat hidden beneath dense stands of trees and situated in a sparse section of town still populated by whites only. At the designated junction, he slowed and turned off the main highway onto a narrow dirt road that jutted from a cluster of trees and wound its way around the edge of a cotton field and along a long, narrow drainage ditch that was marred with weeds and partially hidden by a thicket of thorns. As he turned off the main road, he leaned forward and gripped the wheel tightly. The recent rains had turned the road to a thick, sloppy mush, and there was in him the very real fear of losing control of the truck or becoming ensnared in the soft mud or a hidden bog. Confident, but cautious, he slowed to a snail's pace and followed the deep ruts, staying close to the center of the road, moving to his lane only to avoid an oncoming vehicle or to bypass an ominous puddle of water which his mind cautioned could be concealing soft mud or hiding a deep trench.

He crept along, until finally, near the end of the road, he spotted the tiny trailer nestled close to the edge of the woods and surrounded by a poorly kept yard that was cluttered with old scrap iron and car parts, and other odds and ends that could only be described as junk.

He gazed at the yard, dumbfounded. His lips parted.

"Trailer trash," he mumbled. The thought fired the fury smoldering deep within him as his incensed mind grappled with the unsettling fact that his son had been condemned to die on the word of po' white trash.

He collected the pad and pen and stepped from the truck. He started toward the house, but weak, nervous legs made him stop. What would he say when he got there? How would he get her to talk? His anxious mind hurriedly sorted vague ideas and faint possibilities until it stumbled on an idea that was not good, but under the circumstances seemed better than the others. He was a reporter, not just any reporter, but a sympathetic reporter from Shreveport—no, New Orleans—doing a follow-up story on the imminent execution of Marcus Stokes and its impact on the people of Brownsville.

Calmed by his plan, he approached the house; but before he could mount the steps, the door opened, and a white woman stepped out.

"What you want?" she snapped.

"Looking for Theresa Weatherspoon."

"What you want with her?"

"I'm a reporter," he lied. "I want to ask her a few questions."

"What kind of questions?"

"Questions regarding the execution of Marcus Stokes."

She looked at him, then at his truck.

"Do I look like I was born yesterday?"

"Excuse me?" he said, feigning ignorance.

"You that nigger's daddy, ain't you?"

Her question made him wince. Stupefied, he drew a deep breath to calm himself. He tried to think of a quick response, but his mind was blank; his tongue was tied. Shame made him look away. How did she know? How could she know?

"I heard you was back," she said, unconsciously answering his unspoken question. "And I knowed, sooner or later, you'd be coming 'round here, begging, and pleading, and trying to git me to change my story. But I won't. 'Cause I seen 'im grab her that night. Seen 'im just as good as I see you."

"No." He shook his head. "He wouldn't do nothing like that."

"You calling me a lie?"

"No, ma'am," he recanted. "I ain't disputing your word. It's just

that he my son. And I know he wouldn't do what you said. He just
wouldn't."

"He did it," she growled in a tone void of doubt. "And now he gone
git what's coming to him."

"Ma'am, you must be mistaken."

"Git off my property."

"Ma'am, please. My boy's life at stake."

"I said git!"

He started to say something else, but he saw her reach inside the
house and retrieve a shotgun. The sight of the gun made him submit.
He raised his hands above his head and began to slowly back away. He
turned toward the truck. He could hear her feet descending the steps
as he pulled the truck door open. Then he heard her yell, "You come
back here again, I'm gone put the law on you, you hear?"

Chapter 16

When Tyrone reached the main highway, he pulled to the side of the road and stopped. He looked at the road ahead, then back over his shoulder toward the house. Gun or no gun, he had an overwhelming desire to go back and confront her. Desperation urged him back, but common sense stopped him. It was no use; she would not talk. He looked ahead, then back again. What should he do? His frayed nerves were on edge, and his confused emotions made it difficult for him to think. He straightened, and exhaled hard, then slumped head-long upon the wheel. He was in a whirlwind. He felt himself spinning.

"Daddy, help me."

He straightened again. The cry was clear, but faint. It was as if it had emanated from the deepest, darkest hollow of his tormented consciousness. He clutched the wheel with both hands and gazed abstractedly ahead.

What should he do?

He spurned the force pulling him back and plowed ahead. No, she would not talk to him, but perhaps the girl at the bank would. Through the window, he watched the highway rise and fall before him. Now and then, a car whisked past. Occasionally, a passerby waved, but not him. He saw them, yet he did not notice them. His mind was preoccupied. As the truck slowly swallowed the highway, he thought of the girl. How would he get her to talk to him? Inside his chest, he felt his heart pounding. Inside his head, his mind grappled with the probability that she would not be alone. There would be other white people about her, watching his actions, listening to his words. And if she would not talk to him, he did not know what he would do or what he could do. He longed for the sun to rise and illuminate the darkness that housed the terrible nightmare that had become his life.

At the bank, he parked in the large lot on the north side of the building and stepped down from the truck onto the pavement. He looked around, gawking at the hordes of white people loitering near the entrance of the bank. Though expected, their presence unnerved him, and in an instant he was claimed by a loathing so intense that he had the sensation of being outside of himself, watching them through squinted eyes dimmed by utter contempt. He took a deep breath and advanced toward them, secretly hoping that once inside, as if by some gratuitous act, he would find her momentarily isolated in a discreet area where he might steal a guarded moment of her much demanded time.

Once alone with her, what would he say? Should he pretend to be a potential customer in search of sound financial advice? Or should he identify himself and hope that she would grant him a moment to plead for his condemned son's life? Uncertainty mounted, and the weight of his burden heated his anxious body as warm beads of sweat began to fall from his now tepid skin.

He reached the building, and he felt the muscles in his tense body tighten even more as he swung through the door to the lobby. He stood for a minute, staring at the long counter behind which sat a line of tellers. Which one was she? He shuffled clumsily to the back of the line and strained, staring squint-eyed at distant name tags. The line inched forward until he stood at the forefront, staring at blue eyes, hearing the low drone of a soft voice call "next."

He advanced to the counter, balmy palm clasped against balmy palm.

"How may I help you?"

"Can I see Miss Gautreau?"

"Lori?"

"Yes, ma'am."

"She's in New Accounts."

He squinted.

"Over there."

He followed the line of her eyes to a lone lady sitting unoccupied behind a large, cluttered desk. He looked at her. She was young. Twenty-one, maybe twenty-two. Her dress was professional, a conservative navy blue suit. Her hair was pulled back, and her tan baby face was accented with light make-up. Her thin lips were softly matted with an application of an earth-tone lipstick. He walked to her desk with firm, hurried steps.

"Are you Miss Gautreau?"

She lifted her head, and their eyes met.

"Yes, I am," she said, then rose and extended her right hand. He took her hand in his own, shook it gently, then released it.

"What can I do for you today?" she asked.

"I want to ask you a couple of questions."

"Please have a seat."

He sat on the edge of the chair and scooted close to her desk.

"Are you opening an account with us today?"

"No, ma'am," he said, then waited.

"Well, how can I help you?"

He looked at her. Then paused. She seemed nice enough. Maybe he could be straight with her.

"Ma'am, my name is Stokes," he said. "Tyrone Stokes."

"Glad to make your acquaintance, Mr. Stokes."

"I want to talk to you about my son."

She looked at him with a blank stare. A moment passed; then her confusion faded, and in an instant she was aware of who he was. Suddenly, her face tightened. Her tan skin flushed red, and she looked at him with eyes pronouncing the conversation was over.

She leaned back in her chair, uncomfortable, and said, "Sir, I'm going to have to ask you to leave."

"Ma'am, I just want to ask you a couple of questions." He protested her request while at the same time trying to calm the tension he saw rising in her.

She glanced at him; then her anxious eyes quickly shifted to a uniformed white man lingering near the door. Tyrone looked over his shoulder. The man was a security guard, and he was looking in their direction, alarmed.

Tyrone looked back at the woman, then whispered through clenched teeth, "Ma'am, please."

He saw her nod, and without looking again, he knew that she had signaled the guard, even before he heard him say, "Is there a problem, Lori?"

"Yes," she said. Her tone was low, but serious. "Please remove this man."

Tyrone felt a firm hand grip his shoulder.

"Come on, buddy, let's go."

Defeated, he quietly rose to his feet and walked toward the door, feeling the presence of the guard shadowing his every step, marshaling him out of the building and into the parking lot. Once outside, he stood upon the sidewalk, wondering. Now where should he go? What should he do? The details of his son's crime, though firmly etched in his mind, were not complete. He understood what supposedly happened, but in his mind, he could not visualize it—the store, the streets, the abduction, the murder. Suddenly, there was in him a desire to see the crime scene, and he found himself giving in to a burning impulse to drive to the store. He guided the truck out of the lot and drove west on Main Street, to Hawthorne Avenue, then pulled off the road, parking the truck next to Jones' Grocery. Through roving eyes, he looked at the street, then back at the corner of the store. That was where the witnesses had stood. He leaned back and angled his head, looking toward the entrance. And that was the door out of which the girl had come. Adrenaline surged as he pushed his door open and stepped to the ground. He followed the short sidewalk around the corner, past the large glass window that traversed the front of the building. At the door, he stopped, then pushed through. A single cashier manned the register while several customers milled about the shelves, shopping. Nervous tension guided his steps. He moved between the shelves near the cashier, then lifted an item from the shelf with shaking fingers and pretended to examine it while his eager eyes cased the place. His gaze fell upon the camera. Startled, his eyes widened. His head became light; his chest began to swell. Unexpectedly, and unexplainably, time was transformed, and he was no longer himself, but his son, unaware of the ominous camera watching his every move, recording his every act, sealing his tragic fate.

Suddenly, he couldn't breathe. He needed air. He pushed through the door and out of the store and stood upon the sidewalk, swallowing large gulps of air in short, choppy spurts. He walked past the plate glass window, to the corner, and leaned against the jagged brick wall. He closed his eyes, and though he could not see, he could hear the steady stream of traffic a few yards in front of him on Main Street. He exhaled hard and opened his eyes again. A few seconds passed, and then he realized that he was standing in the exact spot where one of the witnesses reportedly stood. He turned toward the side street. A car passed and when it stopped at the stop sign, he looked hard. It was broad daylight, but from where he stood, he could not see the driver's face. The discovery excited him, and he moved closer to the street and waited. A second car passed. He stared at the vehicle with a concentrated gaze. He watched the vehicle slow and stop at the stop sign. He shielded his eyes from the bright sunlight with his hands and stared. The driver was a man, of that he was sure, but he could not see his face. Inside his chest, he felt his heart pounding. If he could not see him by the light of day, surely they could not have seen Marcus under the cloak of darkness.

Tingling with excitement, he stepped from the building and lingered near the street, his eyes fixated on the stop sign, trying desperately to gauge the distance in his roused mind. Unsure of his calculation, yet determined to know, he paced the distance, counting each long stride, stopping on the shoulder, parallel to the sign. Twenty-seven yards. It was exactly twenty-seven yards. He looked about, his head on a swivel. Across the street, a short distance from the highway, he spied a house. Could someone there have seen something? On an impulse, he went to the door and rang the bell, hearing the soft chiming within. He waited a few anxious seconds, then lifted his finger to press the button a second time; but before he could, the door swung open, and a woman appeared. A black woman.

"Can I help you?" she asked.

He looked at her. She was a worker. Probably the maid.

"Can I see the owner?" he said.

"Miss Mabel?"

He looked at her, then nodded.

"She expecting you?"

"No, ma'am," he said. " She ain't."

"What's your name, honey?"

"Tyrone, ma'am. Tyrone Stokes."

"Awright, Mr. Stokes," she said, "hold on."

She closed the door, and he turned and looked back toward the street. Yes, from inside the house, someone could have seen the whole thing. Behind him, the door opened, and he spun around, startled. It was the maid again.

"Come on in," she said. "Miss Mabel in the parlor."

He followed her down a long corridor, taking in his surroundings as he walked. They were people of standing. He could tell by the shiny hardwood floors and the expensive-looking paintings he spied through open doors, adorning the walls of lavishly decorated rooms, lit by large, imposing chandeliers.

They entered the parlor, and he stopped just inside the door and looked clumsily at the old gray-haired lady the maid had referred to as Miss Mabel. Yes, she was a woman of standing. He could tell by the way she sat with her back straight, and her legs together, and her head held high. There was an open book lying face-down across her lap and a cup of something, possibly tea, sitting on a silver tray on the table before her.

"Miss Mabel, this is the gentleman who wants to see you."

She studied him a moment then spoke.

"Good afternoon," she said.

"Afternoon, ma'am," he said, then politely nodded his head.

"You looking for work?" she asked.

"No, ma'am," he said, then looked away, uncomfortable. There was an empty chair directly across from her; but she did not invite him to sit, nor did he expect her to. In fact, he was amazed that she had ignored old, well-established social mores and invited him this deep into her sanctuary.

"Well, what can I do for you?" she asked.

He opened his mouth to speak, but no words came. He raised an awkward hand to his mouth and cleared his clogged throat.

"There was a crime committed outside your window," he said. "And I was wondering if you saw anything."

"I haven't heard of any crime," she said, puzzled. "What crime are you referencing?"

"Young girl was abducted." He paused to gauge her reaction. She sat poker faced, listening intently. "A white girl," he said. "They say a local black boy did it."

Behind him he heard the maid scurrying about nervously.

"Who are you?" Miss Mabel asked.

"Just an interested citizen."

"Wasn't that boy named Stokes?"

"Yes, ma'am."

"Didn't you say your name was Stokes?"

"Yes, ma'am, I did."

"You related?"

"Yes, ma'am. He my son."

"You talked to the law?"

"No, ma'am. Not yet."

"You best talk to the law," she said. "I can't help you."

"So, you didn't see anything?"

"Didn't see a thing," she said.

"Could anyone else have seen anything? Maybe the maid?"

Behind him, he heard the maid fumble something.

"She didn't see anything either," Miss Mabel said.

He started to asked her if she was sure, but reconsidered. To do so would be deemed an insult. He turned and looked at the maid, but she quickly averted her eyes. He looked at Miss Mabel again, and her eyes told him that the conversation was over.

"Sorry I couldn't be of more help," she said dryly, then politely said, "Irene, show the gentleman out."

In silence, he followed Irene out of the room and into the hall.

Near the front door, he paused and turned to her and whispered, "Can I talk to you a minute?"

She looked around, wide-eyed.

"Can't talk right now," she said.

"But, ma'am, it's important."

"Miss Mabel don't take kindly to socializing on the job," she whispered.

"Ma'am—"

"Can't talk now," she whispered forcefully. "Get off at three."

"Can I talk to you then?"

She nodded and turned to leave.

"Ma'am," he called to her.

"You best go now," she said. " 'Fo Miss Mabel get riled."

He exited the house onto the steps, and she closed the door behind him. He looked at his watch. It was almost noon. He stood upon the stoop, pondering what to do next. He looked toward Main Street. A police car passed. Suddenly, an eerie feeling engulfed him, and he remembered his aunt's stern admonition: "Dot your i's and cross your t's. . . . Them people ain't playing with you."

The thought cleared his confused mind, and he formulated a plan. First, he would renew his driver's license. Then he would grab a quick bite to eat. By that time, it should be time to meet with Irene, the maid.

He descended the steps and walked halfway to his truck, then stopped and looked back at the stop sign, then at the window. Yes, she could have seen something. He looked at the stop sign a second time, then mumbled softly to himself: "God, please let her have seen something."

Inside the truck, he drove to the intersection and braked to a halt at the stop sign, pondering. Why would anyone abduct someone here? It was too close to Main Street. He turned left to make the block. Yes, there were too many houses. Too much traffic. Too many people. And too little cover. It just did not make sense. A black boy and a white girl in a truck this close to town. It just did not make sense. He turned right at the intersection and drove the short distance back to Main Street. He turned left on Main Street and drove toward the Department of Motor Vehicles, more convinced than ever that this thing could not have happened the way it had been portrayed. It just couldn't have.

At the Department of Motor Vehicles, he entered the crowded room and stood at the back of the line, looking about. Before his incarceration, the DMV had been located on the first floor of the courthouse, but now it had been moved to the opposite end of town and was located in the building that had once been the laundromat. The place was not fancy. There was a large plate glass window that spanned the length of the front wall. Several rows of chairs were aligned on the right side of the room, just beyond the entrance. The counter held two clerk stations positioned near the center. At the far end was a camera mounted on a tripod. A few feet in front of the camera was a small wooden stool, behind which stood a large white screen. In the far corner two desks, the kind you usually see in a classroom, were occupied by would-be drivers taking the written portion of the driver's exam. The young white boy appeared to be sixteen, maybe seventeen. The other was an older white man in his late thirties or early forties.

High upon the wall, the clock ticked away the minutes. Tyrone looked at it. It was noon. He glanced around the room at the waiting people. A rather robust white woman was sitting in the first row, on the end seat, bouncing a crying infant on her knee while clutching a white envelope, which more than likely had brought her to the DMV. Obviously, she had been waiting awhile, and her patience was wearing thin. Two rotund white men were standing in the far corner, discussing the price of soybeans and complaining about the time they had wasted this morning. Time that should have been spent in the fields; they were farmers. One woman was reading a book. Another was writing something; it could have been a grocery list. But most were sitting zombielike, occasionally fidgeting in their chairs, staring straight ahead, waiting.

When he finally reached the clerk, he was told that since his license had expired, he was required by law to undergo the entire process anew. The test could be administered today; however, there was at least a forty-five minute wait before he could even sit for the written exam. He could wait or come back tomorrow. It was up to him.

Though the wait was lengthy, he did not leave; instead, he sat quietly in a corner, next to a window, studying a driver's manual and intermittently looking dreamily out into the streets, wondering whether or not things would pan out. He had raised his head to ponder the answer to one of the questions when across the street, his gaze fell on an older white man wearing a suit, carrying a briefcase, scurrying down the sidewalk. Instantly, he thought of Johnson. Why hadn't he questioned the maid? The thought disgusted him. Involuntarily, he began to fidget in his chair, agitated. In his mind flashed a scene, and suddenly he was no longer there. A large white screen had been lowered, before which he sat, watching again that which had already unfolded. He saw Marcus dragged into a courtroom, handcuffed and shackled, standing before the judge, confused, afraid. He heard the judge read the charges. He saw Marcus staring about, dumbfounded. He was in a fight, the rules of which he did not understand, using weapons with which he was unfamiliar. He heard the judge again.

"How do you plead?"

He saw Marcus look at Captain Jack for advice, then look away, confused. The process was fast and beyond him. His lips parted, and he mumbled, "Not guilty."

The words came from his mouth, not his brain. He wasn't thinking. He couldn't think. Fear had rendered him insane. Shock had rendered him mute. Tyrone saw Captain Jack standing next to him, passive, defeated.

Inside the DMV, Tyrone heard the clerk call a name. He turned and watched the large lady up front stand, position the infant in her arms, and move to the counter. He glanced down at the book, then back out of the window. Why hadn't Captain Jack questioned the maid? Why?

Tightness gripped his head. It began to ache. He looked at his watch again. In his mind, he wished time forward. He was anxious to talk to the maid, and at the same time afraid to imagine the outcome. For a long time, he stared at the sample test booklet, examining questions and listening to the sound of strange names being called, until finally, he heard his own. He rose from his seat, and instantly, an eerie silence gripped the room. He looked about cautiously. Yes, they recognized his name, and yes, they were staring at him. He moved stiff-legged toward the counter until he was face-to-face with the young clerk.

"Mr. Stokes."

"Yes, ma'am."

"You can take your test now."

She handed him a pencil and a test booklet and pointed him toward an empty desk. He took a seat and glanced thoughtfully at the clock, then broke the seal on the test booklet and tried to begin. He stared at the words on the page before him, but he could not concentrate. His eyes would not focus. The words seemed blurred; the questions, obscure. He leaned forward, placed both elbows on the desk, and rested his bowed head against the palms of his hands. He stared at the exam, slowly moving his lips as he repeatedly reread the same question, trying desperately to focus his troubled mind long enough to complete the task before him. He closed his eyes, concentrated a moment, then opened them and with a nervous hand marked an unsure answer. He had just begun to read the next question when a loud, shrill wail made him look up. The infant was crying again. His mother had risen to her feet, and the child's arms were draped about her neck, and his head resting on her shoulder. She was bouncing him up and down and gently patting his back with her hand while softly repeating, "Don't cry, honey. Mama's here. Don't cry."

His concentration broken, Tyrone stared blankly at the infant, wondering what his son was doing at this very moment. Was he crying? Was he longing to lay his head on his mother's shoulder? Was he yearning to be comforted by her touch and calmed by the sound of her reassuring voice? Or did he realize that the law had him, and its grip was so tight that neither touches nor words nor his mother's love could comfort him now?

Suddenly, Tyrone felt more intensely the ache of his weary heart. He looked at the clock again. He wanted to rise from his seat and rush from this place. He should be doing something. Yet, there was nothing to do now but wait.

In spite of his tattered nerves, he passed the written exam, then waited another half hour for the driving instructor to return. Then he took and passed the driver's test, had his photograph taken, and once his license was processed, drove to the diner, grabbed a quick bite to eat, then drove back to meet the maid.

When he arrived, she wasn't at work, but had walked across the street and was sitting on a bench in front of the store, waiting. He knew that she was waiting for him, but the way she had positioned her purse and other belongings on the bench next to her, it appeared as if she was waiting on a ride to take her home. In an effort to be discreet, he didn't park near the bench. Instead, he drove his truck to the opposite side of the store and parked near the street. When he was sure that no one was watching, he walked over and stood next to her.

"Miss Irene," he spoke.

"Mr. Stokes."

"Be all right to talk here?" he asked.

"This be fine," she said. "I sats here sometimes and wait for my husband to pick me up. He work down yonder at the locker plant. Got to pass by here anyway. Besides, he ain't too particular 'bout coming over to Miss Mabel's."

"Well, I won't take up much of your time."

"Don't mind talking 'til he get here. Ought to be ten, fifteen minutes yet."

"Well, I wanted to talk to you 'bout that night."

"What about it?"

"Miss Mabel said you didn't see nothing."

"She don't know what I seen. How is she gone tell you what I seen?"

"Did you see anything?"

She paused and looked around before she answered.

"I'm gone tell you what I seen," she said. "But after I tell it to you, I ain't gone tell it no mo'."

"Yes, ma'am," he said. "What did you see?"

"I was satting in the parlor, looking out the window."

"Yes, ma'am."

"The room we was all in a little while ago."

"Yes, ma'am," he said. "What you see?"

"Seen that gal when she come 'round that corner yonder."

"The girl that was killed?"

"That right," she said. "Normally, I wouldn't've paid her no 'tention; but it was raining, and I was wondering whose child that was walking in the rain like that." She paused. "And Lord, the way that gal was dressed. Little ole shorts on. Butt hanging out. And my she was twisting. Twisting like it wasn't no tomorrow. Well, directly a truck come along and stopped at that sign yonder and waited like he was gone give her a ride. When she seen the truck, she come up on the driver's side. And look like she said something to him."

"That's when he grabbed her?"

"He ain't did no such thang. That gal walked 'round that truck, opened the door, and got in on her own accord."

"Are you sure?"

"Honey, I was sitting right there looking at her."

"What color was the truck?"

"Blue."

"Police report say the truck was black."

"Don't care what it say. I seen that truck when it passed under that light yonder. It stopped, and they talked like they knowed each other. Then she got in, and they drove off."

He felt his head spin.

"Witnesses say she struggled."

"Didn't do no such thang. I'm telling you they talked like they knowed one another. Then she opened the door and got in."

A sensation gripped him.

"Then, my son didn't do it."

"Can't say whether he did it or not. 'Cause I don't know that. But I do know what I saw."

"And the truck was blue?"

"That's right."

"You sure it wasn't black?"

"It was blue," she said. "Dark blue."

"You positive?"

"Honey, I know what I seen. That child got in a truck sho' nuff, but it was blue. May've looked black; but it wasn't, it was blue with them ole white tires on it."

"You sure?"

"I know what I seen."

"Why didn't you tell the police?"

"They didn't ask me."

"Ain't nobody talked to you?"

She shook her head. "And to my knowledge, they ain't talked to Miss Mabel either."

Chapter
17

Thrust inside of him, just beneath the surface, was a burning desire to cast his anxious eyes on his son's truck. Suddenly, he was too excited to think. He wanted to believe. Irene had been so sure. She had seemed so positive. Yet there was in him a doubt that he knew could be alleviated only by seeing with his own eyes that which he found so difficult to believe. As he drove, he was hopeful, but not arrogant. This seemed too easy to be real; too good to be true.

At his in-laws' house, he parked on the lawn close to the porch and pushed the door open, then waited. Where was the dog? He cast a cautious eye toward the house, and when he was satisfied that all was clear, he stepped to the ground and on tiptoes gingerly crossed the short distance to the porch and mounted the steps. The front door was open, and as he stepped onto the porch, he heard a mixture of voices mingling together in a low, somber rumble. He made his way next to the door and peeked inside. Through the screen door, he saw several people huddled together in the tiny living room. Mr. Titus, his father-in-law, Miss Gertrude, his mother-in-law, and Pauline, his estranged wife, were sitting on the tiny sofa, and Reverend Jacobs was sitting in the large chair across from them. Suddenly, his muscles stiffened.

"They got company," he mumbled.

What should he do? Maybe he ought to wait until their company left. He turned to leave, but the sound of Reverend Jacobs's voice stopped him.

"There is something above all this," he heard Reverend Jacobs say.

A strange feeling surged through him, and instantly, he knew they were discussing the dim plight of his condemned son. He looked at his watch. No, waiting would not work. The reverend was long winded, and waiting could take too long. There was nothing to do but interrupt them. He raised his right hand and brought it down against the frame of the rickety screen door. The door vibrated. A hush fell over the room, and then the lone sound of his father-in-law's masculine voice rang out.

"Who is it?"

Tyrone didn't answer; instead, he pulled the screen door open and stepped inside. Instantly, his father-in-law snapped to his feet.

"Thought I told you not to come back here?"

"Need to talk to Pauline," Tyrone said.

"Git out my house," the old man demanded.

"Titus!" Tyrone heard Miss Gertrude yell, shocked.

A quiet moment passed. Then Tyrone started toward Pauline, but Mr. Titus stepped in front of him and blocked his path. Tyrone paused, and in the dim light of the room, he could see deep into his father-in-law's fiery red eyes; he could feel the warmth of his hot, stale breath.

"I mean it," the old man said. "Git out."

"Brother Jackson." Reverend Jacobs snapped to his feet. He looked from one man to the other, confused.

"Not 'til I see Pauline," Tyrone said defiantly.

"Boy, if you don't git out my house, you better."

"It's okay, Daddy." Tyrone heard Pauline's voice. It was soft, weak, lifeless. He looked toward her, but he could not see her. She was still sitting on the couch, and Mr. Titus was blocking his view.

"Let 'em talk, Brother Jackson," Reverend Jacobs said. "Let her hear what he got to say."

Mr. Titus stepped aside, and Pauline slowly lifted her eyes to Tyrone.

"What you want?" she said.

She looked at him, and for the first time, he looked directly at her. The ordeal had taken its toll on her. Her too thin face had not only fallen, but her once smooth skin was filled with worry lines. Her beautiful brown eyes had dimmed. Now they were red and weary, and marred with crow's feet.

"We need to talk," Tyrone said.

"Too late for talking," she told him.

"Pauline, can we go somewhere private?"

"Anything you got to say to her, you can say to us," Mr. Titus said.

"This between me and my wife," Tyrone said.

"Ain't nothing you got to say, I want to hear," Pauline said.

"Pauline, listen," Tyrone pleaded.

"No," she interrupted him. "You listen. You the cause of all this."

"Me?" Tyrone said. "Pauline, you know better than that."

"I tried to keep him from you," she said. "It may have been wrong, but Lord knows I tried."

"Pauline!"

"I tried to show him another way."

"Pauline."

"But I wasn't strong enough."

"Pauline."

"You in his blood," she said. "Good God Almighty. You in his blood."

"Pauline, I need to ask you something."

"Guess you satisfied now."

"Pauline, I didn't want this."

"He was a good boy."

"Pauline, where his truck?"

"Truck!" Mr. Titus yelled. "That's what you after?"

"Pauline, I need to see his truck."

"I know you ain't crazy 'nough to think we gone let you take that truck 'way from here," Titus said. "I know you ain't that crazy, is you?"

"Pauline," he called her name again, then knelt before her, but she didn't acknowledge him.

"You asked your question," Mr. Titus said. "Now gone."

"Pauline, where the truck?" Tyrone said.

She started to cry, but she didn't answer.

"Stop aggravating her," Mr. Titus ordered.

"Pauline, it's important," Tyrone said. "Where the truck?"

"Maybe you ought to go," Miss Gertrude said. "Come back some other time. Let her rest now."

"Pauline, I ain't asking for myself," he said. "I'm asking for Marcus."

She looked at him, and her lips began to tremble.

"I met a woman might can help him," he said. "But I need to see the truck. Need to see what color it is."

"What difference that make?" Mr. Titus mumbled.

Pauline opened her mouth to speak, but no words came.

"Pauline, please," he begged. "Please, Pauline, please."

"What woman?" Pauline asked.

"Don't listen to him, honey," Mr. Titus counseled. "Don't listen to his foolishness."

"She say she saw the whole thang."

"Who?"

"She say the truck what picked that girl up was blue, not black."

Pauline stared at him, wide-eyed.

"You know what that mean, don't you?"

"He didn't do it?" Pauline mumbled.

"That's right," Tyrone said. "He didn't do it."

"Git out," he heard Mr. Titus say.

"Titus, you reckon it could be so?" Miss Gertrude asked.

"Git out!" Titus said again.

"Not 'til I see that truck," Tyrone said.

"It's in the pasture," Pauline said. "It's in the pasture. Way back in the woods next to that old shed."

"Baby, don't tie your hopes on this," Mr. Titus said. "Don't listen to him. He don't know what he talking 'bout." He turned to Tyrone. "What the woman's name?"

"Her name Irene."

"Irene what?"

"I don't know."

"You don't know?"

"I don't know," he repeated.

"Where she live?"

"I don't know."

"You don't know?"

"Mr. Titus, you heard me."

"How you know she telling the truth?"

"I just know."

"Is you crazy coming 'round here with this?"

"Maybe this can help him," Tyrone said.

"Why you getting this child hopes up? Why?"

Tyrone looked at Pauline. She was trembling. He felt the need to say more.

"Pauline, I believe her," he said. "She work for some white folks in a house across the street from the store. She was looking out the window when it happened. She seen the truck. She say it was blue, Pauline. She say it was blue, not black."

"She seen Marcus?" Mr. Titus asked.

"No, sir."

"She seen who was driving?"

"No, sir."

"She say it wasn't Marcus?"

"Say she couldn't say one way or the other."

"Why you come here with this?"

"She say the truck was blue."

"They say it was black."

"It's a chance."

"It's her word against theirs."

"It's something."

"She colored?"

"Yes, sir."

"Why you come here with this?"

"I'm trying to help him."

"You making things worse."

There was silence.

"Where this woman been all this time?" Titus asked. "Why she ain't said nothing 'fo now?"

"She been right where I found her," Tyrone said.

"Why she ain't talked to the police?" Titus asked.

" 'Cause the police ain't talked to her," Tyrone told him.

"Maybe she ain't seen what she say she seen," Titus said.

"What reason she got to lie for?" Tyrone asked.

"Maybe it's so, Titus," Miss Gertrude said. "Maybe it's so."

"And maybe it ain't," Mr. Titus snapped.

"But, Titus," Miss Gertrude said.

"But, Titus nothing," Mr. Titus said. "Somebody got to look out for this child, Gertrude. You know what she facing in a few days. Ain't no sense in that boy prancing in here getting her hopes up after all this time. Ain't no sense at all."

"I'm gone go look at that truck," Tyrone said.

"Leave that truck alone," Mr. Titus said.

"Let 'im look at the truck, Brother Titus," Reverend Jacobs said. "Ain't gone hurt nothing to let 'im look at it."

"Reverend Jacobs, this a family matter."

"Titus!" Miss Gertrude exclaimed.

"I'm gone look at that truck," Tyrone said.

"Gertrude, get my gun."

"I ain't gone do no such thang."

Titus wheeled and stared at her, hard.

"Woman, you sassing me?"

"Daddy, please," Pauline said. "This ain't helping nothing."

Mr. Titus turned to his daughter and looked at her with consoling eyes.

"Honey, you getting your hopes up for nothing," he said. "I know this hard on you. God knows I do. But you just got to trust me on this. You just got to trust your ole daddy."

"Sometimes we do better to trust in the Lord," Reverend Jacobs said. "After all, he knows best."

Titus looked at Reverend Jacobs with hard, disdainful eyes.

"Go 'n and look at the truck, son," Miss Gertrude said. "Go 'n and look at it if you want to."

"Woman, you walking over me?" Mr. Titus asked.

"Just doing what I think best," Miss Gertrude said.

"All right," Mr. Titus said. "You gone see. All of you gone see."

Tyrone turned to leave, then stopped.

"Somebody need to hold that dog," he said.

"Dog ain't gone bother you," Mr. Titus grumbled.

Tyrone didn't move. He looked at Miss Gertrude.

"Go 'n," she said. "Blue tied up."

Tyrone started toward the door, then stopped a second time. He looked at Pauline. She was looking down at the floor, crying.

Chapter
18

Tyrone turned and left the room. Outside, he saw the dull red sun hanging low in the early evening sky, and he could hear the faint drone of a tractor in one of the distant fields behind the house. He stepped from the porch and walked toward the pasture. Near the fence, a small herd of cows had gathered around the water trough. Careful not to disturb them, he walked along the dusty road until he found a clear space near the fence, a short distance hence. He paused, then gingerly mashed the middle strand of barbed wire down with his right hand, bent low, and stepped through. Inside the pasture, he walked across the open meadow toward the sparse woods with quick but careful steps. The lush green grass over which he traveled, though evenly cropped by grazing cattle, was sprinkled with what looked to him to be hundreds and hundreds of tiny mounds of fresh cow manure.

In the woods, he advanced over dry twigs and hanging vines until he found himself standing uncertainly before the truck, which was overgrown with weeds and briars and covered with a thick coat of caked-on dirt. He stood still, staring. He wanted to advance, but fear checked him. Was it blue or was it black? From where he stood, he could not tell. Well, there was only one way to find out. He advanced slowly, pushing back weeds with his foot and turning his body sideways, ever careful to avoid being stuck by the sharp-pointed edges of the prickly thorns.

He stopped near the hood of the truck, then raised a steady finger and rubbed hard across the surface until he broke through the crust and saw glimmering beneath the dust, the painted surface of the truck. "Black," he mumbled, half aloud. He wiped hard against the surface of the truck with the palm of his hand, then stepped back and stared, wide-eyed. "It's definitely black." He moved forward again and was examining the spot more closely when he heard someone behind him.

"See you found it."

He whirled and saw Pauline standing at the edge of the woods.

"Found it just fine," he said.

She inched closer, then stopped.

"Got anxious waiting," she said. "Had to know something."

He looked at her, then at the spot again.

"Well, it's black," he said. "No doubt about it."

"Couldn't remember," she said. "Been so long since I seen it."

He looked at her, then looked away. Now that they were alone, he felt uncomfortable.

"What it's doing out here?"

"Papa put it out here after the trial."

"Why?" Tyrone asked.

"Say he didn't want me looking at it."

Tyrone walked to the rear of the truck and bent the weeds back with his foot, then eased down to a squat.

"These the same tires always been on it?"

"Far as I know," she said. "Why?"

"Truck Miss Irene saw had whitewalls," he said. "This one don't."

He looked up at her, but she was staring off, dazed.

"After they give him death, I use to come out here by myself," she mumbled. "Use to sat on that ole stump yonder."

Tyrone looked at the stump, then back at her. He eased to his feet.

"How long this truck been out here?" he asked.

She looked at the truck, then stared off again.

"Use to could see 'im," she said. "Use to could see 'im plain as day."

"Pauline, honey, this important," he said. "Anybody else been using this truck since Marcus been in prison?"

She walked toward the truck, zombielike, and slowly ran her hand across the dirty hood, then stared blankly at the windshield. "Use to see 'im sattin' behind the wheel, just a looking at me, grinning." She paused and turned toward the woods. "Could hear 'im, too," she said, then slowly tilted her head to the side as if listening to a faraway voice. "Git in, Mama," she mumbled. "Git in and let me take you some-where."

She talking out her head, he thought. He walked next to her and laid an unsteady hand gently upon her shoulder. He looked tenderly into her moist eyes.

"Baby, you got to help me," he said. "Time short."

"After a while, I couldn't see 'im no mo'," she said. "I quit coming 'cause I couldn't see 'im no mo'. Couldn't see nothing but that ole truck."

Suddenly, her eyes widened, and Tyrone sensed that she was drift-ing farther away. He tightened his grip about her shoulders and shook her gently. He called her name, and she began to cry.

"Papa and 'em wanting me to turn 'im over to death," she said. Her voice cracked, and she paused to compose herself. "They thank he did it." She paused a second time. Her lips began to quiver. She looked away, and he could tell that her family's stance had produced in her a hurt much too painful to bear.

"Pauline," he whispered her name a second time. "You got to help me."

She turned her head slowly and looked at him as though she was seeing him for the first time. Her eyes were wide, sad.

"If you would have been here, this wouldn't've never happened," she said.

Her pain became his pain, and his body became tense with regret.

"Pauline, ain't no time for this," he said softly. "There just ain't no time."

"You his daddy," she said. "You his daddy, and you supposed to been set a good example for him." She paused and looked longingly into his eyes. "What kind of example you set? Hunh? What you ever give him but a hard way to go?"

Guilt made him drop his head. His eyes began to water, and his nose began to run. He reached up with his hand and wiped his nose with the back of his wrist.

"Ain't no time for this," he repeated. He looked at the truck again, then at the tires. He pulled the door open and looked inside.

"Maybe it's my fault," Pauline said. "If I wouldn't have never sent him to the store, maybe none of this would have happened."

Tyrone pulled the seat forward and looked. The truck was empty. Someone had cleaned it out. He let go of the seat, and it snapped back into place. He looked toward Pauline.

"Did Marcus know the girl?" he asked.

Pauline looked at him strangely but did not answer.

"She knew her killer," Tyrone explained. "The old lady said she got in the truck like she knew her killer." He shut the door and turned and faced Pauline. "Did they know each other?"

"Don't think so," she said.

"You don't know?" he asked.

"Don't know for sure," she said. "But I don't think so."

He opened his mouth to say something else, but at that moment her knees buckled. He watched her sway, then fall back against the front of the truck. Stunned, he raced to her and slipped his arm about her waist. She leaned her head on his shoulder, and he felt the weight of her tired, limp body resting heavily against his own. *She weak from worry and needs to sit down,* he thought. He led her to the stump, and she sat down and leaned sideways against him for support.

"You okay?" he asked.

She closed her eyes and took a deep breath.

"Be all right in a minute," she said. "Just one of them ole dizzy spells."

He placed his arm about her shoulder, and as he did, the tips of his fingers brushed lightly against her naked skin. His downcast eyes glanced lustfully upon her heaving breast. The smooth feel of her skin and the sight of her bulging breast inflamed his senses. He grew light-headed.

"Pauline," he called her name softly.

She opened her eyes and looked up at him.

"Yes," she whispered.

He looked at her, then looked away. He paused, trying desperately to still the fierce battle raging between his warring emotions.

"You ever think about us?" he asked.

She closed her eyes again, then gently laid her head against his body. He paused, waiting for an answer, but none came. He looked at her and saw a single tear slowly rolling down her cheek, glistening in the dull light of the setting sun.

"Do you?" he asked softly, attempting to prod her gently. The fact that she hesitated unnerved him.

"Do I what?" she asked.

"Think about us."

She sighed, and he could see that she was thinking.

"Just all the pain you put me through," she said.

He looked away, hurt. "That was a long time ago."

"Not long enough," she said.

"I still love you," he said.

"Don't say that to me." She rose from the stump and groped forward, her arms extended toward the truck. She reached it and leaned heavily against the hood, her back to him.

"But I do," he said. "You my wife, and I love you."

She turned and faced him.

"I regret the day I laid eyes on you," she said.

"Pauline," he said, his voice cracking. "Don't say that."

"I should have listened to Daddy," she said. "He tried to tell me you weren't no good. But I couldn't see it. I couldn't see you with my eyes, 'cause I was looking at you with my heart."

She paused, and he placed his hands on her shoulders. He could feel her trembling.

"I should have walked away from you, Tyrone. I should have walked away from you a long time ago."

"You don't mean that."

"If I had, I wouldn't be hurting right now," she said. "I wouldn't be hurting, and neither would my child."

"I'm hurting, too, Pauline. I love my family, and I'm hurting, too."

"You don't love us."

"I do," he said.

"No," she denied.

"I do, Pauline. With all my heart."

"If you loved us, you would have stayed in our life instead of in and out the pen," she said. "You don't love us. You love them streets."

"Pauline, I know I screwed up," he said. "But I'm trying to fix that now."

"It's too late," she said.

"No." He shook his head and looked at the truck. "This changes everything."

"This don't change nothing."

"He didn't do it," he said. His eyes were narrow, and his jaw clenched tight.

"You think you telling me something I don't know," she said. "I carried that child inside me for nine months. When something grow inside you that long, you know it. You know what it will and what it won't do. I know my child. Know him better than I know myself. And I can tell you and anybody else who care to listen. He wouldn't hurt a fly. But that don't matter. They gone kill 'im anyway. They done set they minds to it, and ain't nothing you or nobody can do 'bout it."

"Pauline, you can't think like that."

"Daddy right," she said.

"Naw, he ain't."

"I'm too scared to hold on and too scared to turn loose."

"Just hold on to the truth."

"The truth."

"Yes." He nodded. "The truth."

"Them people don't care 'bout the truth."

"It's the only thing that can set him free."

"They don't care 'bout the truth," she repeated. "I went to them people. And I got down on my knees and begged for my child's life. I swallowed my pride and begged them white folks like it wasn't no tomorrow. And they give him death anyway. They don't want the truth. They want revenge."

"Well, they won't get it," he said. "This truck black. The one picked up that child was blue. He didn't do it."

She looked at him with wide, solemn eyes. She wanted to believe, but she was tired, weak, afraid.

"Maybe Papa right," she said. She turned her back and buried her face in her palms and began to weep violently.

"No," he said. He eased forward and grabbed her by both shoulders firmly. "I ain't gone let 'em kill our child, Pauline." He turned her and looked deep into her eyes. "I ain't gone let 'em kill 'im, Pauline. I ain't."

She stared at him with wet eyes. "I'm scared, Tyrone."

"It's gone be all right, Pauline. I swear."

She buried her head in his chest and sobbed. He eased his arms around her and pulled her tight. Over her shoulder he saw a shadowy figure moving toward them through the woods. It was a man. Tyrone focused his eyes without moving his head. The man paused at the mouth of the woods. Tyrone stared at him, and the man stared back. It was Mr. Titus.

"Pauline!" he called sternly.

Startled, she turned and looked.

"Daddy." She pulled away from Tyrone and began drying her eyes with trembling hands.

"Be dark soon," Mr. Titus said. "You best be getting on back to the house."

"It's gone be all right, Pauline," Tyrone said again as she walked away. "I promise you that. It's gone be all right."

Mr. Titus looked at him with angry eyes.

"You got want you come here for," Mr. Titus said. "Now gone."

Chapter
19

He lingered behind a few minutes, giving his wife and father-in-law time to clear the pasture. Then, with his dampened spirit buoyed by his recent discoveries, he walked to his truck, got in, and drove back toward town. He figured that by now Janell had told Captain Jack that he had stopped by, and that maybe, through some small miracle, Captain Jack had hung around the office on the slim chance that he might return. And if Captain Jack had hung around, once he got there, he would tell him about the blue truck, and the white wall tires, and about what the old lady said she had seen that night. And once Captain Jack heard, he would know, beyond a doubt, that Marcus was innocent.

It was after five when Tyrone made it back to town. And for a brief moment, he feared that the office was closed, but when he stopped next to the building, he could see that the lights were still on. From the alley, he recognized the back of Captain Jack's car jutting just beyond the rear of the building. Relieved, he climbed from the truck and walked along the sidewalk toward the door, seeing before his eyes the unnerving image of his broken wife, slumped on the stump, brooding the inevitable fate of their condemned son while hoping against hope that the black truck looming nearby would be enough to awaken her from this dream and end the nightmare that had been her life.

At the door, he knocked, then paused. When the door opened, Captain Jack appeared, and for an awkward moment, he seemed stunned to see Tyrone.

"Mr. Stokes," he said after a brief silence. "Please, come in."

Tyrone entered the room, and Captain Jack closed the door behind him, then motioned to a chair that had been pulled just before the front desk.

"Have a seat," he said.

Tyrone obliged, and after he was seated, Captain Jack came forward, then paused.

"Can I get you anything?" he asked. "Coffee? Soda? Water?"

"No, thank you." Tyrone shook his head. Then he watched Captain Jack make his way behind the desk and lean back uneasily in the chair. Captain Jack opened his mouth to speak, but before he could, Tyrone asked a question.

"Captain Jack, you ever wondered why there was no physical evidence connecting my son to this crime?"

Captain Jack paused, then frowned before answering.

"Yes," he said. "That has always troubled me."

"I think I know why, sir," Tyrone said.

"Why?" Captain Jack asked, his tone seeming to indicate polite indulgence rather than genuine interest.

"Because the girl didn't fight," Tyrone said. "And she didn't fight because she knew her killer."

"There's no proof of that," Captain Jack said.

"Yes, sir, there is," Tyrone said. "Someone saw them."

"Someone other than the two witnesses of record?"

"Yes, sir," Tyrone said.

"Who?" Captain Jack asked.

"The maid."

"What maid?" he asked.

"Miss Mabel's maid."

"Miss Mabel," he repeated, confused.

"Yes, sir," Tyrone said. "Don't remember her last name. But she lives next to the store. In that big white house."

Captain Jack paused, then squinted.

"Mabel Wilkes," Captain Jack said, unsure of himself.

"Yes, sir," Tyrone said. "I believe that's her. She—I mean her maid—was in the window when it happened. She say she saw the girl. She say she saw her get in a blue truck. A blue truck with whitewall tires."

"She told you that?"

"Yes, sir."

"You spoke to her?"

"Yes, sir, I did."

Captain Jack looked at him contemplatively, but did not speak.

"I saw my boy's truck a minute ago," Tyrone said. "It's black, not blue. Black with solid black tires."

Captain Jack leaned back in his chair and brought his hands underneath his chin.

"Did she see the driver?"

"No, sir."

Captain Jack shook his head and sighed softly. "Not enough," he said.

"But she saw the truck."

"It's not enough," Captain Jack repeated. "Just her word against theirs."

"But—"

"Mr. Stokes, I'm sorry. But it's just not enough."

"It's a start," Tyrone said.

"I'm afraid it's too little, too late."

Tyrone looked at him, confused.

"I was going to call you in the morning," Captain Jack said. "I heard from the governor. Our appeal has been denied. The execution will proceed as scheduled."

Tyrone felt a large lump rise from his stomach and lodge in his throat.

"No," Tyrone said, slowly shaking his head. "He didn't do it."

Captain Jack opened his mouth to speak, but before he could, Tyrone interrupted him.

"She said the girl got in the truck like she knew her killer."

"The witnesses said she struggled."

"But the maid say she didn't."

"Her word against theirs."

"But she saw them."

"So did the others."

"But the street light was on, and she was closer than they were."

"A jury of twelve believed they were close enough."

"They're lying," Tyrone said.

"If they are, we can't prove it."

"He didn't do it." Tyrone was adamant.

"Well, if he didn't, who did?"

Tyrone looked at him, stunned. "You think he did it?"

"I didn't say that," Captain Jack said, becoming defensive. "I've worked this case tirelessly for the last five years. I did all I knew to do. I defended him as best I could."

"But you think he did it."

"I didn't say that," Captain Jack repeated.

"Well, what are you saying?" Tyrone asked.

"I am saying that the nature of this crime is so heinous that it's highly unlikely that anyone will believe your son is innocent unless we can tell them who is guilty. Mr. Stokes, a fifteen-year-old girl was raped and strangled, and her nude body was stuffed in a drainage ditch. A jury of twelve found your boy responsible. Public sentiment is firmly against him. . . . I wish that there was something else that I could say or something else that I could do, but there just isn't."

"So, that's it?" Tyrone said.

"There is just no other recourse."

"Just like that."

"I don't want to say that there is absolutely no hope, but, Mr. Stokes, I must be frank. The governor was our last chance. And now that he has refused to intervene, I'm afraid that your son is going to die unless someone can produce irrefutable evidence proving his innocence."

"In other words find the killer?"

"I'm afraid so." Captain Jack nodded. "We have four days."

Tyrone looked at him. His eyes began to water. "I need to see my son again."

"When?"

"Tomorrow."

"I'll see what I can do."

Chapter 20

Tyrone arrived at the prison somewhere around ten o'clock the following morning, and as before, he was searched and led into the visitation room where he sat before the thick Plexiglas window awaiting Marcus. As he waited, he wondered whether Marcus had heard the news about the governor's refusal. Perhaps he should have told Captain Jack not to tell him. At least not right away. At least not until he had a chance to talk to him first.

He was sitting with his head bowed, thinking, when he heard the door clang shut on the other side of the window. He looked up, and instantly, he knew. Yes, Marcus had been told. He could tell by the dazed look he saw in his sad, tired eyes and the lifeless posture of his limp, shackled body. Suddenly, he felt the weight of a thousand pounds pressing tight against his chest, compressing his lungs, constricting his air. He couldn't breathe. His stomach began to churn. He became tense. Nonetheless, he sat perfectly still, trying desperately to conceal the intense agony he felt searing through his tormented soul. Oh, for a cigarette or a shot of whiskey, or anything that could calm his whirling nerves or dull the pulsating pain he felt in his pounding heart.

He watched the guards guide Marcus to the chair, then back away. As Marcus eased awkwardly onto the chair, he did not look directly at Tyrone; instead, he picked up the phone with downcast eyes and spoke into the receiver.

"Papa," he said, then paused. His voice was low and sullen, and though his face was averted, Tyrone could tell that he had been crying.

"Hi, son," Tyrone said; then there was an awkward silence. He felt the need to say more. He searched for words, but none came. As he looked at his son, Tyrone felt himself being overtaken by emotions. He told himself to be steady; he willed himself to be calm.

"You heard?" Tyrone asked.

Marcus nodded and continued to stare off, now visibly struggling to fight back pending tears. Tyrone watched him lower his head and dab the corner of his eye with the back of his chained hand.

"This ain't over," Tyrone said. He tried to sound forceful; he tried to sound assured. "It ain't over by a long shot. You hear me, son? This ain't over."

Again Marcus nodded. He seemed broken, resigned, defeated. A single tear fell from his eye. Yes, he had quit. He had surrendered. Suddenly, Tyrone inched his face closer to the glass. He furrowed his brow and squinted his eyes.

"You ain't giving up, is you?"

Marcus shook his head slowly, then spoke, his voice hardly above a whisper.

"No, sir."

Tyrone looked at him. He could see that his hands were trembling. Deep inside, he wanted to console Marcus but he did not know how.

"Good," he said. "'Cause I'm gone get you out of here. I'm gone get you out of here, I promise."

There was silence.

"You hear me, son?" Tyrone asked.

"Yes, sir," Marcus said, his voice low, lifeless.

"I mean it," Tyrone said. "I'm gone get you out of here."

He paused and waited, but Marcus remained silent. Tyrone leaned away from the glass and adjusted the phone in his hand. He looked at his son for a moment then asked, "You need anything?"

Marcus shook his head.

"You sho'?"

"Yes, sir," he said softly, "I'm sho'."

Tyrone saw one of the officers glance at his watch, then look away. He was still looking at the officers when silence gave way to the weak, feeble drone of his son's voice.

"You seen Mama?"

Tyrone lowered his eyes and looked at his son. "I seen her," he said. "Seen her yesterday."

Marcus lifted his head for the first time. His eyes were red, moist. "How is she?" he asked.

"Holding on," Tyrone told him. "She holding on. And that's just what you got to do, son. Hold on."

Suddenly, Marcus's lip began to quiver. He closed his eyes and dropped his head.

"You hear me, son?"

Tyrone paused and waited, but Marcus did not answer.

"Do you hear me, son?" Tyrone repeated.

"Yes, sir," Marcus said, his low voice cracking under the heavy strain of his frayed emotions.

"Look at me," Tyrone demanded.

As Marcus slowly lifted his head, Tyrone envisioned the maid, remembering her words while trying to piece together in his mind clues that would unlock the mystery and free his son from this hellish nightmare. Somewhere deep inside himself, he believed, even if no one else did, that what the maid had told him was crucial to proving once and for all that his son was innocent. Unconsciously, he blinked and in so doing awakened himself from his momentary daze. His eyes focused. He looked through the glass and saw his son staring back at him.

"Did you know her?" he asked.

Marcus looked at him, confused. He did not understand.

"The girl," Tyrone said. "Did you know her?"

Marcus hesitated and looked at him blankly. When what he was being asked registered, his eyes grew wide, and he shook his head frantically. "No, sir," he mumbled. "I didn't. I swear."

"Ever talk to her before?"

"No, sir, Papa. I ain't never talked to her."

"Ever seen her before?"

"Once or twice."

"Where?"

"School."

"So you did know her?"

"No, sir."

Tyrone appeared confused.

"She was a cheerleader," Marcus explained. "I seen her before. But I didn't know her. I just seen her around."

"What kind of person was she?"

"I don't know."

"Was she fast?"

"I don't know."

"She have any enemies?" Tyrone asked. "Somebody who might've wanted to hurt her?"

"I don't know, Papa. I think she mostly kept to herself. But I'm older than she was, and she wasn't in my class. So I don't know."

"She like black boys?"

He shrugged his shoulders. "I don't know."

"Do you know if she fooled around with any of 'em?"

"I don't know, Papa. I don't know nothing about her."

"You ever hear anything?"

"No, sir."

"Ever seen her with any black girls?"

Marcus paused and looked toward the ceiling.

"I don't know."

"Think, son," Tyrone said. "This important."

"Was one girl," Marcus said. "Another cheerleader."

"Black?" Tyrone asked.

"Yes, sir."

"And they was friends?"

Marcus shrugged his shoulders. "Seen them together sometimes. But don't know if they was friends."

"You remember her name?"

Marcus looked up again, thinking. "Believe her name Terri."

"Terri," Tyrone repeated.

"Yes, sir."

"Terri what?" Tyrone asked.

"La Beaux, I think." He paused. "Yeah, that's it. Terri Lynn La Beaux."

"La Beaux," Tyrone said, pondering. "Don't know no La Beauxs."

"Papa, why you asking me all these questions 'bout her?"

"Somebody else seen her that night."

Marcus gaped at him, stunned.

"At the store?" he asked.

Tyrone nodded. "They seen her when she got in that truck. They figure she knew the driver. And I do, too. Can't see no girl that age getting in no truck with no stranger. Especially no strange black man."

"Papa, did they see him?" Marcus asked. "Did they see the driver?"

"No," Tyrone said. "Least not his face."

"It wasn't me, Papa. I swear."

"I know it wasn't, son."

"I ain't never fooled 'round with her. I keep telling everybody that. But won't nobody believe me."

"I believe you," Tyrone said. "I do." He paused. A thought pierced his consciousness. "What about your friends, son? What about one of them? They ever fooled around with her?"

Marcus thought a moment, then shook his head. "They wouldn't do nothing like that."

"Well, somebody did it," Tyrone said.

Marcus shook his head again. "Not none of them."

"Well, somebody did it," Tyrone repeated. "And they done pinned it on you."

"Maybe this how it supposed to be," Marcus said. "Reverend Jacobs say everything happen for a reason. But I can't find no reason. Except maybe this just how it's supposed to be."

"Naw, son," Tyrone said. "It ain't supposed to be like this."

Marcus looked at Tyrone, then gazed into the distance. "It's gone happen, Papa," he said. "I can feel it."

"You can't think that way."

"Can't help it," he said. "Just got that feeling."

"We still got three days."

"They moving me tomorrow," he said. "Moving me to the death house."

"We still got three days."

"Had to fill out some papers. They wanting to know where I want them to send my body."

"Son, you got to stay positive."

"Captain Jack say it's over."

"We still got three days."

"But . . . the governor . . . he done—"

"Who you know drive a blue truck?" Tyrone interrupted him. "Who you know drive a dark blue truck with whitewall tires?"

Marcus paused. His lips began to tremble again. "They done set things in motion," he said. "They getting things ready."

"Who you know?" Tyrone raised his voice. "Who you know, son?"

"I just want this to be over."

"Marcus, answer me."

"I'm tired and just want this to be over."

"Marcus!"

Marcus lowered his head and sobbed.

"Marcus!"

Tyrone waited, but Marcus did not respond.

"Marcus, look at me."

He looked up, and Tyrone could see that his face was wet.

"Who you know?" Tyrone repeated.

Marcus shook his head.

"That woman what seen him say the killer was driving a dark blue truck. Back then . . . when all this happened . . . who you know drove a blue truck?"

"Nobody, Papa."

"Think, son, think."

He shook his head again.

"None of your friends?"

"Naw, Papa."

"You sho'?"

"Papa—"

"You sho'?" Tyrone raised his voice.

Marcus looked at Tyrone, then averted his eyes.

"Yeah, Papa," he said, dejected. "I'm sho'."

Tyrone opened his mouth as though he was going to say something else, but at the last minute seemed to change his mind. He paused.

"That La Beaux girl. Where she live?"

"I don't know."

"What you mean, you don't know?"

"Use to live 'round by the Mason," Marcus said. "But I don't know now. That was a long time ago."

"You know her people?"

"Daddy name Mr. John. Don't know her mama's name."

"John La Beaux." Tyrone mouthed the name softly.

Through the glass, he saw the officers moving toward Marcus. He heard one of them yell, "Time's up."

He returned his gaze to Marcus, but Marcus had drifted away. He had retreated within himself. He had surrendered his consciousness and was now lost in thought. The officers grabbed him underneath his arms, and Marcus stood, zombielike, and placed the phone in the cradle, then turned to leave. Tyrone tapped on the glass. Marcus looked back; their eyes met.

"Don't give up, son," Tyrone yelled. "We still got three days."

Chapter
21

Outside, he leaned his weary body against the corner of the building, lit a cigarette, and took a long draw. His nerves were frayed. His weary mind whirled. John La Beaux. He didn't know a John La Beaux. He stumbled toward his truck as if in a drunken stupor. His legs were weak. His muscles were taut. Inside the truck he fumbled in his pocket with moist, clammy hands. Anxiety rendered his fingers thick, immobile. Deep in his pocket, he clasped the keys with clumsy fingers, maneuvered them out, and inserted them into the ignition. The engine fired; the truck lurched forward. He cruised down the narrow streets through the desolate area away from the prison and back toward the freeway. Stress caused his head to ache. He lifted his right hand and gently massaged his temples, wondering how he would find the person for whom he was searching and pondering whether her discovery would be the missing piece to the puzzle that would end this nightmare once and for all.

They're moving him to the death house. The thought raced forward and exploded inside his already pounding head. He stiffened. Nervous energy weighted his foot heavy. Subconsciously, he pressed his foot hard against the accelerator. He felt the violent thrust of the steering wheel as the tires of the vibrating truck raced unsteadily over the bumpy road. Instinctively, he tightened his grip, leaned forward on the edge of his seat, and guided the truck up an on-ramp and onto the freeway. As he drove, he stared out into the open vastness. Soon, the smooth, steady motion of the truck lulled his mind until he was no longer seeing the freeway, but instead, was contemplatively exploring his impending course of action. How would he find her? Where would he begin? Ah yes, he thought of something. Beggar Man would know her. He would stop by the club and ask him. That was what he would do. He would ask Beggar Man.

That settled, he leaned back against the seat, loosened his grip on the wheel, and stared headlong into the sunlit highway, anxiously counting mile markers and eagerly anticipating his arrival in Brownsville. In his mind, he saw her clearly—short, petite, and armed with a name, or an address, or some tidbit from the murdered girl's past that would unravel the mystery and right the wrong perpetrated against his son. No, against his family. Oh, why was this happening to him? Why?

When he reached the club, he stumbled out of the truck and hurried toward the tiny, weather-worn building where Beggar Man worked. Through a haze of cigarette smoke, he saw a group of men loitering just east of the porch, underneath an old oak tree. Some of them had splintered off and were drinking and talking amongst themselves, but most of them were standing near two old gray-haired men playing dominoes on a table that had been positioned just beneath the tree. As he passed them, he spoke hastily and readied himself to mount the steps; but before he could, the screen door unexpectedly flew open, and someone leaped forward and grabbed him roughly about the shoulders.

"You old sinner you," the man said. "I heard you was out."

The muscles in Tyrone's tense body tightened. He flinched, then pulled away and looked. Bear Claw, one of his old friends, was standing in front of him, a wide grin lighting up his face.

"What's up, Claw?" Tyrone mumbled. He looked beyond Bear Claw toward the old screen door. His anxious eyes strained, searching the perimeter for Beggar Man.

Bear Claw looked at the door, then back at Tyrone.

"You looking for somebody?" He screwed up his eyes and glanced at Tyrone, then at the door again.

"Where Beggar Man?" Tyrone asked. "Need to talk to 'im. It's important."

"He in there," Claw said. "Least he was a minute ago."

Tyrone looked toward the building again, then back at Claw.

"He busy?"

"Busy," Claw said, then crooned with laughter. "Beggar Man, naw, man. That nigger ain't doing nothing . . . ain't doing nothing but pitling."

Tyrone took a quick, anxious step toward the door, then paused.

"Well, let me holler at you later, Claw," he said apprehensively, then took another hurried step toward the door. "Need to talk to Beggar Man right now. But I'm gone holler at you later, okay."

Tyrone had turned to leave when Claw bellowed, "Everything awright, hunh?"

"It will be," Tyrone said. "Soon as I see Beggar Man."

Inside the club, he spotted Beggar Man standing behind the counter tending the bar. Two men sat before him on high stools drinking.

"Tyrone!" Beggar Man crooned across the small, empty room.

The two men sitting at the bar turned slowly in their seats and looked to see who Beggar Man was talking to. Their gazes fell on Tyrone, but not recognizing him, they quickly turned back to their drinks.

"Need to talk to you," Tyrone said. "Need to talk to you right now."

Without speaking, Beggar Man refilled the two men's glasses, then slid the bottle beneath the counter. He looked at Tyrone and motioned to an empty table. After he wiped it down with an old cloth, both he and Tyrone sat down. Tyrone looked at him, then looked away. At that moment, Tyrone felt his insides churn. He opened his mouth to speak, but the muscles in his throat tightened and choked back his words. He looked away again, then sighed deeply.

"Need your help," he said. Then paused.

"You got it," Beggar Man said. "You know that."

"Seen Marcus," Tyrone said, his somber voice cracking slightly. "Seen 'im a little while ago at the prison."

"Yeah," Beggar Man said, then waited, patiently staring headlong into Tyrone's weary eyes.

"Yeah," Tyrone repeated. He paused. A minute passed. He fidgeted with his fingers; then he spoke again. "He ain't doing too good, man. He ain't doing too good at all."

"Sorry to hear that," Beggar Man said, then averted his eyes. He picked up the cloth and began to wipe the table again.

"They moving 'im tomorrow," Tyrone said. His anguished voice was low, muted. "They moving him to the death house." He dropped his head, then closed his eyes and took a deep, exasperated breath. There was a short, awkward silence, followed by the sound of Beggar Man pushing his chair from the table. He went to the bar and returned with a bottle of whiskey and two empty glasses. He poured the glass half full, then slid it toward Tyrone.

"Here," he said. "Drink this."

Tyrone lifted the glass with an unsteady hand, then tilted his head and gulped down the liquor. The hot, tingling sensation from the soothing liquid loosened his tight palate and calmed his excited nerves. He set the glass on the table and sighed heavily. Beggar Man filled Tyrone's glass a second time and then poured the other for himself. When both men had drained their respective glasses, they set the empties on the table before them.

"More?" Beggar Man asked.

Tyrone shook his head. His nerves now steady, he felt that he could say that which he had come to say.

"You know a girl named La Beaux?" he said. "Terri Lynn La Beaux?"

Beggar Man paused, thinking.

"Believe her daddy name John." Tyrone tried to jar his memory. "Last I heard they lived 'round by the Mason. She ought to be 'round my son's age . . . got to find her. She was friends with that white gal . . . might know something. Got to find her, man. Got to find her or my son gone die."

Beggar Man poured himself another drink, gulped it down, then leaned back in his chair.

"Say her daddy name John?"

"That's right," Tyrone said anxiously. "John La Beaux."

Beggar Man rubbed his fingers underneath his chin and stared blankly ahead, concentrating.

"Was she a cheerleader?" he asked, after several moments of intense thought.

"Yeah," Tyrone said, excited. "She was."

"I know her," Beggar Man said. "She live out in the country. On Route 2."

Tyrone leaned forward, wide-eyed.

"Where 'bout on Route 2?"

"Down by Mason. In a little old trailer. Back behind the railroad tracks."

"Thanks," he said hastily. Then he pushed from the table and snapped to his feet. "Gotta go. Need to check her out. Need to check her out right now."

He turned to leave, but Beggar Man stopped him.

"Tyrone," he shouted.

"Yeah." Tyrone slid to a stop.

"Let me know something, hear?"

"I will," he said, then pushed through the door.

Terri was hanging clothes on the line when Tyrone arrived in front of her old, weather-worn trailer. She was not what he expected. She wasn't fat, but she was plump. She wore a pair of tight blue jean cut-offs, a halter top, and no shoes. She had an old apron around her waist and a tiny wooden clothes pin in her mouth.

When he pulled up, she did not stop what she was doing, nor did she turn around and acknowledge him. Instead, she removed the pin from her mouth and attached a garment to the line, then retrieved another garment from the laundry basket, another pin from the pocket of her apron, and began the process anew.

Tyrone eased from the truck and ambled toward her. He felt anxious. His body told him to hurry, but his mind cautioned restraint. His body, in spite of his best effort to relax, flexed taut. With a concentrated gaze, he strolled toward her with long, easy strides, and when he was close, he paused and spoke.

"I'm looking for Miss La Beaux," he said. "Miss Terri La Beaux."

She turned and faced him. No, she wasn't what he expected. Her hair was short, kinky. Her face was plain. Her bulging brown eyes seemed too large for her round, pudgy face, and her medium brown skin was anything but smooth. Old pimples had been picked, and in their wake had been left small, round blemishes. Perhaps she had been cute once upon a time. If so, time had not been kind to her. She looked at him strangely, then paused. The muscles in her face relaxed.

"Hadn't been called that in a while," she said.

Tyrone didn't understand. "Excuse me?" he said.

"La Beaux," she said. "Hadn't been called that in years."

"Ain't that your name?" he asked. He had assumed that she was the person for whom he was looking.

"Use to be," she said. "Before I married. Name's Zeno now. Terri Zeno."

"Well, Mrs. Zeno, like to ask you a few questions if I can."

"Questions!" she exclaimed.

"Yes, ma'am."

"What kind of questions?"

"'Bout one of your old friends."

She looked at him strangely. "Mister. I don't know you from Adam."

"My name's Stokes," he said. "Tyrone Stokes."

"Stokes," she said. She stopped what she was doing and looked directly at him. Her expression changed. Her smile faded.

"That's right," he said, intuitively reading her mind. "I'm Marcus Stokes's father."

"Ain't got nothing to say to you." She turned her back and resumed her work.

"I need your help."

"Ain't got no help to give," she said. "And wouldn't give it if I had it. She didn't deserve that. Didn't deserve that at all."

"You knew her?" he asked.

"I knew her."

"You two were friends?"

"That's right."

"So you knew her pretty well?"

"Well enough."

"What kind of girl was she?"

"Why you asking?"

"Need to know."

"Why?"

"Just need to know, that's all."

"Ask somebody else."

"Ain't nobody else to ask."

"That ain't my problem."

"I'm asking you to make it your problem."

"Can't help you."

"Was she a slut?"

"What?" She whirled, incensed.

"They tell me she dressed like a slut."

"They told you wrong," she said.

"Say she was real forward."

"She was a class act," she said defensively. "She was pretty. She was smart. She was nice. She was on the squad. She was in the Beta Club. And on top of all that, she worked. She was a class act. She didn't deserve what he did to her. She didn't deserve it at all."

"Where did she work?"

She paused. He could see her chest heaving.

"She worked for Mr. Peterson."

"Who?"

"The guidance counselor."

"What, she was his student helper or something?" Tyrone asked, seeking clarification.

"No, she baby-sit his kids."

He paused. "Was she seeing anybody?"

"Talked about some guy named P. K. But I never saw him. I think he was from out-of-state."

"What state?"

"Don't know," she said. "Never saw him."

"Did he drive a blue truck?"

"Couldn't tell you."

"What does P. K. stand for?"

"Don't know."

"How long was she with this guy?"

"A long time."

"And you never saw him."

"Never saw him," she said.

"Not even a picture?"

"Not even a picture."

"But y'all were friends."

"Best friends," she said.

"How do you explain that?"

"She was a very private person. That's all."

"You been to her house?" he asked.

She nodded. "Been to her house and she been to mine."

"And she told you things."

"We told each other things."

"Personal things."

"That's right."

He paused and studied her. "Girl things."

"Girl things," she said.

"She talked about P. K.?"

"Sometimes."

"She told you how she felt about him . . . and what not?"

"Something like that."

"But she never showed you a picture."

"I already told you she didn't."

"Wonder why?"

"Told you I don't know."

"Was P. K. black?"

She looked at him but did not answer. He could tell that she was thinking, pondering. She didn't know, and she had never considered the possibility.

"No," she said. "She would have told me."

"You sho' 'bout that?"

"She was my friend."

"But that would explain it."

"Explain what?" she asked.

"The secrecy."

"No," she said. "She would have told me."

"I think he was black."

"You don't know that," she said.

"I think he picked her up that night. Not my son."

"You can't prove that."

"I need to find P. K."

"I can't help you."

"You know anybody who can?"

"No," she said. "Don't know nobody."

"Lady, my son's life depends on this."

"Mister, I told you all I know."

"She must've told somebody."

"If she did, I don't know nothing about it."

"She—"

"Mister, I got work to do."

She turned her back, and for a moment he thought about saying something else, but quickly reconsidered. She was finished talking, and to say more would just be wasting time he didn't have to waste. He stared at her for a few seconds. She pinned another garment on the line, then slid the basket of clothes farther along with her foot. Yes, the conversation was over. And yes, he had to find P. K.

Chapter
22

He headed back toward town. A distant bell chimed melodiously
through the air, and he immediately recognized the familiar
sound of the courthouse pipes tolling in the hour. The clock struck
thrice. Instinctively, he looked at his watch. Yes, it was three o'clock.
He clenched the wheel tighter. He could feel himself willing the truck
forward. Though inside his tormented soul the dark, gloomy cloud of
dread still lingered, there was now in him a faint but real ray of optimism. He had a name: P. K. Buoyed by this discovery, he sped back toward the club. P. K. . . . P. K. He felt his subconscious mind tossing the
name around inside his head. P. K. . . . P. K. What could it stand for?
Who could it be?

Suddenly, he hit a pot hole. The violent motion jarred him back to
consciousness, and his feeble mind momentarily surrendered the
thought, only to discover that he was wringing wet with perspiration.
He righted the truck and focused on the road. Then a separate but
even more discomforting thought surged through him. Suppose he
couldn't find him. Suppose somewhere, somehow, too many things
had slipped through the cracks. Too many questions had gone unan-
swered; too many clues had gone unexamined. Oh, would it not have

been better for him had he died behind bars ignorant of his son's horrid plight than to gain his freedom only to live in a world void of the only thing that gave his life meaning.

At the club, he stepped from the truck, and as he passed underneath the large, billowing oak tree, he felt the slight breeze of the warm afternoon wind gently sweep his hot, sweaty face. Directly in front of him, he saw two men carrying wine bottles emerge from behind the building, mount the porch, and stagger through the open door. Yes, their miserable world was still carrying on in spite of his plight, in lieu of his pain. It maddened him to think that to these depraved men, his son's existence was so meaningless as not to cast even the slightest ripple of discontent in this lurid sea of debauchery they all called life. Oh, if he could, he would blot them all out with the stroke of a hand. Yes, he would blot them out with the same temerity with which one would stamp a bug or squash a fly.

Feeling more and more incensed, he pushed through the men toward the opened door his roving eyes scanning the room, seeking out his friend Beggar Man.

"Guess you found her?" Beggar Man called from behind him. He wheeled and stood eye to eye with his friend.

"Yeah, I found her," he said.

Beggar Man nodded, then scanned the room with cold, piercing eyes. His penetrating gaze locked in on a man who had eased behind the unattended bar and was looking underneath the counter, searching for something. The man looked up suspiciously, his right hand locked tightly around a bottle of whiskey. His nonsuspecting eyes fell on Beggar Man. Beggar Man scowled angrily and shook his head slowly. Caught, the man smiled wryly, set the bottle back in place, then nervously backed away.

"Crazy son-of-bitch," Beggar Man mumbled angrily to himself. "Gotta watch 'em every minute or else they'll steal you blind." He turned to Tyrone.

"Find out anything, Ty?"

"Found out she was running 'round with some nigger named P. K."

"P. K.," Beggar Man repeated the name.

"Yeah," Tyrone said eagerly. "You know 'im?"

Beggar Man shook his head. "Never heard of 'im."

"Damn," Tyrone said, disappointed. "I was hoping you knew him." He looked at Beggar Man with wide, pleading eyes. "I think he the one, man. I think he the one that killed her."

"P. K.," Beggar Man whispered the name again, his stark, pensive eyes probing Tyrone's face as if seeking some obscure clue that would help unlock the identity of this mystery man. "What he look like?" Beggar Man asked. He tried to nudge Tyrone and dislodge any fact that might trigger his blank mind or stimulate his failing memory.

"Don't know," Tyrone confessed, then quickly added, "Ain't nobody never seen 'im. Nobody but the girl."

Beggar Man opened his mouth to reply, but when Tyrone's words registered, he paused abruptly and looked at him, bewildered.

"Ty." He called Tyrone's name the way one person calls to another when he or she is confused.

"Yeah," Tyrone mumbled his acknowledgment.

"If ain't nobody seen 'im," he said, "how you know he black?"

Tyrone paused, staring contemplatively. "Must be. Why else would she keep him a secret?"

"P. K." Beggar Man shook his head slowly. "Sorry, home, I don't know 'im." He stared blankly ahead as if hoping for some last-minute revelation, but when none came, he focused his cloudy eyes as his lips parted and he spoke apologetically. "I just don't know 'im, man."

Inside Tyrone, reality set in. He was at a dead end. Suddenly, he felt the muscles in his stomach tighten. A strange feeling engulfed him and he could sense the strong, steady hand of fear gripping his pounding heart, squeezing away hope, choking away optimism. He was in a vise, constricted by time, bound by fear. He waited for his whirling mind to tell him what to do next. He felt confused; he couldn't think. Behind him, he heard the screen door squeak open, then slam shut.

"Tyrone, what you doing in here?"

He wheeled and looked. His sister René was standing near the door, wearing her work uniform, leering at him with angry, hate-filled eyes.

"Nothing," he dismissed her.

"Nothing," she sneered. "Look like something to me." She stood stone still, staring at him with her large, gangly hands pressed hard against her wide, full hips.

"I'm busy, René."

She walked close to him, then paused and sniffed his breath.

"You been drinking?"

"René, what you want?" he snapped. His voice was filled with exasperation. He didn't have time for this. He just didn't.

"Yeah, you been drinking, Mr. I done changed. I can smell it on your breath." She inched closer as if to confirm what she had already proclaimed.

"René, I done told you, I'm busy."

"So much for rehab, hunh?"

"Why don't you shut your mouth and leave me alone René," he said, perturbed. "'Cause you sho' don't know what you talking about."

"I know you need to git home, right now."

"And you need to git out my face."

"Mama say come home," she snapped.

"Come home for what?" he asked angrily.

"Them parole folks looking for you, that's what."

Suddenly his eyes narrowed with disbelief.

"What!" he exclaimed. His whole world was falling apart.

"I *said*"—she intentionally exaggerated the word said—"them parole folks looking for you, fool. And Mama say, they said, if you ain't at that parole office before it close this evening, they gone lock your butt back up first thing in the morning. That's what."

"I don't care," he said defiantly, quickly pulling himself back together.

"What you mean you don't care?" René said, incensed. "You don't care." She repeated his words again. "Mama done called me off my job and got me out here looking for you. And you talking 'bout you don't care. Mister, I ain't got time for this. You going home."

"I ain't going nowhere, René."

"I ain't got time for this," she repeated, turning toward the door as if she expected him to follow her. "Yeah, you going home, mister." She paused and looked back. "Like it or not, you going home."

An awkward moment passed; then Beggar Man spoke and broke the silence.

"Go on, man, and take care of your business. I'll get some of the fellows together. We'll shake some trees and see what fall out."

"And who you supposed to be?" René wheeled back around.

"Folks call me Beggar Man. Me and Ty go way back."

She looked at Beggar Man, then at Tyrone.

"Lord, if this boy done changed, my name ain't René Thompson."

"I don't know, man," Tyrone said. "I got to find P. K."

"You ain't got that to worry about," Beggar Man said. "I'm on it."

Tyrone looked at him with uncertain eyes. He did not know what to do. There was that old feeling he always got just before something bad happened.

"Man, you sure you can find 'im?" he asked, seeking assurance.

"If he live around here, I'll find him," Beggar Man said. "Count on it."

Tyrone looked at Beggar Man, then at his watch. In his heart, he knew that Beggar Man was more than capable, and he wanted to believe in him. But under the circumstances, he just did not know if he could relinquish the reins and allow someone else to drive on a trip that more than likely could mean life or death for his only son.

"Come on, here." René raised her voice. "I ain't got all day to fool 'round with you, Tyrone."

Tyrone looked at his watch again. The portion of his brain that measured time cautioned that he was squandering away time, at a time when every second was precious. He looked at Beggar Man again. Yes, Beggar Man was capable. Yet, there was in Tyrone a lingering feeling that there was one other person he should see before leaving town to deal with his parole officer.

"Go ahead on, René," Tyrone said. "I got one more stop to make."

"Go ahead on!" René squinched up her face. "Tyrone—"

"René," Tyrone interrupted her. "I got one more stop to make. I'm gone go by the parole office soon as I finish my business, okay? Now leave me alone."

"Hope you know it's four o'clock," she said.

"René, I can tell time."

"Fool around and be late if you want to," she issued a warning underneath her breath. "And see if they don't lock your butt back up, crazy nigger."

Shortly after she had left, he went out onto the porch. Outside, he paused briefly underneath the canopy, then looked back toward the door. Should he go back and reconsider his decision, or should he go on and hope for the best? All of his life, he felt as if he had had to make difficult choices, and all of his life, he felt as if he had made the wrong ones. What was he to do? Oh, how he felt the heavy weight of time bearing down hard against his troubled soul. No, he couldn't go back. There was no time. He leaped from the porch and made his way to the truck, ever aware of the ominous tint cast by the dull red sun as it slowly passed behind a cluster of clouds on its final descent from its watchful perch high above the now dimming sky. *Death,* the thought crashed against his skull with reckless abandonment. He had always heard the old folks say that a red sky meant impending death. Could it be a sign? Was it all for naught? Was Marcus's fate sealed? Were foreboding signs telling him that which he cared not to hear? No, he would not entertain such horrific thoughts. No, not for a minute, he would not. He could not. Oh, why was his life a never-ending string of misdeeds and miscalculations strung together in a perpetual cycle of torment and pain. When would he catch a break? When would the undying love of the omnipresent one cast its everlasting light on him?

At Cardinal Street, he turned onto Magellan and then onto the highway leading into town. No, he wouldn't leave until he had seen Captain Jack. He needed to question him about P. K. Maybe he knew him, or had heard of him, or had access to some information that would lead Tyrone to him. And if he hadn't heard of him, he should have heard of him. He should have found him and talked to him before time had gotten short, before the trail had gotten cold, before the situation had become critical. What black person had he spoken to? What black person, from his son's world, had the attorney questioned about what might have happened that night?

Outside the building that housed Captain Jack's office, he parked his truck and bound forward, feeling the effects of living under the constant strain of this most stressful situation on his taut, anxious body. Why hadn't this man done more? He had been on this case for years. Why hadn't he done more?

He pressed through the door and entered the small reception area. To his surprise, unlike previous times, Janell was not there. For what seemed an eternity, he stood uncertainly in the center of the room, staring at Captain Jack's partially closed door. Though he could not see him, he knew that Captain Jack was with a client, for he could hear their muffled voices. They were speaking in low, but serious tones. He looked about, pondering whether he should knock and interrupt their session or wait. Why wasn't someone here to help him? No, he couldn't wait. This was ridiculous. He strode to the door, but before he could knock, Captain Jack appeared. His gray eyes fell on Tyrone.

"Be with you in a second," he said.

Tyrone looked at his watch. "I don't have much time, Mr. Johnson."

Captain Jack cringed, then looked at him strangely, and Tyrone knew that Captain Jack did not like the way he had spoken to him. Yes, he had gotten out of his place. His tone had been too direct, the implication of his words too bold. He was to accommodate Captain Jack; Captain Jack was not to accommodate him.

"Have a seat, Mr. Stokes," Captain Jack spoke out of the corner of his mouth. "I won't be long."

Tyrone looked at him bitterly, then crossed the room and sat lightly on the edge of the sofa, watching helplessly as Captain Jack backed away from the door and disappeared into his office. Several anxious minutes passed, then Captain Jack emerged from his office and followed the slim, well-dressed white man who had been meeting with him to the door. They exchanged pleasantries, the man departed, and then Captain Jack turned his attention to Tyrone.

"What can I do for you, Mr. Stokes?" He waxed formal.

Tyrone rose to his feet. Festering inside of him was a righteous rage that was becoming increasingly more and more difficult to conceal.

"Why didn't you investigate the girl?" he asked.

Captain Jack looked at him in surprise.

"Amy!" he said, his irritated voice slightly raised.

"Yeah," Tyrone said. "Amy."

"I couldn't put her on trial," Captain Jack said, the tone of his voice indicating he thought the question ridiculous.

"Why not?" Tyrone pressed him.

"This town wouldn't have stood for that," he said, his eyes wide, astonished. "It wouldn't have stood for that at all."

"But it would stand for executing an innocent man?" Tyrone said, challenging the absurdity he heard in the statement made by the one designated to fight the battle his son could not wage for himself. He looked at Captain Jack with wild, suspicious eyes. Who was this man? Was he friend or was he foe?

Captain Jack looked at him but chose not to speak.

"Did you know she was dating some guy named P. K.?" Tyrone decided to redirect the conversation. He didn't have time for useless banter. Time was short. He needed answers.

"No," Captain Jack said. "I wasn't aware of that."

"Well, she was."

"I wasn't aware of it," he repeated, and Tyrone sensed that his repetition reflected that he did not know what else to say.

"I'm not surprised." Tyrone let him off the hook. "She kept him a secret."

Captain Jack did not respond.

"Don't you think that's strange?" Tyrone asked.

"What?"

"The secrecy."

"Not particularly," Captain Jack said. He paused, then offered a possible explanation. "Kids that age often hide things. Especially from their parents."

"Why?" Tyrone asked.

"Excuse me?"

"Why would she hide him?"

"I have no idea," Captain Jack said.

"I do," Tyrone snapped.

"By all means, tell me," Captain Jack persuaded him to continue.

"He was black." Tyrone offered an explanation. "She kept him a secret because he was a black man."

Captain Jack looked at him, stunned. "Can you prove that?"

"Not yet," he said. "But I know he was the one."

"Excuse me?"

"He was the one they saw that night."

"Who?" he said. "What do you mean?"

"The two witnesses . . . the maid . . . They saw P. K., not my son."

"Mr. Stokes, you're grasping," Captain Jack said. "We need proof."

"No," Tyrone rejected his assertion. "The blue truck. The way the girl acted that night. It all makes sense."

"We need proof," Captain Jack reiterated. "Not conjecture."

"It was P. K.," Tyrone insisted. "She knew him. That's why she acted the way she did that night. That's why she got in that truck with him. They were dating."

"How do you know that?"

"I just know."

"We need proof."

"Find P. K. and you'll have all the proof you need."

Captain Jack paused and pondered the possibility.

"Why would he kill her?" the attorney asked.

"What!" The questioned agitated Tyrone.

"If they were dating. And he loved her. Why would he kill her?"

"I don't know," Tyrone said, perturbed. "When we find him, you can ask 'im."

"You're grasping."

Tyrone paused and looked at him with frustrated eyes. "Do you believe in my son?"

"Mr. Stokes, your theory just doesn't make any sense."

"Makes sense to me."

"There is no motive."

"How do you know?" Tyrone said. "We don't know what was going on between them two. Maybe they fell out. We don't know."

"Mr. Stokes, lovers don't usually kill their partners and dump their nude bodies in the middle of a field. No, this was no acquaintance murder; this was a rape. A brutal, savage rape probably perpetrated by a stranger."

"I don't have time for this," Tyrone said, his unbridled anger now boiling to the surface.

"I'm sorry, Mr. Stokes. I know you're frustrated. We all are. But in my heart, I just don't think you're on the right track with this."

"So you telling me you ain't gone help me?"

"If you want me to look for P. K., I will. But even if we find him, and I seriously doubt that we will, I don't think we'll be able to build a murder case against him in two days. Especially since your son has been tried and convicted, and that conviction has been upheld by the highest court in the land."

"Well, what would you have me to do?"

"Spend some time with your son."

"What!" he exclaimed, not believing what he was hearing.

"Mr. Stokes, I just had to tell your son that the governor of Louisiana has refused to stay his execution. Right now your son is afraid. Probably more afraid than he has ever been in his life. Tomorrow they're going to move him to the execution building. The next day they're going to allow him a contact visit and a last meal. The day after that, they are going to execute him. In the meantime, there's a phone in his cell. If you want to help him, help him get ready for what's going to happen. Mr. Stokes, they're going to execute your son. He's scared. Spend time with him."

Chapter 23

The parole office was located in Franklin Parish some five miles from Tyrone's mother's house. When he arrived, his parole officer was sitting behind her desk, staring at an open folder. Before he entered the office, he took a deep breath, and from his partially concealed vantage point, just beyond the open door, he stole a nervous glance at her. She appeared to be a tall, burly woman, he guessed, somewhere between one hundred seventy and one hundred eighty pounds. She wasn't old, probably between forty and forty-five. The hue of her skin was dark, her hair was short, and her hard, plain face was such that one immediately got the impression that she was neither friendly nor nice. He cupped the palm of his hand in front of his mouth and blew. On the way, he had sucked a lemon, but he wasn't sure that it had worked. He lowered his hand. Yes, the scent of liquor lingered. It was faint, but still there. Oh, for a stick of gum or a breath mint. Alcohol was a parole violation. One whiff, and it was back to prison. Well, he would not stand close to her. He would try to avoid her without being too conspicuous. He closed his eyes, exhaled, then stepped from behind the door.

"Ms. Dixon," he called her name softly, politely.

"You Tyrone L. Stokes?" She looked up at him with eyes of contempt.

"Yes, ma' am," he said. "I am."

He looked at the empty chair before her desk. He wanted to sit, but she had not asked him to. So, for what seemed an eternity, he stood awkwardly before her desk, wondering whether he should sit or whether he should stand. When no instruction came, he sat timidly on the chair and folded his arms across his lap. Yes, this was uncomfortable. More uncomfortable than it had to be.

"Were you issued a Conditions of Parole pamphlet upon your release?" she snapped. She was no longer looking at him. Her contemptuous eyes were glued to the papers.

"Yes, ma'am," he said. He made his voice soft, subservient, submissive.

"Can you read?" She looked up and glared at him, cold and intimidating. He glanced at her, then dropped his gaze again.

"Yes, ma'am," he said in a small, timid voice. "I can."

There was a long, awkward moment, and he could feel her piercing eyes staring at him for what seemed an eternity. He wanted to move, squirm, but paralyzing fear held him still.

"Did you read it?" she asked.

"Yes, ma'am," he said with averted eyes.

She paused and leaned back in her chair, and he knew it was to let him know that she was in complete control of his destiny. She knew it, and she wanted to insure that he knew it. He glanced at her, then quickly looked away.

"Do you have a problem with comprehension?"

"No, ma'am," he said.

"So you did understand that you were to report to your parole officer within twenty-four hours of your release?"

"Yes, ma'am," he said.

"But you chose not to."

The question was a trap. He looked at her but did not answer.

"Do you think I'm talking to myself?" she asked in a cold, stern voice.

"No, ma'am," he said.

He glanced at her again, then looked away. He knew what was coming. He could see the writing on the wall. He had violated parole, and he was going back to prison. Inside his chest, he could feel his heart pounding. In his tense, frightened mind, he could feel the cool steel cuffs digging into his tightly bound wrists. He could smell the stench of his old cell block, hear the jingling of dangling keys. He could see the puzzled looks; he could anticipate the anxious questions; he could hear all too well the all-knowing "I told you so." Suddenly, he felt his tense body go limp with submission. He felt his frayed emotions sink. He felt his entire body slowly fall under the spell of a gloomy cloud of dread.

"You just decided you weren't coming, is that it?"

"Yes, ma'am," he heard himself say. He wasn't answering now. He was inside of himself, listening to rote responses from that preprogrammed, institutionalized part of himself that knew all too well the futility of challenging absolute authority.

"Explain to me why I shouldn't send you back to the penitentiary right now."

"I can't," he mumbled. There was no explaining. The power was hers to use or not to use. She alone held his fate. She alone would decide.

"You better tell me something," she said angrily, "or that's just what I'm gonna do."

"I should have reported in," he said. "I didn't."

"Why not?" she asked in a tone demanding an explanation.

"My son is on death row."

"What does that have to do with this situation?" she asked.

"I wanted to see him . . . I mean, help him."

"Do you like prison?"

"No, ma'am."

"Do you want to go back to prison?"

"No, ma'am."

"Well, you better start acting like it."

"Yes, ma'am."

"I don't like excuses," she said. "I don't like 'em at all. Parole is a privilege, not a right. You abuse it . . . you lose it. Understand?"

"Yes, ma'am."

"Let's get one thing clear," she said. "I'm not your friend, and I'm not your counselor. My job is to supervise your reacclimation into the free world. I'm here to protect society, not you. Do I make myself clear?"

"Yes, ma'am."

"You're a loser," she said. "This folder I'm looking at tells me so. And that's just how I'm gone deal with you. So, hear me, and hear me good. You so much as sneeze and it's back to the big house for you. Understand?"

"Yes, ma'am."

"Now, let's get down to business."

"Yes, ma'am," he said, then waited.

Deflated, he raised his head and watched her flip through the folder, then pick up a pencil. Yes, now it felt official. He was a parolee, an excon, a nobody. One of a thousand black men, just like himself, living in a white world (one step beyond prison, two steps short of freedom) ever mindful of the watchful eye of the system suspiciously monitoring his movements and blatantly threatening his freedom, seven days a week, twenty-four hours a day. Yes, he was still in the system. Only now he was in prison without bars.

With his wroth emotions teetering somewhere between dread and nervous anticipation, he watched his parole officer lick her thumb, then shuffle through the folder until she had found the document for which she had been searching. Then, as if in a hypnotic state, she studied the document for a moment, lifted it from the folder, and leaned back in her chair.

"Your conditions of parole are as follows:

01. You are not to frequent any establishments that store, sell, or serve alcohol.
02. You are not to be in the company of any person or persons who store, sell, or serve alcohol.
03. You are not to be in the company of any person who is engaging in the consumption of alcohol.
04. You are not permitted to leave the state without written consent from this office.
05. You are not permitted to relocate or change your address without consent from this office.

06. You are not permitted to possess or own a firearm.
07. You are required to obtain and maintain employment.
08. You are required to submit to random drug testing on demand.
09. You will be subjected to random visits at which time you will also be required to submit to searches of your person, your property, and your lodging by this office.
10. You are required to adhere to a nightly eight P.M. curfew.
11. You are required to pay two hundred fifty dollars in restitution to the state.
12. You are required to obey and adhere to all state and federal regulations of these United States of America.
13. You are to report to this office weekly without exception for the next fifteen months.

"Do you understand these conditions as I have explained them to you?"

"Yes, ma'am."

"Do you understand that violation of any one of these conditions will immediately result in a warrant being issued for your arrest?"

"Yes, ma'am."

She removed the document from the folder and slid it to him along with an ink pen.

"Sign it at the bottom near the X, indicating that you have read and understand these conditions as stipulated."

He grasped the pen with trembling fingers and, under the watchful, intimidating eye of his parole officer, scribbled a near illegible name in the appropriate place. He slid the document to her, and she glanced at it, then slid it back.

"Date it," she demanded, frustrated.

"Oh," he muttered anxiously. How had he forgotten that, he thought. He wanted to relax, but his body would not cooperate. With downcast eyes, he hastily scribbled in the date, then pushed the paper back across the desk. Again, she inspected the document. Satisfied, she inserted it in the folder, then selected another.

"Do you have any identifiable marks, scars, piercings, tattoos, etcetera?" she asked in a dry, mechanical voice.

"No, ma'am," he said.

"Have you found a job?"

"No, ma'am."

"Have you looked?"

"No, ma'am."

"Why not?"

"My son," he said. "I've been trying to help my son."

"You understand that you are required to have a job, don't you?"

"Yes, ma'am."

"By our next meeting, I want you to provide this office with proof of employment or proof of your efforts to find employment. Is that understood?"

"Yes, ma'am."

"Now, as far as the necessary tests are concerned, I will personally administer the required blood, urine, and breathalyzer tests, whether it be in this office or out in the field. Understand?"

"Yes, ma'am," he said. Suddenly he began to sweat. Blood test. He had not thought of that. Why had he drank that alcohol? *Please, God,* he silently prayed. *No blood test. Please. Not now. Not today.*

He watched her scribble something on one of the documents, then push away from the desk and rise to her feet.

"Come on," she directed. "Follow me."

Suddenly, his heart plunged. Maybe he should confess and throw himself at her mercy. Wordlessly, he rose from his seat and stood on wobbly, unsteady legs. He looked back at the open door. Maybe he should run. Yes, maybe he should run before she had a chance to test him. No, that would be foolish. *Please God, help me. Please.*

Confused and petrified, he followed her through a side door, out of the office, and into a small adjoining room. Inside the room, he shrank, not knowing what to expect. It was some type of lab. Before him stood a vast, shiny white wall. Next to the wall was a counter upon which were assembled several trays and a strange assortment of plastic cups and bottles. Yes, this was it. She was going to test him. He stood, paralyzed, watching as she moved behind the counter. "Please, God," he whispered to himself. "No blood test. Please."

She stooped and reached underneath the counter, then issued an order.

"Stand in front of the wall and face me."

"Yes, ma'am," he heard himself say.

From in front of the wall, he saw her emerge from behind the counter and walk back to the door, then turn back toward him. She was carrying something. His gaze fell on the object. It was a camera. Yes, she was carrying a camera. She was going to photograph him; that was all. He stood upright and stared longingly into the lens, wishing this was over and he was out of this place. She snapped the picture, and his eyes strayed aimlessly to the large clock on the wall. It was almost five. Maybe this was it. Maybe this was all they would have time for today.

He watched her place the camera on the counter, then examine the photograph, and when she was satisfied, she turned her attention to him.

"I need you over here." She was blunt.

He complied, and when he was near, she spoke again.

"Need to fingerprint you," she barked. "Right hand first."

She took his finger, rolled it in the ink, then pressed it on the page. And as she worked, he knew that she could feel his hand trembling. Why was his hand shaking? At that moment he hated himself. Inside his mind, he willed himself calm, lest his nervous behavior betray him and raise unneeded suspicion in this his most feared adversary. *Please,* he thought. *Let this be over.* Outside, the courthouse bell tolled. She looked at her watch, then at him.

"Your curfew is eight o'clock," she said. "At eight-o-one you're in violation. I catch you in violation, it's back to the penitentiary. Understand?"

"I understand."

"You have any questions?"

"No, ma'am."

She looked at him with eyes that told him that she was serious, and that warned him not to try her.

"The parole board gave you your freedom, and the parole board can take it away. I wouldn't advise you to forget that. Now get out my office."

Chapter
24

Shook up, he hurried from the room and exited the building. Outside, he started to cross the street, then paused. He felt as if she was watching him. He looked back. No, it was just his imagination. He stepped off the curb, out into the street, then stopped again. What was he doing? He couldn't cross here. She could be watching. He quickly stepped back onto the curbing and looked across the street at his parked truck, then turned and looked back over his shoulder at her office complex. No, he couldn't cross here. Suddenly, he felt the heavy thump of his heart pounding inside his chest. He had almost jaywalked. He was on parole, and he had almost jaywalked. He took a deep breath and tried to calm his whirling nerves. What was he thinking? He had to be careful. She could be watching.

On the sidewalk, he walked uneasily back to the intersection, then paused and waited for the light to change. As he waited, he looked at his watch. It was five after five. He had less than three hours. Yes, less than three hours before he had to be home for his court-imposed curfew. The light changed, and as he crossed the street, he thought of something. He should question Pauline. Maybe P. K. had people from Brownsville. Yes, that was it. Maybe he had been visiting relatives for the summer or something, and that was when he met the girl. That would explain it. That would explain everything. Yes, Pauline would know. She had worked all over the parish. If he had people living in Brownsville, she would know.

Across the street, he spied a pay phone. At the phone, he fumbled in his pocket for some coins. Then he inserted the coins in the phone, dialed the number, and waited. The phone rang; then he heard a husky voice on the receiving end answer hello. He recognized the voice. It was Pauline's oldest brother, Levi.

"Need to speak to Pauline," he said. "Need to speak to her right now."

"She ain't here," Levi said.

"Where she at?" Tyrone asked.

"Who is this?" Levi asked; then Tyrone realized that in his haste he had not identified himself.

"Brother-in-law, this Tyrone," he said, his voice anxious. "I need to speak to Pauline. Need to speak to her right now."

There was a pause.

"Brother-in-law," Tyrone called through the receiver.

"She ain't here, I told you." Levi was flip, and Tyrone could tell he was turned off by the fact that he was calling their house.

"I know she there," Tyrone said. "Put her on the phone. I know she in that house."

"You calling me a lie?"

"Levi, I ain't got time for this," Tyrone said, irritated. "Put my wife on the phone. Put my wife on this phone right now."

"Why don't you leave Pauline alone," Levi said. "My God, man. Why don't you just leave her alone!"

"I'm coming 'round there."

"I done told you, she ain't here."

"Then, where she at?"

There was silence, and he could tell that his brother-in-law was thinking, pondering whether to tell or not to tell.

"Brother-in-law, I need to talk to her. It's important. Real important."

There was silence.

"Brother-in-law."

"She ain't in no condition to talk," Levi said, breaking his silence.

"What you mean by that?" Tyrone wanted to know.

"Nothing," Levi hedged again.

"I'm coming 'round there."

"She ain't here, I told you."

"Levi, I ain't got time for this."

There was silence.

"Levi!"

He didn't answer.

"Levi!"

He still didn't answer.

"I'm coming 'round there."

"Man, she in the hospital."

"The hospital!" Tyrone shouted, shocked. "What happened. She all right?"

"She had a breakdown."

"I don't understand," he said, confused.

"They told her about Marcus, and she lost it."

"Who told her?"

"Don't know," he said. "I wasn't here. Think his lawyer called her."

"Called her," he said. "You mean he told her on the phone?"

"I think so."

Tyrone was silent, not believing what he was hearing.

"What did he tell her?" he asked after a long pause.

"Don't know," Levi said. "I was in the field, working. Just know he told her something about Marcus."

"He tell her about the governor?"

"Don't know," Levi said. "Just know he told her something. She got hysterical. And Mama and Papa carried her to the doctor. And he put her in the hospital. That's all I know."

"I don't believe this," Tyrone said. "I just don't believe this."

There was silence.

"Which hospital?" he asked. "Brownsville General?"

"No," Levi said. "Cedar Creek."

When he arrived, Pauline was lying in bed. He entered the room. As he suspected, she was not alone. Her mother, her father, and Reverend Jacobs were also there. Her mother was sitting on the edge of the bed holding her hand; her father and Reverend Jacobs were standing across the room next to the window with their backs to the door. They were talking. Exactly what the conversation was, he could not determine.

"How is she?" he called softly as he approached the bed. He was speaking to his mother-in-law, but his father-in-law answered.

"What you want?" Mr. Titus asked, his husky voice gruff.

"Come to check on my wife," Tyrone said. "Heard she was sick."

"Don't call her that," he said angrily. "Don't you dare call her that."

"Shhh," his mother-in-law shushed them, quiet. "Pauline don't need this right now," she said, sternly. "She just don't need this right now."

"I want you out of here," Titus said.

"No." Tyrone shook his head. "This my wife, and I ain't going nowhere."

He moved next to the bed, then bent over her. Her eyes were closed, and she lay perfectly still. He called her name, low, soft, loving.

"Pauline."

She didn't respond.

"Pauline," he called a second time.

"Leave her alone." Titus crossed the room and confronted him. "Leave her alone, I say."

"Baby, can you hear me?" He paused, but she didn't answer. "It's me, honey, Tyrone. Can you hear me?"

"Leave her alone," Titus said. "I ain't gone tell you no mo'."

"Baby, you got to wake up," Tyrone said.

"Leave her alone," Titus said again.

"Pauline . . . Pauline . . . Baby, we ain't got time for this right now," he said. "I know you scared . . . but we just ain't got time for this."

"She can't hear you." Miss Gertrude tried a different approach. "The doctor gave her something to make her sleep. She can't hear you."

Tyrone took Pauline by the hand and gently tugged her arm.

"Pauline . . . Pauline," he said softly. "Wake up. Please, Pauline, wake up."

"Call the nurse," Titus said angrily. "Call the nurse right now."

"Please, son," Miss Gertrude said. "Let her sleep."

"P. K.," Tyrone said, ignoring them. "Honey, you ever heard of a fellow named P. K. . . . I need to know . . . I need to find 'im."

"Turn her loose," Titus shouted. "Turn her loose right now."

"I need to know, honey," Tyrone said. "I need to know right now."

Titus pulled her hand from Tyrone's.

"Turn her loose, I say."

Tyrone pulled away from his father-in-law and leaned back over the bed.

"Honey," he said coaxingly. "The sooner we find P. K., the sooner Marcus can come home."

"I ain't gone stand for this," Titus warned. "I ain't gone stand for this at all." He spoke directly to Tyrone. "Why don't you leave Pauline alone. You ain't helping nothing. She sick, and you ain't helping nothing."

"Help us, Jesus," Reverend Jacobs prayed out loud. "Help us right now, Master."

The door swung open, and the nurse entered the room.

"What's going on in here?" she asked.

"He vexing her," Titus said. "She trying to sleep, and he keep vexing her."

She looked at Tyrone with confused eyes. She opened her mouth to speak. But before she could, he spoke first.

"This my wife," he said. "Just need to ask her a question."

"Sir, she needs her rest," the nurse said.

"Pauline," Tyrone called to her again.

"See," Titus said. "He hard-headed. He vexing her. Make him leave. Make him leave right now."

"I ain't going nowhere," Tyrone said. "I ain't going nowhere 'til I talk to my wife. Pauline," he called to her again. "Pauline."

"Sir, she's sedated," the nurse said. "She can't hear you."

"Pauline," he called her name again. "Wake up, honey, please wake up."

"He ain't gone listen," Titus said. "Make 'im leave. He ain't gone listen."

"Sir, if you don't stop harassing this patient," she said sternly, "I'm going to call security."

"Call 'em," Titus said imploringly. "Call security."

Suddenly, Pauline's weak, feeble voice broke through the ruckus. "Tyrone." She seemed distant, disoriented. "Tyrone, is that you?"

"Yes, baby," Tyrone answered her, his voice still soft, gentle. "Yes, baby, it's me, Tyrone."

She slowly turned on her pillow and looked at him with glassy brown eyes, and when her eyes focused, and she recognized him, her eyes widened, frightened.

"They gone kill 'im," she said, her weak voice slightly excited. "They gone kill 'im day after tomorrow."

"No," he said. "That ain't true."

"Now you done gone and woke her up," Titus said angrily. "I guess you satisfied now. You done gone and woke her up."

"He gone die." She sat up in bed, visibly agitated. "He gone die . . . My Jesus, he gone die."

"Ma'am." The nurse rushed to her side and restrained her. "You have to calm down. Please, ma'am, you have to calm down."

"He ain't gone die," Tyrone said assuredly. "I ain't gone let that happen. I promise you that."

"Don't tell her that," Titus said. "You ain't helping nothing. Don't tell her that. I mean it. Don't you tell her that."

Pauline became hysterical.

"He just a baby," she cried. "He all I got . . . He just a baby . . . Lord, what I'm gone do now . . . What I'm gone do now?"

"You aggravating her," Titus said.

"Shhh, now, Pauline." Miss Gertrude moved in and tried to comfort her. "Don't go getting all worked up again. You got to stay calm. The nurse say you got to stay calm."

"Pauline," Tyrone spoke to her softly, soothingly. "P. K. . . . Do you know him? Honey, do you know his people?"

"Get out!" Titus said. "Get out right now."

"My baby . . . my baby," Pauline wailed. "Oh, God, my baby."

"Sir, you're upsetting her," the nurse tried pleading. "Think about your wife. You're upsetting her."

"Make him leave," Titus said. "Make him leave right now."

"Pauline, listen," Tyrone said. "You got to listen to me."

"What I'm gone do now?" Pauline moaned. "Oh, God, what I'm gone do now? My baby . . . my baby."

"Help her, Jesus," Reverend Jacobs prayed out loud. "Take her in your loving arms, Master. Take her in your loving arms right now. Please, Master. We know you able. Please, Master, comfort her. Comfort her right now, Lord."

"Sir, you're going to have to leave," the nurse said.

"Git out," Titus said. "You heard the nurse, git out."

"Please, son," Miss Gertrude pleaded. "This ain't the time. Think about Pauline. She sick. This ain't the time."

"Mama Gertrude, I need to know his name," Tyrone explained. "I need to know his name or Marcus gone die."

Suddenly, the nurse pushed the intercom button.

"I need security," she said. "I need security, stat."

"Kane," Pauline mumbled, delirious. "That's what Miss Kane call her boy."

"P. K." Tyrone's voice shook, excited. "Her boy name P. K."

"That's what she call him," Pauline babbled. "Miss Kane's boy. That's what she call him . . . That's what she call him."

Tyrone grabbed her hand and bent over her, excited.

"Miss Kane . . . Who is Miss Kane?"

"My baby," Pauline wailed. "Oh, God, my baby."

"Pauline," Tyrone said forcefully. "Pauline."

"You got your name," Titus said. "Now leave her alone."

"Security," the nurse called again.

"She talkin' 'bout Sybil," Miss Gertrude said. "Don't bother her no more. She talking 'bout Sybil Kane's boy."

Chapter
25

He stepped out of the room and into the hall, his heaving chest rising and falling rapidly. Sybil Kane, he knew of her. He knew of her people, but he did not know of her son. In the corridor, he felt like running. In his excited mind, he could see himself dashing wildly down the long, narrow corridor, out of the hospital, and into the streets. *Sybil Kane. Oh, God, could it be? Please let it be. Oh, God, please let it be.* Outside, the sun had set. It was nearing six o'clock. He had to hurry. He felt panicked. He did not know how he calmed himself enough to drive the truck or how he made it back to Brownsville. Yet, somehow at her small, decrepit-looking house, he found himself walking across her cluttered lawn, and then he found himself standing before her door, knocking. Yes, he knew of her. He knew of her from his days in the streets. He knew of her from the tawdry clubs and vile crack houses. Yes, he knew of her. He knew of fast ass Sybil Kane.

But what of her son? Where was he? Why didn't Beggar Man know him? And how would a boy like this know a girl like that?

He raised his hand back and knocked again.

"Come on," he mumbled to himself. "Come on. Come on. Open the door."

Nervous, he began to rock from side to side. He looked toward the windows. The curtains were drawn. *Maybe she's not at home,* he thought. *Oh, please let her be home. Please let her be home.* Inside the house he heard feet shuffling. Yes, from what he knew of her, he could imagine her son. A young, illegitimate thug not afraid to cross the sacred, age-old boundaries into the forbidden world of white flesh. Yes, in his mind, it all made sense. The secrecy, the intrigue, the violence, the rage, the death. Yes, P. K. It all made sense. Truly, the acorn had not fallen far from the tree. Impatient, he raised his hand and knocked again. He heard chains rattling; then the door flew open. She had been asleep. The skin on the left side of her face was creased. Her eyes were glazed.

"What you want?" she said, not looking directly at him. Her speech was slurred. She looked high. Drunk.

"Sybil Kane," he said, uncertain. She looked much older than he remembered. He was not sure.

"Who wants to know?" she said, swaying slightly. Her equilibrium was off. She was tipsy.

"Sybil, it's me, Tyrone Stokes."

Her unsteady head bobbed, and she looked at him, then smiled slyly.

"How you doing, Tyrone?" She slurred his name, and he sensed that in her present condition she neither remembered nor recognized him. "I was just 'bout to go over to the Silver Dollar," she said. "Why don't you come on to the Silver Dollar with me and buy your cousin a beer?"

"You got company?"

He looked past her trying to see. He wanted to go inside. She was drunk. And being seen with her was a parole violation.

"Ain't got no company," she said. "Ain't had no company all day." Tyrone pushed past her, and she followed him, frustrated.

"Told you I was fixing to go to the Silver Dollar," she said.

"Need to talk to you," he said.

"Give me two dollars," she said. "Give your cousin two dollars so she can buy herself a beer."

"Sybil," he called her name.

"What?" she said.

"Where Mr. Kane?" he asked. Something cautioned him to be careful. He looked around quickly, trying to make sure they were alone.

"Mr. Kane," she said. "Only Mr. Kane I know at home with Mama."

"Your husband," he said. "I'm talking 'bout your ole man."

"Nigger, you know I ain't got no husband."

"What about your son?" he said. "He home?"

"Naw."

"Where he at?"

"What you want with him?" she wanted to know.

"Want to ask him a few questions, that's all."

"You with the police now?"

"Naw, Sybil. Stop talking crazy. You know I ain't with no police."

"He did something to you?" she asked.

"Just want to talk to him, that's all."

"He in trouble?" she asked. "Lawd, what that boy done got into now?"

"Told you I just want to talk to 'im."

"He ain't here."

"Where is he?"

"I don't know," she said. "I don't know where that boy is."

"He working?"

"Working," she said. "That hay burner? Hunh, that thang don't work."

"Well, where is he? I need to talk to him. It's important."

"Give me two dollars," she said.

"What?"

"Come on," she pleaded. "Buy your cousin a beer."

"Sybil," he said. "Your son. Where is he?"

"I don't know."

"When will he be back?"

"I don't know," she said. "That boy got a mind of his own. All I know is when he here, he here, and when he ain't, he ain't."

"Where he hang out?"

Suddenly, she swayed as if she was going to fall. She grabbed her head.

"Sybil." He caught her by the arm and steadied her.

She laughed, drunk, then puckered her lips and moved toward him.

"Tyrone, where you been all this time?" she said, still talking out of her mind. "Why you ain't been by to see me. Hunh? Why you do me this way, Tyrone. Why?"

"Sybil!" He pushed her away, then shook her hard. "Sybil! Girl, you drunk."

"I ain't drunk," she said. "But I been dranking." She paused, staggering. "Come on . . . Let's go to the Silver Dollar. Come on, Tyrone . . . Buy your cousin a beer."

"Where P. K.?" he snapped angrily.

"Who?"

"Your boy," he said. "Where is he?"

"What you call him?" she asked.

"P. K.," he repeated the initials.

"P. K.," she said, then fell into a hysterical laugh. Yes, she was drunk. Silly drunk. "Why you call him that? Why you call him P. K.?"

"Ain't that his name?" Tyrone asked, irritated.

"Naw," she said. "Not P. K., stupid. That boy name Thomas Elroy Kane. T. K., not P. K."

"T. K.," he mumbled, shocked.

"Yeah, T. K."

Maybe he had heard the girl wrong. Maybe Terri had said T. K. not P. K. Maybe he had just heard her wrong. Yes, maybe that was it. He looked at Sybil with hopeful eyes.

"Your son," he said. "How old is he?"

"Fifteen," she said. "Least he was last time I checked."

Suddenly, he felt dizzy, nauseous. It was the wrong person. He was right back where he started. Oh, he was running in circles. What if he could not find him. What if he could not find the killer before it was too late? He felt like leaving, but he did not know where to go. He turned to leave, and Sybil tried to stop him.

"Tyrone!" she shouted his name.

He heard her but did not stop.

"You going to the Silver Dollar?"

He didn't answer. He pulled the door open and stepped outside.

"Wait," she said. "Wait . . . Don't leave me . . . Let me get my shoes."

He went to his truck and climbed inside. He started the engine. He saw Sybil scurry out of the house and onto the porch, her shoes in hand.

"Wait," he heard her scream as he pulled away. "Buy your cousin a beer."

Chapter
26

It was almost eight o'clock when he made it home. His mother, Sarah Ann, and René were all sitting on the porch waiting when he arrived. He parked the truck, and as he made his way to the porch, he could feel their eyes on him. He was tired. He wanted to be alone. He needed to think. He mounted the steps, then opened the screen door and stepped onto the porch.

"How y'all doing?" He spoke, then paused. He was anxious. He did not feel like talking. He wanted to go inside.

"How y'all doing?" René snapped. She looked at him hard, angry. "That's all you got to say? Mama sitting here done worried herself near 'bout half to death. And you talking 'bout how y'all doing. Boy, where you been?"

"René!" Sarah Ann said.

"René nothing," René said. "Boy, you heard me. Where you been all this time? It's almost eight o'clock. Where you been?"

"What's it to you?" he asked. "You ain't my mama."

"Leave him be, René," his mother said. "He here now . . . That's all that matter. Ain't no sense in carrying on so."

"You been to that parole office?" René interrupted. "You been to that parole office like I told you?"

"René, please," Sarah Ann said again.

"Have you?" René said, ignoring her.

"Didn't I say I was going?" Tyrone snapped.

"You say a lot of things," René told him. "But what you say and what you do is two different things."

"René, why don't you go on in the house," Sarah Ann suggested. "Why don't you go in the house so Mama can talk to Tyrone."

"I ain't going nowhere," René said.

There was silence.

"Tyrone, is everything all right?" Sarah Ann asked.

"Everything fine," he said. He looked at the door. He wanted to go in the house. He wanted to be alone.

"That's all you gone say," René snapped. "Everything fine. Folks waiting on you half the night, and that's all you gone say."

"What you want me to say, René?"

"If you had any sense, you'd tell your mama what them folks said, seeing how they done called here and worried her half to death."

"If you'd shut your big mouth, maybe I would."

"Both of y'all need to shut up," Sarah Ann said. "If y'all can't do no better than this, both of you need to shut up."

"Don't tell me to shut up, Sarah Ann," René said angrily. "I'm grown. Don't you dare tell me to shut up."

"Tyrone, honey, you sho' everything all right?" Sarah Ann asked, intentionally ignoring René and attempting to change the tenor of the conversation.

"Honey!" René exclaimed. "Honey!"

"Everything all right, Sarah Ann," he said. "My parole officer blasted me out. But everything fine. She just told me what I need to do . . . That's all. . . . "

His voice trailed off, and he stopped talking, then looked away. He wanted to leave. He wanted to be alone. There was an awkward silence.

"They ain't talking 'bout locking you back up, is they?" His mother broke the silence. He turned to her. She looked scared, worried.

"No, ma'am," he said. "They ain't said nothing like that . . . nothing like that at all."

"Well, thank Gawd," she said. "Thank Gawd."

He looked toward the street, then back toward his mother.

"Anybody call here for me?" he asked.

"Not that I know of," she said. "Sarah Ann, anybody called for your brother since you been here?"

"No, ma'am," Sarah Ann said. "Nobody but that parole officer."

Tyrone looked at her, then away. Where was Beggar Man? What was taking him so long? He looked at his watch and made a quick decision. If Beggar Man did not call in the next few minutes, he was going to call him.

"You expecting a phone call?" René smarted.

He looked at her but did not answer.

"Somebody from the Silver Dollar, I guess." She continued to press the conversation. "One of yo' old drinking buddies, hunh?"

"The Silver Dollar," his mama said, alarmed. "Baby, you ain't fooling 'round that old place again, is you? Please tell me you ain't fooling 'round that old place."

"Yeah, Tyrone, tell her," René said. "Tell her so we all can know how much you done changed. Go on. Tell her."

Tyrone did not respond.

"Ask him if he been drinking, Mama," René said. "Go on . . . ask him. Ask him if he been drinking."

"René, why don't you shut your mouth?" Tyrone said.

"Why don't you answer Mama's question?" René retorted.

His mother looked at him with pleading eyes.

"Baby, you ain't been drinking, is you?" She paused, but Tyrone did not answer. "You told me you quit," she said. "You is done quit, ain't you?"

"Quit!" René said. "Smell his breath, Mama. Smell his breath and see if it don't smell like a distillery."

"Lawd Jesus!" his mother shouted. "It's true. It's true. This child drinking again. Help me, Master. Help me, Master."

"Mama, I just had one drink," he confessed. "Just one drink to calm my nerves. But I ain't drinking. I swear. I ain't."

"That's how it start," René said. "One little drink at a time. That's just how it start."

"Shut up, René," Tyrone shouted.

"First you got to have a drink to calm yo' nerves," René said, ignoring him.

"I mean it, René, shut up."

"Then you got to have one to help you get you through the day."

"Mama, don't listen to her," Tyrone said. "She just trying to start some mess. That's all."

"Then you got to have one to help you go to sleep."

"René!" Sarah Ann shouted. "Please."

"Then you got to have one to help you wake up."

"Shut up, René," Tyrone said. "I mean it . . . shut your mouth."

"Then you just got to have one," René continued. "Yeah, Mama, that's just how it start. Then it's any little excuse to drink."

"I ain't able," his mother said. "Lawd knows I ain't able."

"Don't listen to her, Mama," Tyrone said again. "She don't know what she talking about. She just trying to start mess."

"What you doing at the Silver Dollar?" his mother asked. "That's just asking fo' trouble. You ain't got no business over there."

"Mama, I just needed some information," he tried to explain.

"What kind of information?"

"About Marcus," he said.

"He lying," René said. "He was over there drinking."

"René, why don't you shut yo' mouth?" Tyrone said again.

But before she could answer, an unknown car pulled to the shoulder in front of their house and stopped. Tyrone squinted, looking. It was Beggar Man. Tyrone turned to leave, but René stopped him.

"Guess he looking for you," she smarted.

Tyrone didn't answer.

René looked out toward the car, and when she recognized Beggar Man from the club, she snapped to her feet.

"Ah no," she said. "You ain't gone have them hoodlums coming 'round here worrying Mama. You hear me?"

There was silence.

"Tyrone, you hear me?"

Without answering her, he pushed the door open and walked out to the car and leaned against the window.

"What's the word?" he said, then waited.

Beggar Man shook his head. "No dice, man."

Tyrone looked at him, dejected.

"Cat don't exist, Ty," Beggar Man said. "I checked everywhere. He just don't exist."

"Man, how can that be?" Tyrone wanted to know.

"You sho' you got his name right?"

"P. K.," Tyrone repeated the name. "That's what she said."

"You positive?"

"Man, I'm positive."

Beggar Man shook his head and looked away.

"He don't exist, Ty."

"He exist," Tyrone said. "We just can't find him."

Beggar paused, thinking.

"Maybe his name ain't P. K. Maybe that's just what she called him."

"Maybe," Tyrone said. "But I don't think so."

"Wished we knew something about him."

"I told you all I know."

There was silence.

"What else you know about her?"

"Not much," Tyrone said. "Why?"

"If we knew anything," Beggar Man began. "Where they met? Where they hung out? What kind of work he do? What kind of work she do? Anything, Ty. Anything at all. I could find him. I could find him quicker than you could bat a eye."

"Well, I know where she worked," Tyrone said.

"Where?" Beggar Man asked.

"She use to baby-sit for Mr. Peterson."

Beggar Man sat up in his seat.

"That could be it."

"What?" Tyrone asked, confused.

"Where they met," he said. "Maybe they met up there."

"Naw." Tyrone shook his head. "She was a baby-sitter. She didn't work with nobody else. She work in the house by herself."

"Didn't you just say she worked for Peterson?"

"Yeah," Tyrone said. "She watched his kids."

Beggar looked at him, then smiled.

"Man, Peterson a farmer," Beggar Man said. "A big-time sweet potato farmer. Lot of niggers from these parts work up there."

"I didn't know that," Tyrone said.

"Maybe this cat worked for him." Beggar Man was hopeful.

"Maybe," Tyrone said.

"Won't hurt to check it out," Beggar Man said.

"Man, we running out of time," Tyrone said.

"What you want me to do?" Beggar Man pressed for a decision.

"Check it out," Tyrone said. "That's all you can do."

Beggar Man started the car.

"You coming?" he asked.

Tyrone shook his head. "Can't," he said. "Eight o'clock curfew. Can't afford to get locked up."

"No sweat," Beggar Man said. "Hang tight. I'll check it out and get back with you first thang in the morning."

Chapter
27

A t five A.M. there was an unexpected knock on his bedroom door. He sat up in bed and turned on the light. He wasn't asleep. In fact, he had not slept at all. Instead, for most of the night, he had paced the tiny bedroom floor, too afraid to leave the house and too worked up to sleep, all the while tormented by the horrid fact that he was wasting time he did not have to waste.

"Yeah," he called through his closed bedroom door. "Who is it?"

"Tyrone, it's me. Sarah Ann. Open the door. Somebody here to see you."

"Who?" he said.

"Yo' parole officer."

He crawled out of bed, trembling. He opened the door and spied his parole officer standing soldierlike before him, flanked by two armed police officers.

"Need to search your room," she said.

He stepped aside, wide-eyed and confused. Yes, he was still in prison, and yes, this was her show to run as she so desired. Out in the hallway, he heard his mother talking to Sarah Ann. He heard her ask if they could do this. He heard her ask what they were looking for. He heard her call on Jesus.

"Any contraband in here we need to know about?" his parole officer asked.

He shook his head.

"Any weapons?"

"No, ma'am."

"Any drugs?"

"No, ma'am."

"Any alcohol?"

"No, ma'am."

"All right," she said. "For your sake I hope there's not. Turn around and face the wall."

He complied, feeling ill at ease. He stared at the wall, claimed by so deep a fear that he worried at any minute his entire body would begin to shake, tremble.

"Spread 'em."

He spread his legs and reached high upon the wall, feeling her hand searching his body, exploring his pockets.

Through his bedroom door he heard a familiar voice.

"What's going on in here?"

He turned his head slightly and saw René. She had on her uniform. She was preparing to leave for work.

"What he done got into now?"

"Nothing," Sarah Ann said. "That's his parole officer. Now shut yo' mouth and don't go starting trouble."

"Mama don't need this," Rene said. "Mama got high blood pressure. She don't need this first thang in the morning. I just wish he would leave. I just wish he would leave and take all this trouble with him."

"You ain't helping nothin'," Sarah Ann said. "You ain't doing nothin' but making thangs worse."

"Turn around," Tyrone heard his parole officer say.

He turned, and their eyes met. He immediately dropped his, intimidated. He was in the midst of a nightmare—a never-ending nightmare.

"Open your mouth," she ordered.

He opened his mouth, complying.

"Stick out your tongue."

He stuck out his tongue, then waited.

"Lift it up, and tilt back your head," she issued yet another order.

He lifted his tongue, then tilted back his head, and his parole officer moved closer and examined the inside of his mouth.

"What she doing?" he heard his mother's voice.

"Looking for drugs," he heard René say.

"Oh, my Lawd," came the pained exclamation of his agitated mother. "Oh, Savior, help us," she prayed out loud. "Help us, Savior."

He looked out of the corner of his eye. Why were they letting her watch this? Why didn't they take her out on the porch until it was over? Why?

"All of these your things?" the parole officer asked.

"Yes, ma'am," he said. "They all mine."

Wordlessly, he watched her turn back his bedcovers, remove the mattress, empty his dresser drawers, go through his clothes, and search his shoes. And when she had finished, he saw her stand in the center of the room and look about.

"Where does that door go to," she asked.

"My sister's bedroom."

"Oh, no," he heard René say. "I ain't no convict. And you ain't going through my things."

"Ma'am, as long as he lives here, I am well within my jurisdiction to search every inch of this house to assure that he is abiding by the conditions of his parole."

"Well, he needs to leave, then," she said. "This ain't no prison. This is our home. Our private home."

"René," Sarah Ann said. "Why don't you go to work?"

"Ma'am, do you have any alcohol in your room?" the parole officer asked.

"No," she said. "Don't nobody in this house drank."

"Good," his parole officer said. "Because as a condition of his parole, he is not allowed to be around alcohol or anyone who is engaged in the consumption of alcohol."

René looked at Tyrone. Her eyes widened and her mouth fell open.

"Go to work, René," Sarah Ann said, seeming to sense that René was about to divulge the wrong thing. "Go to work before you be late."

"Are there any firearms in the house?" the parole officer asked.

"No, ma'am," Sarah Ann said. "Ain't no guns in this house. Ain't none nowhere. You can take my word on that."

"I will, this time," the parole officer said. "But understand that I can, and I will, search this entire house anytime I deem necessary."

"Yes, ma'am," Tyrone heard his sister say. He glanced over at her. He saw that she had her arm around their mother. She was holding her up, comforting her. His mother looked worried, frustrated, scared.

"I don't like this," René said. "I don't like it one bit."

Tyrone looked at her. He wanted to say something to her but under the circumstances knew that he could not. Why didn't she just leave? Why didn't she just shut her big mouth and go on to work?

"Do you operate a vehicle?"

"Yes, ma'am."

"Which one?"

"The truck."

"Is it your truck?"

"No, ma'am."

"Whose is it?"

"My mother's . . . use to belong to daddy . . . but he passed not too long ago. So don't nobody drive it. Nobody but me."

"Where is it?"

"Under the car shed."

"You got a driver's license?"

"Yes, ma'am."

"Let me see it."

Tyrone removed his wallet from his pants and then handed her his license. He looked at his mother, and he knew what she was thinking. *Thank God you tended to that before it was too late.* His parole officer handed him his license, then reached in her bag and removed a plastic cup.

"Where is the bathroom?" she asked Tyrone.

Tyrone turned and pointed.

"Down the hall," he said.

"Show me."

He walked out of the room, and when he was in the hallway, he stole a quick, nervous glance at his mother. Their eyes met, and he could see that she was crying. Oh, why did she have to go through this? Somehow it all seemed so unfair. What had she ever done to deserve this? What had she ever done besides love him?

At the bathroom, one of the officers went inside, presumably to inspect the interior. When he returned, he nodded his approval to the parole officer, and she handed Tyrone the cup.

"Need a urine sample," she said.

He took the cup and went into the bathroom, but before he could close the door, he heard his parole officer tell one of the policemen to go in with him and watch him. Feeling thoroughly degraded, he shut the door and turned his back, and under the watchful eye of the police officer, he removed the lid, urinated in the cup, and replaced the lid. Once he was done, he washed his hands, then turned to the officer.

"Now what?" he said.

"Give it to her," he told Tyrone.

Out in the hallway, she took the specimen, secured it in a box, then led the way to the car shed. Once there, she searched the truck, and finding nothing, she turned to him and said, "Keep your nose clean . . . I'm watching you."

Chapter
28

S he left, and though his frightened, tense body was mired in simul-
taneous feelings of degradation, dejection, and humiliation, he
quickly pulled himself together, took a bath, got dressed, and readied
himself to find Beggar Man. In spite of his own personal travails, he
fully realized that to a certain extent, he had placed his son's future in
Beggar Man's hand, and now, he felt deep within his consciousness
that one more dead end would most certainly mean the end for
Marcus, as well as the end of his own life as he had hoped it would
exist beyond the walls of prison.

He dallied at home much longer than he had originally planned. If
his parole officer was lurking, he had to be careful, lest she should
catch him in some minor violation, or should show herself at a most
inopportune time, when he, himself, was mired in some compromis-
ing situation. No, he lingered, being careful to avoid his mother, and
Sarah Ann, until that innate instinct by which he had always lived told
him it was time to go.

As he left for Beggar Man's house, he was plagued by a feeling with
which he had little familiarity. No, his belief in his son had never

waned. No, not for one fleeting moment. Yet, for much of the night, as he had paced back and forth, he had been plagued by one nagging question after the other. What if he was wrong? What if there was no P. K.? And even if P. K. did exist, what if he was not the one? What if someone else killed her? Someone other than P. K. Someone other than his son. Oh, he had been wrong before in his life. He had been wrong many times about many things. But never before had being wrong held such grave consequences for those he loved.

No, P. K. did exist. He picked her up that night. He carried her to that field. He killed her. Yes, he did it. P. K., not Marcus.

It was too early for Beggar Man to be at work. So, Tyrone went to his house. But because of his heightened suspicion, and his awareness that his parole officer now knew his truck, he did not park on the street, nor did he park in the neighborhood. Instead, he parked on the outskirts, at a nearby convenience store, and walked the half mile to Beggar Man's house. When he got there, to his surprise, Beggar Man was sitting on the porch, waiting. Tyrone spoke first.

"Got something for me?" he asked.

"Maybe," Beggar Man said.

"What?"

"A name," he said. "Maybe. I'm not sure."

"What name?" Tyrone asked, curious.

"There's a nigger up there, at Peterson's, 'bout your boy's age," he said. "He looks a little shady."

"What you mean, shady?"

"Well, for one thing," Beggar Man said, "nigger drive a old blue truck."

"Dark blue?" Tyrone asked.

Beggar nodded but did not speak.

"That's it," Tyrone said. "That what I been looking for."

"But check this out," Beggar said. "It ain't his."

Tyrone looked at him questioningly.

"Well, whose is it?" he asked.

"Ole man Peterson's," Beggar Man said. "Way I hear it, nigger his flunky. He runs his errands. And every now and then, Peterson let the nigger keep his truck a day or two. Least that's what I hear."

"It's him," Tyrone said. "Got to be."

"Don't know, man," Beggar Man said, doubtful. "His name ain't P. K. They call him Rooster."

Tyrone was silent, thinking.

"What his real name," he asked. "Maybe P. K. stand for something else. Maybe it's his initials."

Beggar Man shook his head.

"Nigger name Benny," he said. " Benny Earl Jones."

"You talked to him."

"Naw," Beggar Man said, shaking his head again. "I seen 'im downtown, but I didn't talk to him. Wanted to check with you first. See what you wanted to do."

"Wonder if he knew the girl."

"Don't know," Beggar Man said. "Nigger works for Peterson. He could."

"You know where to find him?" Tyrone asked.

"Yeah," Beggar Man said. "I know."

"Let's roll," Tyrone said. "We running out of time."

Beggar Man rose, then stopped. He looked toward the street, then back at Tyrone, and Tyrone could see that he was puzzled. Confused. Tyrone looked out at the empty streets, wondering what he had seen. Why had he stopped?

"Where your truck?" Beggar Man asked with a bewildered look on his face.

Now Tyrone understood. Beggar Man was trying to figure out how he had gotten here. Where he had parked.

"'Cross the tracks," he said, then offered an explanation. "Parole officer sweatin' me, man. Could be following me, I don't know."

"Let's take my ride," Beggar said, expressing an unspoken level of understanding which could only be found in one who, himself, had also had the tenuous task of living life as an ex-con while trying to navigate that monumental obstacle called parole.

Tyrone followed him to his car, and when they both were seated, Beggar Man headed out of town, intuitively taking back roads and obscure streets until they were well away from town and well on their way to Peterson's place. At the little village of Indian Junction, they turned off the main highway, onto a long gravel road, and as they eased along, bypassing one farm after another, they finally came to a vast stretch of land, the bulk of which Beggar Man told him was Peterson's place. And the farther they drove, the more he understood. Yes, this vast, sprawling spread carved into what could only be described as hundreds of acres of pristine wilderness was no farm. No, this was a plantation, the size and scope of which he had not comprehended. As he gaped, wide-eyed, through his lowered window at what appeared to be a never-ending configuration of sweet potato fields, he could only imagine from whence all these workers came. Yes, it made sense. P. K. was one of a thousand black boys, anonymously toiling day after day under the scorching rays of a red-hot sun, invisible to all who cared not to see him.

Yes, she could have met him here. And yes, out here, in the middle of nowhere, theirs could have been whatever they wanted it to be. Visible only to those eyes that cared to see.

They turned off the road and passed under an arch and followed a much narrower road up toward the main house. Near the house, they spotted a lone black man pushing a wheel barrow filled with what could have been sweet potato slips. Beggar Man pulled next to the man and stopped. The man looked up.

"You know Rooster?" Beggar Man asked.

The man nodded and pointed. "He in there."

Beggar followed the road behind the house and stopped before a large building that Peterson used as a storage shed. They got out and walked inside. Rooster was in the shed, loading empty crates on the back of the truck.

"You Rooster?" Tyrone said.

"Some people call me that."

"You work here?"

"Yeah," he said. "Why?"

"That your truck?"

He shook his head. "That's Mr. Peterson's truck. Why?"

"You the only person that drive it? Besides him, I mean?"

"Lots of folks drive it," he said. "It's a work truck. Why you asking me all these questions?"

"How long he had it?"

He furrowed his brow and looked at them, confused.

"'Bout six . . . seven years. Why? You wanting to buy it?"

"How long you been working here?"

"What?"

"How long you been working here?"

"Seven or eight years." He paused. "Who are you? Why you asking me all these questions?"

"I'm Tyrone Stokes."

Rooster appeared even more confused. "Do I know you?"

"Don't think so," Tyrone said.

"Well, what's this all about?" he asked.

"My son," Tyrone said. "Marcus Stokes."

"Marcus Stokes," Rooster repeated the name, then squinted his eyes. "I don't know no Marcus Stokes."

"He supposed to die in a couple of days," Tyrone said. "He supposed to die for killing that white girl."

Rooster's eyes widened, flustered.

"Yeah," he said. His voice cracked. "I heard about that. That's too bad. Hate to see it. Hate to see it happen."

"You know my boy?"

"Naw." Rooster shook his head violently. "I don't know him."

"You know the girl?"

"What girl?"

"The dead girl?"

"Naw." He shook his head again, then averted his eyes, fidgeting.

"Didn't she work up here?"

"I don't know."

"What you mean you don't know, nigger," Beggar Man butted in. "Don't you work for Peterson?"

Rooster looked at Beggar Man, then back at Tyrone.

"Lot of folks work for Mr. Peterson. I don't know all of 'em."

"You know P. K.?" Tyrone asked.

"Who?"

"Who!" Beggar Man shouted. "What's wrong with you, nigger? You can't hear? Answer the man."

"P. K.," Tyrone repeated.

"Naw," Rooster said. "I don't know nobody by that name."

"I think you do." Tyrone dismissed what he heard. "I think you know the girl. And, I think you know P. K."

"Mister, I told you I don't," Rooster said, continuing to adamantly deny any knowledge of that which Tyrone spoke.

"And I told you, I think you lying," Tyrone said.

"Mister, I got work to do."

Rooster started to turn away, but Tyrone stopped him.

"I ain't through talking to you," Tyrone said.

"Well, I'm through talking to you."

"Witness saw that girl get in a blue truck that night," Tyrone said. "Saw her get in it like she knew the driver. What you know about that?"

"Nothing," Rooster said.

"I think you lying," Tyrone pressed him.

"Mister, it's a free world," Rooster said matter-of-factly. "You can think whatever you want to."

"I think that's the blue truck she got in that night," Tyrone said, looking at the blue truck Rooster was loading.

"Mister, I got work to do," Rooster repeated.

"How old are you?" Tyrone asked.

Rooster didn't answer him.

"You ought to be 'bout my son's age, right?" Tyrone ventured a guess.

"I told you, I don't know your son," Rooster said.

"You from 'round here?" Tyrone asked.

"Yeah, I from 'round here," Rooster said.

Tyrone paused and looked at him hard.

"So, you trying to tell me that a white girl 'round here got killed, and the black boy they say killed her got death, and you ain't heard nothing 'bout it."

Rooster returned Tyrone's stare but did not speak.

"Nigger lying," Beggar Man said. "Lying through his goddamn teeth."

"You got any brothers?" Tyrone asked him.

"Yeah, I got brothers," Rooster said.

"Any of them ever drive that truck?" Tyrone said, eyeing the truck on which Rooster had been stacking crates.

Rooster frowned. "Don't none of them work up here," he said, seemingly puzzled by the question.

"Any of them name P. K.?" Tyrone asked, a related question.

"No," Rooster said. "Ain't got no brother named P. K."

"What about cousins?" Tyrone asked.

"Ain't got no cousins either!" Rooster said.

"Partners?" Tyrone said.

"Naw!" Rooster raised his voice, irritated.

"Who, then?" Tyrone asked.

"Nobody, I told you." Rooster lifted another empty crate from the stack and loaded it on the back of the truck. "Mister, I got work to do."

"I think you lying." Tyrone dismissed his attempt to end the conversation.

Frustrated, Rooster turned from the truck and started to leave. Tyrone grabbed him by the arm, hard. "This ain't over," he said. "I think you know something. And this ain't over."

Rooster pulled away and headed toward the door. He stopped before Beggar Man, who was blocking his exit. Tyrone nodded, and Beggar Man stepped aside and let him pass. When he was gone, Tyrone spoke to Beggar Man.

"What you think?" he asked.

"Think he hiding something," Beggar Man said.

"Can you find out what?" Tyrone wanted to know.

"I can find out," Beggar Man told him.

Tyrone paused, then sighed.

"Man, we running out of time."

"I know." Beggar Man nodded sympathetically. "Give me a couple of hours. I'll find out something."

"I'm going with you," Tyrone said.

"No," Beggar Man insisted. "Could get ugly. You on parole . . . don't need to get your hands dirty."

Chapter
29

B ack at his truck, Tyrone made two decisions. First, in a couple of
hours, he and Beggar Man would meet at the old abandoned service station just off Willow Road. And secondly, while he waited, he
would return to Cedar Creek to check on his ailing mother. He was
worried about her. He was worried that the ordeal with his parole officer had been too stressful. Yes, she was too old and her condition
too grave for such aggravation.

After bidding Beggar Man goodbye, he left the convenience store
and drove down a side street for less than a mile, then along another
paved street for another two or three miles, finally connecting to the
main highway back to Cedar Creek. As he drove, he thought of many
things. He wondered if Beggar would be able to uncover anything.
He wondered what he would do if he could not. He wondered how
Marcus was doing. He wondered what he was thinking. He wondered
how he, himself, would go on if the unthinkable happened.

At the intersection near the lake, he turned onto Lake Shore
Avenue and headed toward town. Suddenly, everything stalled.
Something was clogging the road. He inched along in slow-moving
traffic, trying to see. Ah yeah, there was an accident. A big rig had

overturned and spilled a portion of its load on the highway. Up ahead, he saw a police officer and a heavyset white man, who he assumed was the driver, standing on the shoulder talking. Oh, it was an omen, a bad sign. Yes, his life was a big rig, wrecked on some desolate highway, lying prone, desperately trying to avoid the authorities, while waiting helplessly for some merciful soul to happen along and do that which he could not do for himself.

He inched along until he came to Prescott Road. Then he veered off Lake Shore onto Prescott and followed the long, narrow road past the cemetery, around the bend, and into his mother's neighborhood. As he cleared the bend and approached the house, he could see that she had company. An unfamiliar car, a long, white ninety-eight Oldsmobile, was parked out front underneath the pecan tree.

As he exited the truck to go inside, Sarah Ann came out onto the porch and sat down. He figured that she had just finished working in that hot kitchen and was taking a few minutes to cool off. He spoke to her in a low whisper, then asked her who the car belonged to.

"Cousin Daphne," she said.

Cousin Daphne was his mother's first cousin on her father's side. The two of them had grown up close and had always sworn they were more like sisters than cousins. Cousin Daphne was nice, but just like his aunt Babee, she was a talker. And he just did not feel up to her today. There was too much on his mind.

"How long she been here?" he asked.

"Not long," she said.

"Well, what she want?" he wanted to know.

"Just come by to check on Mama," Sarah Ann told him. Then added, "She say she want to see you 'fo she go."

"I don't want to see her," he said. "I don't want to see nobody."

"Well, she want to see you," Sarah Ann repeated. "Heard her tell Mama she gone try to wait for you. Heard her say she ain't seen you in a long time. And she like to see you 'fo she go."

"Where they at?" he asked, still whispering.

"In there." Sarah Ann nodded toward the living room.

He turned and looked.

"I just don't feel like dealing with this today," he whispered. "I just want to go lie down for a few minutes."

"Feel like it or not," Sarah Ann said, "she wants to see you."

"How Mama?" he changed the subject.

"Complaining with her head some."

He paused, then spoke apologetically. "Sorry 'bout this morning."

"Wasn't your fault," Sarah Ann said. "Wasn't nobody's fault."

"It upset her much?" he asked.

"Some," she said. "But she ain't blaming you."

"Just wish it hadn't happened," Tyrone said.

"Wishing ain't gone change nothing," she said. "What's done is done."

He talked to Sarah Ann a little longer, then started toward the living room to check on his mother and to speak to his cousin. But no sooner had he entered the hallway than the phone rang. He heard Sarah Ann answer the phone. He heard her pause, then say, "Yes, I will." He heard her yell, "Tyrone, telephone."

He went back onto the porch. Sarah Ann had taken the phone out there to keep it from bothering their mother. When she gave Tyrone the phone, she immediately went back inside to give him some privacy. When he answered the phone, he fully expected to hear his parole officer's voice or Beggar Man's voice; instead, he heard the low, somber voice of his son, Marcus.

"Papa," Marcus said, then waited.

When Tyrone took the phone from Sarah Ann, he had been standing; but as soon as he heard the sound of Marcus's voice, his trembling legs became weak, and he slowly slid to the floor, clutching the phone in shaky, unsteady hands.

"Marcus," Tyrone finally answered, struggling against surging emotions.

"They moved me, Papa," Marcus said. "They moved me to the death house."

There was silence. Tyrone closed his eyes tight. A tear rolled down his cheek.

"Papa," Marcus called. "Papa, you there?"

"I'm here, son," Tyrone said, his voice cracking slightly. He swallowed and composed himself. "You all right, son."

"I'm all right, Papa."

There was silence.

"Papa."

"Yeah, son."

"I ain't scared no more," he said. Then he was quiet.

Tyrone closed his eyes again, crying. He didn't know what to say. An awkward moment passed. Then Marcus spoke again.

"Just want you to know," he said. "I done made peace with the whole thing. No matter what happens. I ain't scared no more."

"Son, don't talk like this," Tyrone pleaded. "We still got two days."

"Wish we could've known each other, Papa."

"Don't talk like this."

"Wish we could have known each other without all this."

Tyrone was quiet, as tears flowed down his face.

"Seem like its always been something between us, Papa," Marcus said. "Something always keeping us from each other."

Tyrone listened but did not speak.

"A boy need to know his papa," Marcus said. "He need to know his papa proud of him. I want you to be proud of me, Papa . . . That's why I ain't scared no more. I ain't scared no more . . . And I ain't gone cry no more."

"I'm proud of you, son," Tyrone heard himself say. "I always been proud of you. The day you was born—" He paused. His voice cracked. "The day you was born," he started again, then paused. "I promised myself that I was always gone love you, and protect you, and be there for you. I promised myself that, son. And that's what I'm gone do. I—"

"Papa," Marcus interrupted him.

Tyrone didn't answer. He couldn't answer. He was crying.

"Papa," Marcus called again.

"Yeah, son," Tyrone whispered. He was emotional.

"Papa," Marcus said, then paused to collect himself. "Just want you to know, I love you." He paused a second time. "I ain't never had a chance to tell you that. In all these years. I ain't never said it. But I do. I love you, Papa. And I ain't scared no more."

"I love you too, son," Tyrone said, sobbing.

"Come see me, Papa," he said. "Come see me tomorrow."

"I will, son," Tyrone said.

"Papa," Marcus called softly.

"Yeah, son."

"Can you bring Mama," he said. "I want to see my mama."

"I'll try, son," Tyrone said. "I'll try."

Tyrone hung up the phone and was suddenly besieged with an overwhelming desire to speak to his wife. He called the hospital and spoke to the receptionist. She told him that Pauline was much better and that she would be released later that night. The receptionist rang Pauline's room. Tyrone spoke to her. He told her about Marcus . . . He asked if she would go . . . He heard her father protest . . . He heard her say yes . . . He hung up the phone . . . He cried.

Chapter
30

Two hours later, Tyrone sat before the old abandoned building on Willow Street, anxiously watching passing cars and silently praying that Beggar Man had been able to do that which he had not. As he waited, nervously counting every waning second, his tormented mind dangled suspended somewhere between hope and fear, sporadically entertaining distant, yet troubling thoughts seemingly fed to him via some foreign force with which he felt compelled to listen. Yes, he was Marcus's father. And yes, it was his responsibility to help him. Yet, in spite of his best efforts to do just that, his son's grave condition had not been ameliorated, but to the contrary, his dim plight had become dimmer. So dim it seemed that only an unforeseen act of God could stave off his apparent destiny with death.

Why was this happening? Why was his family being punished so? Why?

Suddenly, he bent over the wheel, crying. Of late, he had felt frightened and overwhelmed, but until today he had not cried. No, not once since this nightmare had begun. He had not cried because deep inside of himself, he had believed. In spite of everything, he had believed. But now that the hour was late, and his options few, his emotions erupted, and he cried. No, he did not cry for himself only. But he cried for his son, who never really knew his father. He cried for his wife, whose feeble mind was cracking under the heavy strain of having to bear the unbearable burden of watching her only child be murdered. He cried for his mother, and he cried for his sister, and he cried for his in-laws, and he cried for every black man, woman, and child who, like himself, found themselves at the mercy of this cruel, unjust system of justice. And, yes, he cried because his son would cry no more.

Outside, he could hear the sound of tires on the loose gravel in the parking lot. He looked up, teary-eyed. A white man had pulled next to him and stopped.

"You all right, buddy?" the man asked.

Tyrone wiped his eyes. No, he wasn't all right. How could he be? His whole world was falling apart. Nonetheless, he nodded, fully expecting the man to accept his affirmation and pull off, but instead, the man held pat, staring with wide, curious eyes.

"Car trouble?" the man said blandly.

Tyrone shook his head, but the man still did not budge. Then Tyrone understood. The man could not move and would not move until that innate suspicion with which their kind viewed his kind had been satisfied. No, he expected more; he wanted an explanation. Tyrone looked off, his lips parted, and he felt himself surrender to the unspoken will of his white would-be benefactor.

"Waiting on somebody," he heard himself say.

There was a brief moment of silence, and though Tyrone did not look at him, he could sense the man's gaze upon his face, studying his countenance, processing what he had been told. Tyrone sat still, feeling uncomfortable until he heard the man speak again.

"All right, then," he heard him say. "You have a good day now, you hear?"

As the man drove off, Tyrone watched him, feeling that somehow the stranger's presence, although peaceful, had sparked something that he could not explain. Then he realized what was bothering him. The man's face was that of those responsible for ruining his life. Yes, his face was the face of the girl who was killed. It was the face of the woman who fingered his son. It was the face of the judge who presided over his trial, it was the face of the jurors who convicted him, it was the face of the jailer who held him, and it was the face of the executioner who would kill him. No, he was not all right, and he would not be all right, until he could convince the man behind that face to release his son and end this charade once and for all.

Again, he heard the sound of tires on the loose gravel. He turned and watched Beggar Man pull next to him and stop. He looked at Beggar Man, and Beggar Man looked at him, and intuitively he could tell by Beggar Man's expression that things had not gone well. Yes, somehow he knew that which Beggar Man had to tell him was not what he needed to hear. Suddenly, he wanted a drink. No, for the first time since his release, he wanted to get high. He wanted to get so high that his mind was beyond all of this.

"What's up?" he asked, then braced himself for what Beggar Man had to say. Yes, he wished he was high; he wished he was beyond this place.

Beggar Man shook his head slowly, but he did not speak. His sad, hollow eyes spoke for him. He had run into another dead end; he had hit another brick wall. Tyrone leaned back into the seat and prepared himself to hear the words he did not care to hear. He stared blankly ahead, listening, but not listening.

"The fella I need to see out of town," Beggar Man said. "Won't be back until tomorrow." His voice was low, somber, apologetic.

"Tomorrow," Tyrone said. He still did not look. His voice was dry, distant, mechanical. "Man, I'm running out of tomorrows."

Beggar Man shifted in his car, uncomfortable. "I know," he said.

There was silence, and Tyrone paused, looking far off. He was no longer there; his mind had drifted. A few seconds passed.

"Talked to Marcus," he said. Then it was quiet again. Beggar Man nodded and grunted, then waited. He was uncomfortable. He did not know what to say. He shifted about on the seat; the springs creaked. Tyrone spoke again.

"They moved him today," he said. The sound of his low, sad voice had a faraway drone. "They moved him to the death house."

He turned and looked at Beggar Man, and Beggar Man could see that his red, swollen eyes had begun to fill again. Beggar Man looked at him, then looked away. He wanted to comfort him, but he did not know how.

"I'm sorry," he said.

He waited for Tyrone to say something else, but his friend did not speak. Instead, he slowly turned his head and stared blankly through the windshield. A few awkward seconds passed, then Tyrone's lips parted. His mouth opened.

"He say he ain't scared . . . He say he ain't scared at all."

There was silence. Beggar Man sat stone still, listening.

"But I am," Tyrone confessed. "What if it happens? What if they kill him?"

"Can't think that way, Ty," Beggar Man said. "Just can't think that way."

"How can they do this?" Tyrone asked.

Beggar Man hunched his shoulders, then nodded.

"He innocent," Tyrone said.

Beggar Man looked at him but did not respond.

"I hate 'em," Tyrone said angrily. "I hate all of 'em."

He said that; then it was quiet again. Beggar Man looked far down the road. His eyes narrowed; then his lips parted.

"Me, too, man," he said. "Me, too."

A moment passed. Then Tyrone spoke again.

"He want to see Pauline," he said.

Beggar Man looked at him strangely. His mind had been adrift. "Who?" he asked. He had not heard; he was not sure.

"Marcus," Tyrone said. "He want to see Pauline."

"Oh," he said.

He waited for Tyrone to say more, but he did not. He was quiet, staring straight ahead.

"She going?" Beggar Man prompted him.

Tyrone nodded.

"That's good." Beggar Man tried to sound hopeful. "Probably just what Marcus needs. Probably do him some good."

"I don't know," Tyrone said. "Might make things worse."

"Naw." Beggar Man shook his head. "He need his mama, Ty. He need her now more than ever."

"So do I," Tyrone said.

The words fell from his lips, and instantly he could not breathe. He had not planned to say them. His mouth had simply opened, and they had spilled from some secret place of which he was unaware. Suddenly, he felt like crying again. He opened the door and climbed out of the truck. He scurried behind the building and buried his face in his hands, sobbing. A moment later, he felt a hand on his shoulder. It was Beggar Man. Tyrone did not turn to look at him but raised his head and stared at the distant horizon.

"I love her," he said, his voice trembling. "I still love her."

"Go tell her," Beggar Man advised.

"I can't," he said.

Beggar Man looked at him strangely. "Why not?" he asked.

"I just can't."

"She probably needs to hear it."

"No," he said. "Not now."

"Why not?"

"She sick," Tyrone said. "She don't need this. Not now."

"She ain't sick, Ty." Beggar Man rejected his assertion. "Her heart broke, and can't nobody fix it but you." He paused and gently grabbed Tyrone about the shoulders and turned him until they were facing each other. "Man, this burden you trying to bear is too heavy," he said. "It's just too heavy for one person to carry. You and Pauline created Marcus together, and y'all gone have to see this thing through together. Ty, right now she hurting in a way that don't nobody in the whole world understand but you. She need you, and you need her. Go be with your wife, Ty. Let me handle this."

"She don't want to see me."

"She loves you, Ty."

"No, she don't."

"Yes, she do."

"Not anymore."

"You know better than that, Ty," Beggar Man snapped. "Man, you and me go back a long way. And I love you like a brother. But some of the shit you pulled, man, if I was Pauline, I would have left you a long time ago. But she didn't." Beggar Man shook Tyrone's shoulders. "Man, do you hear what I'm saying?" He looked deep into Tyrone's eyes. "All them years you was down . . . She ain't never went no-where . . . not even on a date." He paused to let what he had said sink in. "She loves you, Ty. You know that. She ain't never loved nobody but you."

"I don't know," Tyrone said. "I just don't know."

"She divorce you?" Beggar Man asked.

"What?" Tyrone said. The question caught him off guard.

"When you was down, did she divorce you?"

Tyrone shook his head.

"Why not?" Beggar Man asked.

Tyrone didn't answer.

"Ty," Beggar Man said, then sighed. "Far as I know, you ain't never done but two things right since you been in this world. That's marry Pauline and father Marcus. Now, for some reason, the good Lord done seen fit to give you another crack at this thing. And for the life of me, I don't know why. But since he has, let me give you a little piece of advice. While you fighting for your son, don't forget to fight for your wife."

Tyrone closed his eyes tight, crying.

"I do love her," he spoke in a whisper.

"Then, fight for her," Beggar Man said.

"Fight for her," Tyrone said. "Hell, I can't even get past her old man."

"This ain't got nothing to do with him." Beggar Man was emphatic.

Tyrone looked at him, then chuckled.

"Man, he her father."

"He gave her to you," Beggar said. "I was there when he did it. I was there when that preacher said, 'Who gives her away.' I was there, Ty. I was there when he stood up tall as you please and said 'I do.' This ain't got nothing to do with him. Nothing at all. Man, buy your wife some roses. Take her for a walk. Tell her you sorry. Tell her you love her . . . Tell her you want your family back."

"I will," Tyrone said. "Soon as all this is over."

Chapter
31

The next morning, Tyrone and Pauline arrived at the prison at a few minutes after nine. They were searched and taken to the warden's office. His office was a large, impersonal room just off the entrance and just beyond the large steel doors leading into the cell block. In his office, they were escorted to two chairs that had been positioned before a large oak desk and were told to have a seat; the warden would be with them shortly. As they waited, Tyrone held Pauline's hand. On the trip up, neither of them had said very much. He had held the wheel, and she had sat silently in her seat, staring ahead, rarely flinching, rarely moving.

Inside the office, Tyrone heard the distant ring of steel against steel as faraway doors clanged shut. He heard the heavy sound of approaching steps resonating off the hard concrete floor. He heard the sound of men talking; then the warden entered. From where he sat, he could see him clearly. He was a tall, well-built, silver-haired man, probably in his late forties or early fifties. Unlike the guards, he did not wear a uniform. Instead, he wore a white long-sleeve shirt, a navy blue neck tie, and a pair of dark trousers. When he entered, he did not cross the room completely, but paused next to them. His light gray eyes settled on Tyrone.

"Mr. and Mrs. Stokes," he said.

"Yes, sir." Tyrone rose and spoke for both of them. Pauline did not speak, nor did she move. She remained quiet, sitting stone still, staring straight ahead. She was there, and yet she was not there.

"I'm Warden Fletcher," he said, then extended his hand.

Tyrone shook his hand, but Pauline did not. She was still, perfectly still. She heard him, yet she did not hear him.

"Thank you for coming," he said politely, then quickly motioned for Tyrone to sit back down. Tyrone took his seat, then watched the warden make his way to the chair behind his desk.

"Can I get either of you anything before we get started?" he asked.

Tyrone shook his head, and Pauline continued to stare.

"Very well," the warden said, then directed his attention to a folder lying prone upon his desk. "As you both know, your son, Marcus Le Roy Stokes, is scheduled to be executed for capital murder at twelve o'clock tomorrow afternoon." He paused.

Tyrone nodded. Suddenly this was real. Too real.

"Let me begin by saying that this is a difficult and trying time for all of us. So, to insure that all goes as well as can be expected under the circumstances, I've asked you to come by before your visit today so that I can explain exactly what will occur over the next thirty or so hours. Now, before I start are there any questions?"

Tyrone shook his head. Pauline did not move.

The warden began again. His voice was dry and methodical.

"Today is your final visit," he said, then paused briefly before he continued. "It will be a contact visit."

Tyrone snapped forward, wide-eyed.

"We can touch him?"

"That's correct," the warden said. Then he leaned back and looked at Tyrone with serious eyes."You will be allowed to sit together." He paused and looked at Pauline, but she did not look at him. "However, for security purposes, armed guards will be posted around the room. And your visit will be closely monitored."

Pauline looked at the warden for the first time. Still, she did not speak. Her red, swollen eyes watered, and a tear rolled down her cheek.

"Right now we have your son in a holding cell. Tonight, he will receive his last meal. Which can consist of anything that he wants as long as it costs less than twenty dollars. Tomorrow, his attorney will be allowed to visit him. But at exactly two hours prior to his scheduled execution, visitation will be terminated. With one exception. A spiritual advisor is allowed to be with him up until the time he is taken to the execution chamber. If he so chooses."

The warden paused again and asked them if they had questions. Tyrone shook his head. Pauline did not respond. She remained still, staring ahead, her eyes wet with tears.

"Now, one hour before his execution, he will be moved from his isolation cell to a small holding cell near the execution chamber," Warden Fletcher resumed. "He will have thirty minutes to collect himself, or to pray, or to write a final note, or talk to his spiritual advisor. Then at exactly thirty minutes before his execution, he will be strip searched, dressed in khaki pants, khaki shirt, and slippers. At exactly fifteen minutes before his execution, his hands and feet will be shackled, and he will be taken to the execution room. In the execution room, he will be strapped to the execution table, and an IV will be inserted into his right arm. Once that has been done, the curtain will open, and he will have an opportunity to make a final statement to the victim's family or to members of the press. When he has concluded his statement, I will signal the executioner. At that time, three injections will be administered. The first will put him to sleep. The second will stop his breathing. And the third will stop his heart. After the final injection has been administered, I will relinquish your son's remains to the coroner. At which time, the coroner will remove the body, and once his office has concluded their procedures, they will turn the body over to the family. The entire process should take less than fifteen minutes. Unfortunately, we do not allow members of the condemned's family to be present during the execution. We do that out of respect for the victim's family." He paused. "Do either of you have any questions?"

"When can I see my child?" Pauline spoke for the first time. Her soft voice trembled, and Tyrone took her hand, trying to comfort her.

"Right now," the warden said. He pressed a button and spoke into the intercom. "Officer Williams, please escort Mr. and Mrs. Stokes to the visitation room."

When the officer arrived, Tyrone and Pauline followed him through a series of clanging doors and into a moderate-size room. It was a drab room with four gray cement walls, a bare concrete floor, and a rather large rectangular table around which were eight or ten plain wooden chairs. Tyrone helped Pauline to her seat. She was frail, so frail that he began to wonder whether or not this was a good idea. What would happen if she broke down again, or if she became too emotional, or if she passed out. No, perhaps this was a bad idea. Perhaps he should have come alone.

They had not been seated long when the door opened again and Marcus walked in, escorted on either side by armed officers. Tyrone studied him. His hair was combed, his face shaven. He was standing tall, erect. He was trying to appear brave, but Tyrone could see that he was scared.

"How are you, son?" Tyrone rose and greeted him.

"I'm fine, Papa." Marcus forced a nervous smile, then turned toward Pauline. She looked at him but did not stand. She appeared solemn and tired, and her frail body seemed wracked with worry. "Hi, Mama," he said. He kissed her on the jaw, and she began to cry. Instantly, Marcus's lips tightened, and he began to tremble. He had come to terms, as best he could, with his own plight, but this image of his frail, suffering mother made him feel that at any minute his own resolve would weaken and like her he, too, would cry. He did not want that. He did not want to cry. He would not cry. He could not cry.

"Mama," he called to her gently. "Don't cry. Please, don't cry."

Tyrone sat next to her and cloaked her in his arms. She buried her head in his chest, and despite his best efforts to settle her, she continued to cry. Marcus sat in the chair directly across from them. He turned and stole a quick glance at the guards. Yes, this was what they desired. They wanted to see them suffer, and they wanted to see them mourn, and they wanted to see them fall on their knees and stretch forth their arms, pleading for mercy that would not come. No, he would not cry. And he would not plead. And he would not beg. Die if he must, but he would not beg. Again, he looked at his mother, and he secretly prayed for God to grant her the strength to face that which would be done.

"Mama," he called to her again.

He waited, but she did not respond.

"I'm all right, Mama," he said. "Please, don't cry."

She continued to sob, and he paused again, searching for the words that would strengthen her. No, comfort her. "Reverend Jacobs brung me a Bible." He paused again, but still she neither looked at him nor stopped crying. Her face remained pressed hard against Tyrone's chest. "I been reading Psalms." Suddenly, her sobbing became heavier. "The twenty-third Psalm . . ." He paused again. "That's what Reverend Jacobs told me to say . . . tomorrow . . . when it happens."

"Ain't nothing gone happen," Tyrone said, his voice forceful.

"He told me to memorize it," Marcus said. His eyes were glassy, his voice detached. He seemed far away.

"Ain't nothing gone happen," Tyrone said again.

"He told me . . . while they was handling me . . . not to think about what they was doing. Just say it over and over again . . . and it would give me courage. And when they was done . . . I would have peace."

"Son." Tyrone looked at him with pleading eyes, but Marcus was not interested in listening to what his father had to say. No, he was staring straight ahead, seeing his future, revisiting his plan. His voice was steady, matter-of-fact.

"Been working on it all night," he said, then paused again.

"Son," Tyrone tried to interrupt him a second time, but the low, steady drone of Marcus's voice plowed on; not stopping, not yielding, not slowing.

"The Lord is my shepherd; I shall not want."

He said that, then paused, meditating on the words, concentrating on their meaning. Pauline still had not raised her head, and Tyrone continued to hold his arm around her shoulder, comforting her. Tyrone lifted his eyes and looked at his son standing before him. There seemed to be in him an impulse to say something, but instead, he closed his eyes, and a tear rolled down his cheek.

Marcus glanced at his parents, then away. Inside his mind, he willed himself strong. He took a deep breath, then concentrated on the words, visualizing the passage. He heard himself speaking in a language not his own, repeating rote words and phrases with which heretofore he had been unfamiliar.

"He maketh me to lie down in green pastures . . ." He lifted his eyes toward the ceiling, feeling the power of the words. No, he was not afraid. Not now. Not anymore. . . . "He leadeth me beside the still waters . . ." He paused again, listening to the words, drawing strength from them. His mind was free, his spirit soaring. . . . "He restoreth my soul . . . He leadeth me in the paths of righteousness for His name's sake. Yea, though I walk through the valley of tho evil: for Thou art with me . . ." He lowered his eyes and paused, allowing the words to resonate off the walls and throughout the room for all to hear. Yes, there was something in him now, something in which he believed that propelled him beyond this place and these men, and this thing which on tomorrow would happen. . . . "Thy rod and thy staff they comfort me . . ." He paused again. His lips began to quiver; his eyes became misty. No, he would not cry. Marcus bowed his head, then concentrated again, hearing that voice inside himself leading him onward. He took a deep breath, summoning the courage to continue. . . . "Thou preparest a table before me in the presence of mine enemies: Thou anointest my head with oil; my cup runneth over." He felt himself becoming full, emotional. He closed his eyes and in the darkness of the moment found that calmness for which he searched. His voice relaxed, and he spoke again in a soft, rhythmic whisper. . . . "Surely goodness and mercy shall follow me all the days of my life." He emphasized the word life, then raised his head, opened his eyes, and gazed at his mother with strong, assuring eyes devoid of doubt, filled with certainty. . . . "And I will dwell in the house of the Lord forever."

Tyrone rose and went to the far corner and turned his back, sobbing. Marcus, looking at him, could see his back twitching, his shoulders jumping. And then, in the next moment, his eyes strayed from his father to his mother. He looked at her, and for the first time, she was looking directly at him.

"Mama," he called to her gently. "Do you still believe in those words?"

She nodded.

"You really believe?"

She nodded again, and he rose and moved next to her. In him was the desire to release her from her pain. To give her back what his ordeal had taken from her. His life was over. Soon to be snuffed out. But she had to live on. In spite of all that had transpired, and all that would transpire, she had to rise the day after tomorrow and live. He looked at her, and somehow he sensed that his was the easy part. He had but to show up tomorrow and follow the script. And when the end came, he would have peace. But for her, there would be no peace, only pain, and angst, and regret, and sadness. And all that she would have to hold on to would be that which he gave her now. He paused again, searching his soul for something he could say to her that would grant her the peace that he so believed, in a few hours, would be his. He took her hands and looked deep into her eyes.

"Then, Mama," he said softly. "I need you to do me a favor . . . I need you to accept this."

"No," Tyrone protested. He started back toward the table; but before he reached them, Pauline's lips parted, and she spoke for the first time.

"I wish I wouldn't've never sent you to that store," she said. She closed her eyes and leaned forward, crying. Marcus put his arms around her.

"Mama, you ain't the blame for this," he said. He held her tight, feeling her face against his chest, her warm tears against his skin. "Mama," he called to her softly, "I don't want you to cry no more." He began to gently caress her arm, still trying to reassure her. "Mama," he spoke in a whisper, "I done made peace with this . . . And I want you to do the same . . . I can't go unless I know you okay."

"Son," Tyrone called to him, his voice trembling.

Marcus ignored him. He had to make his mother understand how he felt.

"Mama . . . I need to hear you say you okay."

Pauline pulled away from him and looked up but did not speak. Her hands began to tremble; her body began to shake.

"No," Tyrone said.

"It's all right, Mama." He squeezed her hands in his own, then rubbed them gently, lovingly. "I ain't scared no more . . . I done made peace . . . I'm ready . . . I'm ready . . . I'm ready."

"No," Tyrone said again.

"Yes," he said. "I'm all right now . . . really . . . I'm not just saying it. It's okay. Ain't no need to cry. We'll see each other again someday."

"No," Tyrone interrupted him. "Son, don't talk like this . . . we close . . . that girl . . . she was seeing a black fella . . . a black fella name P. K. He did it. He the one. Son, do you know him? Do you know anybody named P. K.?"

"Don't want to talk about that no more," Marcus said.

"But, son—"

"No, Papa. I don't want to talk about it. I just want to spend whatever time I got left with you and Mama."

"But, son—"

"No, Papa." He paused, then looked his father in the eye. "I'm a man, Papa. Just like you. I'm a grown man. But I can't go to bed tonight hoping, then get up and face what I got to face tomorrow. No, Papa, I don't want to talk about it."

"Son."

"No, Papa," he said. "I ain't gone talk about it no more. And I ain't gone think about it no more. I'm gone die tomorrow. And ain't nothing nobody can do about it. I just want to enjoy what time we have left."

"Don't talk like this."

"Ain't no other way to talk."

"Son."

"No, Papa. No."

Marcus stood up, not wanting to say any more. His eyes became misty. He did not want to cry. He would not let himself cry.

"Son—"

"Papa, I'm glad I got a chance to see you again," he said. "I been thinking about you all these years. Wanting to see you. Wanting to talk to you. Wanting to know you. I'm just glad I got a chance . . . before I had to go."

Tyrone didn't respond. He wept openly.

"And, Papa, thank you for trying."

Tyrone nodded, then dropped his head, and Marcus turned his attention to his mother. Her sad eyes were full of pain, anguish.

"Mama, I want you to go on," he said. "And I want you and Papa to try to work things out. I want our family to survive."

Tyrone moved next to Pauline, and they put their arms around each other, crying. Marcus stepped just beyond the table. He looked at his parents embraced. The corner of his lip turned up, and he smiled a faint smile. He looked at the guard, and the guard nodded.

"Guess that's it," Marcus said.

Tyrone released his wife as Marcus made his way around the table, and when he was directly opposite his mother, he bent at the waist and gently kissed her on the cheek, then moved his lips close to her ear whispering, "I love you, Mama."

Instantly, he felt her tremble. Then he felt her arms around him, pulling him close, holding him tight.

"I love you, too," she said, sobbing. "You always remember that, son. No matter what . . . Your mama loves you."

"I will, Mama," he said. "I will."

"Son, anything I can do for you?" Tyrone asked.

"Take care of my Mama," Marcus said.

Tyrone nodded, and then the two men embraced.

"Bye, Papa," Marcus said, pushing away.

"Bye, son."

"Bye, Mama."

"Bye, son."

"I love you."

"We love you, too."

Chapter
32

Outside the room, Tyrone could hear the jingling of keys and the fading footsteps of his condemned son striking the hard corridor floor. Then he heard the halls grow quiet. He saw Pauline lean her head upon the table, crying. Gloom and doom swept him, and he closed his eyes against the light, hoping to still the spinning room and quell the waning feeling that the sun was setting, and the sky was falling, and the bowels of the earth were opening, readying themselves to swallow for all eternity that which was his. He opened his eyes and felt himself raging. Raging against his country, his people, his God, his soul, his life.

He rose from the table and led a weak and despondent Pauline back to the truck. They left the prison and he took her home, then went back to Beggar Man's house. When he got there, Beggar was sitting on the porch, waiting. Tyrone pulled to the curb and stopped, and Beggar Man walked out to the car and leaned against the window. They looked at each other; then Beggar Man spoke.

"Stopped by your crib," he said. "Miss Hannah told me you went to the prison."

For an answer, Tyrone nodded.

"How it go?" Beggar Man asked.

Tyrone shook his head, then paused and looked away. He felt like crying. He could feel the tears forming beneath his eyelids.

There was silence. And then, Beggar spoke again.

"Well, I got news," he said.

Tyrone turned his head slowly and looked at him with sad, tired eyes, then spoke for the first time. "Good news, I hope."

"Could be," Beggar Man said. He waited as if he expected Tyrone to say something else, but when he did not, continued, "I talked to Charlie Edwards," he said, then paused again. "You remember Charlie, don't you?"

Tyrone hesitated, then shook his head. He may have known him, but right now his mind was not working.

"You know 'im," Beggar Man insisted. "He a old timer. Been working up there on Peterson's place for years."

Beggar Man paused, and Tyrone screwed up his eyes and furrowed his brow. Then he shook his head a second time and blurted, "Don't believe I know 'im . . . and if I do, I sho' don't remember 'im."

"Well," Beggar Man said, sensing the futility of trying to make Tyrone remember. "He say that nigger knew that girl. He say he seen 'em together before. Say he seen 'em together lots of times."

Beggar Man's words drifted past him, and when their meaning registered, Tyrone leaned forward, his eyes wide, his mouth open.

"Seen 'em where?" he asked.

"Riding in that truck," Beggar Man replied.

"Rooster and the girl," Tyrone said.

Beggar Man nodded.

"He sho'!"

Beggar Man nodded again. "Said he seen 'em that night. Said they was at Peterson's place."

"Together?" Tyrone asked, his voice marred with disbelief.

"That's what he said."

Suddenly, a strange feeling engulfed Tyrone, his moist skin flushed warm, and he discovered that his clammy hands were trembling.

"Get in," he said. "Let's go."

Beggar Man opened the door and started to get in, but before he could, Tyrone stopped him.

"I need a piece," Tyrone said.

Beggar Man lifted his shirt and removed a gun from his waist. "Will this do?" he asked.

Tyrone nodded, and Beggar Man handed him the gun. Tyrone slid the gun underneath the seat. He felt the truck sink as Beggar Man climbed aboard; then he felt the seat give and heard the springs creak. Yes, he had made a decision. Things had gone too far, and now, he would do what needed to be done. And as Marcus had realized, now that the essential nature of this situation seemed clear, Tyrone just became resigned to the fact that his own life was not important, and once he realized that, he, too, was scared no more. He pulled out into the road, staring straight ahead, clutching the wheel with firm, steady hands. His taut body suffered from exhaustion. His head was heavy, and his eyes craved sleep. Silently, he guided the truck over the narrow, bumpy street, his weary mind blank, his unfocused eyes blind to all beyond him. He heard Beggar Man clear his throat and saw him turn slightly in his seat and retrieve a lighter from his pocket, then a cigarette from his shirt.

"Smoke?" Beggar Man offered.

Tyrone shook his head. Beggar Man lit the end of the cigarette and took a long draw, then exhaled. Tyrone watched the smoke slowly drift past Beggar Man's ear, and then, as if caught in a vacuum, it was quickly sucked through the open window and out into the open vast.

"What time is it?" Beggar Man asked.

Tyrone looked at his watch. "Little after three," he said.

Beggar Man lifted the cigarette to his mouth again and took another puff, then turned his head and blew the smoke toward the window. "Reckon he still at Peterson's?"

Tyrone hesitated. He did not know. He had not considered that. Yesterday, they had tipped their hand, and now Rooster knew they were on to him. And if he was involved, as it now appeared that he was, maybe he had gone into hiding, or maybe he was lying low. Instinctively, Tyrone pressed the accelerator, and instantly, the speed of the truck increased. Out of the corner of his eye, he saw Beggar

Man staring at him, and then he realized that he had not answered his friend.

"I don't know," he mumbled in a low, tense tone. "I just don't know."

He guided the truck through the streets, out of the neighborhood, and onto the highway leading to Peterson's place. They were traveling north, and he could feel the warm rays of the evening sun on the left side of his stubbled face reminding him that the hour was getting late and their time was getting short. He glanced at Beggar Man, who had leaned back against the seat, his bent elbow resting on the opened window. The smoldering cigarette lay limp between scissored fingers, and his hallow eyes stared contemplatively out over the passing meadows and grazing cows. Tyrone righted his head and turned his eyes back toward the highway. In his cluttered mind, none of this made sense. Before, he had had a theory of what might have happened: P. K. had picked her up that night. He had driven her out into the country. They had made love. Then something went wrong. And he killed her. But she had not been seen with P. K.; she had been seen with Rooster. And not once, but on any number of occasions. They knew each other. And Rooster had lied. But why had he lied? Who was he protecting? Himself? P. K.? Who? And why was Rooster, a black boy, riding around town with a young white girl. Confused, Tyrone stared headlong into the streets, looking for answers that would not come. And the more he thought, the more muddled things became. And the more muddled things became, the more intense the throbbing pain became inside his aching head.

He arrived at the turnoff and followed the road to the main house. But unlike the day before, he did not stop there. Instead, he drove past the house and stopped next to the large storage shed where he and Beggar Man had previously confronted Rooster. From where he sat, he could see inside the building. A small group of men were milling about, stacking empty crates on empty wooden pallets. Quietly, his eyes surveyed their bent backs, seeking out the now familiar form of the one they all called Rooster.

"Help you?" someone said.

He looked up, hearing the sound of the man's voice. Standing behind him, just beyond the door of his truck, was a middle-aged black man clad in a pair of old, faded blue overalls.

"Looking for Rooster," Tyrone said.

"He ain't here," the man informed him.

Suddenly, Tyrone's worries were realized. He was not here. Was he hiding? Or had he fled? For a brief moment, Tyrone's lips tightened. The thought that Rooster had fled frightened him. It was nearing evening, and he was running out of time.

"Where is he?" Tyrone asked.

"Don't know," the man said. "Didn't show up this morning."

"Reckon he at home?" Tyrone heard himself ask.

"Your guess just as good as mine," the man said. "But I know one thang. This sho' ain't like him. Ain't like him at all. Rooster always been a good worker. Can't say the last time I do remember him missing work. Oh, well," the man said, then paused. "Can I help you with something?"

Tyrone shook his head, then pulled the truck into gear. As he drove off, he could not help thinking that everything was falling apart. This whole ordeal had been nothing but one dead end after another. He headed off the property with no clear idea as to where he was going. Just beyond Peterson's place, Beggar Man lit another cigarette, then took a long, slow drag. A quiet moment passed.

"Well, what you think?" Tyrone asked. Anxiety sapped his strength. He felt drained and unsure of himself.

"He know something," Beggar Man said, then raised the cigarette to his lips again. "That nigger know something real important."

Tyrone leaned back and rested against the back of the seat. He was tired and worn out, and it seemed that his weary mind had finally shut down. He tried to think, but all channels seem clogged, all links disconnected, all functions halted. He needed someone to tell him what to do. He turned to Beggar Man.

"What now?" he asked.

"Let's try his house," Beggar Man said.

At the main highway, he turned right. Rooster did not live in Brownsville proper, but just north of the city limits in the small village of Edna. As Tyrone drove, he glanced at his watch. It was three-fifteen. He thought about Marcus. What was he doing? Well, what did one do when the duration of his life could be measured in hours, and the measure of those hours total less than a day? Did he pray, or did he cry, or did he hope against hope while waiting for those who would end his life to appear and tell him that it was time? And when they told him, how did he feel; what did he think; how did he act?

This was his fault. Had he been a better husband, or a better father, or a better person, none of this would have happened. His father would be alive. His wife would be healthy; his mother would have peace; his son would be free. Yes, Beggar Man was right. Rooster knew something. And what he knew, he would tell. Yes, he would tell or he, too, would die.

They stopped in front of a small wood-frame house just off the main highway a few miles north of Peterson's place. The windows were closed, the curtains were drawn, and there was no visible sign that anyone was home.

"Don't look like he here," Tyrone said. He glanced at the house, then at Beggar Man.

"He here," Beggar Man said. "Check out that curtain."

The moment he looked, he saw the curtain move slightly. Someone in the house was watching them. He retrieved the gun from underneath the seat and stuffed it in the waist of his pants. This was it. Whatever happened now, happened. He opened the door and got out. As he and Beggar approached the house, he kept his eyes on the window. Yes, the man knew something. He was hiding in the house in the middle of the day with the curtains drawn. They neared the steps, and Beggar raised his hand for Tyrone to stop. Confused, Tyrone stopped and looked. Beggar Man pointed to the rear of the house. Yes, he was home; and yes, he was hiding. He had parked his truck behind the house in an effort to conceal it. Tyrone nodded, and Beggar Man motioned him onto the porch. As he mounted the steps, Beggar Man, walking on tiptoes, eased behind the house, lest Rooster should flee through the back door. At the door, Tyrone raised his hand and knocked. He waited. No answer. He knocked a second time. Inside the house, he heard feet scurrying. Rooster was trying to escape. Tyrone lowered his shoulder and rammed the door hard. The lock split, and the door swung open. Inside, the lights were out, but the interior of the house was illuminated by the natural light penetrating the plain sheer curtains. Near the rear, he heard a noise, but before he could react to it, Beggar Man emerged, dragging a struggling Rooster.

"Look what I found," he said, then violently slung Rooster to the floor. Rooster's head struck the floor hard. He looked up; his lip was bleeding.

Tyrone crossed the room and stood over him.

"Get up," he said.

Dazed, Rooster looked up, then struggled to his feet. His eyes were narrowed, and his face was furrowed into a huge, angry frown. "What y'all want?" he snapped.

"Answers," Tyrone said.

"Answers!" Rooster looked at Beggar Man, then at Tyrone. "What kind of answers?"

"Tell me about the girl," Tyrone said.

"I told you . . . I don't know what you talking about."

Tyrone drew closer until the two of them were separated by only inches.

"I think you do," he said.

"And I think you better back up off me." Rooster issued a warning of his own. Suddenly, Beggar Man stepped forward.

"Ah, you a tough guy, hunh . . . a real tough guy."

"Naw," Rooster said. "I ain't tough. I'm just telling y'all to quit riding me . . . that's all."

"And I'm telling you . . . you better start talking," Tyrone said.

"Ain't nothing to talk about," Rooster said. "I told you that before."

"I think you lying," Tyrone said.

"It's a free world," Rooster smarted. "You can think whatever you want to."

Tyrone frowned. A huge wave of anger swelled in him. He drew even closer, until he felt Rooster's breath coming full in his face. He looked deep into Rooster's eyes. Rooster stood motionless, staring back at him. Anger made Tyrone's chest rise and fall, then rise again. He thrust his hand in his waist and removed the gun, then pressed the barrel hard against Rooster's head. He saw Rooster's eyes widen; he heard the breath go out of his lungs; he felt him resign.

"Cap 'im," Beggar Man said.

Rooster's eyes flashed horror. "Hold on, man . . . Wait!"

Tyrone relaxed his grip, yet he held the gun firm against Rooster's temple. In him now was a cold, callous desire to strike out at the world that had stricken him. He felt hopeless, and desperate, and his body was on edge. He sensed himself giving in to a violent impulse; no, a need to hurt, to maim, to kill.

"Talk," he said.

"I done told you all I know."

"Cap 'im," Beggar Man said.

Rooster closed his eyes. His body tensed. And Tyrone tightened his grip on the stock of the pistol. A voice inside his head told him to exact his own justice. His son was going to die. And he would die at the hands of a world he was powerless to touch, and by the deeds of a man, the tracks of whom he could not uncover. He felt his breath coming and going. His chest rising and falling. He heard the intense wail of a raging world echoing loud inside his tormented head. Tyrone wrapped his fingers around the trigger. He felt the tenseness mount. He felt himself squeezing the trigger. He heard Rooster yell.

"Hold on, mister . . . Wait."

"Where P. K.?" Tyrone growled. His jaw was tight. His teeth were clenched. His fiery eyes were red with fury. He was outside of himself now. Yes, Rooster would have to tell him something. He would either tell him something or die. He looked at Rooster, and Rooster looked at him.

"I don't know no P. K.," Rooster said, sticking to his story. "I swear I don't."

"He lying, Ty," Beggar Man said. "Go'n and cap 'im."

Tyrone nodded, and looked at Beggar Man, then at Rooster. Yes, that was what he had to do—kill him. And after him, he would kill others. As many as he could before they came for him. He lowered the gun to his side and stepped back until he was standing directly in front of Rooster. And as he did so, he looked into Rooster's eyes. Then his body stiffened, and as if in a trance, he raised the gun with a slow, steady arm. Inside his chest, he felt his heart pounding. Inside his mind, he heard a calming voice telling him that yes, this was as it had to be. He aimed, then closed one eye, preparing to shoot. He saw Rooster's large brown eyes widened; he saw his mouth opened. He heard his terror-stricken voice scream.

"Wait, mister . . . Please . . . Don't shoot me . . . I'll tell you what I know."

Tyrone lowered the gun.

"Where P. K.?" he asked.

"Mister, I don't know no P. K. I swear I don't."

"He lying," Beggar Man said.

Tyrone looked at him long and hard.

"But you do know the girl, don't you?"

He paused and waited, but Rooster did not answer.

"He know her," Beggar Man said. "He know her. Ole man Charlie said so."

"Is that right?" Tyrone asked.

Rooster lowered his eyes and dropped his head. A quiet moment passed. Then, his lips parted. "Yeah," he whispered. "I know her."

Tyrone looked at him with cold, murderous eyes. "Thought you said you didn't."

"I know," Rooster said in a weak, unsteady voice. "But I do."

"So you lied."

"Yeah, he lied," Beggar Man said. "Nigger ain't been doing nothing but lying since we met him. One goddamn lie after the other one."

"I was scared." Rooster tried to make him understand.

"Scared," Tyrone said. "Scared of what?"

There was silence. Rooster didn't answer.

"What happened that night?" Tyrone asked. His tone was low, menacing.

"I don't know," Rooster said. "I just don't know."

"Don't lie to me," Tyrone said.

"Mister, I ain't lying."

"Give me the gun, Ty," Beggar Man said. "Let me kill 'im . . . Let me kill this sorry ass nigger."

"Mister, I'm telling you the truth," Rooster said. "I swear I am."

"Who killed the girl?" Tyrone was blunt.

"I don't know," Rooster said. "I swear I don't."

"Ole Charlie said he seen you with her," Tyrone said in a tone of voice implying Rooster's involvement. "He said he seen you with her the night she died."

"Well, I'll just be goddamned," Beggar Man said. "He killed her, Ty. This goddamn nigger killed her."

"No," Rooster said. "I picked her up that night . . . and I dropped her off . . . But I didn't hurt her . . . I swear I didn't."

Suddenly, Tyrone could feel his heart pumping fast.

"You picked her up in front of the store?"

"Yeah," he said. "I picked her up. But I didn't hurt her. I didn't."

"In Peterson's blue truck?"

"Yeah," he said. "Mister, you got to believe me. I didn't hurt her. I swear I didn't. I swear before Almighty God."

"He lying, Ty," Beggar Man said. "Nigger lying through his goddamn teeth."

"No, I ain't," he said. "I telling the truth, mister. I swear I am."

"Why?" Tyrone asked.

Rooster looked at him, confused. He did not understand the question. "Why, what?" he said.

"Why did you pick her up?"

"She flagged me down," he said, looking Tyrone directly in the eye. "She wanted a ride. So I picked her up and dropped her off. That's why."

"Dropped her off where?" Tyrone asked.

"At Peterson's house."

"Alive?"

"Yeah!" Rooster exclaimed, his voice high, shrill, excited. "She was alive . . . I didn't hurt her. Mister, you got to believe me . . . I didn't hurt her."

Tyrone paused, thinking. "So, she worked that night?" he said.

"I guess so," he said. "I don't know . . . I just dropped her off . . . I don't know."

"How long was she up there?" Tyrone asked.

"I don't know," he said. "I left."

"But Peterson saw her."

"I guess so."

"What you mean, you guess?"

"Mister, I just dropped her off at the end of the road. His car was home . . . I guess he saw her . . . I don't know."

"But you saw her go in the house."

"Yeah," he said. "I waited just in case he wasn't there. But she went in and didn't come back out. So I left."

"But somebody up there saw her."

"Yeah," he said. "I guess . . . I don't know. She went in the house and didn't come out . . . I guess they did . . . But I don't know."

Tyrone looked at Beggar Man, then at Rooster.

"Come on," he said. "Let's go."

"Go where?" Rooster asked.

"To town," Tyrone said.

"For what?" Rooster wanted to know.

"To see the chief of police," Tyrone told him.

"The chief . . . Hell no!" Rooster shook his head. "I ain't going . . . un unnh . . . noway."

"You going," Tyrone said. "And when you get there, you gone tell this to the police just like you told it to me."

"Un unnh . . . No . . . If I do that, they gone think I did it."

"That ain't my problem," Tyrone said. "That ain't my problem at all."

"I didn't hurt that girl," Rooster said. "I swear I didn't."

"I don't care who hurt her," Tyrone said. "As long as everybody know my son didn't."

"I ain't going," Rooster said.

Tyrone raised the gun so that Rooster could see it.

"You going," he said. "You going one way or the other."

He said that, and then it was quiet. They regarded each other for a moment, and then, as they turned to leave, Tyrone's roving eyes spied a telephone on the small table next to the sofa. Without warning, he crossed the room and lifted the receiver, then dialed Captain Jack's office. A woman answered.

"Captain Jack there?" he said.

"He's with a client." she told him.

"Is this Miss Rainer?" he asked.

"Yes, it is." She identified herself.

"Miss Rainer, this Tyrone," he said. "Tyrone Stokes."

"Hello, Mr. Stokes," she said. "How are you?"

"Fine," he said. "Can you give Captain Jack a message for me?"

"Sure," she said. "What's the message?"

"Tell him to meet me at the police station."

"The police station!" she exclaimed.

"Yeah," he said. His voice was urgent. "I should be there in fifteen minutes."

"What's going on?" she asked, then waited.

"Tell him to hurry," Tyrone said. "Tell him I found the killer."

"No," he heard Rooster protest behind him. "I didn't kill her . . . I swear I didn't."

"Shut up, nigger," Beggar Man said. "Shut the hell up."

Chapter
33

Near the police station, Tyrone walked along the sidewalk with his eyes fixed on the small building just ahead. Rooster was behind him, and Beggar Man was behind Rooster, pressing him close, making sure that he did not do something stupid, like break and run before he had done what they had brought him there to do. At the building, Tyrone opened the door, then stopped abruptly. He looked at Rooster. Rooster's shifty eyes were open wide. And Tyrone could see that he was jumpy, uneasy. He grabbed Rooster underneath the collar and pulled him close.

"Git this right," he said. "Git it right or you gone have to deal with me."

The main office was located on the first floor just off a short hall. As the three of them approached the entrance, Tyrone could hear the sound of two men inside the room talking. And though he could not see them, he was sure they were white. He could tell by the intonations of their voices and by the all too familiar sound of their thick southern drawls. When he appeared before the door, he was all but sure their conversation was not over, but as soon as they saw him, they stopped talking. Both of them were police officers in uniform. The one closest to him could have been performing the duties of a clerk; he was standing behind an elongated counter recording information on a pad. The one farthest away was sitting at a desk in front of a computer screen, typing.

"Can I help you?" the one closest to him muttered. He was big and burly and did not appear to be too friendly.

"Need to see the chief," Tyrone said.

"'Bout what?" the officer asked. He had stopped what he was doing and was looking at Tyrone with large, suspicious eyes.

"It's personal," Tyrone said.

The officer looked at him, then at Rooster, then at Beggar Man. "Chief ain't available," he said. "Maybe I can help."

"No," Tyrone said. "Need to see the chief."

"I told you he ain't available," the officer said.

"Tell 'im my name Stokes," Tyrone said. "Tyrone Stokes."

The officer frowned. "That supposed to mean something?" he asked. The officer sitting farthest away chuckled, amused.

"Just appreciate if you tell him," Tyrone said.

When the officer behind the desk had chuckled, the one standing behind the counter had turned and looked at him and laughed, too. But when Tyrone spoke again, he whirled back around and stared at him, dumbfounded. "You hard of hearing?" he asked.

"Naw," Tyrone said. "I hear just fine."

"Then, what part of he's not available don't you understand?"

"I understand," Tyrone said. "Just need to see the chief, that's all."

Perturbed, the officer opened his mouth to say something else, but before he could, the door behind him opened, and the chief of police walked out, followed by Captain Jack. Tyrone looked at the chief, then at Captain Jack. Captain Jack nodded but did not speak. He and the chief had been drinking coffee. The chief was still holding his cup. Captain Jack was not.

"Chief, these people say they want to see you," the officer said. "They won't tell me what it's about." He paused and looked at Tyrone. "That one there say his name *Stokes*." He emphasized Stokes, and Tyrone knew that he was mocking him. "Tyrone Stokes."

He said that, and the officer at the desk chuckled again. The chief walked around the counter, and Captain Jack followed him.

"What can I do for you?" the chief asked.

Tyrone glanced at the chief and then at Captain Jack. He knew they had been discussing him. He could tell by the expression on Captain Jack's face. Tyrone stepped aside, and Beggar Man nudged Rooster forward.

"He got something to tell you," Tyrone said.

Rooster looked at the chief, then dropped his gaze.

"Well," the chief said after a moment had passed. "What is it?"

Rooster did not look up. His eyes glared at the floor.

"Go 'n," Tyrone said. "Tell 'im."

There was silence.

Tyrone saw the chief look at Captain Jack. Then he saw Captain Jack hunch his shoulders and shake his head.

"Well, you got something to say to me or not?" the chief growled.

"Tell him," Tyrone said. "Tell him right now."

They waited, but Rooster remained quiet.

"Mr. Stokes, what is this all about?" Captain Jack broke the silence. The chief took a sip of his coffee. Tyrone could see that he was agitated.

"He did it," Tyrone said. "He did it . . . not Marcus."

Suddenly, the room grew quiet, and all eyes fell on Rooster.

"No . . . ," he said. "I didn't . . . I swear I didn't."

"Didn't what?" the chief asked, his tone indicating confusion.

"He picked her up that night," Tyrone said. "He did it . . . not Marcus."

Captain Jack looked at Tyrone.

"How do you know that?" he asked, stunned.

"He told me," Tyrone said.

"Jack, what's going on here?" the chief said. He looked at Captain Jack, but Captain Jack was not looking at him. He was looking at Rooster.

"Is that true?" Captain Jack asked Rooster. "Did you know Amy Talbert . . . Did you pick her up that night?"

Rooster's eyes widened; he began to fidget.

"It's true," Tyrone blurted. "He admitted it a little while ago."

Rooster shook his head again. Then looked up, then back down.

"He lying," Tyrone said. "He know he lying."

"What happened to your lip?" the chief asked Rooster.

"Nigger fell," Beggar Man said.

"And who are you?" the chief asked, his angry eyes on Beggar Man.

"A friend," Beggar Man said.

The chief studied Beggar Man; then his eyes strayed back to Rooster's lip.

"They do that to you?" he asked.

Rooster gave a nervous nod but did not speak.

"He lying," Tyrone said. "We didn't touch him."

"Conversation over," the chief said.

"No," Tyrone said. "He did it."

"Conversation over," the chief repeated himself.

"He picked her up that night," Tyrone said. "He already admitted it. Go on and ask him . . . Ask him if he didn't pick her up . . . Ask him."

"Well," Captain Jack said. "Did you?"

Rooster didn't answer. Instead, he kept his eyes averted.

"He did it," Beggar Man said. "I heard him say it with my own ears."

"Did he admit it before or after he fell?" the chief asked.

"We didn't touch him," Tyrone said again.

"Harland, if this is true, you know it changes everything," Captain Jack said.

"Jack, I don't know what in the hell you are trying to pull here," the chief said. "But I don't believe one goddamn word they're saying."

"It's true," Tyrone said. "He did it . . . not Marcus."

"Harland, I resent that," Captain Jack said. "I resent it. I do."

"Well, you're gonna just have to resent it," the chief said. "Because, I don't believe 'em . . . I don't believe 'em one bit." He turned toward Rooster. "Look at that boy's mouth, Jack. Hell, look like they done beat him damn near to death." The chief paused, then looked at Beggar Man. "Boy, ain't I seen you before? Ain't you been in my jail?"

"Ain't been in your jail or nobody else's," Beggar Man lied.

The chief stared at him long and hard; Beggar Man stared back.

"Watch yourself, boy," the chief said. "You best watch yourself, now."

Beggar Man's lips parted as if he was about to say something else, but before he could, Tyrone interrupted him.

"You ain't got to believe us, Chief," he said. "You can go ask Charlie Edwards. He'll tell you them two knew each other . . . He seen 'em together . . . He seen 'em together that night."

"He told you that?" Captain Jack asked.

"Yes, sir," Tyrone said.

"You sure he said he saw them?"

"Yes, sir," Tyrone said again. "He said he saw 'em . . . said he saw just as plain as day . . . go ask him. You ain't got to believe me. He'll tell you."

Captain Jack looked at Rooster. "Is that right?" he said. "Were you with Amy Talbert the day she was murdered?"

"Now, hold on, Jack," the chief said. "What are you trying to pull here?"

"Make him answer my question," Captain Jack said.

"I ain't gone do no such thing."

"Harland, if this boy right here picked that girl up that night, then that changes everything. And you know it."

"That don't change a goddamn thing," the chief said. "Now, I don't know what they trying to pull here . . . But that boy over there in Shreveport done been tried and found guilty in a court of law . . . And I'll be goddamn if I'm gone let y'all come in here and muddy the water with some goddamn stunt like this."

"Make him answer the question, Harland."

"Don't tell me how to do my job, Jack," the chief said. "Last time I looked, I was still the goddamn chief of police around here."

"Harland, I'm just trying to get at the truth."

"The truth. Hell, we already know the truth. That Stokes boy killed Amy Talbert. A jury convicted him. The judge sentenced him. And he gone die tomorrow afternoon. Now, that's the large and the small of it."

"Maybe," Captain Jack said. "And maybe not. Just might be that this fellow here knows a little bit more than he's telling."

"Ain't no might to it," Tyrone said.

The chief looked at Rooster. "Son, did they threaten you?"

Rooster nodded but did not speak.

"That's what I thought," the chief said. "Jack, this is a classic case of coercion. Plain and simple."

"He lying," Tyrone said.

"Like hell he is," the chief said.

"Harland, I don't understand this," Captain Jack said. "I don't understand it at all. We just found out that a witness that none of us knew about saw this man here and Amy Talbert together the night she was killed. Now, I'll be damned if that don't change things."

"Well, Jack, you're just gonna have to be damned," the chief said.

"Come on Harland," Captain Jack said. "Do your job."

"Goddamnit, Jack, don't push me."

"Ask him if he knew her," Tyrone said.

"What?" The chief whirled and looked at him with eyes red with anger.

"My son didn't know her," Tyrone explained. "He didn't know that Talbert girl."

"So," the chief said. "What does that prove?"

"She knew her killer," Tyrone said.

"You don't know that," the chief challenged him.

"Yes, sir," Tyrone said. "She knew him. That's why she got in the truck. She knew the person that picked her up. She didn't know my son."

"She got in the truck because your son abducted her," the chief said.

"No," Tyrone said. "She hitched a ride with Rooster. Ole Charlie seen 'em in the truck together . . . Ask him . . . he'll tell you."

"Don't need to ask him," the chief said. "Two witnesses testified under oath that they saw Amy Talbert get in the truck with your son at that store just before she was killed."

"And ole Charlie said he saw her in the truck with this boy here," Tyrone said. "He said he saw her, and I believe him."

"Can't be," the chief said.

"He saw her," Tyrone said.

"Where?" the chief said. "Where did he say he saw her?"

"At Peterson's place," Tyrone said.

"You mean Mr. Peterson, don't you?" the chief snapped. Tyrone looked at him but did not answer. Out of the corner of his eye, he thought he saw Captain Jack looking at Rooster. He turned his head and looked. Yes, Captain Jack was looking at Rooster. But he wasn't seeing him. He was processing what he was hearing.

"What time?" Captain Jack asked, seeking clarification.

"Sir?" Tyrone said. He did not understand the question.

"What time did he see them?"

"'Bout three-fifteen."

"He told you that?"

"Yes, sir."

"Did ole Charlie fall down, too?" the chief asked.

Tyrone looked at the chief but did not answer.

"Harland, I want Charlie Edwards picked up," Captain Jack said. "I want to talk to him. And I want to talk to him right now."

"Ah, come on, Jack," the chief said. "You can't be serious."

"Harland . . . I mean it . . . I want him picked up."

Tyrone swallowed. He looked at Captain Jack, then at the chief. He heard the chief sigh.

"All right, Jack," the chief said. "You want to play games . . . I'll play 'em with you." The chief turned toward the counter. "Billy Ray . . . go pick him up," he said to one of the officers. The chief looked at his watch. "Ain't five yet. He ought to still be out at Peterson's."

The deputy left, and the chief looked at Captain Jack.

"Hell, Jack," he said. "Even if ole Charlie come in here and say exactly what they say he said, it still won't change a thing. Still be his word against theirs. Two against one."

"That's not true," Tyrone said.

Suddenly the chief whirled toward him. "What did you say, boy?" He asked. His eyes were narrowed; his brow furrowed. "You calling me a lie?"

"No, sir," Tyrone said. "It's just that somebody else saw 'em."

"Somebody else!" the chief exclaimed, perturbed.

"Yes, sir," Tyrone said.

"Who?"

"Miss Irene."

"Miss who?" The chief frowned. He did not recognize the name.

"Irene Chamberland," Captain Jack said. "Mabel Wilkes's maid."

The chief's angry eyes fell on Captain Jack. "Guess you know about this, too, hunh, Jack?"

"I know about it," he said.

There was a brief moment of silence. Then the chief turned his attention back toward Tyrone.

"You talked to Miss Chamberland?" he said.

"Yes, sir," Tyrone said. He paused and waited. When the chief didn't say anything, he resumed again. "She said she was in the window when it happened. She said the girl and the driver acted like they knew each other. She said the two of them talked before the girl got in the truck. She said the truck was dark blue, not black."

There was an interval of silence. Then the chief spoke again.

"Jack," he sighed softly.

"Yeah, Chief?"

"How old would you say Irene is?"

"I don't know," Captain Jack said. "Fifty-five . . . sixty."

"Fifty-five . . . sixty," The chief repeated.

"Something like that."

"And how old would you say the two witnesses were who testified at the trial?" the chief asked.

"I don't know, Harland," Captain Jack said. "They were your witnesses."

"Would you say about fifteen or sixteen?"

"Sounds about right," Captain Jack said. "Why?"

"Well, Jack." The chief smirked. "I don't know about you, but as far as I'm concerned, I'd put my money on them young eyes any day."

"Well, Harland, unfortunately, we're not talking about your money. We're talking about my client's life. Old eyes or not, I want to talk to her."

"All right, Jack," the chief said. "If that's the way you want it."

"That's the way I want it," Captain Jack said.

The chief turned and faced the officer standing behind the counter.

"Randy."

"Yeah, Chief."

"When you get a minute, radio Billy Ray and tell him to pick up Irene Chamberland after he drops Charlie off."

"Sure, Chief."

The chief turned to leave, but Randy stopped him.

"What you want me to do with them?"

The chief looked at Tyrone, then at Beggar Man.

"Put them two in the interview room . . . and put him back there in that spare office."

"Yes, sir, Chief."

"And, Randy."

"Yeah, Chief."

"Call me when Billy Ray makes it back with Charlie. Jack and me will be in my office."

Chapter 34

It was a little before six when the deputy and Charlie made it back to the police station. Tyrone and Beggar Man had been moved to the interview room. Rooster was still out front. And Captain Jack and the chief had gone back into the chief's office. The door to the interview room was open, and Tyrone could see the deputy when he walked in with Charlie. He was walking behind Charlie with his right hand on Charlie's back. And Charlie, tense and stiff, was walking with his shoulders stooped and his head hung. Tyrone, leaning forward, saw the officer guide Charlie to the counter, then stop.

"Is that Charlie Edwards?" he heard the officer behind the desk ask.

"Yeah," Billy Ray told him. "It's him."

"You pick up the lady yet?" he asked.

"Not yet," Billy Ray said. "On my way right now."

There was a brief silence. Then Billy Ray spoke again.

"Well," Billy Ray said, then waited.

"Well what?" the other officer asked.

"What you want me to do with him?"

"Put him in the interview room with the others. I'll tell the chief he's here."

The interview room was a large, rectangular-shaped room that had no windows and no furnishings save for a plain metal table and six wooden chairs that had been placed in the center of the room. Beggar Man and Tyrone had been sitting on either side of the table talking, but as soon as the officer entered with Charlie, Beggar Man rose from the table and moved to the far corner of the room and lit a cigarette. The officer told Charlie to be seated, and the old man sat on the opposite side of the table, directly across from the empty chair that Beggar Man had vacated. After he was seated, Tyrone looked at him. From the looks of things, they had taken him directly out of the potato field. His face and hands were dirty, his hair had not been combed, and his sweaty body reeked of the odor of a man who had been toiling in the hot sun all day. In his eyes was a look that Tyrone had seen a thousand times before. This was the first time that he had been in a police station. No, he had not said so, at least not with his mouth. But he had said so with his eyes, and his posture, and the all too familiar expression etched on his face. Yes, Tyrone had seen that look a thousand times, in a thousand different jails, in a thousand different towns. This was his first time. And they had not told him what this was all about. And he was scared. Real scared.

"You smoke?" Tyrone broke the silence.

Charlie nodded. He couldn't speak. His throat was too dry; his tongue, too thick; his nerves, too frazzled.

"Beggar Man, give the man a smoke."

Beggar Man raised the cigarette to his mouth, took a long draw, then exhaled hard. As the small rings of smoke slowly rose toward the ceiling, he removed another cigarette from the pack, crossed the room, and handed it to Charlie. When Charlie placed the end of the unlit cigarette in his mouth, Beggar Man removed his and touched the hot end to the tip of Charlie's. Instantly, Charlie's dimpled jaws deflated as he sucked hard until the tip of his cigarette glowed red hot with fire. Calmed by the feel of soothing smoke passing over his thick, tense lips, he leaned back against the chair, and the taut muscles in his tense face began to relax. He took a second draw, but before he could exhale, the chief walked in, followed closely by Captain Jack.

"Charlie Edwards," the chief said.

"Yes, sir," Charlie said, leaping to his feet, the cigarette dangling from his hand and smoke seeping from his mouth.

"I'm Chief Jefferies . . . and this is Attorney Johnson."

Charlie nodded timidly but did not speak.

"Please . . . sit down."

"Yes, sir," Charlie said, sitting.

Beggar had been standing also, but when Charlie took his seat, he sat back in his original seat next to Tyrone. And after he was situated, the chief took a seat at one end of the table, the one closest to the door, and Captain Jack took a seat at the other.

"You still work for Paul Peterson?" the chief asked. He was looking at Charlie, but Charlie was avoiding looking at him.

"Yes, sir," Charlie mumbled, then swallowed hard.

The chief turned and looked in Tyrone's direction.

"Do you know these two fellows?"

Charlie glanced at Tyrone and Beggar Man, then quickly lowered his eyes. "Yes, sir," he said.

"What about Amy Talbert?" the chief asked. "You know her?"

"Seen her before," Charlie said. "But I don't know her."

"Where?"

"Sir?"

"Where have you seen her?"

"Up to Mr. Peterson's."

"What was she doing up there?" the chief asked.

"She use to worked up there," Charlie said.

"Doing what?" the chief asked.

"Baby-sitting his kids. Far as I know."

The chief paused. A quiet moment passed.

"You know Benny Jones?" he asked.

"Yes, sir," Charlie said.

"How do you know him?" the chief asked.

"We work together."

There was silence.

"You ever see him and the Talbert girl together?"

"Yes, sir," Charlie said. "I seen 'em together."

"I told you," Tyrone said. "I told you he was with her."

"Where?" The chief asked.

"Up to Mr. Peterson's."

"When?"

"Sir?"

"When did you see them?"

"Seen them lots of time."

"Together?" Captain Jack interrupted.

"Yes, sir," Charlie said. He glanced at Captain Jack, then looked away.

"Benny and the Talbert girl." Captain Jack sought clarity.

"Yes, sir," Charlie said.

"Did you see them the day that Amy Talbert disappeared?" the chief asked.

"Yes, sir."

"Where?"

"They was in Mr. Peterson's truck."

"In his truck?"

"Yes, sir."

"You sure?"

"Yes, sir . . . Rooster . . . I mean Benny . . . let her off in front of the house."

"What house?"

"Mr. Peterson's house."

"You saw that?" the chief said.

"Yes, sir."

"What happened after he let her out?"

"She went in the house, and he waited a little while. Then when she didn't come back out, he pulled off."

"And you saw that?" the chief said.

"Yes, sir."

"About what time was that?" Captain Jack asked.

"Two or three o'clock."

"Well, was it two or three?"the chief wanted to know.

"I believe it was three."

"You believe?" the chief said.

"Yes, sir."

"But you don't know?" the chief said.

"I'm pretty sho'," Charlie said.

"But you're not positive?" The chief pressed him.

"No, sir," Charlie said. "I'm not."

"Well, are you sure it was him that you saw and not somebody else?" The chief continued to challenge him.

"Yes, sir," he said. "I'm sure."

"How close were you?" The chief asked.

"Not too close."

"Then, how do you know it was him."

"I just know."

"You just know," the chief said, his voice slightly raised.

"Yes, sir," Charlie said.

"When did you find out that Amy Talbert was missing?"

"I heard about it the next day."

"Did you tell anybody that you had seen her and Benny Jones together the day before?"

"No, sir."

"Why not?"

"I don't know . . . I just didn't."

"A girl was missing," the chief said. "And you had seen her the day before. And you didn't tell anybody?"

"No, sir."

"What about after her body was found . . . Did you tell anybody then?"

"No, sir."

"Why not?" the chief wanted to know.

"I just didn't."

"You just didn't."

"No, sir."

The chief paused.

"Did these two threaten you?" he asked, looking in Tyrone's direction.

"No, sir."

"They pay you to come in here and say this?"

"No, sir, Chief," Charlie said. "Ain't nobody paid me nothing."

"You're lying."

"No, sir. I ain't."

"You didn't see this boy that night, did you?"

"Yes, sir. I did."

"I think you're lying."

"No, sir, Chief," Charlie said. "I saw him . . . I saw him and the girl."

"So, you're saying Benny Jones here killed her?"

"No, sir."

"Well, what are you saying?"

"Just that I saw them."

"I say you're lying."

"No, sir. I'm telling the truth."

"What time did she leave?"

"I don't know."

"Of course you don't," the chief said. "Because you're lying."

"No, sir," Charlie said. "I ain't."

"What was she wearing?" the chief fired another question.

"Sir?"

"The night you saw her," the chief said. "What was she wearing?"

"I don't remember."

"You don't remember?"

"No, sir."

"You didn't see them, did you?"

"Yes, sir," Charlie said. "I did."

"What time did he leave?"

"Not long after he dropped her off."

"What time was that?" the chief asked.

"I don't know," Charlie said.

"You don't know."

"No, sir," Charlie said. "He didn't stay but a few minutes."

"What time did she leave?"

"I don't know."

"You don't know."

"No, sir."

"Could she have left immediately?"

"Yes, sir . . . I guess."

"Did she?"

"I don't know."

"You don't know?" the chief said again.

"No, sir," Charlie said.

"How long does it take to get to town from Peterson's place?"

"'Bout ten or fifteen minutes . . . I reckon."

"So, if he dropped her off at two, like you said he did, she could have left Peterson's and made it back to town by two-fifteen or two-twenty. Couldn't she?"

"Yes, sir, I guess."

"Just in time for Marcus Stokes to have snatched her and killed her." There was silence.

"Like I said, Jack, this don't change a goddamn thing."

"What color was that truck?" Captain Jack asked Charlie.

"Blue," Charlie said.

"You sure?" Captain Jack said.

"Yes, sir," Charlie said. "Dark blue."

"Harland," Captain Jack said, turning and facing the chief, "I think it does."

Suddenly, the door behind them opened, and the officer poked his head in.

"Chief, Irene Chamberland's here."

The chief looked at Captain Jack.

"You done?" he asked.

"For now," Captain Jack said.

The chief looked at the officer, then at Charlie.

"Put him in the other room . . . and send her in."

Irene walked into the room, clutching her purse and looking about. Unlike Charlie, she did not look timid; instead, she looked angry. Angry because she had put in a long day and she was ready to go home. Angry because they had picked her up, in a police car, in broad daylight, at her house. And angry because she had trusted Tyrone to keep what she had told him to himself or at least to keep her name out of it, and he had betrayed her. Yes, she was angry with him, and she stared at him to let him know.

"Have a seat," the chief said, pointing to the empty chair that Charlie had just vacated. She took her seat without speaking.

"Mrs. Chamberland, I'm Chief Jefferies . . . That's Attorney Johnson . . . That's Mr. Stokes . . . And that's a friend of Mr. Stokes's. I believe Mr. Johnson would like to ask you a couple of questions."

The chief paused, but Irene didn't speak. She was staring at Tyrone.

"Mrs. Chamberland," Captain Jack began. "Mr. Stokes tells me you saw Amy Talbert the day she was abducted."

"Yes, sir," she said. "I did."

"Tell me what you saw."

"I seen a white gal walking down the street. Then I seen a man in a blue truck pass and stop like he knew her. Then I seen her run up to the truck. And they talked a while. Then she got in. And they drove off."

"You say the truck was blue."

"Yes, sir. Dark blue. Dark blue with them ole white wall tires on it."

"Do you remember what the girl was wearing?"

"Yes, sir."

"What?" he asked.

"A pair of them old blue jean shorts. A little ole white top. And no shoes."

"And what time was that?"

"Little bit before three."

Captain Jack looked at the chief, then back at her.

"Are you sure?" he said.

"Yes, sir."

"How sure?" Captain Jack asked.

"I get off at three," Irene said. "And I had gone in the parlor to get my things ready to go—"

"And that's when you looked out of the window," Captain Jack interrupted.

"Yes, sir," she said.

"Any particular reason you remembered Amy Talbert?" he asked.

"Yes, sir," she said, then waited.

"Well," Captain Jack said. "Please tell us."

"The way she was dressed," Irene said. "And the way she was walking."

"What do you mean?"

"That child was half naked," Irene explained. "And doing just some twisting."

"And that stood out for you."

"Yes, sir."

"Mrs. Chamberland, do you remember what day that was?" Captain Jack said.

"Yes, sir."

"What day was it?" he asked.

"Monday."

"Are you sure it was Monday?" he said. "Could it have been Thursday or Friday?"

"No, sir," she said. "It was Monday."

"Well, how can you be so sure?"

"On account of I went to church the night before."

"Excuse me?" he said.

"We had a big program at the church Sunday night. And it didn't turn out 'til late. So I was tired all the next day at work. That's why I was looking out the window. I was looking to see if Albert had made it here yet. He picks me up at that store across the street. And I was hoping that he wasn't late . . . 'cause I was some tired."

"What kind of truck was it?" the chief asked.

"Sir?"

"The truck that you say you saw Amy Talbert get into . . . What kind was it? Ford . . . Chevrolet . . . GMC . . . what?"

"I wouldn't know one from the other," Irene said. "All I know is it was blue."

"Well, what did the driver look like?" the chief asked.

"I don't know," she said. "I couldn't really see him."

"You couldn't see him." The chief repeated her admission.

"No, sir."

"You just saw the truck?"

"Yes, sir," she said. "That's all."

"At the time, did you tell anybody about this?" the chief asked.

"No, sir," she said. "I didn't."

"Why not?" he wanted to know.

"I just didn't."

"A child was missing," the chief said. "And you saw her get in a truck with someone. And you didn't tell it."

"No, sir."

"Don't you think that would have been the Christian thing to do?"

"Yes, sir," she said. "I guess."

There was silence.

"How long have you been wearing glasses?" the chief asked.

"Since I was a child," she said.

"You near-sighted or far-sighted."

"Near-sighted," she said.

"So, you have problems seeing things that are far away?"

"Yes, sir," she said. "If I don't have on my glasses."

"Did you have 'em on that day?"

"Yes, sir," she said.

"How do you know?" the chief asked. "That was five years ago."

"I always wear 'em," she said. " 'cept when I go to bed."

"You do."

"Yes, sir."

The chief looked up toward the ceiling, thinking. Then he looked back at her. "How far would you say Miss Wilkes's house is from the road."

"Not that far," she said.

"About how far?"

"Don't know exactly."

"If you had to guess," the chief said.

"Don't 'spect it's no farther than from here to the other side of the road out yonder," she said. "If I just had to guess."

The chief turned and looked at Captain Jack. "Jack, that's a hundred feet easy."

Captain Jack looked at the chief, then at Irene. "Miss Chamberland, you're not color blind, are you?" he asked.

"No, sir," she said. "Least not far as I know."

"So your eye condition does not affect your ability to see colors, does it?"

"No, sir," she said. "It don't."

"And you saw Amy Talbert get into a blue truck, didn't you?" Captain Jack prodded.

"Yes, sir," she said. "I did."

"You're sure?"

"I'm positive."

"At or around three o'clock?"

"Yes, sir," she said. "Just before three."

"How can you be so sure?" Captain Jack asked.

" 'Cause I get off at three."

Captain paused and looked at the chief. "Harland, bring Benny back in here," he said. "I want to ask him a question."

"Billy Ray," the chief's voice spilled out into the hall.

"Yes, sir, Chief."

"Bring Benny out of that back office."

When they brought him back into the room, he was visibly nervous. The chief did not invite him to sit; instead, Benny remained standing just inside the doorway.

"What color is your truck?" Captain Jack asked him.

"Ain't got no truck," Rooster said.

"He lying," Tyrone said. "That truck behind his house right now. He tried to hide it. But I saw it . . . a blue truck with whitewall tires."

"Come on, Jack," the chief said. "What's the point of all this. She say Amy got into a blue truck. They say she got into a black one. Her word against theirs. What's the point?"

"The point is, he picked her up that night. Not my client."

"She didn't say that," the chief insisted. "She said she saw a blue truck. She didn't say nothing about no driver. Nothing except she didn't see him."

"She said she saw this boy here pick Amy up at three, and ole Charlie said he saw him let her off at Paul's place a few minutes later. Now, that's two unconnected witnesses with two compatible stories."

"Now, Jack, that's not what was said. She said she saw somebody pick Amy up at three. She didn't see the driver. But the witnesses who testified at the trial did. It was Marcus Stokes . . . Now, Charlie said he saw somebody let Amy off at two or three. He don't really know. And even if he did see her with somebody other than Stokes—and I'm not saying he did—more than likely it was two, not three . . . Plenty of time for her to have made it back to town before he abducted her."

"Is there a truck behind your house?" Captain Jack asked Rooster.

Tyrone looked at Rooster, and he could see that the man was sweating.

"It ain't mines," Rooster said. "It's Mr. Peterson's."

"Well, what are you doing with it?"

"It's his work truck . . . He let me keep it sometimes to run his errands."

"Were you running errands in it the day Amy Talbert was killed?" Captain Jack asked.

"I don't remember."

"Chief, I want to see that truck," Captain Jack said.

"Jack, come on."

"This changes everything." Captain Jack repeated his old refrain.

"It don't change nothing." The chief was adamant.

"Harland, you heard 'em. They saw this fellow here with Amy Talbert. They saw him and her together . . . in a blue truck . . . right around the time she was killed. Harland, you heard 'em."

"And I don't believe one word they said," the chief snapped. "I say they are both lying. And I say he's behind it." The chief looked at Tyrone, but Tyrone didn't speak. Captain Jack did.

"Mrs. Chamberland, are you lying to us?" he asked.

"No, sir," she said. "I'm a Christian woman. And I don't lie."

"Maybe not under normal circumstances," the chief challenged her. "But these ain't normal circumstances . . . now, are they?" He paused and looked at Tyrone again. "He threatened you, too . . . didn't he?"

"No, sir," she said. "I'm telling the truth."

"Well, if you knew the truth," the chief said, "why haven't you come forward before now."

"Nobody asked me to," she said. "That's why."

"Jack, I smell a rat."

"I want to see that truck," Captain Jack said.

"For what?" the chief asked. "It won't prove a thing."

"I'd like to be the judge of that."

"Jack, I been in this business a long time. And I know a con when I see one."

"Con or no con, I want to see that truck."

"Jack, the timing of this thing stinks to high heaven. And you know it. It's just too much, too fast, and don't none of it add up."

"I want to see that truck," Captain Jack said a fourth time.

"This ain't nothing but smoke and mirrors," the chief mumbled. "Jack, that Stokes boy killed Amy Talbert. He killed her sure as we're standing here. Hell, Jack, we got him on tape."

"Leaving the store," Captain Jack said. "That's all."

"That's enough."

"No, Harland, it's not."

"Jury thought so," the chief said.

"They didn't have all the facts," Captain Jack said. "This changes things."

"Don't change nothing."

"I want to see that truck."

There was silence.

"Harland, we're wasting time."

"Billy Ray," the chief yelled.

Instantly, Billy Ray appeared before the door.

"Yeah, Chief," he said, then waited.

"Take Mr. Jones to his house," the chief said. "Get his truck and bring it back here."

"What kind of truck is it?" Billy Ray asked.

The chief looked at Rooster.

"Dark blue, Ford, pickup," Rooster mumbled.

"Awright, Chief," Billy Ray said. "I'm on it."

Chapter
35

"Harland, I'd like to speak to Mr. Stokes and Mrs. Chamberland in private, if that's all right," Captain Jack said after Billy Ray and Rooster had left the room.

"Help yourself, Jack," the chief said. "I'll be in my office . . . Let me know when they make it back with that truck."

The chief left, but Beggar Man remained sitting quietly. Tyrone watched Captain Jack remove a pipe from his shirt pocket and place it in his mouth, then cup his hand over the bowl and light it.

"What do you think?" Tyrone asked.

"I would feel better if someone else had seen them together . . . someone other than Charlie." He looked at Irene. "You sure you didn't see his face."

"All I seen was that truck," she said. "I told him that the other day."

"Wish we had something else," Captain Jack said. "Something connecting him to the crime."

"Well, that's all I seen," Irene said a second time.

There was silence.

"Is it enough?" Tyrone asked.

"Maybe to get a stay," Captain Jack said. "That's about it."

"What good will that do?"

"It'll buy us a little time."

"How much time?"

"Maybe a week or two," Captain Jack said. "No more than that."

"He know something," Tyrone said. "If we could just get him to talk."

"Did you hit him?"

"Naw, I didn't hit him."

"Did he?" Captain Jack asked, looking at Beggar Man.

Tyrone shook his head.

"Well, don't," Captain Jack said. "That'll ruin everything. If it hasn't already. A confession is no good if it's coerced."

"Maybe there's another way," Tyrone said. He had an idea.

"Such as?" Captain Jack asked, his interest piqued.

"A lie detector test."

Captain Jack shook his head. "Won't work."

"Why not?"

"It's voluntary," he said. "We can't make him submit to it."

"He doesn't know that," Tyrone said, indicating his willingness to be deceptive.

"The chief would tell him," Captain Jack explained. "It's his duty."

Tyrone paused, thinking.

"What if we could prove that he had been with her before?"

"With Amy Talbert?" Captain Jack asked.

"Yes, sir," Tyrone said.

Captain Jack paused, and Tyrone could see that he was thinking.

"How?" Captain Jack asked after a brief silence.

"Charlie said he seen them together lots of times."

"You think they were an item?"

"Don't know," Tyrone said. "But I know who might."

"Who?" Captain Jack asked.

"The girl," Tyrone told him.

Captain Jack looked at him with confused eyes. "What girl?" he asked.

"The cheerleader," Tyrone said, "Terri La Beaux . . . I mean, Zeno . . . Terri Zeno."

Captain Jack's gray eyes still held a blank stare, and Tyrone could tell that he did not remember.

"I told you about her, remember?"

Captain Jack hesitated, then answered, "She work up there, too?"

"No, sir," Tyrone said. "She was that girl's friend . . . her best friend."

Captain Jack pushed back from the table, then stopped. As he looked at Miss Irene, he raised his hand to his chin, thinking.

"How long did they talk before she got in the truck?"

"Minute or two," Irene said. "Not long."

"Did they touch or act friendly with each other?"

"Not that I remember."

"Excuse me," Captain Jack said, rising to his feet. "I'm going to see if I can get Harland to pick up the girl."

He turned to leave, but Irene stopped him.

"How much longer you gone need me?" she asked.

"Just until the truck comes," Captain Jack said. "Why?"

"Need to call my husband," she said. "He probably worried. I need to let him know what's going on."

"Come with me," he said. "Let's see if they won't let you use the phone."

They left the room, and Beggar Man leaned back in his chair and looked at the clock hanging high on the wall.

"Ty," he called softly.

"Yeah," Tyrone answered him. His voice had a distant drone. He was deep in thought.

"You see the time?"

Tyrone looked at the clock. It was a quarter 'til eight.

"Yeah," he said. "I see it."

Beggar Man lit another cigarette, then lifted it to his mouth and took a puff.

"Well, what you gone do?" he asked.

"Nothing," Tyrone said. "Nothing at all."

He said that, and then it was quiet again. Beggar Man continued to smoke, and Tyrone leaned forward with his elbows on the table and his head resting in his hands. His head was hurting; he closed his eyes and had just begun to massage his temple with the tips of his fingers when Captain Jack walked back in.

"He's on the phone right now . . . But he said he'll send Billy Ray to pick up the girl after he comes back with Benny and the truck."

Tyrone nodded, acknowledging that he had heard him; then all was quiet again. Captain Jack had borrowed a pad and a pen and was feverishly scribbling something on the paper. Tyrone glanced at the pad, but Captain Jack's writing was so bad he could not read it. After a moment of staring at the illegible words, he looked at the clock again. It was eight, his mandated curfew. Suddenly, he felt tense. And in his mind popped a daunting image of his mother anxiously pacing the floor, stopping every now and then to draw back the curtain and look out into the street, all the time frantically praying to God to let her lay eyes on a son that should have been home long ago. In his head, he heard the echoing of a voice. It was loud and clear and menacing: *You gone kill her . . . just like you killed Daddy.*

Inside the other room, he heard the sound of feet on the floor. He turned and looked. They were back. The chief must have already been out front as well, for no sooner had Rooster and the officer entered the station, that the chief poked his head in the interview room and said, "Come on . . . Let's take a look at that truck."

Outside, the moon was out, and the heavens up above were sprinkled with what looked to be thousands of bright shining stars casting their majestic light upon a cool, still night. The chief and Captain Jack led the way. Sandwiched between them was Miss Irene. Tyrone and Beggar Man were behind them. Rooster and Charlie remained inside the building.

In the parking lot, they stopped before the truck which had been parked behind the station, up close to the building, just underneath the light. Both men stepped aside and allowed Irene to step forward.

"Well," Captain Jack said after a moment of silence.

"Looks like it," she said timidly. "But I can't say for sure it's the same truck I saw that night."

"But it was a truck like this?" Captain Jack prodded her.

"Yes, sir," she said. "Just like this."

"Do me a favor," the chief interrupted.

"Yes, sir," she said.

"Turn and face me."

"Yes, sir," she said, complying. And when her back was to the truck, the chief spoke again.

"How long would you say you've been looking at that truck?" he asked.

"You mean, right now, today?"

"Yes, ma'am," he said. "This truck, right here, right now."

"'Bout five minutes . . . I guess."

"Five minutes."

"Yes, sir."

"And how long did you see it that night?"

"A minute or two."

"But nothing like five minutes?" he said.

"No, sir."

"And how close would you say you are to that truck right now?"

"Couple of feet," she said.

"And what about that day?" he asked. "How close were you then?"

"From here to the other side of the road." She repeated her earlier answer.

"About a hundred feet."

"Yes, sir, I guess."

"Without looking," he said, "tell me the make of the truck you just saw."

"I can't."

"What about the model?"

"I don't know."

"What about the year?"

She shook her head.

"Well," he said. "What can you tell me about this truck?"

"It's blue with whitewall tires."

"That's all."

"Yes, sir."

"So any truck that I park here that's blue with whitewall tires would look like the truck you saw that night, wouldn't it?"

"Yes, sir."

"You can't remember anything else?"

She paused, thinking. "No, sir."

"That's it . . . after looking at it for five minutes . . . not more than a couple of feet away . . . just a few minutes ago . . . That's all you can tell me."

"Yes, sir."

"Then, how can you be certain that the truck you say you saw five years ago, from a distance of a hundred feet or more, is identical to this one?"

"It was," she said. "The truck I saw looked just like this one."

"Well, ma'am," the chief said. "I'm almost certain that you would probably say that about any navy blue truck with whitewall tires that I park before you right now. Ma'am, your account just isn't credible."

"Sir, this the truck I saw."

"Ma'am, you can't be sure of that."

"But you are sure that the truck you saw had whitewall tires, aren't you?" Captain Jack said.

"Yes, sir, I am."

"My client's truck had black tires."

"Could've changed them, Jack. He had plenty of time."

"But he didn't," Captain Jack said.

"You can't prove that," the chief said. "No more than you can prove she saw this truck that night. Now, Jack, it's been a long day, and I've gone just about as far as I'm going with this. Miss Irene, thank you for your time. You can go on back inside and wait if you want to. As soon as my officer gets back, I'll have him take you home."

"If it's all right with you," she said, "I'd just as soon call my husband to come get me."

"That'll be just fine," the chief said.

"Harland," Captain Jack said. "I'll be filing a petition for a stay based on these new witnesses first thing in the morning."

"That's your right, Jack. But I won't support it. And I think you know as well as I do that no judge in his right mind will grant it. Not under these circumstances. And not based on what I've seen here."

"I disagree," Captain Jack said.

"Well, that's your right," the chief said again, then paused and looked at his watch. "If you've finished with ole Charlie, I'd just as soon let him go home, too."

"Like to have him look at this truck."

"Don't know why," the chief said. "Don't see what good it'll do."

"Like to have him look at it anyway."

"Suit yourself," the chief said. He removed the walkie-talkie from his waist, raised it to his mouth, and pressed the button.

"Randy."

"Yeah, Chief."

"Send Charlie out here."

"Okay, Chief," Randy's voice boomed through the walkie-talkie. "Will do."

The chief placed the walkie-talkie back on his belt, and a few minutes later, the door to the police station swung open, and Charlie walked out.

"Charlie," Captain Jack spoke first.

"Yes, sir."

"You ever seen this truck before?"

"Yes, sir."

"Where?"

"Up to Mr. Peterson's."

"Is this the truck that Benny was driving the day you saw him and Amy Talbert together?"

"Yes, sir."

"You're sure?"

"Yes, sir, I am."

"Around two o'clock," the chief said.

"Yes, sir . . . I believe so."

There was silence.

"Anything else, Jack?"

Captain Jack shook his head.

"You ride up here with Billy Ray?" the chief asked Charlie.

"No, sir," Charlie said. "I followed him in my truck."

"All right, then," the chief said. "You're free to go."

Chapter 36

After Charlie left, Tyrone did not go back inside the station with the chief. Instead, he lingered near the truck with Beggar Man and Captain Jack, his tense body twisted in knots and his anxious eyes fixated on the highway. Now there was in him no joy or peace, but only fear. For he had seen what he had believed to be two strong witnesses totally dismissed by a chief who, to him, seemed determined to insure that things remained just as they were. As he stood, gazing into the night, a hot wave of rage swept him, and then, as if under a spell, he spun on his heels and kicked the truck hard with his foot. The force of the blow rattled the truck. Captain Jack's eyes bucked; then his lips parted.

"Mr. Stokes," he said, stunned. "Get a hold of yourself. That's not helping matters . . . It's not helping matters at all."

"This ain't right," Tyrone said on the verge of tears. "The chief already got his mind made up. He won't even listen to us."

"Calm down," Captain Jack said. "Let me handle this."

"How can I be calm?" Tyrone asked. "He twisting everything around. He not even trying to hear the truth. He just trying to railroad my son."

"Mr. Stokes, please," Captain Jack pleaded. "I know Harland. You antagonize him, he'll shut this thing down so tight that an army of lawyers won't be able to reopen it. Please . . . Just let me handle it."

"Ty," Beggar Man said. "Think of Marcus."

"But, Mr. Johnson—"

"Mr. Stokes, listen to me," Captain Jack said, his gray eyes staring deep into Tyrone's. "You've got to listen to me."

Tyrone paused and looked at Captain Jack; then his misty eyes fell in surrender.

"With these new developments, we have an excellent chance for a stay," Captain Jack said. "But we don't have much time. And to be honest, we don't have much of a chance without Harland's support . . . We need him." Captain Jack paused to let his words sink in. Then he began again. "Now, I've drafted a letter laying out these new findings. As soon as I've spoken to this last witness, I plan to fax the warden, the D.A.'s office, the governor, the court, Judge Robertson, the media, and any and everybody else who might be able to help. By the airing of the ten o'clock news, I plan to have this broadcast over every news outlet in the state, Mr. Stokes. We have new witnesses. The court will have to consider this . . . The public will demand it. Please, just let me handle this."

Tyrone looked up, thinking. "Do we really have a chance?" he asked.

"I'm not going to lie to you," Captain Jack said. "It's a long shot. But at least it's a shot."

Teary-eyed, Tyrone nodded, then turned and walked to the edge of the road. He needed to be alone. He had gone as far as he could. And now he had but to trust a man for whom he had little trust. And to believe in a system in which he had little belief. He looked at his watch; it was eight-forty. He had just begun to imagine the worst when in the distance he spied two sets of headlights draw nigh, then turn off the highway, and pull into the parking lot.

They were back. And Billy Ray must have alerted the chief from his squad car, for no sooner had Tyrone started back toward them, than he saw the chief exit the police station and approach the squad car. Tyrone looked at Mrs. Zeno. She was still sitting in her car staring straight ahead. Suddenly, a troubling thought occurred to him. What if this did not pan out? What if she had nothing new to add to what had already been said. No, he couldn't think this way, for if she could not say what needed to be said, then he would make Rooster talk. Yes, he would make Rooster admit to them that which he had all ready admitted to him.

A car door opened, then slammed. Mrs. Zeno had climbed out and now stood with uncertainty before the four men.

"Miss Zeno," Captain Jack spoke first.

"Mrs.," she corrected him.

"My apologies," Captain Jack said.

He paused. She remained quiet.

"Did you know Amy Talbert?" he asked.

His question made her squint.

"I knew her," she said. "Why?"

"My apologies again," he said. "Let me introduce myself. My name is Jack Johnson. I'm an attorney. I represent Marcus Stokes."

He paused again, she said nothing.

"How well did you know Amy?"

"We were best friends."

"Do you remember the day she was killed?"

"Yes, sir, I do," she said. She paused and looked at Captain Jack with questioning eyes. "May I ask what this is all about?"

"There have been some new developments," Captain Jack told her. "And we were hoping that maybe you could help us clear some things up."

Terri looked at him, then at Tyrone.

"Did Amy go to school that day?" Captain Jack resumed.

"Yes, sir, she did."

"And what time does school let out?"

"Two-fifteen."

"Two-fifteen." Captain Jack repeated the time.

"Yes, sir," she said. "Two-fifteen."

Captain Jack looked at the chief.

"Harland, Charlie couldn't have seen them at two," he said. "She was still in school . . . had to be three . . . just like Irene said."

"Could have checked out early," the chief said matter-of-factly.

"No, sir," Terri said. "She was there all day. We had last period to-gether."

"Did you talk to her that day?" Captain Jack asked.

"Yes, sir," she said. "We talked."

"She say anything out of the ordinary?"

"I don't know what you mean."

"Did she say anything you found strange?"

"No, sir, she didn't."

"Did Amy Talbert normally discuss her plans with you?" the chief asked.

"Sometimes," Terri said.

There was silence. Then Captain Jack asked his next question.

"Did you know Benny Jones?"

"Yes, sir. I know of him."

"You ever seen him before?"

"Yes, sir. I have."

"You have?"

"Sure," she said. "He picked her up before."

"Excuse me?" Captain Jack said, stunned.

"Amy didn't have a car," she explained. "And if she didn't have a way to work, a lot of times, Mr. Peterson sent Benny to pick her up."

"Were you ever at her house when Benny came to pick her up?"

"Yes, sir."

"Have you ever seen his vehicle?"

"Yes, sir."

"What does he drive?"

"A truck," she said.

"What color?"

She paused and looked up at the ceiling. "Dark blue."

"He did it, Harland . . . He picked her up that day."

"She didn't say that," the chief said.

"You sure the truck was blue?" Captain Jack asked.

"Yes, sir," she said. "I'm sure."

"Would you know the truck if you saw it again?" Captain Jack asked.

"Probably," she said, a little hesitant.

"Well, let's take a look," Captain Jack said.

He led her behind the building, and they stopped in front of the truck.

"Well," Captain Jack said. "What do you think?"

"That looks like it to me," she said.

"Does it look like the truck or is it the truck?" the chief asked.

"Don't know if it is or isn't," she said. "But it sure looks like it."

"That's good enough for me," Captain Jack said, eyeballing the chief. The chief ran his hand over his face, then sighed heavily.

"Did you see Benny Jones pick Amy Talbert up in this truck the day she was killed?"

"No, sir . . . I didn't."

"But you have seen him and her in this truck together?" Captain Jack countered quickly.

"Yes, sir," she said. "Lots of times."

"Well, Jack," the chief said. "I'll admit this makes interesting conversation, but it still don't change the fact that two witnesses saw Marcus Stokes abduct Amy Talbert the day she was killed."

"They saw Benny Jones," Captain Jack said. "Not Marcus Stokes."

The chief shook his head. "They saw Stokes," he said. "Both of them picked him out of a lineup."

"After they had seen his picture plastered all over the news."

"Jury didn't see it that way," the chief said.

"Well, Harland, maybe they saw it wrong," Captain Jack said. "Wouldn't be the first time."

"Mrs. Zeno." The chief turned his attention back to the witness. "Did Amy ever say anything to you about Benny Jones?"

She shook her head. "No, sir, she didn't."

"Nothing at all?" the chief said.

She shook her head again. "Not that I can remember."

"Were they seeing each other?" Captain Jack was blunt.

"God no!" she said. "He took her to work sometimes, that's all."

"How long had she been working for Mr. Peterson?" the chief asked.

Terri paused, thinking.

"About two years."

"During that time, how often would you say that Benny Jones picked her up and carried her to work?"

She looked at the chief, then hesitated, thinking. "A lot of times," she said.

"A dozen or so?" The chief wanted specifics.

"More than that," she said.

"Two dozen?" the chief asked.

"Probably more," she said.

"And during that time," the chief pressed his point, "she never had one problem with him, did she?"

"No, sir," Terri said. "At least not that I know of."

"And if she had," the chief said, "do you think she would have told you?"

"I'm sure she would have," Terri said. "She told me just about everything."

"Did Amy Talbert tell you every time Benny Jones picked her up and carried her to work?" Captain Jack asked.

"No, sir," Terri said. "I'm sure she didn't."

"So, you don't know if Benny Jones picked her up that day or not, do you?"

"No, sir," she said. "I don't . . . but I doubt it."

"Why is that?" Captain Jack asked. Her answer caught him off guard. He hadn't expected her to say that.

"Because it was Monday," she said.

He looked at her strangely. "I don't understand," he said, confused. "I don't understand the significance."

"It's a school night," Terri explained. "And normally Amy only worked on weekends. It was rare for her to work on a school night."

"Rare," Captain Jack said. "But she did . . . sometimes . . . didn't she?"

"I guess," she said. "But I sure can't remember a time she worked up there on a school night."

The chief saw an opening, and he pounced.

"So if someone said they saw Benny Jones pick her up and carry her to work that day, they would be lying, wouldn't they?" the chief said.

"I don't know," she said. "They could have . . . I mean . . . I guess it's possible . . . I just don't know."

"Well, what if I tell you that Benny Jones said he didn't know Amy Talbert," Captain Jack countered.

"Then, he'd be lying," she said.

"What if I tell you that he said he has never picked Amy up in that truck and carried her to work."

"He's lying," she said. "He picked her up lots of times. I've seen him."

"Maybe you're lying." The chief turned hostile.

"What reason I got to lie?" she asked.

"I don't know," the chief snapped. "You tell me."

"I didn't ask to come in here," she said. "Y'all dragged me in here. Besides, Amy was my friend. I wouldn't lie on her. She was my best friend."

"How well do you know Mr. Stokes?" the chief asked.

"Can't say that I know him at all," Terri said. "Just met him a few days ago."

"You and him talk about Amy Talbert?"

"He asked some questions," she said.

"What kind of questions?" the chief wanted to know.

"He just wanted to know about Amy."

"What did you tell him?"

"That she was a wonderful person. That's all I could tell him . . . because she was."

"He threaten you?" the chief asked.

"No," she said.

"Bribe you?"

"Of course not."

"You have any interest in his son?"

"Sir, I'm a married woman."

"Did you see Benny Jones pick Amy Talbert up the day that she was killed?" the chief asked her again.

"No, sir, I didn't."

"Well," the chief said, looking at Captain Jack. "That's all that matters, now, isn't it?"

Captain Jack shook his head. "I don't think so, Harland," he said. "I think something was going on between Benny and Amy. Something that possibly got her killed."

"Pure speculation," the chief said.

"Speculation or not," Captain Jack countered, "I believe it."

"You can believe whatever you want to," the chief said. "But we'll never know, now, will we? . . . Dead folks can't talk."

"Maybe they can," Terri said.

There was silence. And the chief looked at her strangely.

"What?" he finally said.

"Amy kept a diary," Terri explained.

"How do you know that?" Captain Jack asked.

"I saw it," Terri said.

"Are you sure about this?"

"I'm positive."

"Harland, I want that diary."

"Now, hold on, Jack."

"Harland, my client and I have a right to examine any evidence that can prove his innocence. I want to see that diary."

"No, Jack," the chief said. "Enough's enough."

"Harland—"

"No, Jack," the chief said again. "Now, the Talberts have suffered enough. I won't put that family through that, and I won't let you drag that child's name through the mud. I just won't."

"I'll get a court order."

"Don't threaten me, Jack." The chief screwed up his face and stared at Captain Jack with cold, angry eyes. Tyrone had been watching quietly, taking this all in. But now he felt compelled to say something. Here was new evidence that could possibly free his son, and the chief arbitrator of the law, whose express duty it was to protect and serve, was hedging. He opened his mouth to speak, but before he could, Captain Jack spoke again.

"Harland, if something was going on that got Amy Talbert killed," he said, "don't you think her family would want to know about it?"

"Ah, come on, Jack," the chief said, disgusted. "You know this is not about Amy's family. This is about you and that Stokes boy and trying to get away with murder."

"No, Harland," Captain Jack said. "This is about truth and justice. How will it look? We discover a piece of evidence that could exonerate my client, and the chief of police has it withheld."

There was silence. Then the chief looked at Terri. "Do you have any idea what kind of things are in her diary?" he asked.

"Amy was very private. She didn't talk a lot. But she wrote down everything. So, I'm sure it's filled with her innermost thoughts and secrets."

"You ever read it?" the chief asked.

"I saw it," she said. "And I saw her writing in it. But I never read it."

Captain Jack looked at Terri. "If something was going on in her life—something dangerous—do you think she would have written it down?"

"Yes, sir," she said. "I'm sure she would've. Provided she had the time."

The chief and Captain Jack looked at each other. Their eyes met. The chief spoke first.

"Let's say there is a diary, Jack. And let's say I'm able to locate it. And let's say I turn it over to you. How do you plan on handling it?"

"I need to read it," Captain Jack said.

"You and who else?"

"Just me and my client."

"This is sensitive, Jack," the chief said. "I don't want it made public."

"I'm only interested in finding out who killed her."

"I know who killed her." The chief was adamant.

"Well, if you're right, then this won't change a thing, will it?" Captain Jack said. "But if you're wrong, it just might keep an innocent man from dying. Now, I think that's worth making a few people uncomfortable, don't you?"

"I'll ride out there," the chief said.

"I'll go with you," Captain Jack said.

"No," the chief said. "You stay here. Be better for everyone if I go by myself."

Chapter
37

The Talbert house was located near downtown, just off the end of Main Street, not more than a couple of minutes away. So when the chief left, Tyrone did not expect him to be gone long; yet, he was still surprised when the chief returned within minutes with a middle-aged white woman whom he was sure he had never seen before. When they entered the room, he looked at her and at the chief; then he narrowed his eyes and leaned forward, staring. Where was the diary? He did not see the diary. Suddenly, Captain Jack stepped forward and extended his hand.

"Mrs. Talbert."

Tyrone had been searching the chief with his eyes, looking for the diary, but when he heard Mrs. Talbert's name, he halted and with bated breath raised his eyes and peered into the woman's face. His gaze had just fallen on her when her lips parted, and she spoke for the first time.

"Jack, what is this all about?" she asked. As she spoke, she was looking directly at Captain Jack; she never looked at Tyrone.

"Where's Buddy?" Captain Jack inquired about her husband, then lowered his hand.

"At Mike's," she said, then waited.

"Well, I guess there's no easy way to say this," Captain Jack said. "So, I'll just be blunt. We need to see Amy's diary."

"Diary," Mrs. Talbert said. "Jack . . . Amy didn't have a diary."

Shocked, Tyrone looked at her. A voice sounded in him. No diary. His jowls dropped, and just as panic was poised to invade his consciousness, he heard the soft, contradicting sound of Terri's timid voice call from the opposite side of the room.

"Mrs. Talbert . . . she did."

Startled, Mrs. Talbert whirled and looked. She had not noticed Terri when she first entered.

"What are you doing here?" Mrs. Talbert asked.

For a brief moment, Mrs. Talbert paused, observing Terri, and when Terri did not speak, Mrs. Talbert said in an assured tone, "She did not."

"But she did," Terri said in a low, timid voice. "She did have a diary."

"Why are you doing this?" Mrs. Talbert said. She looked at Terri with pained eyes. "I thought you were Amy's friend . . ." She turned to the chief. "Harland, there is no diary."

"You sure?" he said.

"I'm positive."

"It's in her closet," Terri said with downcast eyes.

"What?"

"That's where she kept it," Terri said, still looking at the floor. "It's in a shoe box . . . in the closet . . . near the back."

Mrs. Talbert stared at her, transfixed. Shock had rendered her silent. Then when her mind had fully processed what she had heard, she simply shook her head in disagreement.

"Harland, I want that diary," Captain Jack said.

"Susan," the chief called to Mrs. Talbert softly, then waited.

But she remained quiet, zombielike.

"Susan," the chief called to her again.

The sound of his voice broke her trance and she looked at him with dazed eyes. But still she did not speak.

"Well," the chief said. "What about it? . . . Is it possible?"

"I don't know," she mumbled in a low, dry, distant voice.

The chief frowned, then looked at her with skeptical eyes.

"What do you mean . . . You don't know?"

"I had her things packed up a couple of years ago," Mrs. Talbert said, then paused. Her voice began to shake. "I couldn't bear to look at them anymore."

"Where are they?" Captain Jack asked. "Where did you put them?"

"I don't know," Mrs. Talbert said.

"What do you mean, you don't know?" Captain Jack snapped, his voice stern.

"Jack!" the chief shouted. "What's gotten into you?"

"I need that diary," Captain Jack said.

There was silence.

"Susan," the chief said, his rough voice suddenly becoming soft, compassionate. "Do you still have her things?"

"I don't know," she said. "Maybe." Her hands began to tremble. "I gave some of her things away . . . put the others in the attic."

"Could the diary be in the attic?" the chief asked.

"I don't know," she said. "I gave most of her clothes to the Goodwill."

Tyrone felt his heart sink. Oh, why was this happening. Why?

"Harland—" Captain Jack tried to say something, but the chief cut him off.

"Jack, please!" The chief's voice was stern.

"I don't want nobody rummaging through Amy's things," Mrs. Talbert said through teary eyes. "I won't stand for that . . . I won't."

"Harland, I need that diary," Captain Jack said for the second time.

Mrs. Talbert began to sob heavily, and Terri moved close to her and put her arms about her shoulders, trying to comfort her. They had been standing the entire time, but now that Mrs. Talbert looked faint, the chief got her a chair. She sat down. A minute passed before the chief spoke again.

"Susan." He kneeled before her and gently took her by the hands. "I'm sorry that I have to put you through this," he said. "I know this is difficult . . . But I'm afraid I'm going to have to ask you a few more questions. You up to it?"

She nodded.

The chief started to say something else, then paused. "Can I get you some water or anything?"

She nodded, and the chief motioned to the officer standing behind the counter. On cue, the officer removed a paper cup from the canister and drew some water from the large cooler. When the cup was full, he handed it to Mrs. Talbert; she took a sip, then handed it back.

"Can you continue?" the chief asked.

She nodded again but did not speak.

"Do you know Benny Jones?" Captain Jack asked, approaching her chair. The chief whirled and looked at him with angry eyes.

"Benny!" Mrs. Talbert said. "What does Benny have to do with this?"

"Do you know him?" Captain Jack said sternly.

"Of course," she said. "He works for the Petersons."

"And Amy worked for them, too, right?" Captain Jack fired a follow-up question.

"That's right," she said. "Why?"

"Did Benny ever pick her up?" Captain Jack wanted to know.

"Excuse me?" she said.

"Did Benny Jones ever pick Amy up and take her to work?" Captain Jack repeated the question.

"A few times," she said. "Why?"

Captain Jack paused. "He said he didn't know her."

"That's hard for me to believe," Mrs. Talbert said.

"Well, he said it," Captain Jack told her.

"I can't imagine for the life of me why Benny would say such a thing," she said, becoming frazzled.

"Well, why don't we ask him?" Captain Jack said. He turned toward the chief. The chief looked at him, then slowly turned toward the officer.

"Go get him," the chief barked out an order.

The officer rose and disappeared through the side door. When he returned, he was flanked by Rooster. As Rooster entered the room, Tyrone could see that the uncertainty of the situation was beginning to take its toll. Initially, Rooster had looked nervous; but as soon as he saw Terri and Mrs. Talbert, his face dropped, and he looked terrified.

"Mr. Jones, we have a problem," Captain Jack said. "You see those two women over there?" Captain Jack gestured toward Terri and Mrs. Talbert.

Rooster lifted his head and took a quick look, then dropped his gaze again.

"Well, they just told us that you did know Amy Talbert. Mrs. Talbert even said that you picked Amy up, at their house, on a number of occasions. Now tell me . . . Is she lying, too?"

"Benny," Mrs. Talbert called to him before he had a chance to answer. "What's going on here? What's this all about?"

"It was you, wasn't it?" Captain Jack said. "You picked Amy Talbert up that day, didn't you?"

Rooster looked at him with large, fearful eyes, then shook his head no.

"Harland," Captain Jack said, still gazing at Rooster. "Please tell Mr. Jones the penalty for giving a false statement to a police officer."

"He answered your question, Jack," the chief said. "Just because you don't like his answer, don't mean he's lying."

"All right," Captain Jack said. "I'll tell him." He paused and looked at Rooster. "Five years," he said. "Five years in the state penitentiary."

There was silence.

"He did it, Harland," Captain Jack said. "Not my client."

"You have no evidence of that," the chief said.

"Admit it!" Captain Jack told Rooster. "Admit it or I'll have you thrown under the jail. I mean it . . . I will."

Mrs. Talbert began to cry.

"What's this all about?" she said, her voice trembling.

"Susan," the chief called to her softly. "Did you see this boy pick Amy up the day she was killed?"

"No," Mrs. Talbert said, shaking her head. "I didn't."

"She may not have seen it," Captain Jack said. "But he picked her up, all right . . . He picked her up and dropped her off at the Petersons'."

"Harland, what's this all about?" Mrs. Talbert asked again.

"Well, somehow or another, Jack and Mr. Stokes here come up with the crazy idea that this boy, Benny, picked Amy up at the store that day . . . and dropped her off at the Petersons' house . . . just before she was killed."

"No," Mrs. Talbert said. "He couldn't have."

"Yes, Mrs. Talbert," Captain Jack said. "I know this may be difficult for you to hear right now . . . But it's true. He did it . . . not my client."

"No," she said again. "He didn't . . . It's not possible."

"It is . . . and he did . . . ," Captain Jack said. "They saw him."

"They couldn't have seen him," she said. "Not at the Petersons'."

"Why not?" the chief asked.

"They weren't home."

The chief paused, stunned. "Are you sure?"

Mrs. Talbert nodded. "I'm sure."

Tyrone dropped his head and closed his eyes. . . . No, this was not happening.

"Do you know where they were?" he heard the chief ask.

He opened his eyes and saw Mrs. Talbert nod.

"At Miss Gertrude's house," he heard her say.

"Are you sure?" the chief asked, excited.

"Yes, Harland," Mrs. Talbert said. "I'm sure."

There was a brief pause; then Captain Jack spoke.

"Who is Miss Gertrude?" he asked. He had not heard her name before. He looked at the chief for an answer.

"Carol Peterson's mother," the chief told him.

A long moment passed. Then the chief resumed his interrogation.

"Do you know what time they made it back?" he asked Mrs. Talbert.

"Not until late."

"How late?"

"About eight or nine that night."

"You sure about that?" the chief asked.

"I'm sure," she said.

"How sure?" the chief wanted to know.

"Positive," Mrs. Talbert said.

"How can you be?" the chief asked, hoping to end this once and for all.

"That night . . . When Amy didn't come home, I called Carol and asked if they had seen her." Mrs. Talbert paused and exhaled, hard. Terri rubbed her back consolingly.

"And what time was that?" the chief asked, guiding her.

"About ten," she said. "Just before the news came on."

"And what did she say?"

"She said they hadn't." Mrs. Talbert's voice broke. She paused, remembering, then quickly composed herself. "She said they had been at her mama's all day . . . and that they didn't get home 'til late on account it was Miss Gertrude's birthday."

"They gave Miss Gertrude a party?" the chief asked, filling in the gaps. She nodded.

"Then what," the chief asked, encouraging her to continue.

"Well, after the party was over, she and Paul stayed up there and helped clean up."

"If Paul and her were up there," the chief said, "Where were the children?"

"With them," she said.

"Did Amy have a key to their house?" the chief asked.

"No," she said.

"Did they have a maid or anybody else staying with them?" the chief asked, continuing to chip away at the heart of their story with a renewed enthusiasm until what had once looked promising to Tyrone now looked dim.

Concerned, Tyrone tilted his head and looked at the clock. Yes, they were running out of time. Anxiety swept him, and inside himself, he felt swirling an array of emotions the combination of which made his tension rise. He closed his eyes and took a deep breath, and when again he opened them, he was besieged by a rage, the intensity of which he had seldom felt before. Suddenly, he wanted to kill them all. The chief, the officers, Mrs. Talbert, his lawyer. Yes, he wanted to lunge forward and rip the pistol from the chief's holster, and squeeze the trigger until he had done to them that which they were about to do to his son. Inside his head, his incensed mind told him to move, but practicality made him hold still. Mrs. Talbert shook her head, and the chief asked his next question.

"How long have you known this boy?" the chief said, looking at Benny.

"Few years," she said.

"He ever give you any trouble?"

"Not a bit."

"He ever give your daughter any trouble?"

"No," she said. "Not at all."

"He ever get out his place with her?"

"No!" she said.

"Do you think this boy would hurt your daughter?"

"Of course not," she said. "I know he wouldn't."

"Mrs. Talbert," Captain Jack interrupted. "You didn't know that your daughter kept a diary, did you?"

"No," she said.

"So, it stands to reason that she kept secrets from you, doesn't it?" Captain Jack said.

"I don't know," Mrs. Talbert said.

"Now, Benny and Amy spent a lot of time together, didn't they?"

"Jack, I won't stand for this."

"Perhaps there was more to their relationship than you know."

"Jack! Now that's enough." Mrs. Talbert began to cry. "Amy wasn't like that," she said. "She wasn't like that at all."

"I'm sure that Amy was a nice person," Captain Jack said. "But I'm also sure that she kept secrets. And I believe one of those secrets got her killed. That's why we need that diary." He paused and looked at Rooster. "I'm sorry, but I don't have as much confidence in him as you seem to have."

"Jack," the chief said. "That's it . . . We're through here."

"Ah, come on, Harland," Captain Jack said. "Open your eyes and look at what's sitting right in front of you."

"My eyes are open, Jack. And believe me, I see." He paused and looked at Tyrone. "And, Jack, you want to know what I see? . . . What I see is a situation that borders on the ridiculous. Them two there dragged him in here with a busted lip. Then Charlie says he saw him, but he don't know what time. And, of course, Irene says she knows the time, but she didn't see him . . . just his truck. And you, Jack . . . You threatened him until you got him so intimidated he'll confess to just about anything. Naw, Jack, there's nothing wrong with my eyes, but maybe there's something wrong with your ears. Mrs. Talbert just told you that the Petersons were not home the day Charlie claims he saw Amy go into their house. It didn't happen, Jack. Now, that's it . . . Marcus Stokes killed Amy Talbert. That's what the evidence shows . . . and that's what I know . . case closed."

"You did it," Captain Jack said to Rooster. "I don't know how. But you did it. Didn't you?"

"No," Rooster said.

"Then, why did you lie?" Captain Jack said. "Why did you say you didn't know Amy Talbert?"

"I was scared."

"Scared of what?"

"That everybody would think that I did it."

"Well, if you were so scared, why did you tell Mr. Stokes that you picked her up that day?" Captain Jack asked.

"Because he pulled a gun," Rooster said, looking at Tyrone.

"A gun!" the chief said.

"Yes, sir," Rooster said.

"On you?"

"Yes, sir."

"Where is the gun?" the chief asked.

"In his truck," Rooster said. "Under the seat."

"That's it," the chief said. "Like father . . . like son . . . Lock 'im up."

The officer obeyed. And as a despondent Tyrone made his way to the cell block, Captain Jack approached him, saying, "I'll still look for the diary. But what she said in there hurt us. I'll do what I can. But I think you should prepare yourself for the worst."

Chapter
38

B efore they processed him, they retrieved the gun from the truck, and he admitted everything, for now, there was no reason to lie. They did not book Beggar Man. He had been released, and as a favor to Tyrone, Beggar Man would tell Miss Hannah that Tyrone had violated his parole . . . and that he was back in jail. And for Tyrone, Beggar Man would tell her that he had said not to come to see him. And for Tyrone, he would tell her that he was sorry . . . and Miss Hannah would cry. And for Tyrone, Beggar Man would tell Pauline . . . and Pauline would cry. But no one would tell his son . . . and his son would die.

Yes, it was over . . . done . . . finished. Down in the cell block, they put Tyrone in the cell nearest the entrance. Inside the cell, he climbed upon the cot, curled his taut, tense body into a tight ball, and closed his eyes. And though his eyes were closed, he knew he would not sleep . . . And he did not sleep . . . And as night gave way to dawn and dawn stretched upward toward noon, he held firm, clutching his pillow, lying comatose upon his cot, his weary mind a huge slate of granite, impenetrable to the gloomy forces that now were his reality. Death and dying were far from him now, for he had retreated within himself behind a dark veil where no one or nothing could touch him. He was invisible. And the world was nonexistent. Behind the veil there was no more hurt or pain; or right or wrong. There was neither rejection nor expectation nor hope nor regret. Only one long, continuous space of time shielding him from the dark, painful nightmare that had been his life.

From the cot where he lay, he had heard the comings and goings of the old trustee they called Rusty. And though morning had passed and he knew the hour was drawing nigh, he did not stir. For was it not better for him not to know, but to cut off that part of himself that belonged to a world that he would now leave behind? Was it not better for him to lie dormant in his cocoon, unaware of their comings and goings, their deed and misdeed, until circumstances beyond him forced him to emerge and face the reality that would forever more be his life? Inside the hollows of his head was the loud ticking of a nonexistent clock and the faint image of a time line sprawled across the dark open vast, measuring the journey that never was.

Yes, it was over. No one had to tell him, for though it had happened more than a hundred miles away, he could feel it in that part of his soul from whence all knowledge sprang. He could feel it lingering in the air riding ominously on the invisible currents of the too quiet jail. He could feel it in the dark, hollow void that was now his heart. He could hear it loud and clear, outside his cell, as he had listened to the large courthouse clock strike twelve. Yes, it was over. And he wanted but to lie there. No, he wanted to die. He wanted to die and be free of the cages and the bars and the suffering and the pain.

Toward two o'clock, there was a jingling of keys outside the cell door. Then he heard the booming sound of the officer's voice.

"Stokes . . . You got a visitor."

Tyrone's back was to the bars, and he did not move. Now there was no one he wanted to see. He wanted but to be alone.

"Mr. Stokes," a different voice called to him. One that he had heard before. One that he recognized. It was Captain Jack, but still he did not move.

"Mr. Stokes, I brought someone to see you."

Captain Jack was quiet a moment, and Tyrone was tempted to look; but he did not. There was no one he wanted to see. No voice he wanted to hear. No hands he wanted to touch. It was over, and emotionally he wanted but to live alone, in his self-imposed exile, on an island far from those he loved and free of those he hated.

"Ty," he heard the soft, whimpering whisper of a female's voice cut through the stale jailhouse air. "We don't have but a minute."

Caught off guard, he turned from the wall, raised his head, and focused his weary eyes. Instantly, he felt his heart sink. It was Pauline. And though he did not want to see her, for deep within himself he felt that he could not face her, out of some morbid feeling of obligation, he slowly raised to his feet and moved next to the bars. For a brief moment, he looked into her eyes and saw that she had been crying. And at the moment, he could not look at her anymore. Ashamed, he dropped his head and looked down at the floor. Would it not have been better for her had they never met; had they never loved; had she never borne his child? Suddenly, he felt the need to apologize to her. To free her from her burden. To make her understand that he had never intended for things to be so, and if only he could, he would take upon himself her pain, and her family's pain, and their son's pain, and bear himself that for which he somehow felt responsible. He would if only he could. Feeling convicted, his lips parted, and he heard himself speak.

"I'm sorry," he said.

And no sooner had he spoken than emotions welled inside of him, the force of which he could no longer fight, and he dropped his head and cried. Through the bars he felt Pauline's hand gently upon his own.

"It's okay, Ty." Her voice was consoling. "It's over . . . It's all over now."

She made a strange sound, and he looked up. She was smiling. He continued to stare at her. Yes, this had been hard on her. And he knew that she had not been well. And he knew that she was in mourning. Yet, the way she had said, "It's over," and the way she had smiled evoked something within him . . . something that made his skin cringe . . . something that seemed unreal, and unjust, and out of place. It was as if she was relieved . . . Her only son was dead, and she was relieved. And at that moment, he felt swell in him an anger at a world that could make a mother feel toward her own son that which was not in her nature to feel.

Then as quickly as the feeling came, the feeling passed. What right did he have to be angry, for it was his life that had complicated her life, and his deeds and misdeeds that had ended their son's. And it was a combination of it all that had caused her to feel so. Oh, why was she here? And what was it that she expected him to say? This was all beyond him now. And there was nothing more to say. He wanted but to lie on the cot and face the wall and wait for them to come and take him back to the place that once again would be home.

"It's over," he heard Pauline say again.

Confused, he looked directly at her. Her eyes were glassy. No—spacy. More spacy than he had ever seen them before. And her face was relaxed and her skin was alive and her muscles were no longer taut. He was staring at her with bewildered eyes when from deep in the shadows of the doorway he saw emerge the faint silhouette of a black man. He could not see the man's face, but he could see his clothes. He wore a plain white shirt, a pair of blue jeans, and a pair of white sneakers. His body was stooped, and he walked gingerly as if he was moving about uncertainly in a dark room in which he could not see and in which he knew not what dangers lurked. Tyrone squinted, and then reality set in.

"My God!" he said. "It can't be . . . Marcus."

Suddenly, he felt weak. His knees threatened to betray him, and he grabbed the bars to keep from falling. Then when Marcus was close, Tyrone opened his mouth to speak, but no words came. Out of the shadows, he heard his name.

"Papa."

"Son," he heard himself say. Tears flooded his eyes.

"It's over," Pauline said again. She grabbed Marcus's hand, and they both began to cry.

"I don't understand," Tyrone said. "I don't understand."

Bewildered, Tyrone looked at Captain Jack.

"We found the diary." Captain Jack's words came to him in some strange succession, distorted by senses dulled by his uncomprehending mind. Was this permanent? Or temporary? Was he free? Or out on bond? Tyrone continued to stare. He wanted to speak, but he could not.

"She was pregnant . . . with his child . . ." Captain Jack said.

"Pregnant!" Tyrone said, his mind a whirling mass of confusion. "Who? I don't understand."

"The girl," Captain Jack said. "Amy Talbert . . . She confronted him . . . and he killed her to keep her quiet."

"He, who?" Tyrone asked, trying desperately to control himself. Before an answer could come, his whirling mind flashed an image, and Tyrone ventured a guess. "Rooster!"

"No," Captain Jack said. "P. K."

Tyrone's bulging eyes bucked, and for the first time, he saw Captain Jack smile. Then he saw his lips part, and he heard him say, "Paul Kyle Peterson."

Stunned, Tyrone stared mutely at Captain Jack, his eyes wide, his mouth agape.

"They were having an affair," Captain Jack said. "She was underage . . . and he was married. He killed her to keep her quiet."

Tyrone did not speak, so Captain Jack continued.

"Benny—I mean, Rooster—picked her up in front of the store that night. He admitted it . . . once he was sure that he would not be implicated."

"So they were home," Tyrone said, finding his voice.

"No." Captain Jack shook his head. "At least not Mrs. Talbert and the children. They were at her mother's. Just like she said. But Paul joined them later. He went home after work to change clothes. Amy arrived just before he left. They argued. He killed her . . . then stripped her nude . . . to make it look like a rape. And then he dumped the body in the field where it was found three days later."

"You sure?" Tyrone said. "I mean, it's over?"

Captain Jack nodded, then smiled again.

"It's over," he said. "Paul confessed . . . Besides, we got him dead to right. Amy kept meticulous details about their affair . . . and there is a three-month-old fetus . . . an autopsy would have proven that he was the father. It's over . . . Peterson killed her . . . case closed."

Suddenly, Tyrone buried his face in his hands, crying. Marcus reached through the bars and placed a trembling hand on his father's back. He caressed him but did not speak.

"It's over . . ." Tyrone mumbled, his entire body shaking. "It's over . . ." His voice was soft, unsteady. "It's over . . . my God . . . it's over."

"Mr. Stokes," Captain Jack called to him softly.

Tyrone looked up, and Captain Jack's gray eyes were moist.

"I spoke to Harland," he said. His breath came fast, hard. His voice broke, and he paused, then resumed again. "Your parole has been revoked . . . I'm afraid they're sending you back to prison."

"I know," Tyrone said. "I know."

"Ty," Pauline called to him softly.

Instantly, his head turned and their eyes met.

"I spoke to Mama Hannah . . . I told her what you had done. . . I told her I was proud of you. . . . I told her you done gave me my child back."

"She's alright," Tyrone aked, his lips trembling.

"She's alright," Pauline said. "She say she proud too . . . she say if I see you befo' she do be sho' to tell you she proud too."

"Time's up, Jack," the officer called from the door.

"I'm sorry, Papa," Marcus said.

"No, son," Tyrone said, smiling. "Don't be . . . 'Cause right now, I'm the happiest man in the world."

"You need anything?" Captain Jack asked Tyrone.

Tyrone shook his head.

"Bye, Ty," Pauline said, still crying.

"Bye, Pauline."

"Bye, Papa," Marcus said.

"Bye, son."

They stood for a moment taking each other in; then Captain Jack turned to leave. Marcus slipped his arm around his mother's waist. She leaned her head again in his chest; then they, too, turned to leave.

"Son," Tyrone called through the bars.

"Yeah, Papa."

"Take care of your mama," Tyrone said, his voice reverberating through the hollow halls. "When I get out of here . . . We gone be a family."

CRY ME A RIVER

ERNEST HILL

ABOUT THIS GUIDE

The suggested questions are intended to enhance your group's reading of CRY ME A RIVER by Ernest Hill.

DISCUSSION QUESTIONS

1. Much of the case against Marcus Stokes hinged on the testimony of the two original eye witnesses. Did they lie? And if so, what does their testimony reveal about the reliability of eye witness testimony?

2. What is the significance of the title?

3. What does the underwear symbolize? What plausible explanation can be given for its presence? And how does this fiasco affect your views of circumstantial evidence?

4. What does the plot reveal about the American system of jurisprudence that you were not aware of or that you find most difficult to believe? Especially as it relates to the African-American experience.

5. The relationship between Tyrone, René and Mr. Titus could be described as nothing short of contentious. What was the source of that contention and in what ways, if any, do you think Tyrone's act of heroism will impact his relationship with René and Mr. Titus?

6. Explain the significance of the confrontation in the diner. What does it say about nepotism, politics, and small-town justice? Can you cite other situations in the novel where these elements exist?

7. Pauline and Miss Hannah made independent decisions to keep information from their respective sons. Were they justified? Were their actions helpful or harmful? What do their actions say about African-American women and their views on motherhood?

8. Redemption is a thread that runs throughout the novel. By the conclusion of the novel do you believe that Tyrone's life has

been redeemed? If so, how? Are there others who have been redeemed as well?

9. For centuries religion has played a key role in the African-American community. What role does religion play in sustaining Miss Hannah, Pauline, and Marcus? Explain.

10. Manhood is a central theme in much of African-American literature. How was manhood depicted in the novel? Cite specific examples of references to manhood and the images that those references evoke.

11. Do you think Captain Jack believed in his client's innocence or was his judgement tainted by his own biases and prejudices? If so, did his perceptions affect the quality of service he rendered and is this typical or atypical of the type of representation that men like Marcus receive?

12. What are your perceptions of Janell? What is the significance of her character?

13. Why do you think Pauline never divorced Tyrone? What do you think of the possibility of the two of them reuniting? Will the love that they feel for each other be enough? Or are there simply too many obstacles?

14. Does this novel affect your views on the death penalty? If so, how?

The following is a sample chapter from Ernest Hill's
eagerly anticipated upcoming novel
IT'S ALL ABOUT THE MOON WHEN THE SUN AIN'T SHINING.
Available in June 2004 wherever hardcover books are sold.

ENJOY!

Chapter
1

"**M**aurice, stop it!"
I heard her terse whisper cut through the still darkness and float toward the ceiling. I paused for a moment. My bedroom window was up, and I could feel the breeze from the pond on the back of my neck, and I could hear the crickets chirping and the birds singing and the bullfrogs calling to one another. And she was lying on the bed and I was straddling her. And I looked down at her face and I saw her beautiful brown eyes staring up at me and all I could think of was how much I loved her, and how much I missed her, and how bad I wanted her. And at that moment, I felt my body stiffen at the thought of her and there rose in me an overwhelming desire to possess her as I had done only a few times before. With a movement that was slow and gentle, I eased my sweaty body from atop hers and slid down against the softness of the mattress and, when my mouth was next to her ear, I whispered softly.

"Baby, didn't you miss me?"

I hoped she had, for it was now December and I had not seen her, nor she me, since I had left for the university back in August. But when I asked, I heard her sigh softly then frowned disapprovingly.

And in the quiet of the moment, I hesitated, fearing that I had ruined the moment. I glanced at her, but she was not looking at me. Her dainty shoulders were flat against the bed, her knees were propped up, and her flushed face was tilted toward the dark, ominous hall. And I was lying on my side next to her, and my left arm was underneath her head, and my right arm was draped across her midriff, and my face was only inches from hers. Her blouse was open and her breasts were exposed, and I could see her nipples full and erect. I moved forward and when I was close, I opened my mouth and touched her nipple with the tip of my tongue. She cringed, then recoiled.

"No," she whispered. "They gon' catch us."

"They're gone," I said. "Won't be back for a long time."

I tried to kiss her neck but when I did, she recoiled again and pulled away. And I saw her eyes narrow and her forehead wrinkle.

"Maurice . . . I mean it . . . stop it."

"I can't," I whispered. "Baby, I'm aching for you."

I put my hand in the small of her back and pulled her closer to me. I felt her body become rigid. Then I felt her hands pushing hard against my hips. Again, I moved my lips toward hers but at the last minute she turned her head.

"Maurice, I mean it . . . stop it!"

"Honey," I whispered, "don't do me this way."

An awkward moment passed and I gazed into her eyes and I saw her eyes soften, then her lips parted and she spoke again.

"Not here," she said. "Not in your mama's house."

"We're engaged," I said. "Besides, she's not here."

I pressed closer to her, and her hands came between us.

"Engaged ain't married," she said.

I tried to kiss her again. She turned away.

"No," she said. "I'm not comfortable. I want to leave."

"Come on, Omenita," I said. "Don't be like this."

"No," she said. "Not in your mama's house. Now, I want to go up front. If Miss Audrey catch us back here she'll kill us."

"Ain't nobody gon' catch us," I said. "Mama at the church . . . Won't be back for hours."

"I want to go up front," she said.

"Omenita . . . please!" I said. "Don't do me like this."

"I'm serious," she said. "I want to leave."

"Baby—"

I started to say something else, but before I could, she raised her finger to her lips, then looked toward the door.

"What is it?" I asked. I paused, listening

"I heard something," she said.

Our house was located just off one of the highways leading in and out of Brownsville. We lived well beyond the city limits. I raised my head and looked about, and just as I did a large truck rumbled by. I paused to let it pass and when it did, I heard nothing except the crickets and the birds and the bullfrogs.

"Girl, that's just your imagination," I said.

"No," she said. "I heard something."

I listened again and when I heard nothing, I turned my attention back to her.

"Baby, don't make me beg," I said.

I kissed her on her neck, and she pushed me away.

"Maurice . . . stop it!"

"Okay," I said. "Just let me touch you then."

"You are touching me."

I moved my face closer and instantly I could feel the warmth of her breath upon my face, and I could see the dark pupils of her beautiful brown eyes. And all I could think of was how much I loved her and how much I wanted her and how many hours over the past few weeks I had lain in my small apartment, far from this place, thinking of this moment, longing to feel the touch of her lips on mine and the touch of my fingers on her soft, yearning flesh.

"You know what I mean," I whispered.

I reached for her thigh, and she grabbed my hand.

"No," she said.

"Come on, Omenita," I said.

"No," she said. "I want to go up front."

My room was near the back of the house at the end of a short hall. Mama and Daddy's room was at the other end of the hall. Between the two bedrooms was a bathroom. Directly across from the bathroom was a doorway that led into the living room. My door was ajar, and from where I was lying, I could see into the living room. No one was home except us . . . I tried to reassure her.

"Omenita—" I called to her softly, but before I could say another word she interrupted me.

"I mean it," she said. "If we don't go up front right now, I'm going to leave."

"But baby—"

"That's it," she said, rising from her supine position and placing both of her hands on the bed behind her. "I'm leaving."

"Okay," I said. "Okay . . . we'll go up front."

I slid off the bed and started toward my bedroom door but before I got there, I heard the knob on the front door jiggle.

"Maurice!" I heard Mama shouting my name. "Maurice! You in there?"

Instantly, I fell back against the bed and looked toward the door.

"Goddammit, Maurice," I heard Omenita say. "I told you I heard something."

I looked at Omenita, and her eyes were fiery.

"Now what we gon' do?" she asked.

I looked away, then looked back at her. She was scanning the room, and I knew she was searching for someplace to hide. I paused a minute, thinking. I heard Mama call to me again. Then, suddenly I thought of a plan.

"Go in the bathroom," I said.

She nodded, and no sooner had she bobbed her head yes, than I heard the door jiggle again; then, I heard Mama's key in the lock, and I told Omenita to hurry and she snapped to her feet and raced into the bathroom. I hustled to open the door before Mama could unlock it.

When I pulled the front door open Mama was standing on the stoop cradling a bag of groceries under each arm, and her keys were dangling from the lock. She looked at me, and I could tell she was wondering what was going on.

"What took you so long to open this door?" she asked, and then I saw her looking back toward my bedroom. And when she did, I looked back over my shoulder to make sure the coast was clear. I heard Omenita in the bathroom . . . I heard the toilet flush and then I heard

Omenita turn on the faucet and I knew she was pretending she was washing her hands.

"Nothing," I said. Then I was quiet.

"Whose car is that out there?" she asked. And I knew she knew before she asked, but I answered her anyway.

"Omenita's," I told her.

"Omenita!" she said, her voice slightly elevated.

I saw her looking past me trying to locate Omenita. And I knew she was looking toward my bedroom again, and I was angry at myself because I had left my bedroom door open, and the covers were ruffled. At that moment there was in me no doubt that if Mama saw the condition of my bed, her suspicious mind would quickly conclude what Omenita and I had been doing.

"What she doing over here?" she asked.

"Nothing," I told her.

I became quiet, hoping to say as little as possible.

"Must be something," she said after a moment or two then paused, and I knew she was waiting on an explanation.

"Just visiting," I said. "That's all."

Our eyes met, then I looked away.

"You know better than to bring that gal in this house when Nathaniel and me ain't home," she scolded me. "Don't you?"

"Yes, ma'am," I said submissively. Then I became quiet again and Mama looked at me.

"Where is she?" she wanted to know.

"In the bathroom," I said lamely. "Ought to be out in a minute."

Suddenly, I saw Mama looking past me again, and I knew she was trying to decide whether she believed me. She looked for a moment, then spoke again.

"Reverend Turner took sick," she said, still looking about. "Turned prayer meeting out early. Sister Thompson was kind enough to take me to the store before she brung me home."

"Yes, ma'am," I said. "That was kind of her."

Then, before she could say anything else, I took one of the bags of groceries from her and started toward the kitchen, hoping that she would follow. I heard her feet on the floor behind me and began to relax. Then, I heard her stop and instantly I knew she was still trying to figure out what was going on. I turned and looked and as I suspected, Mama was still looking toward my bedroom, and I knew she was trying to spot Omenita.

"What was y'all doing 'fo I come home?" she asked.

"Just watching TV," I said. "Just watching TV and talking."

Mama frowned, then looked about. The lights were out in the living room, but the television was on. As was the hall light.

"In the dark?" she said.

"The hall light's on," I said, then waited, but Mama did not say anything else, and I knew she was letting me know that I wasn't fooling her. I started back toward the kitchen and I heard Mama behind me. Then I heard her click on the switch, and I saw the living room light go on. I was glad that Omenita was still in the bathroom, for now I only wanted to place the bags in the kitchen and leave before she and Mama had an opportunity to have words.

When I made it to the kitchen, I stopped just inside the door and moved against the wall to let Mama pass. Ours was a small kitchen and Mama had to turn sideways to squeeze by me. And when she had passed, I watched her place the bag of groceries on top of the deep freezer, then turn and open the refrigerator door. I knew she would place it there even before she had, for there was neither room on the tiny counter next to the sink nor on the small table at the opposite end of the freezer, which in actuality, was not a traditional kitchen table, but one similar to those found in a soda shop or a fast food place. Our kitchen was too small for a traditional table. In fact, it was too small for anything except the old stove, which was crammed in the corner just as you entered the room. And the sink that was directly across from the deep freezer and the old late-model refrigerator that sat in the corner just beyond the sink and just before the back door. And in the center of the room there was a walkway between the sink and refrigerator on one side and the deep freezer on the other. The table sat at the end of that alley. And Mama had been standing near the table when she placed her bag atop the freezer.

I set the bag I was carrying on the deep freezer too. Then I heard the bathroom door open and close. Then I heard Omenita walking toward the kitchen. And when she walked in, I looked at her and she appeared nervous, and I knew she was worried that Mama knew what we had been doing.

"Hi, Miss Audrey," Omenita spoke, her voice low and uncertain.

"Omenita," Mama said, then continued putting the groceries in the refrigerator.

"Can I help you with anything?" Omenita asked.

"No, thank you," Mama said. "I can manage."

There was an awkward silence, and Omenita looked at me, and I could tell she was upset. And I knew she was upset with me because she thought Mama was upset with her. I saw her turn toward Mama again.

"Miss Audrey, you sure look nice this evening," she said.

Mama was wearing a navy blue dress with a belt around the waist and she had on heels and her hair was down and she did look good for her age; she was fifty-eight. But I could tell that she was still dissatisfied with us for she neither nodded nor looked up. Just said "Thank you," and kept putting the groceries away.

And when she spoke, her voice was neither kind nor polite but rather cold and dry. And the fact that she had not tried to conceal her feelings bothered Omenita and I saw Omenita drop her eyes and I knew she was feeling ashamed. She was feeling ashamed because she was thinking that Mama knew what we had been doing back in my bedroom before she had come home. It remained quiet for a few minutes, then I saw Omenita raise her head and wipe a small bead of sweat from the center of her brow, and I realized it was getting hot in the kitchen with all of us standing in such a congested space. I reached over and raised the tiny window just above the sink. Mama saw me raise it, and I guess she must have been warm as well for she immediately opened the back door and, instantly, I could feel the cool breeze through the window and I could hear the crickets and the birds and the frogs. And all I could think about was how nice it would be to sit outside by the pond with Omenita.

"Guess Maurice told you the news," Mama said. I looked up, surprised. She was staring at Omenita.

Omenita didn't answer. Instead, she looked at me, confused. And I saw Mama look at her, then at me. And I saw Mama frown. And I forced myself to smile, though it was the last thing I wanted to do at that moment.

"Maurice, you mean to tell me you ain't told that child yet?" Mama said, her tone indicating shock.

"No, ma'am," I said. "Not yet."

I saw Omenita staring at me, and I wished I were somewhere else because I didn't want to discuss it at the moment.

"Didn't know it was a secret," Mama said.

"It's not a secret," I said. "Just haven't told her yet."

"Pretty sure she want to know," Mama said.

She glanced at me, then started toward the bag of groceries that I had placed atop the deep freezer. I was leaning against the counter, but moved aside to let her pass, then I watched as she removed the other bag and lifted the freezer top. I heard the old rusty hinges screech, then I saw the frosty air rising off the meat when the hot air in the kitchen and the cool air in the freezer collided. I saw her remove some pork chops and neck bones from the bag and stuff them in the freezer. I didn't look, but I could still feel Omenita's eyes on me. And when I remained silent, she addressed me directly for the first time since arriving in the kitchen.

"Know what?" she asked.

"Nothing," I said.

Omenita looked at me then at Mama.

"He got news," Mama said.

"News?" Omenita said. "What kind of news?"

"Mama, please!" I said, louder than intended.

I saw Mama's head snap. "What did you say?"

"Nothing," I said.

She looked at me hard, menacingly.

"Boy! As long as you still got what little sense the good Lord gave you, don't you ever raise your voice to me . . . you hear."

"Yes, ma'am," I said. I averted my eyes submissively. Suddenly I was a one-year-old child instead of a twenty-year-old man.

"Damn," I heard Omenita say underneath her breath, and when she did I saw Mama whirl and look at her. Mama's lips were pursed, her eyes narrowed, and her forehead frowned.

"Watch your mouth, missy," she said. "This ain't no bar room."

I saw Omenita's eyes begin to water. Then I saw Omenita's head turn until her sad brown eyes were cast longingly upon my face. And for a brief moment, she looked at me and I looked at her. Then her lips parted.

"I think I better go," she said.

"No!" I said. "You don't have to."

"Maybe that would be best," Mama said.

"Mama!" I said, shocked.

Omenita turned to leave. I followed her.

Chapter
2

By the time I reached the front door, Omenita had already made it outside. And from the doorway, I saw her walking toward the large oak tree just beyond the house and just short of the highway. And I thought that maybe she was going to sit in the swing that Daddy and I had hung from one of the branches but instead she paused in the shadows, and her back was to me, and her tall, slender frame was pointing out toward the darkness, and the moon was bright and the stars were shining. I liked the way she looked basking in the light of the moon. And I liked the look of the soft, subtle glow of the dim light cascading off her long, lustrous hair. And I liked the way her dress was hugging her tiny, delicate waist, and the way it hung off her shoulders and the way it fell down her back and clung to her butt and stopped midway along her full, shapely thighs. And as I looked at her, I wondered why things had to be so difficult between the two of them. Why all the tension? Why all the stress? Why all the strain?

I discretely watched her for a moment, then I stepped out onto the stoop and closed the door behind me. I eased next to her, and when I was close, I slipped my hand about her waist, and my head, like hers, was locked forward. And as I stood beside her, purposely giving her time to collect herself, I could not help but notice that there was a still quietness about and that the night air was filled with the smell of freshly cut grass and that in the distance I could hear the steady hum of rubber tires on the smooth asphalt highway just beyond the yard. As my eyes strayed across the street and beyond the old railroad track, I could see the red glare of the end of a cigarette, and though I could not see the person's face, I knew that someone was sitting on the porch, cloaked in darkness, enjoying the peaceful solitude of a sooth-ing smoke.

And along that street, beyond the tracks, I could see rows of old houses, shacks really, all different, yet all the same. And all following the contours of the street winding unceremoniously through the quaint, depressed, black neighborhood with which I was all too familiar. And as I gazed out upon the horizon, I was anxious to talk to Omenita, but she was still angry, and when she was angry she was mean-spirited, and somewhere deep inside of me a wiser voice cautioned patience, so I remained silent, waiting for some sign from her that she was ready to speak calmly about that which had just transpired. I was secretly afraid that when she did decide to speak, I would not like what she had to say. I would not like it at all.

A moment or two passed and when she remained speechless, I de-cided, against better judgment, and spoke first.

"You okay?" I asked, then waited.

She pulled away, ever so slightly, and turned toward me, but she was not looking at me. She was looking at her car, which was sitting in the yard, on the grass, just off the seashells that were the driveway. I saw her looking and I knew she was contemplating leaving, and I knew she was wishing that she had never come to see me, and that she had never gone in the back room with me and that she had not heard the words that Mama had spoken to her. And she was thinking all this and at the same time, she was trying to hold her face straight and keep her eyes dry, and not let on how bad Mama's words had hurt her.

"What's she so anxious for you to tell me?" she finally asked. Her voice was low, but I could still hear the pain.

"Nothing," I said.

"Must be something," she said. "Something else for Miss Audrey to

throw in my face. What is it?" she continued to push. "Did you win another award? Did you find out you're graduating at the head of your
class? Did some big company offer you a job? Please tell me. What is
it?"

"Nothing," I said again.

She looked at me, and I could tell that my answer had not satisfied
her.

"Must be something or else Miss Audrey wouldn't be carrying on
so."

I remained quiet. I had said all I planned to say.

"What is it?" she asked again, then waited.

I remained quiet.

"I'm leaving," she said.

"All right," I said. "I'll tell you."

She waited for a moment but when I remained silent, she spoke.
"Well," she said.

"I'll tell you later," I said, "when the time is right."

She turned to leave. I grabbed her hand.

"Come on, Omenita," I said. "Don't act like this . . . It's nothing . . .
I swear. Mama's just pulling your chain."

"It's something to me," she said.

"Come on," I said. "Let's just talk about something else. We haven't
seen each other in over four months. . . . Please, let's talk about something else. Okay?"

I felt the tension in her arm loosen and I released my grip, and she
turned toward the street and stared far off into the darkness.

"Can't take Miss Audrey no more," she said. "Can't take her trying
to make me feel like I'm nothing."

"She doesn't know what she's doing," I said. "It's just her way."

"She know," Omenita said.

"No," I said. "It's just her way."

Omenita looked at me, and her eyes began to water.

"Why are you taking up for her?"

"I'm not," I said.

"You are," she said. She had been fighting back tears, but now she
could not fight them any longer, and as the tears descended her face,
I could feel my insides churning, and I could feel my heart aching,

and all I wanted to do was put my arms around her and pull her close to me and make the pain and hurt that was making her cry dissipate.

I reached for her and she pulled away, and I saw her eyes narrow and I saw her nose begin to run and I saw her drop her head and I saw her wipe her nose with the back of her hand and I could see that her hand was trembling and I could hear her sniffling and I knew she was trying to stop crying. I wanted to put my arms around her but I knew she would not let me.

"She know," Omenita said, sobbing heavily. "And you know she know. You were there. You were there just like me."

"I was where?" I asked, confused.

"You saw the way she treated me."

"Treated you when?" I asked. I was at a loss. She was not making sense.

"Could've let me know that she was proud of me . . . seeing how me and you were a couple . . . and seeing how I was the first in my family to graduate."

"Graduate," I mumbled to myself. Then it dawned on me. "High school," I said. "Girl, you talking about high school?"

"But no, she had to be mean. She had to let me know I wasn't nothing."

"She was proud," I said. "She was proud of both of us."

"No," Omenita said. "She wasn't proud. That was the happiest day of my life, and she just had to let me know that I wasn't good enough. Always been that way with Miss Audrey. I graduate from high school and she got to let me know you the val. I go to junior college and she got to let me know you going to the university. I take a job around here so I can be close until we can be together and she got to let me know I didn't need to go to school for no job like that. She know alright. She know just what she doing."

"No," I said. "It's not like you think."

"Yes, it is," she said. "And you know it just as well as I do."

Omenita started crying again and I put my arms around her and pulled her close, and she leaned her head on my shoulders, and my heart was aching because I could hear the hurt in her voice.

"It's not like you think," I said again.

And when I said that, she buried her head into my shoulder, and her tormented body began to pulsate and the tense muscles in her back began to shake. And I could feel her warm tears seeping through my shirt, and I wanted to comfort her, but I didn't know what to say. I pulled her closer and held her tighter and suddenly it seemed quiet again and we were in a dense haze and I could hear the birds singing and the crickets chirping and the bullfrogs calling to one another. And then, in an instance, I heard her voice, above it all, calling my name softly, tenderly.

"Yes," I answered her call, and I looked down and her glazed eyes were wide, gazing out into the darkness of the night. Suddenly, she looked up at me, her face wet with tears.

"When you graduate in a few weeks . . . and find a job . . . and we get married. Promise me we'll move away from here."

"She'll always be my mother," I said.

"But you won't always be her boy," she said, her eyes full of tears. "You'll be my man . . . and we'll have our own family . . . and we'll have our own lives . . . Promise me . . . Promise me we'll move away . . . I can't take her always downing me . . . Promise me."

"I promise," I said.

"No," she said. "Say it like you mean it. Say it like it's true."

"I do mean it," I said. "It is true."

I looked at her as tenderly as I could, and her sad eyes grew wide, and the flesh of her brow furrowed, forming an angry frown.

"How she gon' judge me?" she asked. "And she just a maid."

"That's my mama," I said.

"And I'm your woman."

"She doesn't mean any harm," I said for the third or fourth time.

"The hell she don't," Omenita said, and I heard her voice trembling with a rage that seemed to have emanated from a strange place deep within her soul.

"Shouldn't cuss in front of her," I said.

"So, now it's my fault?"

"I didn't say that," I said.

"Sure sound like it to me."

"Omenita," I said, "you know how she is."

"And!" she said.

"You shouldn't give her a reason," I said.

"What did I do?" she asked.

"You know she's a churchgoing woman," I said.

"So?"

"Just need to watch your mouth," I said. "That's all."

"No," she said. "You need to be a man."

"I am a man," I said, feeling my anger rise.

"No," she said. "A man would protect his woman. He wouldn't duck his head and hide."

"What do you want me to do?" I asked.

"Stand up to her," she said.

"I don't want to talk about this anymore," I said. "I am a man."

In the distance, I saw headlights approaching fast, and when the car was close, it slowed, and as it passed, I recognized the car as belonging to Deacon Fry, and from the appearance of things, Miss Cora had gone to prayer meeting, too, and Deacon Fry was bringing her home, for when he pulled into her yard next door and she got out, she was carrying her Bible and wearing that cream-colored dress that she only wore to church or funerals or prayer meetings. Miss Cora was a portly woman, and it took her a while to get out and when she walked toward her porch, she kept her hand on the car, bracing herself until she was close to the steps that led into her house. There was a vacant lot between our houses, and as she hobbled up the steps onto her porch, I told myself that I was going to mow that lot in the morning because the grass was getting just tall enough to draw snakes. And Omenita was scared of snakes. And tomorrow evening I was going to make some sandwiches and fry some chicken and we were going to sit in the backyard on one of the picnic tables underneath the pecan tree. At least, that was my plan, before all of this confusion with Mama.

I was standing half-dazed watching Deacon Fry back out of the yard when I felt Omenita pull away from me and start toward her car, and I knew that now, not only was she angry at Mama, but she was also angry at me. For in her mind, the conversation was not supposed to be over. I was supposed to tell her that I was going to talk to Mama and that I was going to make things right. She was my woman and I was going to make it right.

"Wait!" I said.

Suddenly, I saw her stop and wheel around, and when I was closer, I looked into her eyes, and in those eyes was anger and sadness and pain.

"Wait!" She repeated my request in a voice tinged with sarcasm.

"Yes," I said. "Wait."

"I'm tired of waiting," she said, and I saw the tears rolling down her face. "That's all I been doing since I met you. Waiting on you to finish college. Waiting on you to find a job. Waiting on you to be a man."

"I am a man," I said.

"Prove it," she said.

I became quiet.

"I'm tired of waiting," she said. "And I'm not going to wait any longer."

"Baby."

"No," she said. "From now on if we're gon' be together, we gon' be together. No more waiting."

"Fine," I said.

"And we gon' start with Miss Audrey," she said. "Either you gon' be her son or you gon' be my husband."

"I won't choose between the two of you," I said.

"You're gon' have to," she said, "if you want me."

"No," I said. "I won't."

"Then it's over," she said.

She turned to leave and I grabbed her arm.

"Don't do this," I said.

"Choose," she said.

I became quiet again and she started to leave.

"Okay," I said. "I'll talk to Mama . . . and I'll make her stop. I will."

"And if she don't?" she said.

"I'll choose."